PENGUIN BOOKS

Warrior Daughter

Janet Paisley is the author of five poetry collections, two of short fiction, a novella and numerous plays, radio, TV and film scripts. Accolades include a prestigious Creative Scotland Award (*Not for Glory*, short stories), the Peggy Ramsay Memorial Award (*Refuge*, a play) and a BAFTA nomination (*Long Haul*, a short film). Her first novel, *White Rose Rebel*, is available from Penguin.

Warrior Daughter

JANET PAISLEY

PENGUIN BOOKS

PENGUIN BOOKS

Published by the Penguin Group
Penguin Books Ltd, 80 Strand, London WC2R ORL, England
Penguin Group (USA) Inc., 375 Hudson Street, New York, New York 10014, USA
Penguin Group (Canada), 90 Eglinton Avenue East, Suite 700, Toronto, Ontario, Canada M4P 2Y3
(a division of Pearson Penguin Canada Inc.)
Penguin Ireland, 25 St Stephen's Green, Dublin 2, Ireland
(a division of Penguin Books Ltd)
Penguin Group (Australia), 250 Camberwell Road, Camberwell, Victoria 3124, Australia
(a division of Pearson Australia Group Pty Ltd)
Penguin Books India Pvt Ltd, 11 Community Centre, Panchsheel Park, New Delhi – 110 017, India
Penguin Group (NZ), 67 Apollo Drive, Rosedale, North Shore 0632, New Zealand
(a division of Pearson New Zealand Ltd)
Penguin Books (South Africa) (Pty) Ltd, 24 Sturdee Avenue, Rosebank, Johannesburg 2196, South Africa

Penguin Books Ltd, Registered Offices: 80 Strand, London WC2R ORL, England

www.penguin.com

First published 2009
3

Copyright © Janet Paisley, 2009

The moral right of the author has been asserted

Set in 11.5/13.25 pt Monotype Garamond
Typeset by Rowland Phototypesetting Ltd, Bury St Edmunds, Suffolk
Printed in England by Clays Ltd, St Ives plc

ISBN: 978-0-141-03304-4

www.greenpenguin.co.uk

Penguin Books is committed to a sustainable future
for our business, our readers and our planet.
The book in your hands is made from paper
certified by the Forest Stewardship Council.

For my friends
warriors all

especially Betty
who fought manic depression
and lost

Sweet darkness, velvet blood
from which you came, as night
will cup you again, again

move you outward into light;
a brilliance to be danced in

is life. Your staggering steps
will grow to trust this earth;
it meets both sure and unsure feet.

That shifting pain will shape
the edges that define you.

Know the body that confines
is a new kind of freedom
to find the fullness of you.

Move through yourself. See,
the future is with child

and needs your labouring.
Be done with pasts, walk away.
I'll watch. I'll guard your back,

blinded by my own time. Go forward
from the shadows mothers cast.

– From *Words for my Daughter*

Dark of the Moon

I

Fog, blue-white like mother's milk, and she was running through it. Each small, naked foot splashed down into the slowing suck of boggy ground and slurped out again, turn by rapid turn. Far behind, a dog howled, holding its long mournful note unbroken except for quick intakes of breath. The slow beat of the great drum sounded, dulled by the dankness. *Boom . . . boom . . . boom . . .* Mewling followed much closer, a thin, protesting wail accompanied by the slap-slap of fast, squelching steps.

'Skaa-haaa! Don't go!'

Skaaha wasn't going. She was running, feet skelping through the dense fog of a dark night, running towards the sea. If she ran hard enough, it couldn't catch her, wouldn't be. She would run till the sea reached her chest, forcing her to swim. Then she would swim until her arms ached, till water filled her mouth and flooded her ears and the seals came to mock. The sea would solve it, washing everything away.

'Wait for me,' the peevish voice behind craiked again.

Skaaha stopped and spun round, ribcage heaving, heart drumming on bone, chest full of thick, white fog. Hair clung to her hot neck and forehead, dripping. Water drops clogged her nostrils. Born in the dark of a Ghost moon, she had lived through forty-five seasons since her birth – eleven circles of the sun. She was Skaaha, the shadow, from the tribe of Danu, daughter of – her fists clenched – daughter of Kerrigen, queen of warriors, and she would not be chased.

'Stop following me,' she shrieked. Her shouted breath barely parted the mist. Mud oozed up through her toes. Now she'd stopped running, she could hear the sea at her back, waves still surging ashore as if nothing had changed.

The shifting, milky cloud in front of her darkened with the shape of her younger sister, who pelted out of it and into her.

'Where're you going?' Eefay grasped Skaaha's sodden dress. 'Can I come?'

'No!' Skaaha pushed her away. 'Go home!'

The smaller girl held on. She was nine seasons younger, half a head shorter, and tenacious. 'I might get lost,' she whined.

'Good.' Skaaha pushed again, harder. 'Go away!'

Eefay stumbled. As she fell, her grip on Skaaha's sleeve brought her sister, staggering, down on top of her. 'I'll tell on you,' the little girl squealed, letting go Skaaha's dress to grab handfuls of her sister's long, wet hair.

'Tell?' Skaaha grunted at the sharp tugs. 'Who will you tell?' With her head yanked close against Eefay's, she scrabbled for purchase in the bog, hands and knees sinking into water on either side of the little girl's writhing body. 'The Shee will get you first!' She grasped her sister's pinkies, slippery with wet, bending them back to force loose the fingers that tore her hair. 'They're watching,' she hissed. 'Can't you smell them? Can you hear them? They'll come for you soon as I get away!'

Eefay sunk her teeth into her sister's arm, biting down hard through the thin cloth of her sleeve. As Skaaha stopped pulling her fingers, she punched her face then clawed at her hair again. 'It's you they'll get,' she yelled. 'They'll smell your blood!'

It was true. Blood ran from Skaaha's nose. She could feel it. With her head twisted awkwardly to one side due to Eefay's grip on her hair, it trickled over her cheek.

'I'll get you for this,' she threatened. She wasn't afraid of the Shee, who rose from their ancient burial mounds to walk the night, but she would not be beaten.

'First blood!' Eefay protested. 'You've got to yield!' though she twisted her fingers tighter in Skaaha's hair in case her sister tried to hit back.

'Not to you.' Skaaha grabbed Eefay's ear and tugged hard. 'Never to you.'

There was a soft snort behind them, a gasp of breath blown

out. Fear widened Eefay's eyes. Her fingers went limp. Hair released, Skaaha turned towards the sound. Not three strides away, a shaggy horse stood in the fog. A human head dangled at its side, severed at the neck. It was a man's head, tied by its long, tangled hair, the eye sockets empty holes. On the horse's back a warrior sat motionless, weapons slung at her waist, face impassive, looking down at the two girls. There was a blue spiral tattooed on to her left cheek. Water dripped from her furs. A hoof squished into the ground next to her mount, a second horse.

Skaaha rolled off the top of her sister, glancing around. Another horse, another warrior, and another, and another. They were encircled. Skaaha stood, feet sinking in the slough, staring up at the lead rider. Beside her, Eefay scrambled upright and moved in close. Feeling the pressure at her side, Skaaha put an arm round Eefay's shoulder. She was only little and would need her big sister's protection.

Now that both were standing, the spiral warrior tightened her one-fisted grip on the horse's reins, eyes unreadable, as they should be.

'Bring them,' she said.

The dozen horses around them all moved at once. Skaaha was plucked into the air and, as Eefay slid from her grasp, was hauled up in front of one of the women. The horse's easy stride didn't falter in the marshy ground, though the warrior shifted her seat to accommodate the girl. Damp fur pressed against Skaaha's face. She hadn't run far enough, fast enough, hadn't reached the sea. Now it was too late. Everything she knew had ended.

The soft ground under the horse became firm as they began the ride up the gentle slope away from the shore. The only warrior who'd spoken, Mara, led the way. The plodding hooves of the other horses followed behind, taking them back towards the beating drum, towards the howling dog. Around the bay, other, more distant dogs had joined in, ululating like Ban Shee, calling each other through the fog. Skaaha felt nothing now, nothing except how wet and cold she was. She wiped the thin trickle of blood from her nose with her sleeve. In case the move was mistaken for tearfulness, she glanced up at the rider whose arms were round each side of her, guiding the horse by the reins, following Mara. It was Jiya who had her, Jiya, who always smiled but who wasn't smiling now.

'I didn't know what to do,' Skaaha said.

'The druids know. It's what they're for.'

That was the wrong answer, but Skaaha's thoughts wouldn't string together, and she could find no words to question with. Between the deep, slow drumbeats, above the howling dogs, the rhythm of hand drums broke through the fog. Faintly, she could hear voices harmonizing the song of celebration. Dark shapes loomed, became fences, paddocks, the roof of the farm roundhouse at the hill-foot. *Boom* . . . The horses plodded on up the slope, past the mound on which the drummer beat out the call.

Boom . . . The curved stone wall of the broch reared above them, feathered with mist, its thatch roof rubbed out in the whiteness. *Boom* . . . Behind it, on the next rise, hidden by fog, sat Doon Mor, the great broch, home of the warriors. But it was the smaller Doon Beck they rode to, home of the warrior queen Kerrigen and her daughters, Skaaha's home, the home she had run from such a short time ago, the home that would not be hers for much longer.

The heavy wooden door stood open, the hallway lamps already lit. In the doorway, a hunting dog waited, watching, a huge beast who seldom barked, and then only at enemies. It was the bitch that howled, Kerrigen's bitch, from the walled cell inside. Seeing the riders come, her mate loped into the broch, wriggled in beside her, and began to yowl in unison, joining the chorus from brochs around the bay. The slow drum spoke to the tribe of Danu. The hounds' eerie keening would pass from dog to dog around the island. No one from any tribe would doubt what it meant.

6

The group of riders rode straight in through the doorway, ducking low over their mounts to avoid the stone lintels. The hollow, circular walls of Doon Beck were three strides thick, high as seven warriors stood on each other's shoulders. Inside, the earth floor of the stockroom was circled with pens that held Kerrigen's cattle, sheep, goats and pigs during the night. Despite the clatter of hooves on hard-packed, rocky ground, the drums and song were louder here, penetrating down through the wooden ceiling from the living quarters above. With a twist of Jiya's arm, Skaaha was slid off the horse, the warrior's sword and spear thrust into her arms. Weapons were not allowed into living quarters where drink might be taken.

Automatically, Skaaha followed Mara to the storeroom, where the woman shrugged off her sodden bearskin and gave it to the door-keeper. The old man turned away to hang the coat on an antler hook. Bent with age and muttering, he moved slowly, but still Mara had to nudge Skaaha to remind her to hand over the weapons when he came back. As she held them out, his watery eyes met hers.

'A god is leaving us,' he mumbled, still talking to himself, 'when sky comes down to grieve.'

'Grieve?' Mara scorned. 'Do you not hear rejoicing?'

'Druids!' The door-keeper spat out the word as if it were gristle. 'They know everything, and nothing.' To Skaaha's bewilderment, he bent lower than his normal stoop and spoke into her ear. 'Mind your mother,' he urged, 'and speak up.'

'She didn't ask your advice!' Mara snapped, tugging her away, pushing past horses, to the doorway on to the stairs.

Skaaha couldn't think what the door-keeper meant. Following the painted warrior up the smooth stone steps between the thick walls, she remembered only one thing – the look on her mother's face when she saw it last, just before she ran. It was the look of the dead, of eyes without the light of life in them, of skin grey and bloodless, the bluish lips. She did not want to see it again.

But there was nowhere to run now. Eefay was behind her, followed by the rest of the warriors. There were thirteen of them, the most feared band of horsewomen in all the islands of Bride. Eleven of them came up the stairs behind her sister. Mara, the chapter's second-in-command, strode on ahead. The thirteenth – Kerrigen, their queen, her mother – lay in the room to which they were going.

On the landing, where the lamplight stuttered in the heated, smoky air, Mara stopped, turned and grasped her hand, squeezing it briefly. The gesture hit like a blow in the pit of Skaaha's stomach. Mara was Kerrigen's rival, ruthless and without pity. She'd never shown any kindness before. Skaaha's throat thickened as the warrior ushered her through the doorway first.

The great room was too warm, its circular wooden floor covered with sheep- and goatskins, a small peat fire glowing in the hearth. On the far side, a group of druids in ceremonial robes played their hand drums and sang the song of rebirth. They had arrived daily for the last week, expecting this. The rhythm of the drums, struck with bone, was rousing. The chanted, joyful song celebrated the baby born in the other-world, a birth made possible by the arrival there of Kerrigen's soul.

Skaaha stopped next the fire but she glanced beyond the druids to her mother's chamber. The woven check curtain was drawn shut. A small, cold hand slid into hers. It was Eefay, who'd come in behind her. The curtain across their mother's chamber twitched. Skaaha gripped Eefay's hand tightly, but it was only Tosk, her mother's druid, who emerged to greet them. As he crossed the floor, Skaaha wondered if it was true that he floated. His feet weren't visible under his robes and he moved smoothly, without the up and down motions of walking.

'There's nothing to be afraid of,' he said as he reached her.

Skaaha stared at him. He appeared to speak without moving his lips too. She'd never noticed this before – his mouth was hidden by his long moustache and grey beard – but she was sure he had lips and that he moved them to talk, so he probably had feet too. Did having feet rule out floating? She frowned – first the door-keeper, now Tosk. No man should speak unless he was addressed, even a priest.

'I'm not afraid,' she lied. 'I wanted to go to the sea.'

He nodded, as if he understood. 'Kerrigen has gone to the otherworld,' he said, to both of them, 'to live a new life there.'

His voice was gentle, his words irritating. She wasn't druid, but she knew her lessons. Time turned a circle: night became day then night; seasons came round repeatedly; the moon grew from dark to full to dark; and life also waxed, waned and waxed again. Death and birth were doorways that all living things passed through as they shifted back and forth between worlds, born in one as they died in the other, both worlds the same. While the great wheel turned, life followed life followed life.

But that wasn't what her mother believed. Kerrigen kept the old faith, believing in a spirit-life, not in reincarnation. When the flesh left her bones, her spirit would join the ancestral afterlife, where she could watch over and guide the living, once the final sacrifice was made. The lump that had threatened when Mara squeezed her hand filled Skaaha's throat. This was what the door-keeper meant. She must speak up.

'Kerrigen will go to the ancestors,' she mumbled.

Tosk smiled, but it wasn't a real smile. It was the kind of smile grown-ups used on small children, the smile of the wise to the foolish. She frowned harder because she had nothing to say, and he turned away as someone else emerged from her mother's chamber. Eefay drew her wet hand out of Skaaha's.

'Donal!' she shrieked, and ran to the tall, blond warrior who crouched, arms held out to swing her up.

Skaaha, her mother's warriors ranged behind her, stood stock still, watching the two of them. Eefay's father must have arrived after she'd run away. The chill inside her grew. Here was the next great change, laughing and hugging her sister. Eefay did not need her now. She, Skaaha, was alone, with no one to protect, and no one to protect her. Mara nudged her from behind, but she couldn't think of the words she should speak. One of the druids, a young novice who had no beard, detached himself from the group, filled a drinking horn from the cauldron that hung over the fire and brought it to her.

'Here,' he said. 'You must be cold.'

The broch was never cold, even mid-winter, when the charcoal-pit heated the hollow walls. Although it wasn't lit in summer, the blood-heat of beasts below still warmed the floor at night and the single peat in the hearth made the room hot. Her clothes steamed. But the inside of her body was chill as the frozen falls in winter, so she took the cup and swallowed a mouthful of the warm liquid. It was beech cordial, sweet and fiery, and it loosened her tongue.

'We're pleased to see you, Donal,' she said to Eefay's father. Her mother had divorced the man many suns ago, and went away when he visited to tutor the warriors and see his daughter. This was not his time to be here. He must have been sent for, after the accident.

'Your mother was a god among warriors,' he answered, courteously, 'but she drove too fast.'

'She likes to win,' Skaaha said, remembering how Mara baited Kerrigen.

'Even the eagles won't race against me,' the second-in-command had taunted. No one dared laugh.

'You have a fine chariot,' Kerrigen countered, and her warriors relaxed.

'The finest,' Mara boasted, 'but the skill is mine. I could race the wind' – her eyes held the queen's – 'and beat it.' Silence thundered into the room; drinking ceased.

'That, I'd like to see.' Kerrigen raised her horn. 'Tomorrow,' she challenged, as she always did, to keep the ambitious warrior in check, 'against me, and the wind in my wake.' Laughter erupted then, with cheers and toasts to the queen.

During the race, Kerrigen's chariot struck a rock on the turn and toppled, throwing her out. Her winged helmet had been knocked aside as she fell. She was very broken when they brought her home, but she was alive. That was seven days ago. Now, she was dead.

Skaaha swallowed the last of the cordial, sat the horn back in its hearth stand and crossed to her mother's chamber. At the curtain, she hesitated, screwed up her courage then slipped inside and stopped again, head down, staring at the floor, at the shadows cast by the lamps that shifted like living things, dancing over the sheepskins.

On the other side of the curtain, the singing ended. They would all talk now, and eat. When she was able to, she looked across at the bed. Her mother had died looking at her. They'd been alone together, Skaaha about to wash her, carefully, ever so carefully, as she'd done every day since the accident. Kerrigen had turned her head a little, reaching out with her unbroken hand. She said one word:

'Skaa-haa.'

Then she was gone, the fire gone out of her eyes, gone from the world. And Skaaha ran.

Someone had straightened Kerrigen. She lay on her back, arms at her sides. Slowly, Skaaha walked over until she felt the edge of the bed against her shins. She looked down, willing herself to be brave. Whoever had straightened the queen also closed her eyes. Skaaha knelt on the sheepskin rug, looking at her mother's beautiful face, framed by the long, braided black hair arranged over her shoulders. She looked real and alive enough, except for the grey pallor. The druids taught that death should be celebrated, but she couldn't. Her mother had wanted help. It was the last thing she asked. Skaaha, her daughter, the daughter she asked it from, had failed her.

'I didn't know what to do,' she whispered.

Still not knowing what to do, she drew over the bowl of water she'd left there when she ran. Squeezing out the rag that floated in it, she began, gently, so as not to disturb its expression, to wash her dead mother's face.

2

For the last time, Skaaha stood on the walkway that topped the broch, looking across Ullinish to its twin ancestral cairns. At her back, the high thatched roof hid the funeral pyre being built by druids on the hilltop behind. Below, the stream flowed past the farm roundhouse and on towards the shore. Sun had chased the fog away, the blue sky clear of cloud. Seals hunted in the bay, diving, leaping, graceful in the water.

The islanded loch of Bracadale spread before her, gateway to the ocean, one of many that formed the ragged coast on the Island of Wings. Like giant jaws open in a war cry, the northern peninsula swept round to flat-topped mountains. Along the south sweep, jagged black peaks ranged like broken teeth. Between those jaws, within easy running distance, several brochs towered above small settlements, a chain that snaked around the green contours of coastal land. The women who kept those brochs were all family, all her tribe. She should have run to one of them. Perhaps she still could.

Jiya came up the stone stairs. The plumpest of the warriors, she was their dead queen's younger sister, Skaaha's aunt. Moonstruck and blessed with a wild, erratic humour, she'd vanished before the accident, going off to wander alone and crazed, as she often did, returning only last night in the fog. Her smile was back, the broad smile she wore to greet friends or when confronted by an enemy. It widened as she looked over the rim of the broch at the rocky ground below.

'Leap only if you trust your wings,' she said.

'I don't trust,' Skaaha muttered. 'Not anything.'

'This is good,' Jiya approved. 'You won't be easily fooled.'

'Have you come to fool me?'

Jiya chuckled, genuinely amused. 'If I say no, maybe I'm

fooling you. The only answer to trust would be yes. But would I answer that, if that was the answer?'

'You talk like a druid.'

'I talk like a warrior. Trust yourself, then you will also become a great warrior like me. Maybe like Kerrigen.'

'Kerrigen's dead,' Skaaha answered bleakly.

'Only to us,' Jiya said, 'if you trust the druids.' She gripped Skaaha's arm, eyes burning with sudden fire. 'Don't be fooled. The blood is yours.' Her words fell over each other. 'It cries out your name. Listen to it. Listen!'

All Skaaha heard was Kerrigen's voice, her mother's last word – *Skaa-haa*. 'Stop it, Jiya,' she said. 'You weren't there, you don't know, and you're hurting me.' Her aunt's fingers dug into her flesh.

'I walked in darkness,' Jiya babbled with the same urgency, 'then I saw.'

Skaaha wrested her arm free. 'What did you see?' It would be nonsense, spirit-talk that no one else could understand.

The fierceness in her aunt's eyes dulled to puzzlement. She stepped back from the edge of the walkway. 'One day you'll leap and let fate choose your future.' Her smile returned. 'Today, talk will do it. They're waiting for you downstairs.'

So it was time, time for her life, and Eefay's, to be decided. Down in the great room shafts of sun scythed through opened skylights in the thatch, illuminating the central feast, making the surrounding gloom more oppressive. The headwomen of the tribe crowded the dim space. A few men-folk hurried in and out, bringing food and drink. Druids waited in small groups. Male and female turn about, they were the priests of Bride, keepers of custom, law and knowledge, advisors, seers and bards.

Skaaha sat down on the goatskins in Kerrigen's place. It was expected. She was the queen's heir until the body was gone, but only till then. She was too young to take her mother's place for longer. When she looked up, she looked into the pale-blue eyes of Suli, the oldest, wisest druid of them all, seated opposite, flanked by Tosk, her mother's priest, and the beardless novice who'd given her cordial the night before. The high priest must have travelled during the night, through that fog. It was said she could see in the dark and needed no moon or star to light her way. It was also said she could see past and future, the hidden thoughts of others and the secrets in their hearts. Skaaha lowered her eyes.

Mara sat down on her left, Jiya on her right. The other warriors divided themselves into the next five places on either side. Beyond them, completing the circle, the spaces filled with Eefay, her father, and the headwomen of the tribe: farmers, fishers, weavers, brewers, thatchers, potters and the smith. When all the shuffling and sorting was done, the chattering that accompanied it ceased.

Skaaha reached forward to lift the ceremonial horn that sat, brimming, in its bronze stand in front of her. It was heavy, and needed two hands. To spill it meant bad luck. The liquid, sweet with honey, swallowed easily then glowed in her belly. It was mead, thick as the silence that had settled. Skaaha looked up again at Suli. The old woman's pale eyes were calm. *Pass the cup*, she said, her voice speaking clear and deep in Skaaha's head though Suli's lips did not move and no one else seemed to hear, though they waited for her to do just that: pass the cup.

It should go to Mara. The horn, as with everything, must pass sunwise. But it was Kerrigen's cup she passed, the Honour of Doon Beck, title to the broch. In passing it, she transferred her home and, with it, leadership of Bracadale warriors. They had already chosen. That's why Mara sat next in line, ready to receive what she could never have won while Kerrigen lived.

Skaaha's hands shook. The ornate glass insets dug into her fingers. A drop of mead spilled over the bronze rim. Her proud and generous mother was gone. Now, she gave up Ullinish, the life she and Eefay would have lived. The drip trickled towards her thumb. She wanted to pass the cup to

Jiya, to prevent that loss, but if her aunt took it, Mara would challenge her. There would be another death, Jiya's. Quickly, Skaaha licked the spillage with her tongue, turned and passed the horn into Mara's hands. A ripple of relaxation ran round the seated circle. The cup followed rapidly.

When it finally reached Jiya, she drank and, as she returned it to Skaaha to replace in the bronze stand, whispered in the girl's ear. 'You did right. Don't make it a habit.' There was a laugh behind the words. 'Wrong is more fun. I can take Mara.'

'Let fate choose,' Skaaha whispered back, 'another day.'

As the drinking horn slotted into its place, Suli spoke. 'Now that our tongues are loosened, we are here to speak for Kerrigen of Danu, foster-daughter of Lethra, whose body cries out to be returned to the earth, to find homes for those of her flesh who live.'

Skaaha stared down at the ceremonial horn, embarrassed. Under druid law, she should have been fostered to other kin before Eefay was born. Then she would have a foster-mother already, with a home that Eefay could join her in.

'Kerrigen shunned our custom to raise both her daughters,' Suli went on. 'Now we see the error of that choice. So who among you will claim them?'

The difficulty was obvious. Two thriving, healthy daughters was a great prize, but to claim it might incur Mara's displeasure. Whoever showed favour to her predecessor's children could find themselves outside her protection.

'Doon Beck is their home,' Mara said. 'They can stay.'

Shocked that she had spoken, Skaaha glanced up at the warrior's taut, expressionless face. Her frozen innards clenched. Mara had never borne or fostered a child. She tolerated Kerrigen's daughters, with bad grace, because she had no choice. Could she have changed? What would they become here, with her? Not warriors. Kerrigen had trained her daughters. Mara wouldn't. Women didn't learn from women. It was strange for her to offer them a home, strange and chilling. A blanket of silence spread. No one else spoke. Breathing seemed to stop.

Beyond Mara, below the warriors, where Eefay sat with her father, there was the slightest movement.

'I want to go with Donal,' Eefay piped up, 'and learn to be a warrior.' Relieved cheers and clapping erupted. Glenelg was safely over the water, on the mainland. Eefay glowed in the approval. 'And Skaaha can come too,' she announced proudly. It was a good answer. More loud approbation followed.

Beside Skaaha, Mara remained silent, though her breathing deepened to the rhythm used before battle. As the shouts of approval frittered away, Suli considered Kerrigen's elder daughter.

'And what does Skaaha say?' she prompted.

'I don't want to be a warrior.' Skaaha glared at Eefay. 'Warriors die broken.'

Everyone but Suli gasped. Nothing seemed to surprise the old woman. In the rising mutter of comment, Jiya chuckled at Skaaha's side.

'Beautifully wrong,' she snorted. 'I love it. Tell them we should have beer.'

'We should have beer,' Skaaha said loudly.

The potboy scurried to fill the waiting horns. There was some coming and going on the stairs, gossips rushing out, latecomers entering. Seated beside Suli, Tosk looked furious but, unless spoken to, he had no voice in this gathering. On the old woman's other side, the young druid who'd given birch cordial to Skaaha the night before lowered his head to hide a smile. Skaaha wondered why he was in the circle when more senior druids sat apart. But now she'd found her voice, she had other things to say and didn't wonder long.

'Kerrigen won't go through fire into the earth or the water,' she said. 'She'll go to the sky, to the ancestors.'

Beside her, Mara tensed. At her other side, Jiya whooped with joy.

'That cannot be!' Tosk couldn't contain himself. 'It offends Bride. The corpse must be cleansed by her flames. This is not a matter for debate!'

Suli ignored him, still unperturbed. Her concentration on

Skaaha didn't alter. 'Such things have not been done for longer than we remember,' she said. 'The way of the ancients is not our way.'

'But it was Kerrigen's way, what she believed.' The lump was back in Skaaha's throat. 'My mother wasn't druid.' Her eyes stung. 'And you know how.' The resolve in her voice wavered, uncertain now that no one spoke to support her. 'You know everything.'

'We know many things that should not be done.'

There was movement behind Skaaha, from shadows near the doorway.

'But you will do this one,' a man's voice thundered across the room.

Mara and Jiya, weaponless, grabbed eating knives and were half-way to their feet before Skaaha's head turned. The man who stepped into the shafts of sunlight was a stranger, broad-shouldered and muscular, with a gold torc round his throat. He wore the leather garb of a metalsmith, and was clearly a master of his craft, his travelling cloak pinned with an elaborately wrought gold and bronze brooch. The frisson of alarm in the room dissipated. Smiths were magicians who turned rock into tools, weapons and art. All warriors depended on them; their magic was second only to that of druids, next to whom their own smith sat.

'You're welcome to speak, Ard,' Suli said. She stood. The other women rose with her. In unison, they lifted the front of their skirts to the waist in a ceremonial gesture, asserting both domination and munificence in one swift flash of naked flesh. 'We're pleased to see you,' Suli continued, dropping her robes. 'It's been many moons.' Seats were retaken, leaving a space for the man between the warriors and the farmers, opposite Eefay and Donal.

'It was that or have Kerrigen feed me to the eagles,' he joked as he sat.

'Piece by tiny piece,' Mara muttered, settling back next Skaaha.

'Now the sparks will fly,' Jiya giggled, flopping down and reaching for beer.

'Who is he?' Skaaha hissed. Master-smith or not, men served women. They did not speak at council or give orders to druids.

'Ard Greimme of Kylerhea, foster-son of Lethra, born of Suli.' Jiya raised her drinking horn, eyes gleaming. 'He's your father.'

The interrupted discussion resumed. It seemed everyone now agreed with Skaaha that excarnation was Kerrigen's right. Their own smith smoothed the path. The tribe of Danu honoured the goddess, Bride, and respected druid law, she said. But Danu people also kept many older customs.

'This is true,' Mara agreed, glaring at Ard. 'We've heard of new habits among tribes who sit to talk with men among their number.'

'In equal numbers,' Ard said smoothly, 'as the druids teach.'

'While the fires go out and wolves take the sheep?' the farm-keeper asked.

'Men can speak,' Donal pointed out, though he had no right to.

'A drum speaks,' snapped the boat-keeper, 'but it, too, is skin stretched over empty air!'

Skaaha was entranced by Ard. She had a father. Kerrigen had never mentioned this. No one had. Yet here he was, and everyone seemed to know. He looked like her mother – dark hair, dark eyes, a strong forehead and straight nose. Like her, too, and not at all like Eefay, whose name meant beautiful, with the fair hair and green eyes of Donal. In the centre of the heavy weight of sorrow that filled Skaaha, a small, bright flame of joy began to burn. She had a father, just like Eefay, but hers worked the magic art and was not afraid to answer priest or warrior.

'Kerrigen upheld the law,' Ard was saying, 'and valued druid knowledge, but she kept the ancient faith of our ancestors. The Islands of Bride were safe and prosperous while she lived. Now, in death, we should honour her, and not ourselves.'

Suli nodded agreement. 'You speak well, Ard, and wisely.'

'For a man,' Mara conceded, though her knuckles turned white.

'We can take Kerrigen to sacred ground,' Suli continued, 'and offer her body to the sky, if it will have her, but we cannot open the mounds of the dead to make a place for her bones. That is forbidden.' For the first time, she sounded stern and fierce, drawing a line the druids would stop anyone from crossing. The burial mounds of the ancestors dotted the landscape but, while new settlements were built near by to benefit from the spiritual protection, they had all been sealed and filled with soil long ago. It was believed the Shee who inhabited them still walked the land. Although their name meant peace, no one risked disturbing them. 'Forbidden,' Suli repeated.

'There will be no bones,' Tosk said quietly.

'And no one keeps my sister's head,' Jiya insisted.

'No.' Tosk shook his own, his grey beard sweeping his knees. 'There will be nothing to keep her here. Kerrigen will go' – the briefest pause – 'to the ancestors.'

'Aye-yie-yaa!' Skaaha exclaimed, clapping her hands together.

Despite grumbles about profanity from priests outside the circle, there was agreement within it. Tosk, to whom the honour belonged, agreed magnanimously to conduct the disposal at High Sun. The mid-summer quarter-day marked the solstice, when the sun's slow fall into winter began, its ancient rites conducted now by druids. Joyful, the longest day also brought the sorrow of returning darkness. Kerrigen had picked a fitting time to die. Chatter began, with more to-ing and fro-ing to fill beer into horns. Again, it was Suli who brought attention back to their purpose.

'Now that her mind is free of worry over her mother's remains, what does Skaaha say for herself?'

When the rites were over, she couldn't stay in Doon Beck. Mara's offer was false. Kerrigen's daughter wouldn't live long under her roof. Jiya's arm pressed against hers. Was it a warning? Her aunt hadn't offered them a home with her, in Doon Mor with the warriors, to work in their household. The headwomen's familiar faces all turned towards her. Now that Suli made the choice hers and not theirs, she could go to any of their homes. None would refuse. Her future craft was determined by this choice – hunter, farmer, fisher, weaver, potter – but she would never feel safe in Mara's domain. Despite her aunt's boast, Jiya couldn't protect her.

She glanced at her sister. Eefay's eyes pleaded, her hands clasped in hope. Please, please, please, she mouthed, begging silently. Donal would take them both to the mainland of Alba. They would learn the honour code and how to be protectors of their people, but she would always be second to Eefay, to her little sister who was Donal's child and had been their mother's favourite. Eefay, the fair, the beautiful one. Skaaha, the shadowy one – again. Even though she had rejected it earlier, that had been her best hope when she entered this gathering. Now, she had a better option.

'I will go with Ard Greimme,' she said, 'and learn to be a smith.'

3

It began with a crow. As the light of morning bled into the sky, the black and white hooded bird flapped down on to the headstone of the circle, and cawed. Other wings flapped past, fluttered down. Claws scrabbled, dancing on top of the standing stones. *Kaah . . . kaah . . . kaah . . .* they called. They'd come to feed. Below them, Kerrigen's body lay on the low offering stone, stripped naked, head shaved, her abdomen split by a deep cut that ran from breast to pubis and another from side to side above her navel, the released decomposition gases an irresistible signal of carrion.

The journey north to the sacred stones had taken two days. A ring of massive monoliths, the stones stood upright in flat, open pasture, placed there by the ancients. Behind them, on the north side, the long water of a sea loch snaked on to a shingle beach. Craggy mountains towered in the east. Thick woodland crowded the west. Tosk had led the way there, on foot, taking the smoothest path between mountains and sea, leading Kerrigen's chariot, mended and draped with her bearskin, on which lay the dead queen's fully armed, helmeted body.

Skaaha rode behind the chariot, Eefay alongside, Ard and Donal at their backs. The warriors of Bracadale, headed by Mara, came next. Naked and painted, wearing short sash cloaks, they bore full honours, spears and swords glistening, hair spiked white with lime, enemy heads dangling at their horses' sides. Other warrior chapters followed: Donal's school; the men from north and south of the island. The tribe walked, a procession that grew as more clans swelled their ranks. Two carts carried cauldrons, barrels of beer, pitchers of mead, food for the feast. The druids brought up the rear, chanting and singing to reed pipes and hand drums, using rhythm to keep the long train of people high-spirited and in step.

Now they stood silent in a wide ring around the sacred ground, witnesses waiting for sunrise. Tosk was the only druid still inside the circle of stones. The others had carried the body in, waited on him while the preparation was done then left to join the watching tribe while he stood guard, back to his dead queen, facing the wake-stone over which the sun would rise. He would not leave her till it did. *Kaah . . . kaah . . .* In the pale half-light, the crows gathered, eyeing him, calling.

Tosk chanted quietly. The rhythmic sound carried in the stillness, making the birds uncertain. As the glow of sun slid up from the horizon, he raised his arms, rod in hand, towards it, following its rise to the crown of the distant stone. When the light struck his face and the stone behind, he dropped his arms, ceased chanting and strode, in his strange gliding fashion, away from the queen's sunlit body, out through the gateway stones of the circle to join the wider ring of watchers. Before he was half-way, the crows were down off their high perches, strutting, squabbling, pecking.

Gulls already wheeled above, shrieking, raucous, their white wings flashing. They dived now on the feeding crows to disperse them, making space to land. Facing the gateway stones, as chief witness, Skaaha watched the fluttering wings. She hadn't known what she asked. No one, not even Tosk, had ever witnessed the ancient rite. Now she knew. Falling felt like this. Once, while trying to master a leap, she'd fallen. It was the wrong place to practise, on the beach, from one rock to another, both studded with sharp barnacles. Blood oozed from grazing on her shin and hands.

'Pain is the teacher,' her mother said. 'If it hurts, it's meant to hurt. Listen to what the pain tells you, else what do you learn?'

'How to die bravely,' she answered, blinking back tears.

'And young,' her mother retorted, 'very young.'

She hadn't understood. Warriors fought with courage. 'Live the day well,' they said when parting, and added before battle,

'It might be your last.' Death wasn't feared. It meant new life. So the druids said. Her mother's face faded from her mind. It lived only in her memory. Now she understood pain. Death meant loss for those left behind.

Biting her lip, Skaaha hoped for eagles. High above, raptors arrived, soaring, circling. A few kites darted down, in and out quickly, scattering gulls, pointlessly chased after by a handful of annoyed crows. The air filled with brown wings as a wake of buzzards mobbed the crows in return, screeching, swooping in to land and jostle for space at the feast. Beating, heavy as her heart, thumped overhead. The vast black wings of a raven carried it past her to the circle of stones, stones that were alive with fluttering feathers, hawking cries and quarrelling. Another raven followed, and another. The stone circle boiled like a cauldron of birds.

Then they came, down the valley of the sea loch, giant white-tailed eagles, so many she couldn't count – more than she had fingers on her hands. *Rau . . . rau . . . Yip – yip – yipp.* Barking and yelping like dogs, wings bigger than broch doors and barely beating, at last, they came.

'They're coming, they're coming!' she squealed at Ard, so excited she forgot to keep the silence.

'Aye,' he said. 'Did you think they wouldn't, for a queen?'

'No.' She shook her head. 'I knew they would.' But tears filled her eyes. There was an ocean between hope and certainty. That gulf had been safely crossed. Most of the smaller birds swarmed into the air as the convocation of eagles swung down to land. Though tears spilled over her cheeks, Skaaha began to laugh.

'Look,' she giggled. 'They're like the warriors.'

On the ground, the sea eagles were indeed like warriors, with white, limed hair and wearing bearskin coats, all strut and feathers, well-armed warriors with sharp beaks and talons who coolly ignored the odd hoodie crow that thought to make a fight of it, just as cattle ignored flies.

'We'll not stand long now,' Ard said. 'Do you hear that?'

High above was a new call. *Kya . . . kya . . . kya . . .* Golden eagles, come from the mountains, soared overhead. They might not come down, but they paid their tribute. Kerrigen had been offered to the sky, and the sky had answered. Skaaha buried her face in her father's tunic and wept.

Tosk picked his moment with care. The departure of the first crow, a handful of gulls rising, the first eagle to lift and land on the headstone, preening its feathers. He lifted the heavy iron mallet from the queen's redundant chariot. With its weight resting on his shoulder, he set out back to the circle. A step behind, two companion priests matched his pace, one playing a slow rhythm on the hand drum, the other a soft, haunting tune on a reed pipe. There was a great fluttering inside the stones. Screeching in protest, the remaining birds lifted into the sky, finding different heights to hover at. Tosk drew breath deep and steady with every step. Kerrigen had been his charge from her childhood. He was an old man then and expected her to outlive him. Now his beard was grey and she was white bones, picked almost clean.

It was said their ancestors came from the sky. It was said eagles were born from the sun and died among the stars. Tosk eschewed such superstition. He'd seen many dead eagles and didn't believe in ancestors. Everyone who lived was alive still, here or in the otherworld. The spirit couldn't exist without mind and body, or be separated from them, as this ancient ceremony intended, with flesh from bone. Yet, as he swung the mallet from his shoulder to balance in his hands, he turned his face to a sky dark with wheeling birds and willed the progenitors pleased to receive this woman. Then he swung the mallet high and brought it down, hard and heavy, smashing the bones. Over and over he swung, shattering all that was left of the queen he adored into sharp shards and leaking marrow.

Skaaha squirmed, watching the rhythmic movement of Tosk's back. The sun climbed high, the pipes played on, the hand drum beat out quiet and steady, every fourth beat joined by a heavier thud from the mallet.

'What's he doing?' she asked Ard. It took so long.

'Making a great sacrifice,' her father replied. 'Making sure it will be finished today.' She saw his body stiffen, the fist nearest her clench. He turned to look west. 'There's a bear coming,' he said. 'Keep still.'

As he stepped forward, scanning for it, Skaaha froze. The wide human circle that allowed birds to come down should also deter land predators who might chase them away. A bear wouldn't come near people, unless it was sick or very hungry. Maybe this one was. She glanced around, looking for Kerrigen to protect them, and caught herself, the shock of absence sudden and alarming. Ard had no such hesitation. Spotting it, he signed 'bear' to Mara, who stood further round the ring, pointing its whereabouts. Skaaha stared in that direction. At first she could see nothing, but as she heard the faint click of weapons released, she saw the shambling movement on a low mound in front of a wooded copse.

Drawn to the possibility of an easy meal by squawking, circling birds, the bear stopped, surveying the sky to pinpoint the food source. Then he reared to sniff. His nose told him all was not well. The warriors rearranged themselves between him and the people, spears held ready. Ard stepped back into place beside Skaaha.

'Mara might want a new coat,' she said, worried by the warrior's leadership.

'They won't hunt today,' her father said, 'unless they must.'

As they watched, the bear decided otherwise. Affecting an air of sudden indifference, he swung around and headed off, out of sight behind the hillock.

Inside the circle, Tosk reached the end of his task. He was too old for this, the work long and hard, the mallet heavy. Only the skull remained, slivers of skin and sinew still attached, eye sockets empty, brain intact, the accident damage to it now obvious in the cracked cup-shaped depression on the rear mound of bone.

He rested the mallet against the keeper at the head end of

the offering stone and wiped sweat from his face and hands with the rim of his stained robe. Tenderly, he lifted the skull and placed it in the centre, clearing a space among shards of rib and spine. The warriors preserved the heads of enemies because the soul couldn't pass to the otherworld while the mind remained in this one. His hands trembled, the ageing muscles in his arms protesting at the effort they'd expended. Again, he raised the iron mallet. Again, he swung it.

'Mara doesn't like you,' Skaaha told Ard, in case he thought otherwise. 'She gives you the evil eye.'

Her father laughed. 'She liked me well enough once,' he chuckled. 'In her bed. And a wildcat she is too, as I remember it.'

Skaaha's mouth fell open. 'She bedded you!' He was even braver than she thought. Mara's lovers rarely lasted long. One was found at the foot of cliffs where she'd thrown him when he displeased her. The druids banned her from a full circle of Bride's four festivals over that.

'Until your mother took a notion for me instead,' Ard said. 'For which Mara only had her own boasting to blame, though she never saw it that way.'

'She boasted of bedding you?' Skaaha puzzled. Men were easy to bed, and warriors took any they wanted. 'Because you're a smith?'

'No, of how well I pleased her.'

The look on his face made Skaaha wonder if he boasted now. He was beautiful to look at, strong with broad, sinewy muscles in his arms and thighs. No doubt he could swing a hammer, stand up to great heat, forge and shape rock into metal. In the jewellery he wore, there was also something fine and delicate about his craftsmanship. But she was far too young to know a man and couldn't guess what he meant.

'You didn't please my mother,' she corrected.

Again he laughed out loud. 'Oh, I think I did,' he said. 'Perhaps too much.' But he would say no more.

The druids returned from the sacred stones. Silence fell

again. This time the birds came down quicker, the eagles landing almost before the smaller birds settled. The sun approached mid-day but it didn't take so long this time – a short period of screeching, squawking, fluttering and flapping. The high *kikikiki* scream of golden eagles usurped by their bigger kin ripped through the day. This time when the birds left, they didn't circle but swept off, back to their different roosts and territories, leaving only a few disappointed gulls wandering among the stones.

Tosk made his third trip into the ring. It was brief. When he emerged, he stopped in the gateway, took the cord from his waist and raised his arms. Two priests carried a bronze pot with a burning peat in it to him. They pulled off his ruined robe and dropped it on the peat so it flamed. A new robe was pulled over his head, covering his nakedness. It was then Skaaha saw that the sash Tosk held was not the usual knotted cord druids wore but hair – long, dark, plaited hair: Kerrigen's. The old druid held it high for a moment, then he dropped it into the heart of the flame. It smoked and burned, the acrid stench drifting up in the warm air.

'Kerrigen of the tribe of Danu, queen of warriors, foster-child of Lethra, born of Oohaa, blood descendant of the goddess, is gone to her ancestors,' the old man called. 'She lives now in the skies and is no more among us. It is finished.'

'Aye-yaa!' The crowd cheered the triumph of beliefs older even than druid faith, old as the standing stones themselves. Kerrigen's spirit was freed from the endless burden of life. 'Aye-yie-yaa!' Some hugged each other with joy. Others wept. Most crowded forward to see the proof that nothing remained. The priests, relieved that the profane ritual was over, struck up a lively tune. Children, relieved of the need for silence, skipped about. Young women ran to pick flowers for garlands, men to collect wood for the solstice fire. Barrels of beer were broken open, food laid out for the feast. When they'd eaten, the warriors would pledge their honours to a new queen.

4

'I pledge allegiance to Mara!' One by one, warriors from every chapter on the island clenched their right fist to their heart and took the oath of honour. No man could challenge Mara, and none of the women did. Jiya wasn't among them. On the far side of the field, she paced back and forth behind her niece, murmuring incomprehensibly to herself. Protected by her disorder, with the freedom of those blessed in such ways, if she chose to make no pledge, no one would insist.

Ignoring her aunt, Skaaha frowned as the new queen swore to protect and uphold the druid peace throughout the Islands of Bride. Ard, who stood beside his daughter, wore an identical expression, brow dark as a moonless night.

'I think we should go,' he prompted, 'before drink reminds Mara of her spite against me, and she exerts her new authority.'

Suli hurried over, swinging her long staff to prod the ground ahead as she walked. 'We'll restrain Mara,' she assured him. 'A queen serves the will of her warriors or she does not lead for long. Don't miss the sun-dance.' The celebration would last all night, the shortest on the wheel. 'Stay till morning, my son. You have a long road and there will be many goodbyes.'

'Not my favourite thing,' said Ard, declining.

Jiya slid round behind him, wrapping her arms around his waist. 'Not even with me?' she whispered in his ear.

Ard clasped his arms over hers, leant his head back against her hair. 'Now that would be a long goodbye,' he teased.

Watching the two of them, Skaaha felt a surge of inspiration. Her aunt liked her father, perhaps enough to marry him for a time. 'Jiya can come with us,' she exclaimed, looking to Suli for confirmation. 'Can't she?'

Ard pushed the warrior's arms away. 'We've trouble enough,' he protested.

'But I will come.' Jiya grinned, and turned to Suli. 'We should make sure our little shadow settles only where she's safe.'

'And what happens when visions torment her?' Ard demanded of the elderly high priest. 'There are no warriors in Kylerhea.'

Visions? Skaaha frowned again. Jiya couldn't be a visionary. Seers, like Suli, were always priests. A small body thumped into her, grabbing her tunic. It was Eefay.

'Don't go, Skaaha,' she begged. 'Don't leave me.' Her green eyes filled with tears. 'You've to look after me.' Her mouth trembled. 'Kerrigen said.'

All Skaaha's certainties deserted her. She had often resented their mother's insistence that she protect Eefay. But now, unable to imagine life without her sister, she threw her arms round the little girl and hugged her tight.

'You can come with us too, Eefay,' she assured her, 'be a smith like me.' It wasn't right they should be separated. She glared at Eefay's father, arriving from his oath-taking to fetch her. 'You don't have to go with Donal.'

Suli thumped her staff on a rock. 'Enough,' she insisted. 'We will not go over old ground.' She called on Tosk to fetch Kerrigen's chariot. Then, sternly, she laid down the law for Skaaha. 'You can't solve losing what you love by taking half of Ullinish with you,' she said. 'Jiya can accompany you.' She raised a hand to forestall Ard's further objection. 'But Ruan,' – she indicated the blond, beardless druid who had sat next her in the council – 'will go too, as your advisor and teacher.' She glanced at the blacksmith. 'He will bring Jiya to me, if the need arises, before returning to you.'

Skaaha hesitated. She could tolerate the druid if Jiya was the reward. But Eefay clung to her, still pleading. A life among strangers without her little sister to share it yawned suddenly before her, alien and lonely.

'You both have futures to embrace,' Suli went on. 'All that comes between you is a strip of sea. Blood is surely thicker than the water of the sound between Kylerhea and Glenelg. You'll meet often, this much I see. Your bond will be tested. It need not break. Eefay chose to be a warrior, to follow Kerrigen's path. She goes with Donal. And you, Skaaha, have a sacrifice to make.'

Tosk arrived beside them, leading the chariot ponies. Mara rode alongside, bearing the torch to light the solstice fire. Eefay clung tighter to her sister.

Halting her skittish horse, the new queen looked down on them. 'The warriors of Bracadale,' she announced, 'would be honoured to make the final sacrifice for Kerrigen in her homeland.'

Wordless, Skaaha stared up at her, at the cold eyes, the blue spiral on her cheek. The answer formed in her gut, shrieking through her flesh, but no sound came out of her mouth. Eefay shivered against her, mouth open, gazing at the warrior.

Suli spoke for them. 'Your offer is generous,' she said calmly, 'for it will be a hard task, but by hard tasks we learn, and that one falls to Skaaha who will do it.'

'Yes.' Skaaha nodded furiously. 'Yes, I will.'

'So be it,' Mara said. Tugging her mount's head round, she kicked the horse away, scattering clods of turf around them.

'Bitch,' Jiya cursed, flicking spatters of soil from her breast.

Suli tapped her rod again. 'Ruan will keep the honours till the time comes,' she said, continuing as if the interruption hadn't occurred.

The novice druid took the dead queen's helmet, shield and weapons from the chariot. Her bearskin was gone, burned to ashes in the fire cauldron. Tosk held out the reins, offering them to Eefay. The little girl's grasp of Skaaha slackened.

'It's mine?' she gasped.

'If you mean to be a warrior,' the old man said. 'If not, they'll be sacrificed.'

Letting go of her sister, Eefay grasped the reins and clambered on to the platform behind the ponies. 'It's mine,' she shouted gleefully. 'Look, Donal, it's mine,' she yelled, 'mine!' as her father led the chariot away.

Anger flared in Skaaha. The water in the kyle should freeze over before she'd go visit Glenelg if she was so easily replaced! Impotent, she watched her sister go, the tears of loss barely dry on her cheeks, hair gleaming golden in the sun, the wheels of their mother's chariot spinning over the grass.

'The size of her,' Erith complained, 'and knows nothing!'

'She'll learn,' Ard protested. 'And she's a girl, worth two boys, maybe more.' They'd been back a fortnight, and still his wife raged, growing more annoyed each day.

'Kerrigen's girl.' Erith was scathing as a crone despite her child-bearing prime. 'Her life spent learning the wrong things!' She tutted at the youth responsible as the cauldron banged down on the hearthstone of the peat fire in the centre of their home. 'We have men aplenty for warriors.'

'And few wives for them,' Ard pointed out. 'I thought you'd be pleased. Skaaha's not to blame for how she was raised. Be fair, Erith.' He changed tack. 'The druids thought you'd be good for her.'

'Don't try getting round me, Ard Greimme. This was your idea. You didn't ask before you left.'

'I didn't know,' he objected. 'She chose me.'

'And you couldn't say no. Now why does that not surprise me?'

'She'll make a fine smith.' Ard ignored the jibe. Erith's ire was due more to Jiya's presence than Skaaha's. 'I'll teach her myself.'

'You better,' Erith warned, 'or you'll be without a wife yourself!' It was no idle threat. Unlike Jiya, Ard was not a guest who must be given shelter. He was her husband, the second one of three, and divorce was easily done. If Ard lost favour, he could lose home and livelihood, become dependent on some other woman to take him in.

Outside, Skaaha went through her morning routine of turns and leaps, of handstands, cartwheels, back flips and somersaults. A light sea-breeze kissed her naked skin. In the unfamiliar landscape, she improvised, using a peat stack instead of rock to gain enough lift for a double turn in mid-air before landing. Dew shimmered on the grass, making it slippery under her bare feet. No broch towered near by, only squat roundhouses, their huge thatched roofs almost skirting the ground.

The ironworks of Kylerhea sat on the south coast of the island, separated from the mainland of Alba by a narrow strait. Sheltered on three sides by comfortingly high but passable, rounded hills, the flat river valley of the foreshore looked out across the sound to the bay of Glenelg. Once across the water, it was a short journey to Donal's school for warriors, where Skaaha's sister had settled.

'Don't care,' she'd said when Ard had pointed out its position for her.

Alongside her, naked as the girl, Jiya went through the same exercises, except for the warrior's use of spear, shield and sword. Raised voices reached them through the roundhouse thatch. Skaaha had never heard a row before. Warriors settled disputes with competitive feats. Argument, like the one she'd been hearing for days, would have ended swiftly, with bloody finality. It made Skaaha nervous for Ard, and scornful of Erith's authority.

The welcome had been warm at first, excited, yet the people here were wary, distant, and men spoke out of turn, without waiting to be addressed. Her newly prized father lessened in stature when she discovered he shared a wife. Warriors took one husband at a time, and only if they wanted to breed. But she was now the daughter of a man who must do as men did, and took comfort in Erith's jealousy. The forge-keeper had two other husbands. If she divorced Ard, Jiya would steal him to her bed in no time. Then they'd all be happy.

A small, bemused crowd watched the two newcomers go

through their paces. Ard came to the door of the house. Equally bemused to find himself guardian to his daughter, he watched her now, lithe and slender, so like her mother, though a child without breasts or buttocks. She was good, confident in her movements, and quick, using the land the way a seal used water. Such talent could be channelled.

Jiya – he frowned – the moonstruck warrior was joyous in training, buoyed up by a strange lightness despite her heavier flesh. The globes of her full breasts swung as she turned in the air, buttocks bouncing as she landed. A fine sweat misted her skin like haar hugging the early-morning valleys. How well he remembered the saltiness of that skin, the firm rounded warmth of those buttocks – and Kerrigen coming in to look for her sister to find she was astride her husband. He shuddered. This was not good.

'Breakfast,' he called, his voice rougher than usual.

Both child and woman came to abrupt, poised halts. They looked at each other, not at him. Each thrust a fist forward to head height.

'Hyaaa-aaaaa,' they screamed together, then took off towards the sea, yelling as they went, legs scything, feet flashing over the grass.

Although the bystanders had witnessed this every morning since Skaaha arrived, it grew more and more compelling. Today, Ard couldn't help himself. He, too, thrust a fist forward, as did several of the watching women and men, girls and boys.

'Hyaaa-aaaaa,' they screamed, and followed their strange guests, pelting towards the lapping waves.

'Aaaaa-yaaaaa,' Jiya and Skaaha yelled, plunging in and ploughing on till the depth around their armpits slowed their assault and cold bit into their flesh. Swimming wasn't possible here. Further out, a strong current dragged the tide rapidly through the rocky spout of the narrow Kyle of Rhea. Instead, they drew deep breaths, ducked under, twisted, turned then came up for air, splashing, laughing, chittering before the stumbled, scrambled rush back to land.

Only a few who'd followed them down the shore had actually run into the sea: a couple of children, a woman and two men, one of whom was Ard. He reared up, water running from clothes and hair, to realize, of course, the warriors were naked, their clothes, dry, waiting, conveniently placed on a sandy hummock. He hauled the children out and plodded, dripping, back to the roundhouse. Erith would not be pleased. No matter. They'd dry out round the fire or in the forge after eating.

'With salt in your clothes, is it?' Erith complained. 'You' – she nodded at Jiya – 'can wash them in the river. We've nothing else for you to do.'

The insult was gross. Warriors were waited on. It was their due for giving their lives over to defend the island people. Jiya's fleshy lids flickered up till her eyes met the forge-keeper's. The warrior's face creased, and she laughed, roaring, hollering and hooting until everyone joined in, even Erith, who tried not to. Skaaha giggled and chuckled with the rest, though sense told her nothing funny was happening. But everything seemed fine. Breakfast was eventually eaten, punctuated by continued snorts and repeated outbreaks of laughter.

When the meal was over, the sun was fully up. While the damp among them went to their curtained chambers to change, Skaaha and Jiya dressed each other's hair. The rest scattered to their various jobs. When Ard appeared, changed and ready for work, he asked Skaaha to accompany him. Jiya fell in behind. They were outside when Erith called.

'Wait.'

As they turned, she dumped a pile of sodden clothes in the doorway.

'Your work for the day,' she said to Jiya.

'I cannot laugh twice at the same joke,' the warrior said. Her hand went to her sword, drawing it from the scabbard in a single, smooth slash of steel, and her face lit with the wide smile she kept for dear friends or when facing an enemy. 'So I will wash your clothes.'

'Jiya,' Skaaha gasped, more shocked than if the warrior had ended Erith's life.

Her aunt held up her other hand to silence her. 'I am not trained for this,' she said, keeping her gaze fixed on Erith and sounding strangely pompous, 'but I am not above it.' She drew the sword. 'Only the truly great can stoop with humility so that others may learn the error of their ways.' She plunged the sword straight through the centre of the bundle, raised it like a traveller's pack over her shoulder and strode off towards the river, cackling as she went. Erith's jaw dropped. Ard grabbed Skaaha by the shoulder of her tunic and whisked her away.

At the river, Jiya found a deep pool, slid the bundle off her sword and crouched to stir the clothes around in the clear water with the blade. This washing was a mysterious chore, and one that merited time. To ensure the sea-salt dissolved thoroughly, she poked and prodded her weapon into air bubbles that formed in the garments. Now and then, she hauled one out to whack it soundly. To entertain herself, she turned the task into training, assigning names to items, issuing challenges, delivering thrusts.

5

Ard led Skaaha past the forge, past the smelting house, on up the river course away from the settlement, until they reached a wider valley, most of which was peat bog. They came to a group of cutters busy at work, lifting and stacking the cut blocks of peat to where they'd drain before being carted down to the village to be piled up to dry ready for winter.

'I'm not to be a peat-cutter,' Skaaha objected. 'I'm to be a smith.'

'If peat-cutting is needed, peat-cutting you will do,' Ard said, walking on to where the water grew murkier. 'But we're here so you can learn about smithing.' He pulled off one of the leather bags he carried on his shoulder and put the strap over her head, tying it so it hung at her waist rather than her knees. 'And the first thing to learn is to value what you work with.' He stopped where the water was coloured a milky orange. Lurid scum crusted the surface among the grasses. 'Would you tie your skirt up between your legs?'

'Why?'

'Because we're going in the bog.'

As she tied the cloth to keep it out of the brackish water, Skaaha grinned up at her father. 'It will be all right to get dirty,' she said. 'Jiya's doing the washing.'

Ard almost chuckled, before he remembered his fatherly responsibilities. 'Do not be getting ideas,' he said. 'Erith's my wife, and keeper of the forge. She's also with child, and you must mind her.'

Skaaha gaped. Pregnant women merited great respect. Druids believed those who died in the otherworld came back through them and, often, birthing women were born into the otherworld as their child arrived in this one. Even though

Skaaha doubted druid teachings, Erith became instantly admirable. She tied the knot in her skirt tighter between her legs. Ard was already calf-deep in the orange bog-water, reaching into it. He pulled out a small lump of rough sandy-brown pitted rock.

'Feel it,' he said, putting it in her hand. 'Feel it, look at it, smell it. Taste it, too. Know it when you find it, exactly that. That's iron, good iron.'

She studied the nugget. It was the size of a chestnut but heavier, jaggy and brittle. The earthy, peaty smell was tinged with the smell of metal, metallic on her tongue, too. Sometimes, when the potter at Bracadale allowed, she had played with clay. It was special, a slippery, squidgy soil that baked hard in the hot oven to become bowls and jugs. But the rock she held now was even more magical. It could become cauldrons, spearheads, swords, and rims for chariot wheels. The art of working it would become hers, a magic art warriors depended on, hers to give or to withhold.

'See if you can find some,' Ard said. Skaaha stuck the iron nodule in her bag and searched about in the rust-coloured water with her hands, drawing up silt, soil, pebbles. Eventually she had three pieces of ore, and her back ached. Ard talked as they worked. 'Best you use your hands,' he said. 'Eyes are no use in this murk, but fingers see what they touch, once they know the feel of it.' As morning wore on she found the right lumps more quickly. They took a break then. Ard showed her how to find the bubbling source where springs of orange water brought iron up from the otherworld.

'If you believe the druids,' Skaaha said.

'But you can see it rise.'

'It comes from the ground is what I see,' Skaaha argued.

'So where do we come from?' he asked, humouring her.

Rau . . . rau . . . yip. Yip . . . yip . . . Skaaha looked up at the sky, where a pair of white-tailed sea eagles drifted lazily above the coastline. 'Out of women,' she answered. 'You plant the seed, so you must know.'

'And some seed grows wilder than others,' he chided. 'If you want to talk chickens and eggs, talk to Ruan. With me, talk iron.' They were walking back down the side of the bog, where the water was clearer. 'You see that?' He pointed to an oily slick on the surface.

'The rainbow on the water?'

'Aye, there's iron there too. Any time you see that slick.'

He sent her into the marsh again, fingers searching through sharp reeds, the greasy slick sticking to the hairs on her arms, making a rim round her legs. She felt like a treasure-hunter, rewarded now and then with a nugget and her father's quiet nod of approval. The ache in her back from constant bending made straightening up difficult when he called a halt. They walked on, heading home, a satisfying weight in the bag at her side. When they passed the peat-cutters, she saw the youngsters with them all had similar leather pouches slung at their waists, some bulging with nuggets of iron, heavier than her own.

'They bring down most of it,' Ard explained. 'Two birds with one stone. But you have to learn.'

She felt cheated of something indefinable, her victory quashed. No one in the village would greet her as if she were a hunter bringing home a stag, after all, especially not Erith, whom she'd hoped to impress. Her joy in her finds shrank.

'Where is Eefay?' she asked. They were high above the settlement, with its three large houses, smoke drifting from the cooking fires through their great thatched roofs. Other buildings nearer the hills housed the smelter furnace and forge. Standing between the village and the burial mound of the ancestors, the druid cell's three huts seemed small and isolated. But it was across the water she looked, where the narrow strait widened towards the open sea in the west, to the land beyond.

Ard crouched beside her, pointing. 'See those hills, like breasts, one larger?'

She nodded, unable to speak for the sudden tightness in her chest.

'She's in the valley between,' he said, straightening up.

'They'll put a fire on top of the smaller hill come Sowen. You'll see your sister then.'

All the way back, she kept looking over at the twin peaks. The cross-quarter festival of blood was a long way off. Lunasa came first, the reaper's moon followed by the hunter's moon. Both would pack the larder for the coming winter. Only when the third, final red moon of harvest died would it be Sowen.

When they reached the valley floor, there were raised voices. She needn't have worried about attracting Erith's disapproval. Jiya had finished the washing. It hung neatly on ropes of twine between the trees, barely recognizable strips swaying in the slight breeze.

'Rags,' Erith screeched. 'They're rags!'

'Clean rags,' Jiya corrected, proudly. She sat astride the anvil stone outside the forge, feet planted on the cobbled path, putting an edge back on her sword with a flint rubber. 'This clothes-washing is a fine thing. I will do more tomorrow.'

'You'll do no such thing,' Erith yelled, 'or we'll all be naked by winter!'

'And a fine hardy bunch we'd be, the better for it,' Jiya announced, swinging her leg over the anvil and standing to sheathe her sword when she spotted Skaaha. 'Hey, iron hunter,' she cried. 'Look at you with your heavy pack!' She patted it approvingly. 'Soon, you will make me a spear, and they will talk of this great new smith the length of the island.'

'I might just about have enough for a spearhead,' Skaaha agreed ruefully.

'Excellent!' Jiya crowed. 'You learned to find iron. I learned how to wash clothes. We have lived the day well.' She put her beaming face down to Skaaha's till the heat of her cheek touched the girl's, and whispered, 'And it won't be our last.'

Sunset was when the new day began, as it always did, with everyone reclining round the hearth after eating, supping ale. This time Jiya was begged for a story. Delighted, she began, telling of a man who saw a handsome naked woman wandering the beach and chased after her into the sea. The woman didn't run too fast, because he was a fine-looking man, and she didn't swim too hard, because she could tell, under his clothes, the man had smooth, sensuous muscles and strong thighs. But, in his haste to catch her, the man forgot he was clothed. So, while the irresistible woman plunged further and further out, the man got into great difficulty in the current, a current much like the one that so easily carried coracles across Kyle of Rhea. The weight of water in the man's clothes slowed him down so that the waves lashed over his head and seaweed wrapped round his legs, drawing him deeper and deeper into the salty depths until his lungs burned for breath.

The woman turned in the waves to see why the man was taking so long to catch her and saw he was drowning. She dived to rescue him but couldn't. He was down too deep and she, too, felt her lungs burn for breath. She looked into his dark, drowning eyes and knew she would lose him for ever, no matter what she did now, yet she loved him and couldn't let him drown. So she left him tangled in the weed and sinking, and swam for the shore faster than she had swum away from it. There, on a sand dune where she'd left it, lay her slick, smooth coat. Grabbing it, she ran back to the waves, pulled it on and plunged in. Now she was more at home in the water than the fish. Now she was master of the waves.

'She's a selkie, a selkie,' shouted the children, recognizing the mythical creature that could change from seal to human and back again.

And that's what she was, of course, and she reached the man just as his lungs gave up and drew deep for breath so the water flooded into them. But the selkie plunged straight at him, thrusting her silk nose hard into his middle so the water was forced back out of him again. With her sharp seal teeth, she caught hold of his tunic and rose fast, leaping out of the water, trailing the helpless, limp man with her as she soared through the air, spilling salty drops like a rainbow of beads in the arc she made. This time, when the man's lungs drew deep for breath, it was sweet salt air that filled them.

'And he lived, he lived!' yelled the adults.

And, indeed, he did. Tugging and tearing at his clothes, the selkie dragged the beautiful man up on to the beach, where she rolled him on his back and nudged him so he coughed up all the cauldrons of sea water he had swallowed. As he shook the water from his eyes, the man looked around for the woman who had saved him, but all he saw was a seal. He gazed in astonishment at the shredded rags he now wore that once had been his clothes. 'Did you see a woman,' he begged the seal, 'a beautiful woman who swims like a fish and has hair that drifts like seaweed down her back? Where is she, where did she go?'

'She's there, she's there,' everybody shouted. 'It's the seal. She's a selkie!'

But a seal cannot speak. And having put her seal coat on again, seven circles of the sun must pass before the selkie could take it off and be a woman again. All she could do was nudge the rescued man one last time, and with a sad look from her luminous dark eyes, she turned towards the sea and vanished into the waves.

'And,' Jiya finished, her own eyes glowing like the peats in the hearth, 'if you would see the proof' – she slapped Ard's chest with the back of her hand – 'here is the man, and there' – she pointed to the pile of rags in a basket by the door – 'are his tattered clothes.'

'Aye-yie-yaa!' There was delighted applause, from the children for the nail-biting story complete with props to prove it, and from the adults for Jiya's aplomb in turning a source of discontent to advantage.

'Bardic,' a cracked old voice cackled. It was Lethra the crone, clan chief, head of the village and larder-keeper, whose people had come over from her house to hear the story. 'You must stay with us through winter, when fine stories are most needed.' She patted the warrior's shoulder as she shuffled past, going home to sleep.

Ard put his arm round Jiya, giving her a celebratory squeeze. 'A brave lesson in storytelling,' he said. 'You did well.'

Erith glared at the pair of them. 'And perhaps tomorrow,' she snapped, 'our guest will put her mind to the story of a selkie with needle and thread who can do the mending!' Then she shooed Skaaha and the other children off to bed and got ready for her own, throwing Ard's clothes out of her chamber and calling for another of her husbands to come keep her warm.

'Does that mean you're without a bed, beautiful man?' Jiya breathed, nuzzling Ard's neck and nibbling his earlobe, 'for I have a bed, over there.' She nodded to the curtained guest chamber further round the room. 'A bed sizeable enough for two, providing they lie close enough together.'

'I can take Gern's bed,' Ard answered, 'now that he shares Erith's. I might be out of my depth in yours.' But as he spoke, he had moved into her, not away, pushing aside the knot of hair against her neck and with his mouth kissing the hollow of the curve at the side of it, the point where she would aim a sword to kill a man, and with a kiss that was killing her.

'Then I must help you ride the waves,' she murmured, pressing her cheek against his dark head, her voice thick and heavy as the ocean pressing on its floor. They both rose together, holding close to each other as they moved to the curtained chamber on the farthest side of the room.

When first light woke Skaaha, she rose and went out to strip off and start her routine. Jiya hadn't risen yet. A boy, several seasons older than her, stood watching.

'Will you show me how?' he said.

'How to take your night clothes off?'

He shook his head, flushing. 'I can do that.' To prove it, he did, revealing bony ribs and the skinny muscles of a youth.

'How to jump and turn in the air,' he explained. He raised his chin proudly. 'I want to be a warrior.'

'Then you're in the wrong place,' Skaaha said, but she showed him how to stand, kicking his feet to the right space apart. 'Now copy me.' She did the moves slowly so he could follow, running through all the easy ones, which were about stretching and loosening up. He managed them easily enough, though she could see he was tense from trying too hard. 'You would do the warrior steps well,' she said. 'They're about being fierce in battle. Look.' She stood square, stuck her elbows out and pushed down with flattened palms on to nothing. 'Push down,' she told him. 'Push down on to the anvil.'

'It's over there,' he said, pointing.

She shook her head. 'No, it's where you think it is. Push down.'

And he did, and got it. The warrior steps were easy after that, the strong strides, the set arm movements. But the chill of the morning began to bite.

'Now we must speed up,' she said, and did three rolling somersaults over the grass then leapt up neatly to cartwheel back. 'Together,' she said, and went again. The boy started beside her, but his first roll went squint, and he flopped about as he landed. Skaaha cartwheeled back, showed him how to place hands and feet. 'Think small,' she said. 'Think ball, then you will roll. It's up here.' She tapped her head, and off they set again. This time was better. 'Now you practise that, while I get on.'

'But I want to leap and turn,' the boy protested.

'And break your neck?'

He shook his head, flushed and miserable again.

'You can't learn everything in one morning,' she said kindly. 'When you can roll forward like a ball, and backwards just as well, and to one side or the other, then you'll begin to know how to fall. But only a fool leaps in the air without knowing how to come down, for down you will surely come, unless you have wings, of course.'

43

'I don't, but I would like to have – invisible wings like yours.'

'Then roll.'

He set off, inexpertly. Skaaha continued her routine. From the roundhouse, she heard Erith's angry voice, the sound of Ard trying to soothe. It must be their habit. Eventually, Jiya appeared. Grinning joyfully, the warrior glanced briefly at the boy who rolled around all elbows and knees and ankles, but said nothing. Stripping off, she warmed up vigorously. When breakfast was called, the three of them dashed into the sea. The few who watched controlled themselves this time, and went instead to eat.

6

After breakfast, when Jiya combed and re-plaited Skaaha's hair, the warrior worked quickly, her mind elsewhere. The girl, stoical as ever, gritted her teeth rather than yelp when tugs were harshly yanked out. None of the usual banter passed between them, though Jiya chuckled often, deep in her throat, and wouldn't say what amused her. Erith glared, drawing them dark looks. Skaaha was sure they finished sooner than usual, but by the time she'd redone the warrior's braids, Ard was already gone to the forge. Outside, it was Ruan who waited, leaning on a long staff twice the length of the carved rods druids usually walked with, a staff like Suli's.

'I'll come with you today,' he said, slipping the bag Ard had given him over Skaaha's head.

'I don't want a druid for company,' she said, pulling the bag into place. His eyes were a disturbing blue. They watched her always. She was aware of that and didn't like it, but it was bearable while he kept his distance. 'What do you know of iron-hunting?'

'You can test me,' he suggested, and when she frowned, added, 'Look, where you go, I will go. You're my charge. That's the way things are.'

Skaaha ignored him. 'Come with me, Jiya,' she said. 'Then I don't have to listen to druid lessons all day.'

Jiya declined. 'I'm going to hug my happiness,' she grinned, 'before it's taken away.' She strode off towards the beach.

'What does that mean,' Skaaha demanded, 'and where's she going?'

'That's for Jiya to know,' Ruan said. 'It's enough you should know where you're going.'

Skaaha glanced skyward, snorted and set off, following the

river up the valley. Ruan kept pace with her, chatting about the forge and her place in it.

'I'm not druid,' she interrupted. Like Kerrigen, she kept the old faith.

'No.'

'I'll never be druid.'

'No?'

Skaaha shut her ears, there was no point, and watched golden eagles hover above the hills. Every now and then, one would plummet to the ground. Her heart swooped too, experiencing with the dive a frisson of fear that it might not pull up, but they always did and rose again, usually with a rabbit clutched in their claws.

Eventually, the priest stopped talking. Earth-song took over. The river gargled over rock. A breeze whispered through reeds and treetops. Birds chirruped, warbled and twittered. From hill pastures, sheep bleated, quavering against the deeper lowing of cattle. Skaaha walked on beyond the peat-cutters, beyond the spring of yesterday, looking for a place of her own to harvest, one that would yield much more. Though she wanted the priest to feel superfluous, she also wanted to impress.

The riverbank grew rockier and drier as they climbed. It began to seem she'd been too clever and might look a fool instead when they rounded a bend and there, spread out, was a curved wetland valley. Spotting the telltale orange crust around the reeds, Skaaha bent to tie her skirts up. Ruan slung his staff on his back and copied by pulling his robe up through the cord at his waist so it hung just above his knees.

'Do you think Thum will make a warrior?' he asked.

Skaaha stopped tying and stared up at him. 'Who's Thum?'

'The boy you were teaching this morning.'

'Why should I care?'

'Because you're a good teacher.' That it was the first response he'd had since they left the settlement hung unsaid. 'Patient.'

Skaaha shrugged. 'He works in the forge.'

'The smelter, and isn't happy there.'

She considered. 'He's gangly.'

'But won't always be.'

'And old to be starting.'

'But not much, four seasons more than most. It was different for you.'

Different, right enough. She had played at warriors' feet since she could crawl, copying their routines since she could stand. The druid didn't sound disapproving, though he must be. Kerrigen taught her what she knew. *Rau . . . rau . . . Yip . . . yip . . . yip . . .* Above, a white-tail barked on its way to the sea. Skaaha stepped into the chilly water.

'If Thum truly wants to be a warrior,' she concluded, 'then he will be.' Sliding each foot turn by turn along the marsh bottom to avoid the danger of a pothole, she decided to work around the edges, leaving the deeper water for the priest. He seemed to know fine what was iron and what was stone.

They worked for some time, the sun half-way to noon before Skaaha felt her back begin to object to constant stooping, her bag heavy. She'd made a good choice. This bog had not been harvested for a long time. She was a quarter-way round it, on the furthest side, the water growing deeper with every step, and stopped to push her sleeves up further. Her foot slipped, a sludgy pothole sucking her suddenly down.

Unaware that she yelled, she clawed for a handhold in the reeds, floundering for anything in the silt that would give her purchase. As her weight drew her deeper down, she threw her arms over a hummock, grasped the blind side of it and pulled. Among the mosses, a thick strand of root gave her something to grip. She wound her hand around it and, with her other hand gripping sharp blades of marsh reeds, dragged her chest up on to the clump. As she rose, something reared from the other side of the hummock to look at her – a hooded thatch of muddied hair, leather-brown skin, wicked eyes, crook nose, a mouth curved in a warped leer. A drum battered in her chest, thundered in her ears. Just as she recognized the face that loomed into hers was human, a hand swung up, fingers reaching for her.

'Aaaaaargh!' she screamed, jerking back as it lurched towards her. 'Aaaaargh!' She stumbled sideways. The face swung closer, leering into hers. 'Aaaaargh!'

'Let go the rope,' Ruan shouted, splashing through the bog. 'Skaaha, let go the rope!'

Rope, what rope? Wild with terror, she looked at the root she had wrapped round her hand. It was rope! Frantically, she pushed it off her fingers. The reaching hand of the bog creature swung backwards, its shoulders slipped below the water, the face sank back – and Ruan was pulling her out of the bog, out of the water, to the firm dry grass at the edge. Shaking, whimpering, she clung to him, looking past his shoulder in case the monstrous thing would rise again and run at them.

'It's all right,' Ruan was saying, holding and rocking her. 'It's all right.'

There was nothing, a bubble, a ripple or two, the marsh undisturbed.

'Was that the Shee?' She shuddered, still watching. 'Is it coming again?'

'No. You disturbed a sleeper, that's all.'

'A sleeper? It was somebody,' she squealed. 'What are they doing sleeping in the bog? It was coming for me!' She was losing it again, arms round his neck, clambering higher into his living warmth.

'Hush, no. It's dead and can't harm you.' He stood, lifting her with him, and carried her away up the slope to a rocky outcrop where a stream of clear water trickled down. Once there, he sat, still holding her, for there was no way she would loosen the grip of her hands round his neck, and began to wash her face, throat, legs and feet with the cold, fresh water. 'Fool that I am,' he muttered as he cleaned her. 'I should have thought.'

'You knew that was there?' Anger rose easily on the back of fear.

48

'No.' He shook his head. 'But I might have guessed. Look.' He pointed up the hill to the mountain path where a great boulder marked the boundary between the ironworkers' land and the next tribe's. 'Sleepers are put in bogs on the edges of clan land, as far away as possible without trespassing on another's land. They're bad people who were killed three times, mind, body and spirit, so their soul is trapped.'

'Is that why he – she – had a rope round its neck?' She was calmer now, a dead stranger less alarming than incomprehensible monsters. But she kept her head turned to keep an eye on the bog, just in case. Ruan unwound her arms from his neck, bending her closer to the stream to clean her hands.

'The rope has many purposes,' he said. 'It's left on to lower them in, and so anyone who finds them will know. Even to pull them up, if need be.'

A shiver ran through her. She didn't even want to know why anyone would pull them up on purpose.

'Come,' he said, taking her bag and holding out his hand. 'We'll go back home, get you changed. I think you've learned enough about iron for today.'

They wound their way back down the hill, returning to the riverside well below the marsh. With a safe distance between it and them, Skaaha ran ahead, did a few confident cartwheels then paused, waiting for the druid to catch up.

'If it was tied to a tree up on the path,' she said, 'that would warn other bad people to stay away. Not many folk come visiting through the bog.'

'That's my little warrior,' he said. 'But it wouldn't be a sleeper out of the bog. Its flesh would rot and its spirit pass to the otherworld, to do harm there.'

'So it's trapped for ever and will still be there when you're old and grey?'

'Yes, when you are too.'

'I'll never be old,' she grinned, and turned a few more cartwheels to prove it. Returning to reclaim her bag, she studied the priest. 'When I make the sacrifice, Kerrigen's spirit will waken in the afterlife,' she said, 'and watch over us again.'

'As you believe,' he said, tapping his steps with the staff, 'so it will be.'

'But you don't believe it.' She frowned. Druids usually ignored anything said about ancient beliefs. Without nourishment, the faith of their forebears shrivelled to a stump. 'Shouldn't you tell me I'm wrong?'

'No,' he said. 'I trust the nature of things. And no, beliefs can't be wrong. They're stories we use to explain the world, to help us understand ourselves. Every story has its own truth, and truth is always right, never wrong.'

His answer was unexpected, and puzzling, but she understood what stories were.

'I have a story now,' she exclaimed, beaming.

'You have, indeed,' he agreed. 'A good one, if it's well told.'

She skipped on ahead, eager for home. Tonight, in the safety and warmth of the roundhouse, she would be the storyteller – one who awakened a sleeper in the bog, who outran it, outjumped it, and who led it around by its rope, dancing in tumbling circles till the monster tired and could be slipped safely back into the mire. Jiya would be surprised and proud. Erith would see she wasn't just a burden.

Running down the slope into the village, she couldn't see Jiya, and called her. 'Jiya!' Her voice echoed, unanswered by her aunt's cheerful bellow. In the forge, the smiths were still busy, but not with Jiya. Ard shrugged, his mind on other matters.

'She'll come back when she's ready.' He took Skaaha's bag, weighed it in his hand, impressed. 'You did well.'

The praise went over her head. She ran to Erith's house but Jiya wasn't there.

'Better she stays away,' Erith grumbled, 'for all of us.'

The smelters were clearing up. None of them had seen her aunt. Thum came to help her look. They checked the other roundhouses and all three druid lodges. No one had seen

Jiya since morning, nor did anyone seem troubled by her disappearance.

'She wanders,' Ruan reminded her. 'You know that.'

'Not here, she doesn't,' Skaaha yelled. 'She wouldn't leave me!' But Jiya would, when the mood took her, and she knew that too. Dread settled in her belly. Pushing through beasts returning for the night, she and Thum searched animal pens, disturbing cattle, annoying the milkers. They scoured the copse, the riverbank, the shore. Climbing half-way up the slope, they scanned the hills, the valley, the sea, even the far shores of Alba. There was no sign of Jiya.

Supper was fresh mussels and salty oysters followed by mutton stew. Skaaha ate little. Jiya didn't return to eat. The atmosphere was tense. Erith had ostracized Ard, shunning him. The evening story was told by her new bedmate, Gern. It was a story of a great battle between wind and fire that began with a careless boy in the forge. A dull story from a dull man, Skaaha huffed, only half listening. She wouldn't tell hers, not without Jiya to hear it.

Nights passed. Jiya didn't reappear to join their morning routine. Days came and went. Skaaha learned more new things: how to make charcoal, how to smelt iron, how to beat cold metal. Tides rose and fell. When work was over, she and Thum played games, climbed trees and rockfaces or raced each other through moor or marshland. The moon waxed and waned. Ruan stayed close by wherever she went, and in the evenings, taught her the meaning of night, the patterns and movement of stars. The cross-quarter day approached, the great fire-festival of Lunasa grew near and Skaaha forgot the story she might have told.

Once morning, as the moon grew full again, the dripping of rain woke her. Rising, she peered out at the grey drizzle. Water puddled in the draining ditch around the house, dripping from the thatch. It was warm and dry inside, cold and wet out. *A warrior who can't move is finished*, Kerrigen's voice said, deep and strong in Skaaha's head. But that life, like her mother, was dead. She was becoming a smith, not a warrior. There was no point to her routine now. A weight had settled in her heart since Jiya left, stealing her lightness. Maybe it was time to stop.

Thum came splashing over from the smelters' house, already stripped.

'Come on,' he yelled. 'It's only rain.'

'A curse on your blood,' she yelled back, but unwilling to appear weak, she hauled off her nightshirt, hung it inside the doorway so it would stay dry, and ran out.

The boy had improved greatly during the last moon. He rolled almost as fast as she did, limbs tucked well in. His handstands and cartwheels grew confident, but he remained weak in the jumps. His eagerness was infectious, dispelling Skaaha's black mood. She showed him how to use rising ground to gain height, to run and push off from it. Intending only to demonstrate how to rise higher, on landing she couldn't resist following with three handsprings. When she stopped, almost at the shore, she was looking at a longboat drawn up on it, at Jiya, who sat in it looking back at her, wild and ferocious, and at a dozen helmeted warriors with bristling moustaches, all fully armed for battle, who strode up the beach towards her.

7

Thinking she saw a vision, Skaaha wiped the drizzle from her eyes. The warriors were still coming, and almost on her. She turned her head towards Thum.

'Invaders!' she shrieked. 'Invaders!' She ran towards him, still shouting. 'They've got Jiya. Wake everybody!' As the boy ran to the forge-keeper's roundhouse, Skaaha dashed into the forge, grabbed the nearest weapon and skelped back towards the shore. The unwelcome visitors had just stepped off the shingle on to the grass when she pelted at them, a wet, naked girl with long plaited hair flying out behind her, brandishing a sword.

'What the blazes!' the leader exclaimed. The iron blade plunged into his middle. The girl, unable to stop on the slippery ground, thumped into him as he doubled over, clutching his gut. The men on either side of him drew their swords.

Skaaha, shocked at her success, stepped backwards, looking for blood spurting through the warrior's fingers. An arm caught her round the throat. It was Ard, pinning her against him as he pulled her back out of reach of the assaulted man.

'What are you doing,' he spluttered, 'trying to get hurt?'

The leader of the warriors wheezed, pushing away the support offered by one of his men. 'I'm only winded,' he said. 'Are we needing swords for child's play? Put those away.' He slapped at the nearest blade and the weapons were hastily sheathed.

'There is no edge on this,' Ard said, yanking the half-made weapon from Skaaha's wet fingers. 'As well for you,' he threatened in her ear.

'You don't understand,' she yelped, wriggling. 'They've got Jiya!' Her head slipped through the crook of Ard's arm. She darted forwards, and seeing the lead warrior stoop to catch her, dropped on to her back and slid the last stride-length over the sodden grass. As she slid, she drew her right knee back, aimed for his testicles and kicked out hard with the ball of her right foot.

'Name of Luna,' the warrior gasped, collapsing to his knees, hands clutching his throbbing genitals.

Skaaha turned over, rapidly scrabbling out of the way. Her head jerked, her hands and feet lost purchase on the wet ground. She was lifted, by her plait, into the air and held there, at arm's length, kicking.

'Wherever you got this, Ard,' the red-haired warrior who held her said, 'you should tie it up when you have callers, to a branch of yon tree.'

Hands gripped Skaaha's ankles, Ruan's hands, before she got the measure of her situation and lashed out again.

'Be still, Skaaha,' he said. 'These men are from Ardvasar, protectors, not enemies.' And to the warrior, 'I'll take her now, Fion.'

As she was lowered, cautiously, into Ruan's keeping, Ard helped the grimacing leader to his feet, apologizing for his daughter.

'Sorry you're hurt, Vass,' he added, 'not that she has spirit.'

'Daughter?' Vass grunted. 'Fast as a hare and slippery as a seal with a kick like a thrawn mare! If you could sell me that as a weapon, I'd pay any price.'

'The daughter I made with Kerrigen,' Ard explained.

'Ah, that explains it.' Vass looked at the bedraggled, muddy girl with new respect. 'Kerrigen's daughter.' He limped a careful step towards her. 'I would've wished your mother a longer life,' he said, 'and that she'd taught you sweeter ways to greet an uncle.'

'Kerrigen had no brother.' Skaaha wasn't fooled. 'And you have her only sister in your boat!'

'Bites *and* barks,' the warrior said, turning to Ard. 'Next time you're in a Danu bed, brother, best keep that' – he gripped

Ard's genitals – 'between your own legs.' Then he hollered with laughter, and the two men embraced each other.

Skaaha stood in the rain in front of Ruan, watching her father usher the warriors into the roundhouse like honoured guests. Ruan still had a grip of her plait, the only part she could be held by in the wet. She felt a fool. Not only that, but Thum stood watching, hopping from one foot to the other, looking shamed.

'I should've said,' he muttered. 'Lunasa.' He pointed vaguely skywards. 'They always come.'

'But you ran!'

'To tell Erith they were here. I couldn't find her.'

'You knew and didn't tell me!' she shrieked. Ruan's grip of her plait tugged.

'Enough,' the druid said. 'Go home, Thum.' The boy ran off. Ruan turned Skaaha by her hair to face him. 'I will let you go and you will dress. Then you will serve your uncle and our guardians with ale. Understand?'

'What about Jiya?'

'What about me?' Jiya strode towards them, out of the boat and unrestrained, every inch herself except for the wildness in her eyes.

'Jiya!' Skaaha jerked towards her. Ruan let go her hair, and she ran to throw her arms round her aunt, drawing instant comfort from the bite of leather and the smear of wet fur against her bare skin. 'I thought they had you tied.'

Jiya glanced at the priest. 'Not yet,' she said, beaming, before resting her cheek on the girl's wet hair. 'I went to train the Ardvasar warriors. They've had no one since Kerrigen died.'

'My mother taught those men?'

Jiya nodded. 'Where did you think she went when Donal came to tutor us?'

'Out of his way.' No one had said. 'I thought she just didn't like him.'

'That too,' Jiya agreed. 'Come, you're shivering.'

Ruan stood in the rain, watching them go inside. Suli, his

high priest, believed Jiya guarded Skaaha, and helped guide her. But the woman's body, mind and spirit were not balanced. Capricious, with unknowable ways, she was a gifted warrior made dangerous by erratic moods and visions she couldn't control. Her return threatened the progress he'd made with his task. He let his breath slow. His life had lasted twenty suns, almost twice that of Skaaha. About the time she was born, his priesthood had begun. Ten more circles of the sun would pass before he ceased to be a novice and could let his beard grow. There was much to learn, and his burden was heavy.

The warriors had come to celebrate Lunasa, the festival of fostering and fecundity which marked the end of summer. Reclining in the forge-keeper's house beside his brother, their leader, Vass, tucked into steaming fish stew and watched a subdued Skaaha serve drink to his men.

'Mara won't be pleased she's here,' he observed. 'Grudges cling to her.'

'I've been Erith's a long time,' Ard reminded him. 'She lived with that.'

'You think it was about you?' Vass snorted. 'A bone for Kerrigen and Mara to fight over is all you were. So's your daughter.' He swallowed a mouthful of ale. 'Kerrigen married you to get that girl.'

'And now she's in the afterlife where Mara can't get at her.' Ard gestured a toast with his horn. 'Haven't you more to worry about, with Mara controlling you lot?'

'Ignoring us,' Vass corrected, wiping froth from his long moustache. 'We heard she hunted a thief. But she's not been near, or sent a tutor. Jiya was a gift.'

'That'll cheer Erith' – Ard hauled his wife's young son back from the hearth – 'if Jiya stays with you.'

His brother glanced around the vast, shadowy interior of the roundhouse. 'Where is Erith? I haven't had my welcome yet.'

'Shh.' Ard covered the child's ears, mouthing words. 'She's the goddess.'

At each of Bride's four festivals, the creator appeared from her underground home, transfigured with the season to sanctify that stage of life. At Lunasa, as the moon waxed red with summer's failing sunlight, she came as Telsha, the foster-mother, who began the harvest. Preparing to play her, Erith lodged, hidden for the last three days, in the hillside cavern behind the village, its entrance screened by curtains of corn garlanded with plaited corn-dollies and rowan branches rich with red berries. In the larder-keeper's house, Lethra the crone supervised the cauldron of Luna, aided by the settlement's two female druids. The Telsha honey stewed, small flesh-coloured, nippled mushrooms simmering slowly in bubbling mead.

When the rain stopped, Ruan led the men up the hill to choose a strong tree whose straight trunk would form the pillar round which the fire would be built. The honour of placing it fell to the person who could throw it so it turned over on its end to fall pointing directly at the waiting hole. The honour of bedding Telsha went to whoever came closest. Erith was much prized. Pregnant women were renowned for their appetites, experienced in giving and receiving pleasure, their swollen bellies voluptuous, breasts firm with the promise of milk.

Skaaha watched the competitors line up to toss the caber, Jiya among them. Her aunt was not the only woman. Some liked to bed other women, just as men sometimes preferred other males. It was the way of things. She had already disturbed one of the warriors mounting one of the smelters among the scrub while she searched for kindling, kindling that would need to be dried on the hearth after the morning's rain before the bonfire could be lit. The two men were unperturbed, unable to contain their excitement at meeting again. Skaaha didn't care what adults did for pleasure. But Erith didn't like Jiya, and she was sure her aunt disliked the forge-keeper equally.

'Are you really going to throw?' she asked, when Jiya called her over to tie on the leather wristbands.

'If I can lift it, I can throw it,' Jiya said. 'Pull them tighter.'

Skaaha tugged the thongs, wondering at the broad white scars around her aunt's wrists as she tightened the bands. 'But it's Erith,' she said, frowning.

'That's why,' Jiya said. 'I want to make the bitch squeal, and I want him' – she nodded to Ard who stood in line with his arm round Vass's shoulder – 'to hear.'

'You can't hurt her,' Skaaha was shocked. 'She's pregnant.'

'The pain of pleasure,' Jiya grinned. 'One day you'll know.'

The furnace-keeper, a huge noman whose dual gender gave her female status, was third in line. A lover of shiny things, Kenna dripped with beads and rings. Despite her powerful arms, she couldn't throw the caber. Her legs gave out. The tree trunk toppled sideways. Everyone ran screaming, mostly with delight, out of the way. When Ard's turn came, he had the advantage. He'd cut the tree to suit himself and made a good toss. It landed almost true, half a stride left of the waiting hole. His brother, Vass, was next, but he stood aside to let Jiya go first.

The four carriers trotted back with the caber. Jiya linked her fingers. The base was lowered into her hands, trunk resting on her shoulder. The weight told on her immediately, but her strong warrior stance kept her balanced. She breathed deep and set off, taking rapid strides to the mark where she stopped, planted her feet and squatted. The caber swung forwards, naturally, off her shoulder. It drew a sweet line. Then came the toss. Jiya straightened her legs, thrust upwards, and as the far end swung towards the ground, pulled the small end back above her head and let go. It rose beautifully. For a moment the trunk was planted upright again then it went over.

'Aye-yie-yaa!' the crowd called, applauding wildly as the caber swung gracefully down to land, half a stride to the right of the hole. Ruan, who, with the two female druids, was judging, declared a draw with Ard.

The smith congratulated Jiya. 'Unless Vass does better,' he offered, 'we might toss something smaller to decide.' He drew a silver coin from his pocket, held it out. Bedding Telsha might repair his marriage. Jiya flipped the coin over. It had the same design on both sides.

'We'll throw dice,' she said.

Vass decided the matter with a perfect toss, howling his triumph before setting the caber in the hole. As the druids played a lively jig, the fire was quickly built.

When darkness fell, just before moonrise, everyone gathered on the green. Skaaha stood with Jiya, gripping her aunt's tunic as excitement grew. Dressed in ceremonial robes, the druids beat their drums and began to chant, invoking the goddess. Warriors and villagers joined in, the rhythm rising in the dark, echoing from the hills, calling on Telsha. As the full moon rose behind them, its light illuminated the cavern entrance. Drums and voices ceased. The shimmering curtain of corn parted. Wearing a moon-yellow dress and plaited corn wreath, the sacred foster-mother emerged. A great roar of joy rose from the crowd. Beside her disgruntled aunt, Skaaha controlled her urge to bellow with the rest. It was only Erith, pretending.

Exuberant music struck up. The goddess took the blazing torch from Vass, carried it to the waiting stack and thrust it into the dry kindling. Soon the fire roared. Telsha crowned Vass her Lord of Harvest. Together, they toasted Lunasa. Summer was over.

'Never mind, Jiya,' Skaaha commiserated with her aunt. 'Vass won't please her in bed as much as you would have.'

'I don't care about her,' Jiya groaned. 'It was for Ard. So he would know pain in his groin like the ache he planted in me.' She stalked over to the drink cauldrons.

Skaaha hurried behind. 'Erith keeps him out of her bed,' she said, hoping to cheer the despondent warrior. 'And hardly speaks to him, just about work.'

'But she doesn't divorce him.' Jiya snatched up a goblet and held it out to be filled with Telsha honey. 'Sorry – he said sorry, to her – for lying with me!'

Ruan was serving. His ladle hovered over the narcotic brew. 'The cordial is better,' he suggested, nodding to the other cauldron.

Jiya grinned, showing her teeth. 'For babies at the breast and druid priests,' she agreed. Plunging her cup into the headier liquid, she drew it out, brimming over. 'I drink for Lunasa' – she leaned over the cauldron, nose to nose with Ruan, still grinning as if she made a great joke – 'then maybe I come to your lodge tonight and fuck with you. What then, druid? What then?' Without waiting for an answer, she strode off to seat herself near the bonfire.

Not knowing what to say, Skaaha held out her goblet, teeth bared, grinning widely with pretend humour, just like her aunt. Ruan filled her cup with cordial.

Next morning, the games began. Skaaha joined in, her physical dexterity a winning gift. Villagers ran races, walked hot charcoal, jumped hurdles and threw hammers, rocks and boulders the size of cauldrons. All three druids joined in sling-shot competitions. Days passed. The warriors' prowess with bows and spears was tested. They wrestled, boxed and fought with blind swords. Nights were spent eating, drinking, dancing and singing, storytelling, reciting poetry and, for those with wits, energy, desire and a willing partner, copulating.

By the last evening, most people had won something, along with headaches or bruises, but the warriors were stars. A final tug-of-war crowned them champions of Lunasa. Telsha gathered children who were leaving birth mothers and gifted them, in turn, to the foster-mothers who would rear them. Finally, she raised a celebratory horn with Vass before the last consummation of their brief union. Come morning, Lunasa would be over and autumn's work begun. Before that, there was more festival brew to drink, and a last night of dancing to enjoy.

Skaaha joined the ring round the fire, linking arms with Thum. Four steps deasil, three steps widdershins, the chain danced sunwise round the flames to the beat of druid drums.

Firelight flickered on the dancers. Woodsmoke drifted between them. From behind, a hand caught Skaaha's wrist.

'Come, come away,' Jiya hissed, hauling her out of the dance.

'No.' Skaaha tried to shake her aunt's iron grip from her wrist. 'I like that dance.' Her aunt, obviously crazed, would not be shaken off. Skaaha was pulled away from the fire, across the grass and round the cobbled path.

'You have to know.' Jiya drew her behind the smelters' house. 'I saw what happened.' Her eyes stared with horror. 'Danger walks beside him.'

'Who, Ard?'

'The druid, Ruan. He watches me. That's why he's here.'

Skaaha sighed. It was spirit talk, nonsense. Back at the shore, Ruan sat on a rock behind the fire, playing his reed pipes. 'No, he came to teach me. Suli said so.'

'You can't learn what he knows. Don't be fooled.' Jiya's words came in a rush. 'He tried to make me drink poison. You saw!'

'It was cordial,' Skaaha explained. 'I drank it.'

Her aunt let go her wrist. 'That was a trick,' she shrieked. 'Suli sent him to take me back.' She clutched her head. 'Remember.'

Skaaha remembered. *He will bring Jiya to me*, Suli told Ard at the solstice. 'But why?' Except in battle, no one would harm Jiya. Anyone who did brought her malady on themselves, destined to live out its purpose instead.

'His magic is strong,' Jiya babbled. 'He's from the north, like Suli. He can see inside your head.' She crouched, terrified. 'He puts thoughts in mine.' Her hands slapped her skull. 'Things I don't want to think.'

'He can't do that' – Skaaha felt fear creep up her spine – 'can he?' They were alone on the opposite side of the round-house from the festivities, but she looked around in the gathering gloom, half expecting to see Ruan lurking in the shadows, exuding malevolence, watching them.

8

'Help me,' Jiya begged. 'I need to stay.' She punched her head 'Remember.' She punched herself again. 'Something, you need me, need to know.' Another punch. 'He'll take me away.'

Skaaha stared at her aunt, cowering in the shadow of the building, hands clamped on her head, shaking it now. A familiar helplessness rose from her gut into her chest, threatening to choke her, the same fearful feeling she'd had when Kerrigen died. Without forming the thought, she instinctively did what she'd done then. She ran, but not to the sea. Not this time. This time she ran, as she'd eventually done then, to the only haven on offer. She ran to her father.

Ard was among the group still dancing hypnotically round the bonfire, and reluctant to leave it.

'You have to come,' Skaaha tugged at his hand as he tried to whirl her round instead. 'Dad, please!'

He stopped then, looking down at her as they both realized it was the first time she'd called him anything other than Ard.

'Come on!' She urged him towards the smelters' house. 'Jiya needs help.'

'Too much Telsha honey?' He resisted. 'I'm in enough trouble.'

'No, she's afraid. I don't know what to do.'

He pulled back from her. 'Then we should fetch Ruan.'

'It's him she's scared of. Come on.'

Reluctantly, he followed. When they rounded the building, Jiya was crouched, huddled against it, moaning. But when she saw them she stood, her stance strange, almost arrogantly erect.

'Skaaha says you need –' Ard began.

Jiya cut him off, raising the flat of her hand towards him, as if to shield her face from him, or his from her. 'I don't hear you,' she said, walking past them. 'I don't hear you. I don't see you.' As she passed, she stopped and leaned towards him, without dropping her hand. 'Stay away,' she hissed from behind it, 'or I'll slit your gizzard in your sleep.'

Skaaha, looking up, saw ugly, unsmiling hatred on her aunt's normally joyous face. Hairs on the back of her neck rose, prickling. Then Jiya was gone, round the house and out of sight.

'Will she go away again?' she asked Ard, fearful now for him.

'Maybe,' he said. 'Maybe it's drink. Those mushrooms don't suit everyone. If it is, she'll sleep it off. If not, Ruan will solve it.' He squeezed her hand. 'And you, daughter, should come to dance. One last dance for Lunasa, then off to bed.'

Through the deep blanket of sleep, a hand shook Skaaha awake.

'Come on, Lazybed,' Jiya urged. 'Your pupil is waiting, and my warriors. Is slacking what you do if I'm not here?' It was the morning after Lunasa.

Outside, as they stripped off, her aunt beamed, full of joy, restored to her usual, exuberant self. Behind the playing field, Ruan emerged from his lodge. He raised a hand in greeting and Jiya waved back, cheerfully, quite undisturbed by his presence. As the druid walked on past the burial mound, Skaaha's spirits rose. Slotting into the perfectly choreographed team, delight in her physical skill returned. Jiya was with her again. Warriors ran through their routines alongside her. Apart from dangling genitals, which at other times were strapped in leather pouches for protection during hand-to-hand combat, it was like being back in Ullinish, like being home.

Kylerhea grew busier in autumn. Fishers and farmers came to trade fresh, smoked and salted fish or wheat, barley, rye and oats for hooks, ploughs, gaffs, scythes and other tools. The warriors stayed on, waiting for the hunter's moon. By day, they patrolled the coast to keep the island safe from robbers and deter foreign raiders in sailing ships, a rare sight for many suns. Nights were spent gambling with dice, reciting heroic verse or stories of amazing feats. Women threw husbands out of bed, filling the empty space with one, or maybe more, of their guests.

Skaaha helped pack the larder – a long, narrow tunnel dug below ground, lined with stone. Earth-covered and overgrown with grass, it wasn't discernible from normal ground except for a low, iron-plated wooden door. The interior was no higher, its darkness alleviated by guttering lamps. She had to stoop all the way, being careful not to bang her head where one stone beam was lower than the rest. It smelled familiar, of earth and produce, like the great larder of Ullinish, creating the illusion she would emerge from the gloom to see Doon Beck on the slopes above. Spare milk, butter and cheeses were kept there in summer, along with game that needed to be hung. As winter approached, the amounts multiplied.

Lethra, the chief, conducted the storage operation from outside. Everything had to be stacked exactly as she said, fish kept well away from butter, spaces left for meat that would be dried or smoked before storing, and the fruits, fresh or stewed with honey, that would be picked between now and Sowen. Her husband – she had only one – saw to the grain pits.

'And this is?' Lethra screeched, gripping and twisting.

'My ear!' Skaaha squealed.

'Ah.' The old chief let go. 'So you do know. Then use it. I said hang the smokies above the barrel of herring. What's in that barrel?'

'Buttermilk?' This time she was grabbed by the nose. 'Oww!'

'What's this for then?' Lethra pushed the girl back into the larder.

It was mead in the barrel. Skaaha located the pickled herring and moved the smokies. 'Did Kerrigen do this?' she asked, coming out again. She had felt sorry for herself earlier, seeing the warriors set off on the first hunt without her. Now she felt sorry for her mother, fostered by this narky crone. No wonder Kerrigen refused to send her daughter to someone else to rear.

'Kerrigen.' Lethra's weathered face softened. 'That was my girl. The islands lost a great queen when she died. A fine worker, determined never to be beaten, not by anything. By your age, she'd gone to be a warrior. A pity you're not like her. Here' – she thrust a basket into Skaaha's arms – 'go pick some Great herb, and if you bring back a handful of Ribwort leaves, I'll make us a brew.'

Skaaha's ear smarted. Her nose stung. She would give the brew a miss for as long as possible. Hurrying away, basket over her arm, she started up the hill. It was only mid-day, the warm air cooled by a light breeze blowing in off the sea. If she found the warriors, they'd let her stay. Coming back with a wild pig or pointed stag would be better than returning with a few limp leaves.

When she reached the crest of the hill, the basket already held Lethra's herbs, but there was no sight or sound of hunters. They must be stalking among trees. Tentatively, she walked into the nearest thicket. Wild boars might be around, dangerous beasts who would attack a human unprovoked, and she was weaponless. She moved the way she'd been taught, walking quickly from one scaleable tree trunk to another, checking undergrowth for movement or rustling before moving to the next. The only frightening sound was a moose moving away as it scented her. When a polecat darted across her path, a squeal leapt to her throat, quickly stifled. Startled, a red squirrel scampered off. But as the trees opened into a clearing, she relaxed, about to retrace her steps. Wherever the warriors hunted, it wasn't here. Around the glade, blue-black berries gleamed on low plants, succulent, delicious fruit. A basketful of it would show Lethra she wasn't useless.

Lifting the Great herb from the basket, she spread the Ribwort leaves in the bottom to prevent the small, plump fruit filling the wickerwork. Nimbly, she began to strip the thin woody stems, barely glancing up when a couple of roe deer passed behind her. The stillness of the forest, drowsy with droning insects, settled round her. Eventually, the basket was half full and satisfyingly heavy. Her back hurt, her fingers were stained deep purple. Sitting down on a hummock, she pulled a few berries to eat and looked up for the sun. It would soon be time to leave. A rustle that wasn't wind, bird or deer made her look towards it. She was looking at a bear.

Across the clearing, the bear also looked at her. Fear raced through her limbs like ice-fire in her blood. She averted her eyes, hoping it would turn back into the forest. It didn't. Instead, it pushed its brown snout into the plants, nipping blaeberries with its sharp teeth. Perhaps it hadn't seen her. She was upwind. That wasn't good. The bear snuffled around, feeding, coming towards her. She should speak, let it know there was a human in its way. Her throat, clagged with berries, couldn't produce a cough. The bear's shoulders were massive, forelegs powerful, its claws could rip a face off in one . . . she mustn't scream. Maybe if she ate more berries . . . maybe it would be happy to share the patch . . . surely it heard her heart thunder. She swallowed. The bear's head swung round. Black eyes glinted at her.

Outside the forge, Lethra complained to Ard. 'How long does it take to fetch a handful of herbs from up on the rocks?'

Ard shrugged. 'Maybe she met Vass and the others.'

'And what would they be hunting just there' – the chief waved her hand to the rocky rise behind the smelter – 'shrews? We'll feed fat on those this winter!'

'I was only suggesting . . .'

'I know what you're suggesting – that it's fine for her to wander off, forget work, do as she pleases.'

'Not at all. But she's young, used to being with warriors, a child . . .'

Noise from behind the smelter interrupted him, loud, joyful noise, and many voices. Lethra hobbled round the house to see. Ard followed. It was the warriors returning, a reindeer slung below a pole carried by two of them, two wild boars hanging below another. The sun was low, too low.

'Is Skaaha with you?' Ard called to Vass.

She wasn't. Jiya, bloodied spear in hand, was first to react. Dropping her shouldered pole, she turned to scan the hills. A crow lifted above a patch of woodland, drifted to another. Jiya was off and running. Ard snatched a finished spear and sword from the forge. It was almost dusk. Birds should be settling. The warriors dumped their cargo and followed Ard, fast.

Across the clearing, the bear reared up, sniffing. Its fur rippled like grass in the wind. It might drop down and charge. Skaaha wanted to turn, scramble away, get to her feet, run. But she couldn't move. The bear dropped, swung its dark head left then right, uttered a low moan. It wanted her to leave. She couldn't move. She couldn't move, but her mind raced now. The bear could easily outrun her. It could climb as well or better than she could. She should stand, raise her arms, make herself look big, talk to it, back away. She couldn't move. The bear paced forward a step, reared on its hind legs, pushed its nose up, sniffed again.

Skaaha rose slowly to her feet, head half-turned away from the bear. Her lowered gaze lighted on the traitorous basket of berries. The bear could smell it, so much fruit in one place, at her feet. Cautiously, she raised her arms as high as she could.

'I don't want fruit,' she lied, keeping her voice low. 'You have it, bear.' She stepped backwards, away from the basket, slowly. 'You eat. I'll go.' She took another step back. The bear dropped and charged, a brown blur roaring towards her. She wasn't sure if it was making that growling, thundering sound or if the roar was her blood surging, the thudding her rapid heart. She froze.

In his lodge, following the woman priest's instructions as he ground chopped herbs to a paste, Ruan heard a commotion from the village, shouts of panic and running feet. Dropping the pestle, he snatched his long staff and ran out. Bloodied game lay, abandoned next the forge. Warriors pelted back up the slope. People stood around, fretful, the evidence of interrupted chores in their hands.

'Skaaha,' Lethra said, her weathered face gone grey, pointing. A pair of rooks put up from the patch of trees.

Cursing himself for thinking her safely occupied, Ruan sped after the warriors. The time of day, unsettled birds and the nature of beasts, all informed his mind and muscles. Racing upwards, he deepened his breathing, beginning to overtake the line of running Ardvasar men.

Skaaha's breath caught as the charging bear rushed straight for her. On the last lope, it veered off, hurtling past. She turned to face it, keeping it within sight. If she ran, it would chase and kill her. Stealing half-glances, she took another step, to the side this time, away from basket and bear, nearer the trees, and another step. The bear turned too, swinging its head from side to side again, moaning.

'I'm leaving, bear,' Skaaha said. 'You have the fruit.' Now she kept moving, slowly, evenly. Everything in her wanted to run. The bear reared up again, watching, sniffing. Skaaha was into the trees, still backing off, glancing down, trying not to stumble. If it charged a second time, she'd have to drop, curl up, play dead.

Racing up the slope, Jiya kept her eyes on the spot she wanted to arrive at. Boulders and outcrops kept getting in her line of sight. Other birds put up from the same trees. Her legs pumped, muscles burned. Wolves would be stirring. Something disturbed those birds. There were lynx, boar and bears in the island's woods, and a girl, defenceless.

The warrior leapt a burn, ran on, rounded another outcrop. A shriek pierced her ears. Skaaha, a terrified, pelting, screaming Skaaha, burst out of the scrub and thumped into her, arms grasping round her waist.

'Jiya, Jiya,' she sobbed. 'There was,' her voice gabbled, 'a bear.'

Jiya pushed the girl behind her, butted the base of her spear against the rock at their backs, aiming the point forwards, scanning the tree-line. 'A bear, where?'

'It was . . . it's eating . . . it got my basket.' Now she wailed. 'I had blaeberries!'

'When I stick it, you go,' Jiya ordered, tense, braced. 'Don't run till then. Then go fast. Don't look back.' One spear in a bear wouldn't stop it, only enrage. Her mind played the moves, rapidly. Thrust for the throat as it rears, let go, draw sword, go in fast, into those powerful arms, past the mauling claws, right into the gut, thrusting up to the heart, in and up.

No rapidly darkening shadow rushed from among the tree trunks, nothing emerged, nothing. The only sound was feet coming up the hill behind them. Ruan arrived, with Ard a step behind, the smith breathing hard.

'Bear?' Ruan asked, voice steady, taking in her stance, her trembling niece. He wasn't even out of breath.

'It was.' Jiya shifted her gaze from the forest to glare at him. Had it come, saving Skaaha would have cost her life. 'Where were you?'

In the village, Lethra and Erith formed an unholy alliance, bolstering each other against fear with complaints about Skaaha's unruliness and warriors who dropped food to go look for her. Thum was first to return, skittering down the slope.

'She's fine,' he called to the two headwomen. 'They have her.'

'Well, that's a blessing,' Erith said, and went to supervise the evening meal. The youthful cook was prone to burnt offerings if she didn't stand over him.

Lethra nagged the men skinning and butchering the aban-doned deer and pigs, despite their efficiency, until the hunters arrived back with Skaaha perched on her father's shoulders. 'I don't know what you're all so pleased about,' the crone snapped, wiping the smiles off all their faces, 'back without herbs or basket!'

But when Skaaha embroidered the story of the bear that night, telling how they ate berries together after the many charges, so close she could feel the brute's hot breath fan her cheeks, and, by shouting that it should be thankful she'd shared her find and behave better, how her boldness had tamed the beast and won her safety from the threatened mauling with its great claws, everyone delighted in the telling. Ruan smiled, despite his failure. Jiya hooted with joy. No one, not even Lethra, commented on the different tale told by the white tracks of tears left in the purple blaeberry juice dyed on those same cheeks.

9

'I'm floating,' Skaaha said.

'You're not,' Lethra snapped. They were in the cavern, sitting by the hearth, finally sharing that brew. 'But if you start, you'll get no more of this.' Then, in case Skaaha forgot the chief had picked the Ribwort herself: 'Not that you deserve any. It's your throw.' She put the two dice in front of the girl.

Skaaha cupped them between both hands and shook. She didn't understand this game – an elaborate arrangement of carved wooden pieces on a chequered board. Not that it mattered; Lethra would win. The crone won every game they played. 'Tosk floats,' she said. 'Maybe he drinks this.' She threw – a two and a one – and moved her pieces. 'Do you know him?'

'Of course. Too well.' Lethra scooped up the dice. 'That was a stupid move.' She threw and captured three of Skaaha's pieces in one hopping jump.

Nights drew in, the warriors long gone back to Ardvasar. Jiya had stayed, buoyant and joyful, sticking close to Skaaha until the third full moon of harvest. As it waned, her agitation grew again. Fully armed, she sat cross-legged in the middle of the playing ground, chanting all night, sleeping in snatches. Sowen approached, festival of the dead, and blood harvest. The oldest woman in the village, Lethra would play the goddess, who appeared this time as Carlin, the blue hag of winter. She was confined out of sight till the time came.

'Who will you be?' she asked.

'A druid, like Tosk.' Skaaha stood and tried to walk around the bed without bending her knees or bobbing. Because the dead might come, no one should be recognized at Sowen. Everyone dressed up, dyed their faces, tried to look frightening or funny. Thum would play Kerrigen, with black horse-tail plaits. She had made Tosk's grey beard with goat hair. 'I have a long stick and a hammer.'

'Be careful what you conjure,' Lethra warned. 'It may come to you.' She scooped up the dice.

Skaaha frowned. 'I have the sacrifice to make.'

The old woman considered her. 'Aye, it's time. You've ghosts to lay if you're to settle.' She held the dice out. 'Your mind is elsewhere. It's your go, though if you'd any sense, you'd concede.'

Soundly thrashed, Skaaha left for bed, heading down the slope. Below, in the dusk, Jiya sat, chanting on the green. Ruan walked towards her with a cup. Her aunt reared back, hand raised to shield her eyes from seeing the druid. The priest hesitated, sat the cup down and returned to his lodge. Skaaha ran to the disturbed warrior.

'What did Ruan want?' she asked, crouching down.

'To stop me,' Jiya moaned, tipping the drink into the grass. 'Says he'll take me back' – rocking – 'can't. I can't go.' She resumed her chant, staring out to sea.

Skaaha ran home, prepared a travel pack, and stuffed it below her bed. At Sowen, they could slip away unnoticed. Ruan wouldn't take Jiya anywhere.

'Is that for my costume?' Thum hovered in the forge doorway, not sure if he was interrupting. Next the glowing furnace, bellows puffed and blew.

Skaaha squinted at him, her attention on the piece she worked. 'Have you been cuffed by a bear? It's gold.' Ard had given her just enough to make the bracelet, and a lot of help. He engraved a triskele on the flat-ended keepers, while she had twisted the fine strips into ropes then twisted them together for thickness.

'It can't be for you,' Thum said, coming in. 'Druids don't wear armlets.'

'It's for Eefay, my sister,' she said, showing him the keepers.

'Don't tell anyone,' she confided, lowering her voice. 'But I'm going back to Glenelg with her. Jiya will be wanted there, and me.' Her aunt provided refuge from the bear, a debt of honour Skaaha would repay. 'You too, if you like.'

'What,' the boy exclaimed, 'you're leaving?'

'Shh!' Skaaha glanced around in case Ard had overheard, but he was busy at the fire, melting bronze. 'Is any of your family coming for Sowen?'

Thum nodded. 'Erith, Calum, my father maybe.'

'Erith? But she's here anyway, and Calum.' The boy was Erith's son by Gern, the toddler fostered at Lunasa now his mother carried Ard's child.

'She's still my blood mother, and Calum my brother.'

Skaaha was shocked. She'd never have guessed. 'But you live with . . .'

'My foster-mother, of course.' Thum arched his eyebrow, cheekily. 'Is it you has been cuffed by a bear?'

Skaaha plonked the bracelet down and chased him out of the forge, catching him easily despite his longer legs. 'Swear you won't tell Erith!'

'I swear,' Thum promised. They wrestled with playful seriousness, both wanting to win yet submitting whenever the other had the upper hand. Jiya exercised around them, obsessively repeating her routine. As she leapt on the boy's prostrate body for the third time, Skaaha saw a familiar figure glide down the hill path.

'It's Tosk,' she cried, shoving away the arm Thum had jammed across her throat.

The boy rolled over to look as the old druid, rod tapping the ground, reached the foot of the slope. 'Yes,' he agreed, 'it's my father.'

Skaaha ran to her aunt. 'Go somewhere else,' she hissed. 'Hide!'

As Jiya glanced, wild-eyed, towards the master druid, Skaaha and Thum followed him into the forge-keeper's house. Erith settled the old man by the hearth with a horn of ale and a dish of mussels to refresh him after the journey. Ruan and the other two druids came to greet him. Tosk had come for the festival, to prepare the sacrifice of Kerrigen's honours, still stored in Ruan's lodge.

'Then I'm going south,' he said, 'to end my days at Ynys Mon.' The island grove was a druid sanctuary. 'But first, Sowen.' He glanced at Thum, who hopped about, too shy to speak. The boy was the result of Erith's coming-of-age, a service she'd asked Tosk to perform, much to his, even then, aged surprise and pleasure. 'Have you something to say, my son?'

Standing beside Skaaha, Thum tried. His tongue tangled itself.

'He wants to be a warrior.' Skaaha spoke instead. 'I've been training him.'

'Have you indeed?' Tosk studied her. 'You've grown well. It suits you here?'

She nodded, lying. Erith barely tolerated her. Lethra thought her a fool. The people saw her and Jiya as odd. 'What about Thum? It doesn't suit him.'

Tosk glanced at Erith. The forge-keeper's baby was not far off. 'If Mara will teach him, Thum can go to be a warrior,' he said.

The boy whooped, punching the air. Skaaha frowned. She'd forgotten about Mara, and since the school taught women, that Tosk wouldn't consider Glenelg. The old priest turned to Ruan.

'Perhaps you'd take him to Bracadale? Jiya might be ready to go with you.'

'Jiya likes it here with me.' Skaaha stared at Ruan, daring him to contradict. 'She's been calling down the moon for Sowen, and practising new feats.'

'I made her a cordial,' Ruan said, smoothly. 'Chanting is thirsty work.'

'The ground is thirstier,' Skaaha replied. 'That's where it went.'

*

Jiya watched the druids gather in the forge-keeper's house. Blood harvest was a dangerous time. Robbers often sought to fill their winter bellies from the larders of other tribes. But these priests would rob her. While they plotted, she sat cross-legged among gorse bushes above the cavern, rocking herself, spear at the ready, murmuring to dark shadows in her mind. What was dream, what was memory, what was vision, she couldn't tell. Pictures buzzed like bees in her brain. A bright chariot raced past. Darkness came down. A horse screamed. Silence descended. There was blood, a shattered wheel. She clucked her tongue.

'Tluck-tluck-tluck.' It was the only sound she could recall. Someone looked for it. She saw the broken weapon tucked in a safe place. It was herself doing it. Someone searched. The fine blue cloth stained red. It wasn't here.

'Tluck-tluck-tluck.' Something she knew couldn't remember itself. Enemies plotted. She saw it happen. Time ran out. The priests came to make her silent, put chains on, head opened, light shone in dark places. Ard rejected then betrayed her.

'Tluck-tluck-tluck.' She couldn't remember forgetting. There was blood. More blood spilled. She must tell, warn Skaaha. The priests made her forget remembering. The dark earth opened. Light came in. The Ban Shee stirred. She heard them whisper below the sod. *Stay with us*, they hissed. *Remember. See.*

'Look, look!' Skaaha danced excitedly, pulling at Ard's arm, pointing across the narrow strait to Alba. At the crossing on the opposite coast, a group of people climbed into coracles, among them a little girl with golden hair. 'It's Eefay!'

'Is it?' Ard peered. 'Won't they come as guisers?'

Skaaha wore her druid outfit. The goat-hair beard tickled her nose. She tried to pick out features as the small boats moved off westwards before turning into the fast-flowing current that would draw them rapidly back down to the landing at Kylerhea. It wasn't far. She ought to know her sister. Only five moons had passed since they last saw each other. But, at

Sowen, it was hard to recognize anyone. Even Ard looked strange, with breasts, corn-coloured wig and blue face dye, his bulky muscles bulging inside the sleeves of a dress. She would miss him, and the forge, but no one else.

The first coracle arrived, the boatman in it splashing through the shallows, dragging it ashore. The little girl with golden hair was not Eefay. It was a boy brought by his foster-mother to visit his blood-mother. Sowen was a time of family reunions. Overland visitors came through the hills. Several villagers left by the same path days before. Some waited to cross to Alba. The second coracle arrived. The small person in it wore a warrior's helmet, tattered tunic, a face stained with bloody wounds.

'Eefay?' It had to be. Skaaha pulled aside her grey beard. 'Look, it's me!'

The battle-scarred face lit up with recognition. 'Skaaha! You look funny.' Eefay drew a short broken sword. 'See my blade. I'm a dead warrior.'

'So you are.' Skaaha hugged her close. 'I've got a surprise for you.'

'It is a present?' Eefay asked. 'I've got one for you.'

'More than just a present,' Skaaha answered, grabbing her hand. 'Come on, we've got loads to eat, and lots to do first.'

At sunset, they laid offerings of food on the mound so the ancestors might join the festivities, a superstition from the old faith. Jiya had disappeared. Darkness fell. Village fires were doused. The torch-lit rites began. Dressed as beasts, the priests invoked the goddess. Erith, in Telsha's autumn-yellow dress, swollen with child, was led to the cavern. As she vanished inside, the slow drumming surged like thunder. The pipes changed to eerie urgency, calling the Carlin. Hoping her aunt stayed hidden, Skaaha stood at the front of the crowd with Eefay, grasping her little sister's hand.

The broom that screened the cavern entrance didn't stir. The drums softened, pipes soared and wept, haunting the night. No one appeared. Something was wrong. Skaaha gripped Eefay's hand tighter. Maybe Jiya was in the cave. Maybe the Shee had taken Lethra. Maybe it was her. Did she let her mother down? The spirit dead took revenge if wrong was done them, and the Carlin brought death. But without it, there was no birth; without winter, no spring. If the goddess abandoned them, the world would end, and life was over, for everything, for ever.

Tension grew in the crowd. There was no moonlight. Sowen began when the last crescent of old moon died in the rising sun. It ended three days later when the new moon was born at sunset. Darkness deepened, lit by stars and the flames of thirteen torches. Music soared. Beside the cavern mouth, the torch bearers whirled. A frantic roll beat from the drums. All the torches came together, held aloft in a blaze of light. The broom screen swept aside. The Carlin, the blue hag of winter, strode out. Dressed in black, wearing the pointed hat of lost-time, she raised her long-handled bessom.

'Aye-yie-yaa!' the crowd shrieked, relieved. Skaaha sagged against her sister.

The Carlin swung her broom, chasing the fire-bearers ahead so she was stalked downhill by her own giant shadow. As she walked she struck at boulders, each one turning white, edging her path with frost. In the darkness behind her, a straw effigy in Telsha's yellow dress danced grotesquely.

Skaaha's spine shivered with a delicious tremor of fear. Eefay's fingers dug into her arm. The music became a breathless whisper. Barely recognizable in their disguises, all the girls stood in a row fronting the adults. Bending to peer at each in turn, the hag shuffled along it. She would touch just one – the one who would succeed her when spring came – gifting them the sprig of mistletoe at her waist.

Some children darted behind their foster-mothers. Others squealed to be lifted into safe arms as the crone bent and breathed her chill breath on their faces. Skaaha held her ground, hanging on to Eefay. It was Lethra. She was sure it was still Lethra. Nippy though the old chief was, she was human. But when the haggard blue face thrust into hers, she stared into eyes rimmed red as the bloodiest harvest moon.

'You,' the Carlin said, and put her wizened hand on Skaaha's head.

'Aye-yie-yaa!' the crowd roared. Drums boomed. The hag put the sprig of mistletoe in Skaaha's hand and turned towards Loup hill, where the unlit bonfire waited. Skaaha stared, stunned, at the sacred plant with its ghostly white berries. The shadow behind the crone reached out, like night shifting, to grip her arm.

'Come on,' it urged. It was Erith, hidden in voluminous black, carrying the effigy of Telsha. Up the hill they went, following the Carlin. Her emotions in disarray, Skaaha saw the frosted boulders were crouching villagers. Last Sowen, at Doon Beck, she had believed the Carlin trailed real ice and snow. Now, the magic of this night was for children. Her childhood was over. She'd been chosen.

Disguised villagers and visitors surged after them, cheering. On the hilltop, the effigy of Telsha was hooked over the fire-post. The Carlin seized the offered torch.

'In death, we live!' she screeched, before plunging it into the kindling hole. Autumn ended. The veil of time lifted. Their dead walked among them. This world and the otherworld were one. The remaining twelve torches, signifying the moons that had passed since last Sowen, were tossed into the stack.

As the fire consumed Telsha, the Carlin joined Skaaha for the first blood harvest. Dressed in a hide cape and stag antlers, Tosk straddled an old sheep. A blade flashed in his hand. Blood spurted, gushing from the beast's throat into the bronze cauldron held by Ruan, disguised as a hare. Mixed with oats, it would be cooked on flat stones by the fire. Nothing was wasted. The dead ewe would provide the spit-roast for tomorrow's feast. Pungent, the smell of iron filled Skaaha's nostrils. Dedicating the death to the continuance of life, Tosk smeared the blood-mark on her forehead.

Beer horns filled. The dead were praised and liberally toasted, just in case. Songs began the entertainment. All over the island and across the water, bonfires glittered on other hills as the whole druid world celebrated.

'I wanted to be chosen,' Eefay complained. 'I should be Bride.'

'You're too young,' Skaaha said, spitting aside goat hair from her beard. Not that it mattered. She wouldn't be here to play the goddess in spring. She'd be in Glenelg, with Jiya. Bride, in all her guises, was druid anyway. 'And you were scared.' Her arm still hurt where Eefay's nails dug in.

'Was not,' Eefay denied. 'I'm a warrior.'

'A heroic warrior too,' Erith said, pushing back her black hood to admire the child's outfit. 'And a wonderful singer, so Skaaha is always telling us.'

'Is she?' the little girl asked.

'Night and day,' Erith lied. 'Why don't you go next?'

Eefay *was* a good singer. Her clear childish voice lilted through the night, backed only by the crackle of flame. Hearty applause followed. Skaaha and Thum made a little play of Kerrigen and Tosk arguing about the queen's disposal. Laughter rippled round the watchers as the protesting druid fought off the irate corpse with his rod before being given a thorough drubbing with his own hammer.

'Hyaaa-aaaaa!' A terrifying shriek ripped through the night, silencing both performers and their laughing audience. Everybody turned from the bonfire to stare down at the village below. Flames licked the thatch of the forge-keeper's house. The flickering light illuminated a screeching figure running across the playing ground, sword glittering in hand. Skaaha froze. She knew that howl, that stride. It was Jiya.

10

From the slope above the cavern she saw them rise from the ground, growing out of the dark – shapes that shifted where nothing should, in and out of houses, through the deserted village. One came from the druid's lodge, a shimmer of light on its back like a half moon. Kerrigen's voice cried out to her. Training took over from the swirling fog in Jiya's brain. Twisting dry grass around an arrowhead, she sparked it alight with her flint and fired the flaming missile down among the shadows. That moon was a shield, one that called with her dead sister's voice. These were not Shee, not the dead rising for Sowen. They came to rob, seeking what she knew.

Before the arrow stabbed into the roundhouse thatch, Jiya's spear followed. She didn't wait to see it slice into the nearest moving shape, bringing it down, but was off the slope running, sword drawn. Shadows scattered as she screamed towards them. The shield bearer turned, pulling the circle of metal round to ward off the attack, white eyes staring from blue-painted skin. Jiya leapt and spun around, behind the man before he realized, her sword slicing in where neck joined shoulder. His body crumpled to the ground, but she was already gone, chasing others.

As the robbers reached the jetty, stumbling, splashing and falling into their boat, the slowest of them heard her feet close behind. Dropping his haul, he reached for a sling at his waist, loaded and swung it above his head. His hand flew off into the rocks, still gripping the cord. Jiya's blade glittered. The man stared in horror at the stump, at blood he couldn't see in the murk, not yet feeling pain he would never feel. Jiya thrust her sword into his middle and drew back before his dead weight pulled her weapon down. She was still too late. The boat was out into the current, rapidly carried away, blotted out by dark sea.

There were voices behind her now, running feet. 'Water, fetch water!' shouted from among the houses where a roof was on fire. Turning, she saw more shadows rush towards her, lit from behind: the great long ears of a giant hare, antlers. She squared up, balanced the weight of her weapon. The advancing beasts halted, eye to eye with her. She must have shrunk, small as a rabbit.

'Jiya?' It was the hare that spoke. 'It's all right. They've gone.'

'I hid it,' she said. 'It's not here.' She did hide something but couldn't remember what it was. 'I knew they'd come. You can't take me. I know.'

The hare removed its ears. It was the druid, Ruan. Her body stretched back to normal size. 'I will only take you if you're ready to go,' he said.

Tosk pushed in front of the beasts, half the size he should be. 'Jiya's all right,' he shouted with Skaaha's voice. 'Leave her alone.' He came to stand in front of her. 'It's not her fault. They were robbing us. Look!' He held up a sword taken from the first man she'd killed. 'It's Kerrigen's. They stole it from Ruan's hut. She stopped them.' He looked up at her, beard twisted to one side of his strangely young face, a blood-mark on his forehead. 'You're fine, aren't you, Jiya?'

'I'm growing into the sky,' she said, feeling her body do it, looking down. Kerrigen's sword was too large for this small Tosk, too big for Kerrigen, who stood to one side, shifting from foot to foot. 'You called to me,' she told her dead sister. 'I heard you.' She dropped her own sword and fell to her knees, reaching out to the apparition. 'I saw what happened.' But what she saw had forgotten itself. Her head still buzzed, full of bees. 'I hear it.' She clucked her tongue. 'Tluck-tluck-tluck.' She clamped her hands over her skull. 'Tluck-tluck-tluck. Do you hear it?' She grasped Ruan's fur cloak. 'Do you hear?'

'I hear,' Ruan assured her. 'Time will tell what it means.' He put his arm round her shoulder, drew her close. 'Come, I'll give you something to quiet it now.'

Skaaha's heart hurt. Jiya couldn't be saved; her aunt shut away in Ruan's lodge. Shamed, she helped clear the mess. Damage to the roundhouse roof was minor, the fire quickly extinguished with cauldrons of sea water, smouldering thatch cut out to be replaced come daylight. Inside houses, bedding and clothes were tossed around, baskets tipped out, contents rifled, Skaaha's hidden pack scattered. Villagers raged.

'Swine.'

'Can't trust anybody these days.'

'Wouldn't have happened while Kerrigen lived.'

'On Sowen too!'

'What kind of person desecrates a festival?'

'It's the bog for them when we catch them.' The threat was empty, a symptom of anger. Eternal death was for treasonable crimes, like killing a priest. Physical death was extreme, yet three intruders were corpses. If islanders stole, druids punished them by exclusion from festivals till reparation was made. Strangers were branded or lost a hand. Feelings ran high, and in all directions.

'Where were the Ardvasar men?'

'Never here when you need them!'

'In their cups, I bet.'

'So much for patrolling the coast.'

'Is this what we keep warriors for?'

'Kerrigen would have sorted them out, and hunted down the thieves!'

'If they'd got to my larder, I'd take a coracle and follow them to the end of the world myself,' Lethra threatened. 'I'd give them what for!' But there was also relief. They faced a harsh winter if the stores had gone, their debt to Jiya troubling but immense. Even Erith recognized it.

'Though I don't know why she had to fire a flaming arrow into my roof!'

'I expect that was an accident,' Ard soothed. 'She needed light to see by to throw the spear.'

'So she gets it by burning us out of house and home' – the exaggeration was out before Erith could stop it – 'while you defend her?'

'That's unjust,' Ard said. 'I admit my shame. Do you have none?'

Erith calmed herself 'I'm just saying she might have aimed better. Why did it have to be *my* roof?'

Hearth fires were re-lit and the council met. The three house-keepers, Lethra, Erith and Kenna, were joined by one man from each home, with the druids as advisors. Ard favoured going after the gang, but the current would have carried them rapidly up the coast of Alba. They could be anywhere on the mainland.

'Only a few small treasures are missing,' Ruan reported. Jiya had prevented Kenna's jewellery being taken to the boat; the basket was found beside one corpse. The other two had carried all of Kerrigen's honours. 'So we have those back.'

'But why steal them in the first place?' Erith asked. 'They can't be used.'

Ruan shrugged. 'I doubt they knew the owner had died.'

'Warrior honours in a druid lodge,' Lethra snorted, 'and they couldn't tell?'

'The forge store is full if they wanted weapons,' Kenna added. It made no sense. Metalwork could be sold, but the store was untouched. 'The state of my house,' she grumbled, 'like they looked for something.' The others agreed but could think of nothing in their houses worth the effort the robbers had expended on the search. There was also nothing to distinguish the corpses, the trade tattoos below their left ears burned out, a druid custom to exile persistent troublemakers from society.

'Outsiders,' Tosk said. One body bore a second tattoo. 'If it's a clan mark, it's been altered,' he added, examining it, 'or we'd know who they were. But they're from Alba, not beyond it. No one would take the open sea in a sail-less craft.'

Ard engraved a copy of the design on to a metal disc, in case the record would help to identify the escaped thieves some day. If they were found, druid law would be applied.

Despite mutterings that the otherworld was too good for them, the priests cremated the dead in the bonfire. Villagers threw the charred bones in the bottom of the new rubbish pit. This insult to their remains meant the robbers should arrive tainted in the next life, ready to make amends. The druids had Jiya, drugged and tied in Ruan's lodge. They would decide the justice of the deaths.

Next morning, as he stripped off, Thum bent close to Skaaha. 'What will you do now?' he whispered. It was first light. The smell of roasting mutton for the evening feast already drifted round the village.

'I don't know.' She watched him go to exercise with Eefay, unable to join in. Her aunt was in trouble. Not knowing who they were, she'd killed three unarmed men. They might have been visitors from the otherworld, or villagers in disguise playing a trick for Sowen. Despite anger at the thieves, people were uneasy.

At breakfast, Ruan came looking for her, staff slung on his back. With him he brought her mother's weapons, shield and winged helmet. For the first time, she wanted to speak with him, to ask his advice. Guilt stood in the way.

'It's good you've eaten,' he assured her. 'After the spoiling, we have a long walk. But you must fast now till evening.'

'I want to come,' Eefay piped up.

Skaaha shifted uncomfortably as the druid considered the little girl. He would say yes. People always said yes to Eefay.

'This is for Skaaha alone to do,' he said.

'But I can watch, can't I?' Eefay persisted. 'It's not fair. She

84

gets to make the sacrifice *and* be the chosen one.' Her petulance became aggressive. 'Donal would make you take me.'

'Your father has no say in this.' Ruan spoke calmly, yet the manner of his speech did not allow for argument. 'And you have a lesson to learn. Life is fair with one gift only.'

'But I want to go!' Eefay wailed.

Erith came over. 'Wants and gets are two different things,' she said, taking the little girl's hand. 'Come, we've chosen you to sing at the feast tonight. You have to learn a special song.' She winked at Skaaha and led her sister away.

The spoiling took place in the forge, where Tosk waited, chanting, dressed for the ceremony. Kerrigen's weapons were put beyond use, the shaft of the spear burned, its iron tip and the blade of her sword heated, beaten out of shape, and cooled in sea water. Ruan slung them, with the shield and winged helmet, in a pack on Skaaha's back. This was her burden: a large one, but not heavy, not like her aunt.

'If Jiya hadn't killed those men, I couldn't make the sacrifice,' she said.

'You owe her a debt,' Ruan agreed, puncturing her defiance.

Up on the hill path, the smell of woodsmoke drifted from the bonfire. The air was cold with the promise of frost, the sky a clear, sharp blue. North of them, the rounded red mountains were redder. The jagged, black mountains beyond jumped closer. Home lay far behind them: the sweeping curve of Loch Bracadale, the green peninsula of Ullinish, the solid, reassuring brochs of Doon Beck and Doon Mor.

'Does your sister always get what she wants?' Ruan asked as they walked.

'Mostly. She's very pretty.' Skaaha shrugged. 'Everybody loves her.'

'Yet she's angry with you.'

'Is she?'

'You have what she wants.'

Skaaha couldn't think what she had, but it was true that Eefay always asked to go where she went, do as she did, have whatever she might have. 'Aren't fostered children the same?' she asked.

Ruan shook his head. 'Does Calum chase after Thum?'

The youngster sometimes rolled about the grass in the mornings, copying them, but it was just child's play, not because Thum was doing it. Skaaha had been surprised to discover they were brothers. There was warmth between them, but no passion, none of the anger that swelled between her and Eefay. The boys' lives were not tied together, sharing a home and mother, as hers had been tied to her sister's.

The track was not demanding, mostly flat plateau between low peaks. Where it passed through forest, Ruan played his reed flute as they walked.

'To please the beasts,' he joked when she asked.

'Do they like to dance?'

'They like to know we're about.'

Gradually, she relaxed. Her worry for Jiya could wait. In front of them, the land spread out into a wide green valley. Before long, they reached a clustered group of small lochs. The druid led the way around the rocky shore, keeping them upwind of trees on the opposite bank. She spotted a lynx in one, and knew it saw them. There would be bears here too but, though his only useful weapon was a sling and a bag of stones, the druid was unperturbed. His confidence inspired hers. Bears would think they were parent and cub and steer clear.

'What are you grinning about?' Ruan asked.

'You don't look much like Mummy bear,' she said, giggling.

'There's always something to be grateful for.' He smiled back. 'We're here.' They were on a rocky outcrop above the loch. Below, there was no shore, only deep water gently lapping the sheer stone face. 'Will I stay with you?'

'It doesn't matter. I'm fine.'

'Don't fall in.'

She stepped back from the edge, shook her mother's honours off her back on to the sparse grass. Images filled her head: the old door-keeper; peats burning in the fire-pit; curving stone steps; smoky lamps; curtained chambers; a voice. *Pain is the teacher.* Extricating the spearhead, she walked back to the edge, paused to get her grip – she did this for Kerrigen, so her spirit would wake in the afterlife – and threw. In spite of the bent tip, it flew down into the loch, slicing through the water. Next, she lifted the bronze shield. Throwing it was more difficult. She swung around. The disc spun away from the cliff edge, falling with a splash. Aghast, she turned to the druid.

'It's floating,' she said.

Without a word, he stepped forward, put a stone in his sling, swung it over his head and jerked it forwards. The stone clunked against the rim of the shield, tilting it. As it dipped below the surface, water filled the boss. In moments, it was gone.

'There is no need to throw,' he said gently. 'Just hold them out over the edge and let go.'

A lump formed in Skaaha's throat. She lifted the winged helmet. Like all her mother's accoutrements, it was beautifully made. Kerrigen loved fine things, skilled workmanship. Skaaha had envied her only this, with its bronze feathered wings and delicate roped edging. She could see now who had made it. The craft was Ard's, from the time when they made her. Her eyes filled with tears.

'It wouldn't be a sacrifice if it was easy.' Ruan's quiet voice neither prompted nor insisted. 'No one will make you do what you don't wish to,' he added. 'Keep it if you must, but think first how well it protected your mother.'

Skaaha blinked furiously. Tears spilled down her cheeks. If the helmet had stayed in place her mother would have lived. Bending, she lifted a heavy stone, put it in the helmet then dropped it over the edge. Gleaming, it fell, splashing into the water, sinking out of sight. Only the sword remained. She gripped the haft in both hands and held it out over the edge, the buckled blade pointing downwards. She held it a long time, this last reminder of the warrior queen who was her mother. Then she let go.

Ruan joined her at the cliff edge, putting his arm round her shoulder as they gazed at the ripples fading out over the loch below.

'Bravely done,' he murmured. 'Brave girl.'

'She'll watch over us now,' she said, 'me and Eefay.' But she knew he didn't believe it and turned on him. 'Why do druids sacrifice when you don't believe?'

'The dead need to be let go. Keeping their treasured possessions is a way to keep them here. Would that be good for anyone?'

She considered. 'No. If they're in the afterlife, or,' she added doubtfully, 'if there is an otherworld, they'd be unhappy if they still wanted to be here.'

'And so would we, wanting that,' he said.

Half-way home, they stopped to break their fast with cold water from a mountain stream. The days were short now, the light already fading. A great white-tailed sea eagle flew overhead, barking as it went. *Rau . . . rau . . . rau . . .*

'A good omen,' Ruan said, watching it head inland to roost.

'I know what it is,' Skaaha said. The wet rock under her hand was knobbly, like the bones in Eefay's shoulder when she'd pushed on it to raise herself and saw the warriors surrounding them. 'It's death.'

'The eagle?' Ruan looked puzzled.

'The only gift life gives to everyone.'

Like water, his eyes took on the colour of the sky. At the loch-side, they had been sharp winter blue. Now they were warm grey. He smiled. 'Wise as well as brave,' he said. 'You'll keep me on my toes.'

'What happened to Jiya?'

'Her spirit doesn't fit well into her mind and body. She sees the world differently. Sometimes that frightens her.'

'I know. I mean, what did you do?'

'I gave her cordial to calm her, but she can't have it for long.'

'You'll take her to Suli.'

'Yes. She'll be safe there.'

Desperation gripped her. 'I could take her to Glenelg.'

'Is that what you planned?'

Caught out, Skaaha stared down at the sparkling water. 'Will I see her again?'

'Maybe.' He gripped her shoulder. 'Be where you are, Skaaha, always. There is nothing you can do for Jiya.' They rose and walked on. Soon, the smell of roasting mutton would have drawn them to the village, even if they'd been sightless.

The feast was held in Lethra's roundhouse. As larder-keeper, the chief's home smelled of beasts from the pens outside, and of milk, cheeses, smoked fish and drying meats or, depending on the tasks in hand, of mead, ale, beer, berries, fruit or herbs. To enter it was an assault on the senses, one that whetted appetite.

Backed by other children, her thwarted desire forgotten, Eefay sang the rest-and-be-thankful blessing for the harvest bounty and basked in delighted applause. In the quiet time after the feast, family gifts were exchanged. Skaaha fixed the gold armlet she'd made round the top of Eefay's arm.

'There,' she said. 'Now you'll be even more beautiful.'

Eefay stared at it, amazed. It was the first piece of jewellery she'd owned. 'I'll never take it off,' she vowed. Then her eyes clouded. 'The bad men took my present for you. It was a dagger.'

'That's all right,' Skaaha assured her stoutly. 'They nearly had yours too, except for Jiya.' But when her sister ran to show off her present to the others, the ache of disappointment swelled. Even where no one favoured either of them, Eefay always got and she didn't. That was the way of things.

I I

Huddled in the cove, out of sight of his boat or the broch, Mara raged. 'Nothing?' she hissed, furious. 'You found nothing?'

'Weapons, but not that one.' The outsider spat on stones. 'I lost three men. Half of us. Dead, I'm sure. You never said about a warrior. Crazed, that one is.'

The stink of him offended her. Even in pitch dark, grease shone on his beard. 'She has it. I know she has.'

'Then it's well hid.' He blew his nose with his fingers. 'Reward, you said.'

Mara forgot caution. 'You had the honours, and lost them!' she snapped. They would have been some consolation. But the sacrifice was made by now, Kerrigen's spirit awake in an afterlife from where the dead could be vengeful. 'You owed me,' she snarled. 'I should've taken your hand off when I first caught you. Be grateful I don't take your head!'

'Hasty, that is.' He held up grimy hands then quickly dropped them, shoving them into the pockets of his ragged coat. 'There's other uses we could be.'

The truth of this kept her in check. Warrior queens made enemies. Those who lived by stealth could do what others couldn't. There could be other opportunities to recover her possession. Clearly, Jiya didn't recall what or where it was. As for Kerrigen, the druids might be right, her dead rival safely in the otherworld, a mewling baby at its mother's breast. 'Your mouth stays shut,' she said, 'even with your men, or I will hunt you down. Now get out of my sight.'

He scurried away, stumbling over pebbles, his bulk a blacker shadow in the dark. The smell of him remained.

*

The last day of Sowen was spent culling older beasts, the carcases salted, dried or smoked except for one fat porker, spit-roasted for the evening feast. Skins were stretched, scraped and set to dry inside roundhouse roofs, sheepskins washed in the freezing river, scrubbed with soapwort, oiled then steeped with herbs to protect against moths. During winter, they would be routinely worked to keep them supple.

At sunset, everyone cheered the new moon born into the western sky. The bonfire flared again, its embers raked down for the Carlin's leap into the future. She danced around, sweeping glowing cinders into the low heap. Finally, with a roll of drums, she leapt, blacks trailing out, only just clearing the flickering flames, her pointed hat held in place with one gnarled hand. As she landed, the rift between the two worlds healed. Hands drew her forward to safety.

'Aye-yie-yaa!' the people cheered. Winter had begun. The blue hag screeched her prophecy of snow to come before the moon was full. Everybody queued to jump. The Carlin swatted each one as they landed, her broom applied more vigorously to any who fell short and were hauled out, smoking.

'Jump with me,' Thum said, shyly, holding out his hand to Skaaha, 'into our new lives, for luck.'

'I'm staying in Kylerhea.' She made a wry face. 'I'm the chosen one.'

'Then you'll need luck,' he grinned.

She took his hand, and they jumped together, making a clean leap of it. When the last had leapt, the hag stomped back to the cave, muttering all the way about being unnecessarily manhandled over an easy jump. She would not be seen again till spring.

First light also brought departures, as visiting family and friends were waved off home. When they were gone, houses would be swept clean, fresh herbs scattered to deter pests or pestilence, rubbish thrown into the new pit on top of the charred bones of the robbers. About to leave, Thum came running over to find Skaaha.

'I wanted to give you something,' he said, embarrassed, 'for teaching me and persuading Tosk. But I can't make things like you can.'

'Make yourself a warrior,' Skaaha said, 'and protect us.'

'I'll do that,' the boy said. 'But I also found this for you.' He held out his hand. 'Gern showed me how to pan the streams for it.' In his palm nestled three large shining nuggets of silver. 'Ard promised to make you a brooch with it, for Imbolc.'

Skaaha had trouble closing her mouth to speak. This was Bride's metal, the silver of winter moon reflecting a pale spring sun whose low light silvered trees, grass, hills and sea. Her eyes flitted from the coveted nuggets to the boy's flushed face. Before she could say anything, or hug him, he thrust the nuggets into her hand.

'Well, take it then,' he said, gruffly, and scurried back to Ruan.

The druid rode one of the shaggy ponies that brought them to Kylerhea, and led another. On it sat Jiya, head hanging. Her face had changed, features dragged down, heavy, immobile, the wildness gone from her eyes and replaced with a vast emptiness. A rope bound her wrists together. Skaaha went over, put a hand on her aunt's thigh and looked up into the dreadful lifelessness of her expression.

'It'll be all right, Jiya,' she whispered, but nothing seemed all right about the warrior, and she did not reply. An arm went round Skaaha's shoulders.

'It will be all right,' a voice said. 'Visions should be a blessing.' It was Erith, the bulge of her pregnant belly pressing against Skaaha's side. 'The druids will make her well.'

'Will they?' Unconvinced, Skaaha shook off the forge-keeper's arm. Erith had never wanted her or her aunt to be here. Thum waved furiously from his seat behind Ruan as they rode off. Jiya did not look up or round.

Saying goodbye to Eefay was infinitely easier. It had taken just those few short days to remember how annoying she was.

'When they see I'm wearing gold,' the little girl crowed, 'they'll think it's a warrior queen coming back!'

'Well, you are,' Skaaha assured her. 'You just have to grow a bit.' With nuggets of Bride's silver nestled in her pocket, she envied her sister nothing except her innocence. They exchanged hugs, kisses and promises of future visits. Tosk helped the little girl into a coracle. He was crossing too, making his way to Cairnpapple in the navel of Alba. As the small boat rowed above the current before being allowed to pick it up and be pulled down and across to the opposite coast, where Donal already waited, the sisters waved till they could wave no more.

'Live the day well, Eefay,' Skaaha shouted. The answer, if there was one, drowned in the swell. She watched the craft dock safely on the other side, and waved again till Donal put her sister up on his horse and rode off out of sight. Cold began to bite, and with it, loss. None of her own people were here now; no Jiya or Eefay, not even Ruan, and not Thum, the best friend she'd made. A hollow space opened inside her. Drawing her cloak tight, she hurried home. Inside, two older girls waited.

'Erith says you can come with us,' Kaitlyn, the taller, blonde girl said.

'Where to?' Chittering, Skaaha just wanted to stay by the fire.

'The cavern,' the red-haired girl answered. Freya, her name was. She worked in the smelter. Kaitlyn trained with the crone, milking ewes, goats and cows.

'I don't want to sit with Lethra,' Skaaha complained. 'Not again.'

'Shhh.' Kaitlyn put a finger to her lips, in case the children in the house heard. 'She's gone home,' she whispered. 'It's ours now. Any time we want to be there.'

Skaaha couldn't imagine wanting to be in a smoky cave halfway up a freezing hill. But the two girls were keen, and the alternative was clearing up, so she went with them. On the way, they explained. Freya had played Bride last Imbolc, Kaitlyn at

Imbolc two suns before that. The Bride in between, from the nearest fishing village, had gone to be a druid. Now it was Skaaha's turn. She would bring the gift of fire, bless babies with their names and grant wishes. They would be her companions.

'It will be Kaitlyn's last time,' Freya confided. 'She comes of age at Beltane.'

'If I can wait that long,' Kaitlyn said, rolling her eyes. 'I keep looking at men and thinking, Mmm, bet he'd be good.'

'Good for what?' Skaaha asked.

The others laughed.

'You'll find out,' Kaitlyn assured her. 'That's what we're for.'

'There's a reason why you were chosen,' Freya added. 'Lethra always knows, says she can smell it.'

'Smell what?'

'The change coming. You wait. You'll be fine till Imbolc is past, then you'll bleed. The old witch is never wrong.'

Kaitlyn pushed aside the curtain of broom that screened the cavern entrance. All evidence of their chief's seven-day occupation was gone. There was food laid out, a jug of ale, a fresh straw mattress and peat smouldering in the hearth. It was warm enough, cosy and private. Kaitlyn sprawled on the bed.

'Peace,' she sighed. 'No Lethra to nag and complain.' She glanced at Skaaha. 'No Erith to bug you. And' – she turned to Freya – 'no Kenna waiting to pounce when you come of age.' Kenna, the noman furnace-keeper, liked an occasional young woman in her bed to break the monotony of men. Anticipation lit Kaitlyn's face. 'We could even sneak some boys in.'

'That's the last thing we want,' Freya objected.

'Only because you're too young yet.' Kaitlyn rolled on to her stomach and considered the redhead. 'You could watch and learn.'

'Like I haven't seen that a million times already,' Freya exaggerated. 'And even if I see it a million times more, I'm still not doing it. Ever.' She turned to the food. 'Cakes and ale,' she drooled. 'That's a lot more fun.'

Girls, apart from her sister, were a mystery to Skaaha. At Doon Beck, she spent her time with women, or sometimes with young men in training. Girls of her age were rare. If she saw any, it was at festivals or when visiting family homes with her mother. Having two for company was new and exciting. There was no privacy in the village, only on hills and moors, in forests, or further down the shore. Meeting the bear had taught her to stay in sight of houses. Now, she was growing up, and for a few moons over winter, she had a special place to go and two friends to share it with.

'Boys are all right,' she said, 'if they bring something we want.'

'Like?' Kaitlyn asked.

'Peats for the fire,' Skaaha shrugged. 'Hazelnuts to roast.' She looked at Freya, who was busy pouring ale into the three horns. 'Beer?'

Kaitlyn sat up, spreading her hands to indicate length. 'And a good stiff –' the two younger girls stared '– broom to sweep the place out.' All three began to giggle.

Stockpiled charcoal meant the ironworks wasn't idle over winter. Forge and furnace were the warmest places to be. Work filled the long evenings. Bride-in-waiting and her maidens spent every spare moment in the cavern. Though they didn't dare invite boys, they talked about them plenty, grumbled about their respective house-keepers, shared life histories and secrets, did each other's hair and played games. It was treasured time. Anything that intruded was resented.

The full moon brought the promised snow. Skaaha hurried through it, heading for the cavern. Icy flakes stung her cheeks like tiny needles. Erith, wrapped up against the chill, stood outside the larder entrance, a bowl of pickled herring for the evening meal in her arms. The forge-keeper still shunned Ard, though his child was due soon.

'Skaaha,' she called, her voice strangely strangled. 'Would you take this?'

Skaaha turned, annoyed to be distracted. In Erith's footsteps, the slush was bloodied. At her feet it melted steamily in a pool of warm water. Annoyance became fear. 'What's happening,' she gasped. 'What's wrong?'

'It's just the baby coming,' Erith grunted. 'I don't want to drop the food.'

Skaaha took the bowl, and gripped the forge-keeper's arm. 'I'll help you back.' Together, they walked slowly to the roundhouse. At the doorway, Erith stopped, gripped by pain. Skaaha ran in, dumped the bowl and ran back.

'Go fetch the druid.' Erith groaned, still unable to take the next step.

Skaaha pelted through the slushy snow to the druid huts. Erith hadn't said which one so, with Ruan gone, she went to the older woman's, unceremoniously bursting in the door. She'd never been in a druid lodge before. The small round room was larger than she expected, festooned with drying herbs, bark, mushrooms and other shrivelled fruits. It smelled of spiced smoke. The startled druid stared up at her from where she sat grinding something in a bowl behind the central hearth.

'Erith's baby's coming,' Skaaha gasped. 'I'm to fetch you.'

'Ah, right.' Although she appeared bumbling, Nechta was rapidly on her feet, wrapped in a cloak, searching among pots for those she wanted. 'Now, yes, and this.' Having found the required creams and brews, she turned to Skaaha. 'Don't stand dithering, child. Go tell Yona to bring her needles.'

Yona was the third druid in the cell. Skaaha dashed off next door. This lodge was quite different, cluttered with rocks and crystals instead of plants, sweet with the smell of soap. Skaaha didn't wait this time, but scampered back to the roundhouse. The ground was slippery, but Nechta had beaten her to it. There was no time to wonder how she'd moved so quickly. Nechta shooed everyone else out and issued orders.

'Keep the door closed. You' – to the cook – 'take the food to Lethra's. Feed your people there. You' – to Skaaha – 'put another peat on. Come now' – taking Erith into her curtained chamber – 'we'll get you sorted, see how close it is.'

Skaaha put two peats on, lit some lamps and waited. Yona hurried in, bringing a cold blast of air and closing the door tight behind her. Skaaha sat on, pushing away the selfish thought of her friends waiting in the cavern. This baby who was being born would be her sister or brother, sharing Ard as their father. It would link her to Thum, his sister or brother too, Erith his blood-mother. As Bride, she would bless it with the chosen name – a good omen.

Nechta came out of Erith's chamber to warm a pot of foul-smelling cream by the fire while Yona inserted her witching needles into different points of the labouring woman's limbs and trunk. The druids' presence was calming, soothing, but the grunts and moans of the birthing forge-keeper caused Skaaha's stomach to clench. Following instructions, she boiled water then set it to cool. Then she waited, and waited, trying not to hear the urgent groans of delivery or the frantic gasps that came between. It seemed to go on and on. Erith began to panic.

'Something's wrong,' Skahaa heard her groan. 'This isn't right.'

Yona started to croon, a rhythmic chanting that did nothing to quiet the rising fear in the room. The baby was coming into the world the wrong way round, and it was, indeed, taking far too long. Eventually, the last sounds of birth assaulted Skaaha's ears, then an interminable silence that was full of noise: Yona crooning, Erith begging reassurance about her baby, Nechta not giving it but taking the warm water, cleaning the little blue body, rubbing it, shaking it, smacking it, but still that one unbroken silence settled among darkening shadows around the room.

When everything was done in the birth-bed, Nechta left to fetch something to help the bereft mother forget, Yona to tell

Ard and the others. Told to sit with Erith, Skaaha eased aside the chequered curtain. Propped up, the exhausted forge-keeper held the shawl-wrapped body of her dead daughter in the crook of her arm, her fingers pushing the cover aside to check the perfect little body, the limp arms, the tiny fists, stroking the baby's legs, cupping the small feet. Faint sounds escaped her lips, like the whimpering of an injured beast.

'I'm sorry,' Skaaha whispered. There was a long quietness. Erith rested her pale cheek on the baby's head. It looked asleep. Not knowing what else to say or do, Skaaha repeated what the druid had told her. 'Nechta said her spirit wasn't ready to leave the otherworld yet. She's still alive there.'

Erith looked through, or beyond, her. Her haunted eyes filled with tears. 'If that's true,' her voice cracked, 'why can my heart not hold the pain?' A sob shook her shoulders, then another, great gut-wrenching sobs that shuddered the whole length of her body and emerged in howling cries akin to rage.

12

The fine blue cloth was stained, the marks brown like rust. Sitting on her pallet bed in Erith's house, Skaaha unravelled it. Inside were two, almost evenly shattered, pieces of a spear, the ends splintered. She frowned. 'Jiya sent me a broken spear?'

Ruan shrugged. 'She galloped off while I took Thum to Mara. When I caught up, that was hidden in her clothes. Before I left her with Suli, she insisted I bring it to you, that you keep it.'

'That's all she said?'

'Not all.'

'Then what else?'

The priest clucked his tongue. 'Tluck-tluck-tluck.' Then, with lengthening pauses between, 'Tluck – tluck – tluck – tluck.'

'What does that mean?'

Again his shoulders rose and fell. 'Only Jiya knows.'

'Maybe she means to come back, and wants me to mend it.'

'Maybe.' He shifted, embarrassed. 'Does it help to know she' – he cleared his throat – 'forgave me?'

'Maybe.' Skaaha re-wrapped the weapon. 'I'll keep it safe till she comes.' She tucked it under her bed. The tattered cloth was familiar. Kerrigen had a sash cloak of similar fine blue wool, but she couldn't say so in case the druid insisted she burn it.

With the package delivered, Ruan went in to see Erith. The full moon had waned to a dying crescent since the baby, but she was not recovering. It had been three days before she gave up the body for cremation. The ashes and remaining bones were stored in a clay pot which she kept in her chamber. Her

99

husbands were still banished to other beds, the rift with Ard, her baby's father, not repaired. Ard, distraught, worked late in the forge, the lamps guttering long after everyone else rested. Nechta's potions quieted Erith's grief but did not restore her spirit. Healing was needed, or winter would take another life from them.

Lounging listlessly in her chamber, the forge-keeper was neither pleased nor displeased to see the druid. She was pale, lips colourless, eyes heavy. Ruan squatted cross-legged beside her bed.

'I missed seeing your baby,' he said. 'Tell me about her.'

Making flat-bread on the hearthstone, Skaaha listened to the murmur of his voice. He spoke as if expecting response, as if genuinely interested. When no answer came, he chatted amiably about the child, surmising the colour of her hair, eyes, the length she measured, who she was most like. Skaaha was about to go tell him, for she remembered every detail of that baby, when she heard Erith speak in reply. It was just a word, then a stumbling phrase, then a flood. The relief was immense. Responsibility for Erith's life lifted from her shoulders. Ruan had taken the weight. He knew what to do. Skaaha wrapped the hot bread in cloth and headed for the cavern.

Freya had brought honey, a small pot sneaked out before Kenna, the furnace-keeper, returned from the smelter. The golden liquid dripped from the warm bread.

'Why did you stop that stuff you did in the mornings?' Kaitlyn asked Skaaha, licking the sweet drops from her fingers.

'Yeh, I noticed that,' Freya said. 'Is it too cold?'

'No.' With Thum and Jiya gone, her routines had been lonely, purposeless. After the baby died, she stopped. 'It's for warriors. I'm a smith now.'

'Not just warriors,' Kaitlyn said. 'That Ruan does it, twice every day.'

'Does he?' Skaaha said, astounded that a druid would, or could.

'Sun-up, and sunset,' Kaitlyn said. 'Round the point, on the shore. I've seen him when we bring the beasts in. Sometimes I go to watch.'

'Why?' Freya asked, dribbling honey on another chunk of bread.

'Grow up, you.' Kaitlyn couldn't believe she needed to be told. 'The man's a god.'

'I mean, why does he do it?' Freya corrected between bites of bread. 'And on his own. That can't be much fun.'

'It's fun for some of us,' Kaitlyn said. 'I'm glad he's back. If you want, we could all go watch him tomorrow morning, if it's dry.'

They met at the cavern before anyone else woke. Skaaha almost encountered Ard, who was outside emptying his bladder when she sneaked out, but he had his back turned and didn't see her. It was less cold than it had been, the first light snowfall long gone, and not raining. Giggling and shushing each other, the girls climbed above the cavern, making use of what cover remained in the stunted trees and scrub on the low slopes. Above them, a grizzled wolf watched their creeping progress then loped off. The grey dawn behind Glenelg blackened the hills but lightened the sea.

'What if he sees us?' Freya asked.

'Shh,' Kaitlyn warned. 'He's got ears like an owl.'

'Are you sure he'll come?' Skaaha whispered.

For answer Kaitlyn dropped on her belly behind a gorse bush. 'Get down,' she hissed. They collapsed beside her. Ruan was already on the beach, naked except for a knotted cord around his waist that carried a pouch of stones tied close to one thigh with his sling. The girls peered past the prickly gorse, through long blades of grass. The druid was more muscular than Skaaha expected, though she remembered how strong he'd been that day at the bog, lifting and carrying her as if she weighed less than a feather. Not the bulkiness of Ard's muscles but lithe, sinewy. His movements echoed like song and dance in her. She watched, awed, her own muscles tensing and relaxing to the familiar rhythms.

Beside her, Kaitlyn grunted softly and wriggled, rocking her hips against the rough ground. Engrossed, like Freya, in the man on the shore, Skaaha barely noticed. Ruan's tempo changed. He leapt and spun, turning in the air and landing to a series of handsprings from which he rose easily into an aerial spin, kicking out as he turned. His moves were far advanced on hers, graceful, light and sure. As the low sun lit golden ripples on the waves of the kyle, the priest completed the routine facing the sea, right fist raised high above his head.

'Hyaaa-aaaaa!'

Freya's hand clamped over Skaaha's opening mouth. 'No,' she hissed, stopping the girl from uttering the same, familiar shriek. On the shore below, the druid raced into the water. 'Wow,' Freya whispered, 'he is a god!'

'Told you,' Kaitlyn gasped, her body shuddering with pleasure.

That afternoon, in the forge, Ard laid down his tools early, took the sickle Skaaha worked on from her hands and plunged it in the bucket of sea water to cool it.

'Come,' he said. 'We're wanted.' He looked gaunt, still estranged from Erith, grieving alone, these few words as many as he'd spoken to Skaaha since the confinement. As they walked towards the roundhouse, she slid her hand into his. For whose comfort, she couldn't have said. His sorrow made her guilty. Immediately, his fingers tightened around hers, saying what speech did not. Whatever they were wanted for, she felt forgiven.

In the doorway, Ruan waited with Erith. The druid looked serious, the forge-keeper sombre. Fright caught in Skaaha's throat. Erith might formally divorce Ard. Or, worse, Ruan might have seen her at the beach. But they had concerns other than the preoccupations of pubescent girls. In her arms, Erith held the pot with the baby's ashes and the remains of its bones, now ground to powder by the druid. Ruan carried a spade and a birch sapling. Ard lifted a cauldron of water, and they walked to the edge of the settlement, stopping before the tree-line began. A spot fronting a small copse was already marked. It could be seen from both forge and roundhouse.

'I will dig,' Ard said, giving Skaaha the cauldron and taking the spade from the druid.

Skaaha stood beside Erith, watching her father put his foot against the step of the spade, his back into raising the earth. When the hole was deep and wide enough, he plunged the blade into the soil so the tool stood upright and held his hands out to his wife. Erith handed him the pot. Carefully, Ard shook the contents into the hole. He beckoned Skaaha to bring the water, and she tipped it into the pot to be swirled clean before being poured over the ashes. Ruan positioned the sapling for Erith to hold while Ard backfilled the hole with the excavated soil. When it was pressed down, the last of the water was poured around the trunk. It was a fine, straight tree. A fitting memorial with delicate, weeping branches that would yield many medicines as it grew.

Ruan raised his flute and began to play, not the song of celebration but one of sleep, a lullaby. For a moment, Skaaha thought Erith would cry again, or that she would, but the forge-keeper took hold of her husband's hand instead, and both of them began to sing, softly, unwavering. Skaaha could not. The lump in her throat would not allow a squeak to pass.

When the song ended, Ard and Erith didn't move, except the blacksmith put an arm round his wife's shoulder and she rested her head against his chest. Ruan took up the spade and gave Skaaha the empty cauldron. Leaving the couple by the tree, they walked towards home.

'They'll be fine now,' the druid said.

'Erith didn't believe.' It was out before she meant to speak it, but she could not forget the forge-keeper's wail of grief, the intensity of pain, or her own for a sister here then gone.

'We don't own people, Skaaha. Erith's body cried out to nurse its baby at her breast. But the spirit of the child chose otherwise. Respect that, and there is nothing to grieve. Death demands we let go. That's what it teaches. Erith accepts that now.'

They walked on in silence. The truth in the priest's words chimed with Skaaha's sense of self. Her life had come through others but wasn't owed to them. It was hers alone. The baby, too, was only itself. Not hers, not Ard's, not Erith's. Sensing the care with which the priest had guided them, guilt grew about the morning's adventure with her friends. Miserable at the childishness of it, she stared down at the shards of grass underfoot as she walked, all too conscious of his longer strides beside her. They were almost back at the house before he spoke again.

'You can join me if you wish.'

'What?' Panic tore through her.

'At the beach. Skills shouldn't be lost for lack of practice.'

Embarrassed, she hung her head. 'I can't do the things you can.'

'Neither could I at your age. In fact, I doubt I could do as much. My foster-parents are warriors, in the north, but when I reached my ten suns, I left to be a priest. I've learned more since, from other warriors.'

'But why, if you don't want to be one?'

He stopped walking, having reached the point where he'd turn to head for his hut. 'The body has its own wisdom,' he said, 'and another way of remembering. Come in the mornings,' he suggested. 'My evenings are solitary, for meditation, and you have Imbolc to prepare for.' He paused, leaning on the spade. 'I don't suppose your friends want to learn?'

Skaaha flushed. 'I don't know,' she muttered. 'I'll ask them.'

Low Sun arrived, the mid-winter feast, tormented by a hard frost.

'This is crazy,' Freya muttered, from the shelter of white-rimed bushes well beyond the light of the bonfire on Carlin's Loup, as she shifted in the chill.

'You're so joyful,' Kaitlyn chided. 'Hush, I want to see.'

Skaaha yawned, tired from earlier rises to train with Ruan

on the beach. It was even earlier now, well before sun-up. The men round the fire had drunk and danced all night to the throb of drums. Druids apart, women were excluded from the solstice wake, the only reason Kaitlyn wanted to be here, as near as they dared but well beyond any heat.

'I'm bored to freezing,' Freya muttered. The ceremony seemed to consist of young lads leaping the dwindling fire. Those who achieved it began learning with the druids how to come of age at mid-summer's High Sun. Only one youth easily cleared the flames. Freya perked up. 'Oh, I like him,' she whispered.

'Not wasted time then,' Kaitlyn muttered, vindicated. 'She's alive, after all.'

'I'm not,' Skaaha hissed, chittering. Between them and the glowing embers, shadowy men cheered. One of them raised a holly wreath to crown the boy. It was Ruan. Skaaha ducked. 'Come on, before we're caught.'

Keeping low, they scampered back towards the cavern, giggling once they were out of earshot, more excited by the thrill of clandestine danger than by what they'd seen. Back on Loup hill, as the men killed the fire and began to sing, the huddled knot of druids watched the girls go, running like shadows over frosted heath.

'Lethra was right,' Nechta said. 'She's more at home now, and spirited.'

'Kaitlyn's curiosity helped,' Ruan added, 'and things improve without Jiya.' His face darkened. 'Mara asked how Skaaha fared, and of her sister.'

'You didn't say she was our Bride?'

'No.' Mara's interest was better not roused. 'Her attention should be on security, with outsiders about. Stock is stolen under her nose.' Across the sound, the coming dawn blued the sky. 'And we have a long way to go yet.'

'But Skaaha trains with you,' Yona approved, 'and you gain her trust. The first steps are taken. Suli will be pleased.'

'Time will tell,' Ruan cautioned. Time would tell. Down below, the headwomen woke and opened house doors to let in the first light.

At the cavern entrance, wrapped in blankets, Skaaha and her friends raised the screen to watch the renewed sun rise over Alba's hills.

'They won't come here,' Freya groaned, watching the men descend to the village carrying fresh peats, food and drink, and led by the holly-wreathed youth.

'No first foot over the threshold,' Skaaha objected. 'Where's the luck in that?'

'Hard luck,' Kaitlyn said. 'Men aren't allowed in here, remember?'

'Then let's go home.' Freya plunged down the path, slithering on icy patches. The other two followed. For twelve days, while everything in the larder that would keep no longer was consumed, there would be celebration and little work.

Skaaha fretted till it was over, her impatience mediated by joining Ruan at every dawn. Winter bit deep. Icicles hung from roundhouse thatch, waterfalls petrified, the burn froze. Preparations began for Imbolc, festival of birth and rebirth, which brought the end of winter, when the goddess returned as Bride, the creator. While Ard changed the broom screening the cavern entrance for pine, Erith added sprigs of holly heavy with blood-red berries.

'I'll do that,' Skaaha offered, shamed by the forge-keeper's willingness to work in the freezing cold.

'We'll do it together,' Erith said, showing her how. Fixing the twigs wasn't as easy as she made it look. 'It's such a blessing, you being here.'

'Me?' Skaaha couldn't believe her ears, especially after the woman's loss.

'No,' Erith teased, 'that girl behind you. Of course, you. Lethra says you're even smarter than your mother.'

Skaaha gawped, wordless, fumbling inexpertly with the greenery.

'Mind your fingers,' the forge-keeper warned. 'It's jaggy.'

The Wolf moon waned. Around the hearth, the priests told stories of Bride who brought the sun, who forged the world from a ball of flame, and who inhabited the furnace in its centre. Every spring, long before the young sun had heat in it, she returned from underground, through the cavern, bringing warmth and growth back to the land. The Snow moon waxed. Soon it would be full. Skaaha was confined to the cave for all seven days and nights of its second quarter, waited on by her friends.

'Don't you miss your priest?' Kaitlyn warmed food in the cauldron over the fire, her mind preoccupied by her favourite subject. The others sprawled on the bed.

'I miss the practice,' Skaaha agreed. It was a poor truth. Ruan's undivided attention was rewarding. Unlike Jiya, he could teach her. Under his intense discipline, she worked hard to gain approval and learned fast. 'Maybe I could sneak out. No one else is up that early.'

'No, you can't,' Freya corrected, shocked. 'Nobody should see you.'

'There speaks don't-rock-the-boat Freya,' Kaitlyn teased. 'You're such a druid. She has to sneak to the latrine anyway.'

'Only because neither of us wants to carry smelly pots,' Freya reminded her.

'Because I wouldn't let you!' Skaaha shrieked.

Kaitlyn served the food, a thick venison stew. 'That proves it,' she grinned. 'Not everything is carved in stone. In here, Bride rules, and we' – she planked the plates down in front of them – 'are her trusted maidens. So eat up because, afterwards, we do her bidding.'

'What bidding?' Skaaha frowned.

'What are you up to?' Freya asked.

Kaitlyn would say no more. 'Eat, and find out.'

Tender venison was never eaten so fast. The girls cleaned the gravy from their plates with hot bread, downed some ale and waited, expectantly. Then they waited some more.

'What are we waiting for?' Freya asked.

'You eat too fast,' Kaitlyn answered.

'At this rate, I'll be eating again,' Freya complained.

There was a cough from outside, beyond the screen. 'Kaitlyn,' a voice grunted, a male voice.

'You didn't!' Freya gasped.

'You haven't asked Ruan up here!' Skaaha squeaked, terrified the druid would confront them with disapproval, and even more terrified that he might respond to Kaitlyn's seductions.

'Don't be silly,' her friend said. 'You have to start with one you can handle.' She went to the entrance and pulled the string that swung the thick curtain of pine aside. 'Don't stand out there like a torch in the moonlight,' she said. 'Come in.' It was Hanick, the young fisherman who'd won the holly crown, who came in. Kaitlyn had chosen wisely. Freya had confessed her erotic fancies for the youth. Skaaha was not about to appear intimidated by him.

'A boy?' she said, in much the same way she might have said, 'A fish?'

'You said boys were all right,' Kaitlyn reminded her, settling on to a cushion by the hearth.

'If they brought something we wanted.'

'I'm not a boy,' Hanick boasted, though he still lacked the tattooed mark of maturity below his left ear. 'I'm a man. Soon, anyway. The druids teach me how. And I brought beer,' he added, holding up a jug. 'Man' was anticipation. Hanick was gangly and angular, a few suns short of twenty, with knuckles too big for his fingers and a large knot in his throat. But he was also fair, fresh-skinned and forbidden.

Freya took the beer, filled the horns, gave hers, nervously, to the youth, who had remained standing, and sat with Skaaha on the bed to share hers. The drink was taken in silence, with great concentration. The small sounds of the cave became a nightsong: the smoulder of peat, spitting lamps. An owl hooted outside.

'All right,' Kaitlyn said, grasping the initiative. 'Show them.'

The boy put the horn in its stand and dropped the front flap of his leggings. His penis jutted out, semi-erect. The three girls stared, watched it deflate.

'Is that it?' Skaaha asked, unimpressed. 'It's just the same as any boy's.'

'Make it grow again,' Freya demanded. 'I want to know how you do that.'

Hanick concentrated. His organ twitched but remained dangling. 'I can't while you're all staring,' he said. 'Do something else.'

'Like what?' Skaaha asked.

Kaitlyn sighed. 'Like this?' she said, and pulled the front of her dress open to reveal pert young breasts. She stroked one of them with her hand.

'Yeh, that helps,' the boy said. His penis jerked and began to rise.

Skaaha stared at Kaitlyn's bosom. Unlike Jiya's plump, heavy breasts, these were half-grown, youthful. 'They're nice,' she said. 'I haven't got any yet.'

'D'you want to feel?' Kaitlyn offered, moving closer so her friend could reach. Skaaha cupped a hand over the warm mound. The flesh was smooth, silky, the dark nipple softer. In the cooler air, it tightened to a hard nub. Hanick groaned.

'That's working!' Freya yelled. She hadn't taken her eyes of the boy's organ, which was now fully erect and swaying slightly. 'Can I touch it?' she asked.

'Course,' he said, generously, 'you all can.'

Tentatively, Freya put her fingertips against the shaft. 'Oh,' she said, 'it's hard inside.' She closed her fist around it, squeezing. 'Really hard.'

Skaaha lost all interest in Kaitlyn's breasts. The youth was trembling. 'Let me feel,' she said. Freya relinquished her grip and Skaaha took over. It felt like flexed muscle but not the same. The skin was loose. When she slid her hand down a little, it came too, revealing a swollen arrowhead of reddish, tender-looking flesh at the top. 'Is it supposed to do that?' she asked, worriedly.

'Don't stop,' Hanick urged, 'pull harder,' and put his hand on top of hers, moving it rapidly up and down.

Skaaha started to giggle. 'Kaitlyn, you should do this,' she spluttered. 'You're used to pulling the cows' teats.' The boy moaned, shuddering. Under her hand, Skaaha felt the hard flesh throb, swell and pulsate. 'Oh no!' she yelled, jerking her hand back. 'It's burst! Look, it's bursting.' The instruction to look was superfluous. Freya and Kaitlyn were mesmerized as semen spurted in front of them. Hanick was transported, eyes closed, groaning.

'What's going on?' Ard's voice cut through the moment of fascination like a hot knife through butter. All three girls jumped. They hadn't heard the pine screen rustle, or his footsteps. Hanick gasped, staring at the blacksmith as if one or other of them didn't occupy the real world. 'Go practise elsewhere,' Ard told him. 'And don't come back here.' As the youth stumbled out, the smith glanced at the cave occupants. His gaze settled on Kaitlyn, who'd drawn her dress guiltily back over her bare breasts when he entered. 'Was this your idea?'

'No,' Skaaha said bravely, jumping to her feet. 'It was mine. There were things I needed to know.'

'Things that couldn't wait several suns?' her father asked. 'What were they?'

Skaaha didn't know. Her curiosity about the boy had been mild and of the moment, though the worrying behaviour of his penis left her with a question now. Kaitlyn got up and came to stand beside her.

'It was my idea, Ard,' she confessed. 'Not Skaaha's.'

'But we didn't say no,' Freya added, getting up beside them. The display of solidarity affected the man strangely. He seemed to struggle to get words out. Finally, he succeeded. 'No more boys,' he said. 'And' – to Kaitlyn – 'if you can't wait till Beltane, choose a man, not a beginner.' Then he turned to Skaaha. 'I came to bring a gift for Bride,' he said. 'You might want to wear it for your day.' He held out his hand. In the palm lay a silver brooch, intricately worked from the nuggets Thum had given her at Sowen. It was the full moon of Imbolc, engraved with its hare and delicately edged with bronze shading.

As her friends gaped with admiration, Skaaha let her father put the shining gift into her hand. It was perfect, as if the real orb, in miniature, had been plucked from the sky and placed in her keeping.

'It's beautiful,' she said, looking up at him, her eyes also shining in the lamplight.

He pulled her to him in a hug. 'And only a little less beautiful than my daughter,' he said. She walked with him to the door. As she pulled the string to raise the screen, she glanced at him again, still worried.

'Will Hanick be all right?' she whispered.

Her father leaned down to her. 'Hanick will be over that moon' – he tapped the brooch in her open hand – 'and will still be dreaming of this Imbolc when he's old and grey.' He left then. Skaaha let the curtain fall. Back in the cavern, her two friends sat shaking on the bed. Freya's hand was clamped over her mouth. Kaitlyn hugged herself, face contorted as if in pain.

'What's wrong?' Skaaha asked.

'You,' Kaitlyn shrieked. 'Oh, it's bursting!' she mimicked. 'Haven't you been to High Sun?'

'Yes.' Skaaha frowned. All she could recollect was Kerrigen's excarnation, the gnawing pain of grief, birds fluttering, and her dismay at Mara's accession.

'Without seeing the sun-dance?' Freya squealed, hugging her belly.

Skaaha shook her head, mystified. The girls on the bed could hold their laughter in no longer. Yelping and squeaking, they rolled about, thumping their heels. A shudder ran through Skaaha's abdomen. She doubled over, chuckling and snorting. The three of them made so much noise they still didn't hear the man who, this time, walked away down the slope, hurrying to share the story with Erith. Safe beyond the constraint of parental duty, he, too, broke out in hoots of laughter.

Snow fell like drifting feathers. Among the crowding ewes penned against Lethra's roundhouse the first lamb was born – a good omen for Imbolc. The shepherd pushed other pregnant beasts away so none adopted the newborn, depriving its recovering mother. Left alone, they stole lambs to ease milk-swollen teats and then rejected their own or abandoned fostered ones when theirs arrived, leaving them orphaned, forgotten by that time by birth mothers.

In the cavern, Skaaha huddled naked beside the hearth.

'Will you hurry up?' she complained. 'I'm freezing.'

'It's ready now.' Kaitlyn stirred a pot of oily cream. 'You'll have to stand.'

Gritting her teeth, Skaaha stretched upright.

'Turn round a bit,' Freya insisted, ready with a second pot. 'Then I can do your front while Kaitlyn does your back.'

'It better work,' Skaaha threatened, doing as she was told. Kaitlyn rubbed the concoction into her shoulders. It smelt spicy, rich.

'Course it'll work,' Kaitlyn said. 'Nechta's an expert.'

The druid's cream was to keep the cold out. Already Skaaha could feel it working, the skin on her back tingling, and on her throat where Freya smoothed it, rubbing it well in as she worked across breastbone and chest.

'Ow!' Skaaha yelped. 'What did you do?'

'Sorry,' Freya said. 'It's your breasts. They're starting to come.'

Skaaha glanced down. It was true. Small bumps had formed behind her nipples. That explained the recent tenderness, an ache she'd blamed on the rough bed in the cave. She pushed her chest out. Freya laughed.

'You've nothing to stick out yet,' she said. 'Put your arms up.'

'Have I got hair too?' Skaaha asked hopefully, peering into her bald armpit.

'Yes, on your brooch,' Kaitlyn teased. 'The hare of the moon.'

'A little bit,' Freya confirmed, working down over her friend's belly. 'Keep still!' she chided, as Skaaha tried to look down to see for herself. "You can look when we're finished.'

'My legs are still cold.'

'We'll get them now,' Kaitlyn said, slapping Skaaha's feet apart. 'Step.'

When they'd finished, they dressed her. Bride's colour was white. A fine, wool undershift went on first. White leggings were wrapped round her calves up to her knees and held in place with criss-crossed ties. The dress was warm, woven wool.

'We'll do the cloak once we're done,' Kaitlyn said, as Freya stripped off, ready for the warming cream to be applied. They worked quickly, first one, then the other, then dressed themselves hurriedly in the handmaiden's traditional blue.

'You look beautiful,' Skaaha said, when they'd finished. 'Both of you.'

'You should see yourself,' Freya said.

Skaaha felt beautiful. The girls had braided her long black hair first, weaving the braids around her head. It made her feel tall, grown-up almost. They shared a horn of nippy brew sent by Lethra to complement Nechta's cream in helping keep them warm. Then Kaitlyn went off to check outside and came hurrying back.

'Boots on,' she said. 'The moon's well up.' Timing was everything. Bride must visit every home before the village woke. Quickly, they pulled on sheepskin boots and donned cloaks. Kaitlyn fastened Skaaha's with the silver brooch.

'Now, remember, nobody must see you, or us,' she warned, pulling the hood of the white cloak carefully over her friend's hair.

'I'll be invisible,' Skaaha grinned as it flopped over her eyes. 'If I fall in a drift you'll never find me.'

'Don't yell if you do,' Kaitlyn warned. 'We need to be quiet, or somebody might wake and come out to look.'

'Thum came out last Imbolc,' Freya said, handing out small baskets which they each looped over an arm, 'to pee. We had to hide behind the smelter till he went back in. He took ages!'

'Wish he was here,' Skaaha said, touching the brooch. 'No, not now,' she corrected, as her friends gasped at the bad luck which would follow if he were, 'in the morning. So he could see how well Ard used the silver.'

'You can show him some day,' Kaitlyn said. 'Time to go.'

Bride's fire, lit with flame brought from the forge, burned on the playing field, in case the goddess and her maidens got cold or needed light. The light wasn't necessary. More snow cloud blossomed on the horizon, but the sky above was clear and bright, the land a luminous white, the night eerily still. Although she'd sometimes peered through the screen to watch the Kylerheans go about each day's work, after seven days' of incarceration in the confined cavern the sudden enormity of landscape, sky and sea stunned Skaaha.

She stood for several moments, assaulted by the smells of earth, air and water, awe-struck. It felt as if the top of her head was sliced off, as if moon and stars shone into her skull. Once she had her bearings, they set out, treading carefully through the drifts, stifling giggles. Outside the three roundhouse doors lay offerings of food and drink. On the doors, ribbons of cloth torn from old clothes were tacked. Each carried a wish for someone sleeping inside. Collecting these into their baskets, the girls hurried to the riverbank.

Kaitlyn led Skaaha to the easiest spot to dip the ribbons. For speed, the baskets were lowered into the chill water so it seeped in through the wickerwork, the rims kept above the surface so no piece of cloth could escape and float away.

'Why do they have to be wet?' Skaaha asked. 'Our fingers will freeze.'

'Because water's magic,' Freya whispered back, reciting, 'Rag of hope, freeze and thaw, blow in the wind, dry in the sun, fall from the tree when the wish is done.'

'Because we can tie them tighter wet,' Kaitlyn countered. The tree of hope hung over the pool. 'Just watch you don't end up in the river,' she hissed again, as they wrung out the wet rags before tying them to its snow-covered branches.

Skaaha recognized some, guessing their wishes as she worked: Erith's, Ard's, Gern's, Lethra's, Hanick's, Kenna's, Calum's.

'Oh, help,' Freya squeaked. 'We forgot the priests!'

'They won't have wishes,' Skaaha said, fingers already growing numb.

'You bet they do,' Kaitlyn corrected.

Freya scampered off to fetch and dip the strips of cloth from the druid huts. When the baskets were empty and the tree fully beribboned, the girls warmed their frozen hands at the low bonfire. Kaitlyn gave each a dollop of Nechta's cream to rub into their tingling fingers. Standing by the flames, exposed in the open centre of the village, their nervousness grew into fits of giggles.

Skaaha nudged Kaitlyn. 'Maybe you're Ruan's wish,' she chuckled.

'I'm off him now,' Kaitlyn said. 'There's someone I like better.'

'I still want Hanick.' Sniggering, Freya touched chilled

fingers against Skaaha's cheek. 'Imagine these hands on him.'

'It'd freeze and fall off.' Kaitlyn mimed the drop. 'Clunk! Imagine you – "Oooh, help, it's broken. Anybody got needle and thread?"'

'Stop it!' Skaaha stifled a snort. 'Somebody'll wake.'

Kaitlyn shushed them both. 'Let's get the food and go.' She put the pot of cream back in her basket. 'Drink the drinks, leave the dishes.'

Hurrying now, they took the druid offerings first, then scattered, one to each roundhouse. Fresh flakes of snow began to fall as Skaaha reached the larder-keeper's door. Quickly, she drank the mouthful of mead then crouched to replace the empty cup. As she reached to lift the cloth-wrapped food from its dish, the door swung inwards a crack and stopped. She looked up. Young Calum, eyes full of sleep, stood looking at her. The child blinked, beginning to realize he looked into the face of Bride framed by her white hood. His mouth fell open. Skaaha put a finger to her lips.

'Shh,' she whispered. 'Blessings on your house.' Scooping up the food parcel, she scurried off, leaving the little boy standing in the doorway, mouth still open. All the way back to the cavern, with her handmaids following, she expected to hear him call out, to shout he'd seen Bride, but no sound came. Safely inside, they collapsed round the hearth, laughing out loud at the adventure of it all.

The sound of voices reached them just before dawn. Children called. 'The food's gone. Look, she drank the ale!' and 'She's been, look! My wish is on the tree!' Quickly the girls straightened dresses, wiped each other's faces, patted hair back into place. Pipes began to play, chasing the hag of winter. Kaitlyn snatched up the rag torch that Skaaha would light from Bride's fire just as Lethra, dressed again in Carlin blacks and carrying her broom, hurried into the cave.

'You better all be ready,' the chief snapped. They were. She gazed at Skaaha, her old eyes watering from the cold air outside. After a long moment, she nodded. 'I expect you'll do.'

She held out a bunch of mistletoe, gleaming white berries nestling in its waxy green leaves. 'From the druids.'

'Blessings on you, Lethra.' Skaaha took the sacred plant. At the entrance, the crone fixed a wreath of mistletoe around the girl's braided hair. Carefully, she pulled the white hood over it, and down over Skaaha's eyes to veil them from the sun.

'Keep it there till you're indoors,' Lethra advised, 'or you'll go blind.' Her gnarled hands gripped the cord to lift the screen. She would wait inside, stuffing her hag's robes with the straw mattress for ritual burning when Bride called her down. Winter was done. The young, weak sun had no warmth in it, but heat rose from underground. Green shoots pushed through the snow, the ewes gave milk.

From outside, the music changed to Bride's song, clear and pure in the frosty air. The screen rose. The first rays of morning sun rising over Alba shone directly into the cave. A great cheer went up from villagers crowding the playing field below.

'Aye-yie-yaa!'

Children shrieked. 'It's Bride! It's Bride!'

Stepping out into the blinding light of dawn, in the glare of snow, whiteness rushed into Skaaha's brain, blotting out thought, memory and sight, as if she were absorbed by brightness. She gasped, stopped – she, and all existence, wiped out, cleansed into pure light. Realization flooded her. This was birth, and rebirth. The gift of fire brought the extinction of dark. It took some time, blinking, staring down at her feet from below the hood, before she could raise her head.

Wanting to see, she pushed the hood back, blinking until she could squint through the rush of light. Frosted and sparkling, a world of white homes, trees and hills spread out before her in the morning sun, backed by shimmering water. Beside the river, the wishing tree's neatly dusted naked branches hung festooned with brightly coloured ribbons of hope.

Familiar faces looked up at her, cheering. Ard and Erith hugged each other, glowing with pride. Kenna, the furnace-keeper, swung little Calum on to her shoulders so he could see better. Parents with babies born since last Imbolc waited, eager for name-blessing. Children gaped in awe, other girls, who might soon menstruate, with envy. Hanick, Gern and the rest of the men yelled themselves hoarse.

Even the three druids beamed as they played. Ruan raised a hand in salute. A shiver ran up her spine. *Danger walks beside him.* But that was madness, Jiya's voice. Inside dark homes, cold hearths waited with fresh kindling. She would take the gift of fire to each house in turn. With her maidens following, she began to walk down the snowy hillside.

'Aye-yie-yaa!' The people cheered. 'Bride, Bride, Bride!'

Skaaha strode towards them unafraid, no longer the grieving, resentful child, not the odd, unwelcome stranger. For the first time, she understood druid celebrations. Change and renewal were blessings, ordinary but miraculous. She left childhood behind in the cavern, childhood and the past. This was where she belonged. These people had become her people. She hung their wishes on the tree. Their hopes were hers. It was Imbolc, the first day of spring, and she, the bringer of life, she was Bride.

Leap of Faith

14

Skaaha stood in Nechta's lodge. Several suns had passed since her time as Bride. Proving the crone's intuition correct, she'd bled at every moon since. Slim as a whip, her muscles lithe and supple, she was almost a woman now, shapely, with good bones, and strong, with the strength of willow. In her hands, she held a parting gift, a fat, curved blade set in an ornate stubby handle – ideal for chopping herbs.

Nechta was leaving. As the eldest priest, her herbal knowledge now imparted to Ruan, she'd be replaced, with a new post assigned her at the sanctuary of Tokavaig.

'It will be strong,' Skaaha said, handing her the gift. 'I made it from the iron of a fallen star.' The blade, finely sharpened, gleamed. Three bronze hares chased each other round a mushroom handle.

Nechta cupped it in her palm. 'A perfect fit,' she purred, 'and fine, very fine.' She examined the workmanship. 'You have Ard's gift with metalwork, right enough.'

'My father is a great smith, who gifts me with teaching,' Skaaha boasted.

'Good pupils make good teachers.' Nechta bustled around, finding a place among her packs to safely tuck the chopper. Gusting wind rattled the door. 'Ruan says you stretch even him.'

Skaaha flushed, searching for politeness that escaped her brain like disturbed mice running from the grain store. Ruan had discussed her? The druid's hut seemed smaller, fragile against the wild wind outside, the spicy scent richer than ever.

Nechta watched her, head cocked. 'Will you come of age at Beltane?'

Skaaha's discomfort deepened. 'I don't know.' She looked

into the older woman's enquiring eyes, genuinely puzzled. 'How will I tell?'

'If you have to ask, you're not ready,' the priest chuckled. 'The body knows its needs. Let nothing else persuade you, least of all some lovesick fool.' She changed her mind about the chopper, retrieving it and rummaging for space in her other packs. 'Run along then, Ruan's waiting. I'll be here till after breakfast, if there's anything else you want to know.'

Skaaha left, questions whirling, unformed. Outside, the wind caught her hair and clothes. Ruan was indeed waiting, leaning on his staff, though she'd heard nothing to indicate his presence. Without speaking, they crossed the river by the stepping stones, skirted the mound of the ancestors, walking round the coast to the beach with the morning sun behind them. The only sound was their clothes flapping, the howl in the heavens and the crash of waves.

Beltane, the festival of mating, celebrated fertility. Marriages were made, or unmade. First-time couples handfasted till next Beltane. Of the four druid feasts, it was liveliest, the time when Bride became Danu, spring turned into summer, and girls embraced maturity. Skaaha had never envied the participants, nor wished to be one. Though atmosphere and music were powerful, the dance compelling, copulation looked and sounded painful. Kaitlyn shrugged it off, unimpressed, but had since chosen two husbands. Freya, who became wordless in praise of its pleasures, carried Hanick's child. What Beltane gifted in the coming-of-age obviously bore repeating.

'Do you mean to work or watch?' Ruan asked. He was already stripped, robes weighed down with a rock, re-tying the knotted cord round his waist.

Realizing she was staring at him, Skaaha stood to haul her dress off, but as the druid looped the sling around the pouch of shot and tied it round his thigh, her gaze kept straying back again. Like iron from the sky, he, too, was strong, his hands lean, fingers nimble. The smooth line of his thigh muscle made her breath catch.

'Ready?' He straightened up, fair strands of hair flapping in his face.

She nodded, befuddled as if ale addled her wits, and began to warm up, shaking tension out of her limbs, running on the spot, stretching, her skin pummelled by wind. From long practice, they moved into the routines in unison, matching their movements through the warrior steps then tumbling and leaping across the sand as if twinned in dance. As they began the more difficult aerials, a thought rose in her head. Ruan must have lovers. Who, she didn't know. Caught off guard, she landed badly. He hurried over, but she was on her feet before he offered a hand. Small hairs glistened on his forearm, trapping sunlight. She felt feverish.

'You try too hard,' he said. 'Go with it, like a leaf in the wind.' He moved away to demonstrate. 'Don't force. Allow.'

Even as she tried to note the position of arms and legs, what she saw was the litheness of his back, tautness in his buttocks. A ripple of foreign feeling surged up through her abdomen, like a spring tide. Her breath caught in her throat again.

'Now you,' he said, hair whipping across his eyes. 'Show me.'

She took up the start position, raised her arms. Glancing down briefly, it was her breasts she saw, not her stance. Firm, youthful, much like Kaitlyn's in the cavern when Hanick had been aroused. The fisherman's response was still a mystery, bare skin commonplace. She assumed it was the cave, enclosed, clandestine, the forbidden encounter. An image flared in her head – Ruan's fingers deftly tying the sling to his thigh, the ends of thong slapping. Another surge stabbed through her belly, upwards from between her thighs. Weakness trembled through her muscles.

'I can't do it,' she said, dropping her arms.

'Breathe.' He came to her, tilted her chin, put a hand on her diaphragm. 'Deep and steady. That's it.' He moved behind, raised her arms to the start position then placed his hands over her hip bones. His touch felt like fire. 'Breathing,' he reminded, as hers became shallow again. 'Fold here,' he said, rocking her pelvis, 'where the weight is. Balance is everything.'

When he stepped back, she ran, leapt upwards and folded for the spin. As her pelvis swung, wind fingering her skin, it remembered the pressure of his hands. Her abdominal muscles clenched. She wobbled, falling out of the air to land heavily on her back foot. A sharp pain jagged up through her heel. She stumbled, limping to a rock to sit. Pulling her foot up across her knee, she brushed the sand off. A shard of razor-shell was embedded in the flesh. Blood oozed round it.

Ruan flopped on his knees beside her. 'Let me see.' Cupping her foot in his hand, he gripped the end of broken shell between thumb and forefinger to ease it out.

'Aahaa!' she yelled, wincing. The flesh rose when he pulled, the spike of shell firmly fixed.

'Wait.' The druid ran to his clothes, raked his pouch for knife and flint.

Skaaha watched him twist a loose torch of dried grass, shielding it with his body as he sparked it alight. When the flame flared, he ran it along the blade before dousing it and returning to crouch, knife poised, in front of her. Light glinted again on small hairs on the back of his hand. Her limbs became water.

'It needs cut out,' he said.

'Why did you burn the blade?' Her voice thickened in her throat.

He glanced at her. 'Fire cleanses.' Turning his gaze to her foot, he gripped her ankle with his free hand, pressing his knee against hers. A flash of sensation ran up her calf and thigh, burning across her belly. He looked up again, as if he felt it too, a long, intense look, as if he gazed into her soul, eyes deep and dark, their faces so close he would know her breath shortened.

He can see inside your head. So Jiya had said. Heat flushed Skaaha's cheeks. Her foot throbbed with the warmth of his hand cradling it. Wind tossed the hair back off his neck.

Below his ear, the small tattoo of manhood was druid – the cross-quartered wheel of life.

'Watch the hills,' he said, nodding towards Alba.

Vaguely disappointed, she did as instructed, trying to think of Eefay rising in one of the brochs that nestled in the valley opposite. There was a sharp stab into her heel, but she was ready and contained her reaction, no quick intake of breath to break the deep rhythm that controlled pain.

'There,' he said, showing her. 'That's why it wouldn't come out.' The sharp point of the shell was barbed on one side. He placed it on the rock to smash it.

'I want it.' She stopped him. A question rose in his eyes. 'It hurt me so it's mine,' she answered, before he spoke, holding out her hand. He put the shard in her palm. She scanned his face, amazed that it pleased her just to look at him.

'Bathe the wound in the sea,' he said brusquely. 'We're done for today.' Springing to his feet, he turned his back, raised his fist. 'Hyaaa-aaaaa!' he screamed, and belted down the beach into the waves without waiting for her to join him.

On the way home, dressed and limping a little, she tried to regain his attention. 'We never do weapon training.' She raised her voice so the wind wouldn't steal it. 'I could bring swords.'

He shook his head. 'I'm druid, Skaaha. We don't fight people' – a brief glance towards her – 'sickness and cruelty, troubling thoughts or feelings, but not people.'

'Nechta asks if I'll come of age.' It wasn't intended but blurted out, the only thought that formed into words. He didn't respond. 'Maybe I will,' she persisted. Still nothing. 'Maybe I won't.' He didn't speak. 'Have you no advice?'

'The choice is yours.' They skirted the burial mound, approaching the village. 'Take time to make it.' A loaded cart sat outside the druid huts. 'I'll go with Nechta to Tokavaig. Rest your foot. Bathe it in the sea. I'll leave a paste in case it needs binding.' Before she could ask why he was going, he was gone into Nechta's lodge.

Skaaha hobbled on to the roundhouse, into her chamber.

Dragging the curtain shut, she threw herself on the pallet, the bloodied shard of shell clenched in her palm. High in the thatch, the wind whoofed, creating puffs of dust. Let him go to Tokavaig. She wanted to be alone, to recreate those sensations, to understand what had happened to her on the beach.

When the priests were ready to leave, Skaaha stood lounging in the doorway. Ruan came over from the cart to put a pot of lotion in her hand.

'I'm not a child,' she said, disdaining it.

'Flesh and blood, all the same,' he replied, robes slapping his body.

That strange sensation rippled through her belly again. There was something different in the way he looked at her, a hesitation before he turned away. She didn't know what it was.

'Live the day well, Nechta,' she called when the cart pulled away. The wind snatched her breath.

'Blessings on you, Skaaha,' the old woman called back, 'blessings on all of you.' The crowding villagers waved; she'd been with them a long time. A few children ran behind till the cart reached the rise. Skaaha didn't wave, but she watched, moving to the shoreline where it might look like she'd gone to bathe her foot, if he turned round. Her hair tugged, skirts flapped. The cart climbed the hill path to the top, vanishing behind the trees. The wind howled like a wolf. Ruan did not look back.

The warriors arrived with the vernal equinox, the end of the sun's first quarter, when feasts marked the changes from child to youth. Their dues were paid in weapons. They brought seabird eggs to clear gambling debts, and frightening news. There had been raids in the north-west – a village burnt, men killed, women and girls taken – the first since before Kerrigen's time. Mara and her warriors stopped one boat that slipped past into Loch Bracadale, engaging the foreigners where they put ashore. Two of her women were killed, some injured. Most of the enemy escaped back to their ship. The men of Ardvasar were stepping up patrols.

'So you'll be seeing more of us,' Vass explained grimly at the evening meal in Erith's house. 'We'll build you a warning stack up on the Loup, green for smoke.'

'What about Jiya?' Skaaha asked, alarmed. 'She's with Suli. And Thum, he's training at Doon Beck. Is he all right?' No one knew for certain. Suli might be anywhere, and Jiya with her. Thum was probably safe. They'd heard no reports of death or injury among novice warriors, or priests for that matter, but they could tell her the names of the two from Bracadale who died. Skaaha left them to their cups, wandering outside to be alone in the dark with her thoughts.

High above, a fat waxing moon ducked behind heavy cloud. She perched on a rock, dangling her bare foot in the shifting water. The short, neat cut healed well. Wind tugged her hair. If only a storm might whip up. Then they would all be safer. Raiders stayed in port while the sea raged. She heard feet on the rocks behind, approaching, the muffled clink of weapons carried. The red-haired warrior, Fion, settled himself on the rock beside her, a horn of ale in his hand.

'The dead warriors,' he said, 'they were friends of yours?'

She nodded. 'Like foster-mothers,' she realized.

'They will be proud to have died in battle.'

That was true. All warriors hoped for a glorious death – to arrive a hero in the otherworld, their feats praised in ballad in this one.

'We'll drink to them.' He passed her the cup.

'Death in glory,' she toasted, and drank.

Fion's skill was the axe. Though younger than Ard, his shoulders were broad and bulky as the smith's. It was Fion who'd lifted her, one-handed, by her plait the day they first met. He, too, wore a plait, in his beard, into which were braided the ends of his long moustache. Amused had turned out to be his usual state. She passed the cup back.

'The warrior, Thum,' he asked, after drinking, 'is he your man?'

'He's my friend. I don't have a man.'

'This is good.' He smiled broadly. 'I will be your man. Here' – he offered the cup – 'we'll drink to us.'

'No, we won't.' She drank anyway. 'I'm not of age yet.' This was hedging. She glanced at the gibbous moon. It was less than five quarters from Beltane, not three fortnights. No law compelled her to wait. She could do as she chose. Fion was a fine man. Warriors were rarely refused.

He leaned into her, pushed the fold of her bodice aside. His huge hand cupped her bare breast. 'But you're ready to be a woman,' he said, puzzled by her reluctance. 'And will be more pleased by me than any three men here.' The boast was a common one but, in his case, might be true.

His breath deepened as his hand stroked her breast, tension growing in his body. The effect pleased her, that she was the cause. His touch was warm, intimate and not unpleasant. Already her body arched of its own accord towards him. Her head tilted into the crook of his neck, nose rubbing the skin below his earlobe, nuzzling into the male scent of him.

'You see?' he murmured. 'You want a man.' His arm pressed round her back, drew her close. 'I will teach you.' Taking the beer horn from her, he drank it empty, laid it aside. Then he tilted her chin, and put his mouth on hers, the hairs of his moustache damp against her face. It was a strange thing to be kissed, his lips moving against hers, the pressure growing, hair tickling her cheek, breath mingling with the taste of ale. Urgency welled up from the pit of her stomach, wanting what she didn't yet know. His hand stroked her naked thigh, a touch that increased the ache in her for more. With it came something else.

'No,' she said, gripping his wrist to stop his hand moving, and drawing back. 'I'm not ready.'

'Ach, Skaaha,' he groaned. 'That was a fine night we were almost having.'

'You'll have it with someone else,' she consoled. 'Kaitlyn would enjoy a change and Freya would even throw Hanick out of bed for you.'

'A shrew or a wet rag,' he complained. 'You have fire in you. I would be the one to make it blaze.'

'When I choose a man, it won't be by accident,' she said, getting to her feet. 'I'll wait till Beltane.'

'You'll only choose me then,' he protested.

'Maybe, or maybe somebody else.'

'So I will fight for you.'

She leaned over, grabbed his plaited beard in her fist. 'Do that,' she dared, 'and I'll blunt your axe.'

A deep groan issued from his throat. 'That's wicked,' he said, both appalled and impressed that she could think it. 'And you the spawn of warrior and smith?' He pressed for advantage, undaunted. 'You wouldn't.'

'Try me,' she invited, letting go his beard, 'but don't roll dice on it.'

15

'Blood is not all,' Ruan said. 'Look at Jiya. Can you be sure?'

'You were at Doon Beck.' Suli leaned on her staff. 'You saw her work out the consequences before she passed that cup, and of her choice.' Despite their exertions, the high priest's voice was steady as ever. 'A child, yet she put wisdom before desire. Surely you can do no less?'

Ruan hesitated, uncertain what his truth would be. 'Not easily, not with her.'

'What sacrifice is easy, especially if the reward is great?' Her pale eyes were calm, as if he presented no risk. 'You accepted the task.'

'Four circles since,' he protested. 'Things change.'

'And by doing so, remain constant.' She inclined her head towards Tokavaig, lying between them and the bay, the sanctuary busy with injured from the raid. 'She must be quite a beauty by now.'

'She is,' Ruan agreed. 'But unaware of her grace, or the impact of her presence.' The foreign ships had tested the water for the last sun. Now they probed the island's defences, and found them weak. 'Which doesn't help,' he added. 'I am tormented.' If he gave in to his own weakness, his task would fail.

'Do as you will, Ruan, but do no harm.' The old woman's staff smacked against his as he moved, just in time, to protect his shin. 'That is the law.'

Smoke stacks were built on three hills behind Kylerhea, dry kindling to quickly catch flame blanketed by branches of green pine. The warriors left, returning south to continue patrolling the seaward coast. Skaaha stood with Ard, watching their longboat run before the sun to dwindle on the horizon.

When it became a distant speck in the waves, they still stood, gazing at nothing, for no apparent reason, as if reluctant to walk to the forge. A sea breeze tossed spume, tugged their clothes. Skaaha curled her bare toes round a crack in the damp rock, pressing the bulbs of bladder wrack that clung to it.

'I'll come of age at Beltane,' she said. No justification was needed, but the lack of immediate response compelled her to add one. 'It's time I was a woman.'

Ard nodded, though he now seemed more interested in the hills of Glenelg across the water. 'And this is your choice, or did Fion make it for you?'

'I have the measure of Fion,' she snorted. 'Nobody chooses for me.'

He looked at her then, his usual scrutiny tinged with pride. 'Good, that's how it should be.' He cleared his throat. 'You come of age once. Be sure the man who'll honour you deserves to.' When her mouth opened with a question, he stopped it. 'Talk to Erith. You can bring the water.'

Erith brimmed with excitement. 'About time! We hoped it would be this sun. The council will meet. Wait till they hear in Torrin. We'll have to do some travelling. You don't just want the men here to choose from, unless you know. Do you know?'

Skaaha shook her head. 'I should ask the women.'

'We'll have a night for you,' Erith laughed, anticipating. 'Advice enough to make your head spin.' She drew Skaaha conspiratorially into her chamber, away from the houseboy's ears. 'Don't tell him I said so, but Ard's the best around here, which is no help to you. Fion would be good – believe his boasts – if you want him.'

'I don't know.' She could still feel his touch, desire for it rising then dying. 'He wants me.'

'Well, of course he does,' Erith exclaimed. 'Who wouldn't want to honour you?' She gripped Skaaha's shoulders, ran her gaze over the girl's face and body. 'Look at you. Think who you are! Just don't choose someone wet behind the ears.' Delight lit her face. 'Wait till the council hears.' Putting an arm round Skaaha's shoulders, she squeezed tightly. 'This will be the finest Beltane!'

Skaaha took the cauldron to the sea, bemused by what she'd set in motion. Tying her skirt up between her legs, she waded out till the water reached her knees. Peering down, she saw little bubbles attached to the fine hairs on her calves, sand ooze up between her toes. To avoid scooping any into the pot, she stepped sideways on to smooth rock, placing her feet carefully to avoid the sharp peaks of barnacles.

A crab scurried over her toes. Waves rippled past, caressing her skin. She closed her eyes, tried to conjure a lover's touch, like the water, the waves, the pale warmth of sun in her face, on her throat. But it was easier to imagine her hands on him, gripping the ball of his shoulder, feeling the hardness of his chest. Hugging the empty cauldron close, she imagined hips pressed against her own.

'Ho, Skaaha!'

The call broke the spell. Hanick rowed a small coracle towards her, coming in from the bay.

'Did you catch much?' she called back.

'Enough,' he said, jumping into the water to pull the boat past her, showing off the gleaming white bellies of fish, some still thrashing. 'The best one got away.'

'They always do,' she grinned.

'No' – the young man would not be deprived of his story – 'he was twice the size of these. I saw him go under the boat.' He beached the coracle and waded back to her. 'A real smart fish, went with the hook and pulled free. Here' – he reached for the cauldron – 'I'll get that for you.' His hand touched against hers on the iron handle.

When she didn't immediately let go, he tilted his head, looking at her through a flop of fair hair. That time in the cavern rose between them, when his hand had covered hers.

Skaaha let go, startled by a quite different discovery. He wasn't reacting to Kaitlyn now, or Freya who carried his child, but to her.

Hanick dipped the cauldron, carefully to avoid creatures and seaweed, and they waded back to the beached boat, him carrying water for her that she was well able to carry for herself.

'You have fish to gut,' she said, as they reached the grass. Taking the pot, she flashed him a smile. 'But thank you.' She walked away to the forge, smiling more widely now he couldn't see her face, knowing he watched her go. This becoming a woman held many pleasures, when a glance or a touch was all it took to make strong men weak with wanting. A sense of power swept through her. If it hadn't been for the weight of the cauldron, she might have skipped into the heat of the forge.

Inside, the smell of hot metal and clatter of iron turned her attention to work. Something nagged at the edge of her mind, like a forgotten line of poetry. She tied on her leather apron and went to study fish hooks. Gern made most of them. They were fiddly to work on, and in various sizes suitable to different fish, but all were the same – thin, deeply curved hooks with sharp, flattened points, the stem ending with a loop for tying them to gut. The forgotten words remembered themselves. *That's why it wouldn't come out.* Ruan's words on the beach.

Running from forge to roundhouse, she snatched up the shard of shell from the stone shelf behind her bed and hurried back. Explaining her idea to Gern, she begged a rolled rod of metal from him and began to heat, beat and shape the end. With his help, it was sharpened down to a fine point, but with a barb on it like the shell, bent into shape, the eyelet made and the slender hook cut from the rod. Everyone in the forge was intrigued. To test it, the bellows boy ran to fetch one of Hanick's fish before Lethra cooked them. Carefully, the hook was pushed into the roof of its gaping mouth. Mentally crossing her fingers, Skaaha tried to ease it back out. It wouldn't come. Several others tried, and failed. The hook held firm.

'Well done!' Gern congratulated her.

She was beating out a second hook when Ard returned from council.

'A fine idea,' he praised when she demonstrated. 'Clever, indeed. But' – he sucked his cheeks in thoughtfully – 'fishers can't lose a hook for every fish. They need to come out to be baited again.'

'Could they cut it out?' Skaaha was reluctant to abandon her invention. 'That's what Ruan did with the shell.'

'A gutting knife would do it,' Gern said, trying. 'No, wait' – as the hook moved and he saw how it would go – 'it would push through.' He tried, easing the hook fully out. 'The gut is easier to cut, easy to retie.' He held up the freed hook triumphantly.

That afternoon, buoyed up by pride in her craftsmanship, Skaaha went looking for Hanick. She found him on the shore, tying his lines for the next morning.

'Here,' she said, opening her hand and carefully attaching each of the three hooks she held to the cloth of his tunic. 'Try these tomorrow.' Delight bubbled inside her. The tautness of his body told her she could make him do anything. He'd swim to Glenelg if she said so. 'You might catch that big one.'

'If I can get them out my tunic,' he said, tugging.

'Like this.' She showed him, her forearms resting on his chest. Looking down, his flopping hair brushed the top of her head. 'Be careful of your fingers too,' she murmured, glancing up into his eyes. 'The only way out is through.' Instinct she'd never possessed before told her to go now. Patting his chest, she tossed her head, threw him a half smile and turned towards the village. Freya stood in Kenna's doorway, swollen with child, watching them.

'You want Hanick, don't you?' she asked when Skaaha reached her.

'No, I was only teasing. You're handfasted.' Women didn't share their men unless their interest was exhausted. 'I don't want your man.'

'He'd look good with you.'

'And he looks better with you.' Skaaha looped her arm in her friend's and they walked towards the copse at the edge of the village. Freya and Hanick handfasted last Beltane. This time, they'd jump between the fires again, wrists bound together to enter marriage, or untied to separate. 'Don't you mean to marry?'

'What difference does that make?' Freya would not be cheered. 'You can have any man, especially now they can't say no.'

'What?' Skaaha halted. Only the goddess couldn't be refused.

'You'll become Danu. The priest, Yona, told the council.' Freya frowned. 'What else did you expect?'

'Not that. There will be other girls.' She was puzzled. Villages chose their own goddess for the autumn, winter and spring festivals, but in summer there was only one, chosen by the druid cell at Torrin. 'Word can't have come already.'

Amazement spread over Freya's face. 'You don't know, do you? Danu's blood runs in your veins. You chose yourself soon as you spoke. The priests have waited for this since you were born' – significance larded her voice – 'in the dark of a Ghost moon.' The thirteenth moon came every third circle. Legend said the goddess was also born from the dark of it. 'They say it will make powerful magic,' Freya rambled on. 'Folk will come from all the islands. It'll be the biggest Beltane ever.'

Skaaha sat down on a tussock of grass. That explained what Erith meant. She'd been here so long she'd forgotten. These people were not her people. She was a daughter of the tribe of Danu, born of the blood-line through a warrior queen. This was why a priest had been assigned her, why she was allowed her father's care instead of being fostered. The druids protected Danu's heir. Not her. Not Skaaha, but the spirit of the goddess in her – a spirit they expected to release at Beltane.

'You're not an ordinary person,' Freya whispered. 'Didn't you know that?'

Rau . . . rau . . . rau . . . High above, two white-tailed sea eagles linked their claws and spun into their mating dance. *Yip . . . yip . . . yip . . .* Skaaha's heart battered inside her chest. It was all clear now – she and Eefay sent to separate places of safety, both with blood-tied warrior protection. It was no accident and not their choice, as it had seemed, but designed by Suli, the high priest. Bride made the world, but Danu was its protector – a fecund, fierce warrior who gave birth to the future. So the druids said.

'Stories for children,' she muttered. That's how Kerrigen had dismissed druid beliefs. But she'd kept Tosk with her at Doon Beck, just the same.

'Not stories,' Freya denied. 'You're not like us. You never were.' Behind them, voices called, whistled, as the shaggy black cattle were brought in off the hills.

'I'm me.' Skaaha thumped a clenched fist against her knee. 'A blacksmith, like Bride.' The world spun. Bride became Danu. Her voice rose. 'Danu is fierce, and battle-scarred – a warrior!'

'Give it time,' Freya cautioned. 'Bride, Danu, Carlin – even Telsha – they're all the sacred mother, just different ages.'

'But she's not real,' Skaaha persisted.

'Believe what you like.' Freya shrugged. 'It won't change anything.'

'I can change this.' Anger burned in Skaaha's eyes. 'I can refuse!'

Freya's chin dropped. Turning down the role of goddess was unthinkable. Beasts streamed past, heading for the stockades. Kaitlyn peeled off from driving them and flopped on the ground next Skaaha.

'What's new?' she asked. 'Anything good?' She was joking. Even the herdsmen who guarded flocks all day already knew. Announcements were unnecessary formalities. Among Kylerheans, the difference between a secret and news was that the former travelled faster. 'Don't be daft!' she exclaimed, when she heard Skaaha's intention. 'You get to choose the consort.'

'And that's so great?' Skaaha asked. Both her friends wore small tattoos of womanhood on their necks. It seemed like a conspiracy.

'Yes.' Kaitlyn had no doubts. 'I wanted Ard to come of age with, but Erith refused. If I'd been Danu, she couldn't have.' The goddess should be partnered by an experienced lover. If that man was married, the honour was as much his wife's as his. Kaitlyn hunkered up on her knees, leaning her elbows on Skaaha's thigh. 'Forget druids,' she urged, 'and all this goddess nonsense. You can have any man you want. That's better than good. Believe me, they're not all the same.'

'If I'd been Danu, I would've picked Hanick anyway,' Freya said. 'We fucked all seven days and nights.' The others stared at her. 'Mostly,' she added. 'When we weren't eating or sleeping.' Her friends still stared, speechless. 'It's true. I could hardly walk afterwards.' She giggled. 'Nor could he.'

'And on the seventh night,' Kaitlyn intoned, 'he lasted more than two thrusts.' She and Skaaha dissolved into fits of giggles.

'That's not fair,' Freya protested. 'He learned lots after that time in the cave.'

'So' – Kaitlyn feigned innocence – 'do you suggest Skaaha choose Hanick?'

'That's what started this,' Skaaha yelped, pushing Kaitlyn's shoulder.

'Yes.' Confused, Freya quickly corrected herself. 'No.' She puffed her breath, glaring at them both. 'Actually' – she thrust her chest out, held her head high – 'I will be proud to see my man honour the goddess. You can have Hanick,' she told Skaaha. 'But only once,' she added, pointedly, 'then you give him back.'

The teasing fell flat. Freya's jealousy was misplaced, her attempt to overcome it bungled, lacking respect. Danu forgotten, Skaaha leapt to her feet and spread the palm of her hand over her friend's bulging abdomen.

'You have his child in you,' she said coldly. 'So he served you well, and I won't take him from you if you beg. But don't you, ever, tell me what to do again!' She stalked off to the forge, leaving Kaitlyn shaking her head in disbelief at Freya.

'Are you soft in the head?' she asked. 'Be glad you're pregnant. If she was still a warrior, she'd kill you for ordering her about like that.'

'She is a warrior still.' Freya, hands clasped over her belly, gazed awestruck at Skaaha's retreating back. 'Anyone else would have thanked me.'

'What?' Kaitlyn jumped up, gasping with exaggerated astonishment. 'She really is becoming Danu?' She shook her head, gazing in despair at her friend. 'You're such a druid, Freya. Beltane, big party, ho, that's it.'

'Boat! Boat!' Calum screeched, rattling the metal rod around the circle that topped the pole beside him. 'Boat!'

Below him, on the hillside, Lethra dumped the basket she'd been filling with herbs and charged up the slope towards the boy. Yesterday it had been the shadow of a cloud, the day before a pod of dolphins. *Clang-clang-clang!* The racket drove her, and everybody else in the village, crazy.

'Do you want a thick ear?' the crone yelled with all the breath she had left as soon as she was near enough to make herself heard over the din. The clatter stopped.

'No,' the boy said.

'Well, you're going the wrong way about it!' Age ached in her limbs but hadn't yet reached her tongue. The chief thrust her hand out. 'Give me that rod!'

Calum's lip trembled. 'Skaaha made it for me.'

'To stop you lighting the stacks every second breath ' – she grabbed the bar from his reluctant hands – 'not to drive us daft!' Making a V of her first two fingers, she poked them perilously close to the terrified lad's eyes. 'What are these for?'

'To see with,' Calum quavered.

'Then use them,' she snarled, 'or I'll poke them out!' She straightened up, easing stiffness out of her back. Youngsters these days — they knew nothing. 'Do you even know what a boat looks like?'

Trembling, the boy pointed. 'It looks like that,' he said tearfully.

Lethra spun round. In the middle of the bay was a sizeable boat, square sail billowing, its prow ploughing towards them. She swung the metal bar into the hoop, clattering it from side to side. 'Boat! Boat!' she shrieked.

Down in the village, people swarmed from buildings, running to the shore.

'Not that way!' Lethra roared. Fools! The boat struck sail. 'Get that going!' she yelled at the hapless Calum, on his knees next the fire stack, all fingers and thumbs with the flint. Oars dipped in the waves. Lethra counted — six, eight of them. Not an alarming number. No war helmets in sight, the only glitter came from . . . 'What are you doing?' she yelled at the boy, snatching the smouldering tinder from his hands and stamping on it.

'Making smoke,' Calum protested. 'So the warriors come.'

'Warriors don't want metal bars,' she blustered. 'Can't you tell a trading ship when you see one?'

16

Needing deeper water for its hull, the boat passed the beaching point near the village which was used by fishers and warriors, to tie up at the landing pier where coracles for the crossing to Alba were kept. The trader, a rotund little man who wore a long, brightly patterned coat, had called cheerful halloos since they'd come into earshot. Now he leapt nimbly ashore, waving a short cane with a bone handle carved into a perching eagle.

As furnace and forge-keepers, Kenna and Erith waited to greet him, greedy for the tin he brought from the south but wise enough not to appear over-eager and push the price up. Food and drink were consumed, news and stories told, and a great deal of disinterest in trading displayed, before haggling began.

'It's been a long time, Beric,' Erith said, 'and we're pleased to see you, but we make little bronze now.'

'What we need, we re-smelt from old goods,' Kenna added casually, cracking a bone with bejewelled fists to suck out the marrow. 'Saves on copper as well as tin.'

The trader downed his mead. 'No matter. A visit to the Island of Wings is never wasted. There's a fine wind out on the water will carry us west with our cargo. And we might pick up a southerly to take us beyond the Islands of Bride.' He paused while his drinking horn was refilled.

Fascinated by the strangeness of the man and the glamour of his travels, Skaaha brimmed with questions, but she knew better than to interrupt negotiations.

'Besides, I have a few trinkets that might take your fancy,' Beric continued, 'a Greek pot, Roman swords, jewellery from Egypt, a bottle or two of wine.'

'Roman swords?' Skaaha queried, forgetting restraint. 'What are they like?'

'Short,' Beric said. 'With an edge to split a hair.' A troubled look passed over his face. 'I fancy these split a few hairs in Germanica of late.' He didn't trust the Romans, though they'd traded for his tin over many suns. They warred on every land they marched into. 'One day, when it suits them, they'll ship their legions to Alba and take what they want, as casually as they do elsewhere.'

'And how will they do that?' Skaaha scoffed. 'They must be poor warriors to trade their weapons.'

'They didn't,' Beric corrected. 'One of the ships taking them home from that campaign was blown off course, landed in the south-east, with their Emperor's son on board. The swords belonged to their deceased, gambled away by the crew.'

Ard, as curious as his daughter, took Skaaha to see the foreign weapons. There were two swords. While he tested the metal, she swung and thrust.

'A good size,' she said, 'for in close.'

'Good steel,' he said, 'strong.' He rung the blade with the hilt of his knife, sniffed along the flat then licked it, mindful of his tongue, tasting the carbon.

'Sharp, too,' Skaaha said, trying the edge on a rope. By the time they'd fully assessed the quality of alloy, the layered welds, workmanship and design, Beric was back on board to oversee the exchange of goods, including much of his tin.

'She strikes a hard bargain, that wife of yours,' he complained to Ard. 'Blood from a stone, she would get. Will you take the swords?'

'And bring bad luck on us?' Ard answered. 'Trade them to someone who needs to make a sacrifice. The weapons of the dead have no other use.'

Beric threw a few friendly curses at them as they left his boat. Happy enough with the morning's trade, he'd cut his own throat rather than admit it. With the tin offloaded, the additional cargo stowed, he could still be heard, cheerfully calling them down this time, when the oars berthed and the sail ran up, from far out in the bay.

Erith was also in a jovial mood, issuing orders, making plans. They had been out of tin for some time, and even the most mundane iron objects increased in value and desirability when made beautiful by the addition of bronze designs. Her third husband, who spent most of his time up at the woodland charcoal clamps, was sent extra woodcutters and word to step up supply.

'If we work the forge flat out,' she told Ard and Gern, 'we can fill our larder from trade at Torrin.' She lowered her voice. 'You know what you must do tonight.'

Ard nodded. 'Which also, very neatly, keeps us out of the way.'

'But short-handed,' Gern added.

'Neither of you would like being cock in a henhouse,' Erith assured them. 'You'll be fed at Kenna's.' She spread her hands in thankfulness. 'I could've kissed Beric when he showed up.'

'Then we'd have paid double,' Gern pointed out.

'The most beautiful things, Ard,' she reminded him. 'We can't stint on this.'

He tapped his temple. 'I have it all planned. Fit for a goddess.'

On the playing ground in the centre of the village, Skaaha worked through the warrior steps. It contained her rising apprehension, the strong firm strides, deep rhythmic breathing. A party of women should not have this effect, but the last time such a group met to focus on her future, the change had been momentous. This change, too, would hurtle her from one state to another, shifting her status from novice to adult woman, able to take lovers, handfast, marry, have children – set up her own forge, if she chose. She felt ready for none of those now, unable to envisage beyond the first hurdle – an evening of ribald, chattering wives.

'I am Skaaha, the shadow,' she breathed, squaring off into a strike, 'of the tribe of Danu, daughter of Kerrigen, queen of warriors.' The sun was setting behind her, the sky over the sea a misty purple. Squawking birds headed home to roost.

'Skaaha, Skaaha!' Calum's voice shrilled.

'And I will not be interrupted,' she growled, quartering smoothly to face him.

'Look, look!' Calum jumped up and down at the far side of the field, his arm stretched, pointing to the hill path. A cart, with a spare horse tied behind, jolted down the slope. Even at this distance, with the setting sun in her face, she could see it was Ruan who drove it. Her gut clenched. Automatically, she took several steps in his direction, and stopped. A second person rode the cart with him – a dark head next his fair one, the tilt and shape familiar and strangely out of place in druid robes.

'Jiya,' she gasped, and then she ran, feet pounding across the grass, slapping over the cobbled path, dodging past the forge. 'Jiya!' she called, as she emerged from behind it. Ruan stopped the cart at the foot of the slope to let his passenger dismount. The woman threw her arms wide, beaming a wider smile. Skaaha thumped into her, hugging and being held, feasting her eyes on her aunt's appearance.

'I thought you'd never come back,' she cried.

'All good things come round again,' Jiya said, chuckling. 'Sure as the sun.'

'But it can't be you.' Bewildered, Skaaha stroked the priest robes. 'Not dressed like this.'

'It's half of me,' Jiya assured her. 'The other half learns to be quiet.'

Ruan had sat silent, watching the reunion. Now he clicked the horse forward a few steps, level with them. 'Suli thought you might like your aunt with you for Beltane. Seems she was right.' Before Skaaha could respond, he slapped the reins, sending the horse forward, on into the village.

Disappointed that he revealed no obvious pleasure in seeing

her again, Skaaha turned her attention back to her aunt. 'No sword, no spear,' she puzzled. 'What have they done to you?'

'Filled my head with light,' Jiya said, bending down and parting her hair behind the crown to show Skaaha a circular scar. 'Feel that.'

Skaaha did. The skin was softer inside the circle than the skull around it, a hole cut in the bone beneath. 'What is it?'

'Salvation,' Jiya said, tossing her hair back. 'And this hole' – she clamped a hand on her stomach – 'is hunger. Come, we will eat, drink.'

Skaaha explained that a feast awaited, and the reason for it.

'Then fate had a hand in my coming,' Jiya grinned. 'We will eat, drink and we will talk about men.'

The clan chief, Lethra, and the women of her house, were first to arrive.

'Though it's wasted time,' she grumbled, directing Kaitlyn to sit the cauldron of special brew down on the hearth. 'The problem with men is they start as boys.'

'And stay boys,' Erith added, 'in spite of our best efforts.' Ruan had spoken to her when he returned, so she expected Jiya when Skaaha rushed in, dragging her aunt by the hand. 'Perfect timing,' she said, smiling with a delight she didn't feel. Even though the ex-warrior would be accommodated in the vacant druid lodge, her unexpected re-appearance took the shine off proceedings, distancing the forge-keeper from Skaaha just when the girl's glory reflected on her too.

'Ha!' Jiya exclaimed. 'You smile like the wolf when the sun should be in your heart.' She spread out her hands. 'I use these to do washing now.'

Erith's smile thinned. Lethra thrust a brimming cup towards Jiya.

'But not tonight,' the crone said. 'Tonight we expect good stories of other uses for women's hands.' Tittering broke out among the younger women.

The druid, Yona, witching needles set aside, brought one of her own brews. Guests trickled in from nearby farming communities. Everyone brought food, or drink, or both. Several brought stringed harps, and other instruments, to play. Unexpectedly, three armed novice warriors appeared, having crossed from Glenelg. The youngest of them wore a mane of braided blond hair.

'Eefay!' Skaaha shrieked. The last person she had expected was her sister. 'You shouldn't be here, you're not of age.' Everyone under-age had been shooed to other houses for the night.

'Nor are you, yet,' Eefay said. 'Nor will I miss your celebrations.' The passing suns had stretched her, adding muscle and arrogance to her determination. She glanced around, friendly enough but with a hard glint in her eye. 'Who here is going to throw me out?'

'No one,' Erith intervened. Eefay's two companions wore the warrior mark of womanhood. The girl, almost as well developed as her older sister, might easily come of age next Beltane. 'But, if you want to drink, leave your weapons at the door.'

The rule was standard. Acceding to it, Eefay took her rightful place, reclining casually beside Skaaha. Kenna's household came last, having stored tin and stacked charcoal first. Crowded with women, the roundhouse filled with raucous chatter.

Out in the forge, the din could be heard above the roaring furnace and constant hammering. Nodding in the direction of the racket, Gern clucked like a hen.

'Pooook – pook-pook-pook.'

Ard grinned, briefly glancing up from the mould into which he carefully poured glowing liquid bronze. 'Except it's us they're picking over.'

Walking back from the beach alone, Ruan heard music and voices over the rushing waves. A bawdy song was being sung. The waning gibbous moon cast a path of golden light on the water. Three quarters, and it would be almost full again. He hesitated at his hut, looking over at the noisy roundhouse. Before then, when it was moon-dark, Skaaha would choose a consort. A fortnight later, they would all be in Torrin, and she'd become a woman. The song ended. Gales of laughter split the night but no smile lit his face. He went into his lodge, and shut the door.

'I had a husband once,' Kenna protested, frowning. 'Just can't remember where I left him.' More howls of laughter erupted. Twisting the strands of gold and glass beads round her throat with heavily-ringed fingers, the noman shrugged. 'Now, if I want a man, I go get a man.'

'Or a woman,' Kaitlyn called from the other side of the hearth.

'Pleasure's where you find it.' The furnace-keeper made great play of ogling Skaaha. 'There are many ways to be a woman.'

'Except it must be a man for Beltane,' Skaaha demurred.

'And you better learn how to put them in their place first,' Lethra muttered.

'Aye-yie-yaa!' the women shrieked in agreement.

'Show her,' Erith suggested to the crone.

Lethra stood, yanked up her skirt to reveal her pubis, and dropped the hem again with a dismissive toss of her head. Applause exploded at her aplomb.

'Now you try.' Erith offered Skaaha the floor. More cheers arose.

'Go, Skaaha.' Jiya put a hand under her niece's backside, helping push her to her feet. 'Show them how.'

Skaaha raised her skirts and dropped them, tossing her head as she did so.

'No, no, no!' Lethra barked. 'Don't apologize, announce.'

'You're not offering sex.' Kenna grinned.

'Or showing him a secret,' Freya giggled, clutching her belly.

'More like this,' Erith said, rising to demonstrate the quick flash of lower abdomen, a dismissive look. 'Imagine you're silencing his argument.'

'Reminding him who's in charge,' Jiya offered.

'Showing where he came from,' Kaitlyn added, 'and where he wants to be.'

'Saying you're the bringer of life,' Yona pointed out.

'Telling him he's a dick,' Eefay chimed in, jumping up to drop her leggings and wiggle her rear, while everybody hooted and squealed.

Annoyed to be outdone by her sister, Skaaha tried again. It didn't quite come off. 'Ach, maybe there needs to be a reason,' she complained.

'Or a man,' one of the farmers suggested.

'That would help,' another agreed. 'Somebody get one.'

'They're all busy.' Erith leapt in front of the doorway, barring the exit.

'Ruan isn't.' Yona stood. 'I'll fetch him.'

'No!' Skaaha yelled.

The druid stopped dead. Erith looked shocked. There was silence, heads turned towards her, puzzled faces.

'I couldn't,' she explained, embarrassed. 'Not with a priest.'

'A man just the same,' Yona said. The druid spoke quietly, a small furrow deepening between her brows as she gazed at Skaaha.

'Hah,' Jiya exclaimed. 'This is the man you want!'

'No,' Skaaha protested. 'He's not.'

'But that would be perfect,' Erith cried. 'Why didn't we think of him? That's why I picked Tosk when it was my time. Who makes a better consort at Beltane than a priest, especially for the goddess?'

'Especially this priest,' Yona murmured, returning to her seat, her comment lost in the growing clamour. The circle of women all talked at once, praising Ruan's attributes: his temperament, self-control, physical form and his expected prowess. Druids were well versed in the art of love. It was the perfect solution.

'So who has bedded him?' Jiya asked.

Silence fell, broken by some uncomfortable shuffling.

'None of you?' Eefay scoffed, amazed.

'Send him to Glenelg,' one of her fellow warriors proposed. 'We'll soon find out how well he does.'

Kaitlyn shrugged. 'He hasn't the interest.'

'Or inclination,' Kenna added. 'Maybe he prefers men.'

Freya wrapped her arms tighter round her swollen belly. 'No,' she corrected, blushing. 'He showed Hanick . . .' She faltered. 'He helped us.'

A torrent of questions assailed Freya from the excitable group.

'Stop this!' Yona insisted. Compliance was instant. Every voice stilled. The priest let a moment pass before she spoke again. 'Ruan embraced celibacy to come here.' Her hand rose, to quiet further interruption. 'It was required till his charge comes of age.' Her eyes met and held Skaaha's. 'But if he's chosen, he will serve.'

Every face turned to Skaaha, hopeful, urging, expectant. Celibacy had only one purpose, to increase potency upon release – for the working of magic. For Bride to become Danu, her consort must be pure, but potent. To achieve both, he abstained from selection till the ceremony, denied all forms of sex bar the pleasure of his own hands. One who'd been abstinent for so long would bring powerful magic, if chosen.

Skaaha returned Yona's gaze, but her mind raced. If celibacy was required, then Suli had required it. The high priest made people do things. *Pass the cup.* She gave druids their posts. *Ruan will go too.* Jiya huddled, frightened at Lunasa. *He can see into your head.* Nechta, before she left. *Will you come of age at Beltane?* Her aunt terrified, punching her skull. *He puts thoughts in mine.* Desire first came to her on the beach. The druids wanted this. Suli intended it. Ruan prepared for it. Fear of having her feelings exposed turned to fury. She was Skaaha, not a tool to druid belief.

'Will you choose him?' Yona prompted.

'No,' she said coldly. No druid would exploit her. It was her life, her choice. She would make it. Not Ruan, and not Suli. 'I don't want him.' She sat down.

Disappointment murmured round the room. Jiya leaned into her, mouth close to her ear. 'That lie will turn on you,' she whispered.

'Danger walks beside him,' Skaaha hissed back. 'You said so!' *Don't be fooled*, her aunt had warned, long ago at Doon Beck.

'Maybe you're the danger,' Jiya hazarded. 'It's you he walks with.'

Her aunt had changed. 'Or maybe they took out what you saw and planted other seeds inside your head.' She'd come to trust Ruan, to believe, and he was only using her. 'There are other men, men who want me.'

'Who cares what they want?' Jiya rocked back. 'Take what *you* want, or the day goes against you.' She ladled a beverage into both their cups.

Erith clapped her hands. 'Right,' she said brightly. 'Fill your cups and let's give Skaaha our advice. Champion one man each, one who isn't already rejected or of her blood. Lethra' – she deferred to the wisdom and experience of age – 'will you start?'

The crone balked. 'You don't want my man,' she grunted. 'I have to show him where to put everything these days.' Again, laughter exploded round the room.

17

In the darkness, glowing stones hissed as water poured over them. Ruan sat naked, cross-legged, bathed in rising steam. Drops condensed in his nostrils. Moist heat filled his lungs. Beads of sweat ran over his closed eyelids. Perspiration trickled down his back. The slow, steady thump of heartbeat pumped like a fist beating the rhythm of life against the inside wall of his chest. The sound of it beat louder in his ears. *Do as you will*, Suli had said, *but do no harm. That is the law.* Seduction was harm done. It breached trust, trespassed the will of the goddess, made the choice his. The power of Beltane was released through her. The up-fire surged through him. When it flared in Skaaha, he'd quelled his own – duty mastering desire, as it must. In the dark of the moon, she would choose, as she must. It would not be him. Through the fire and water of earth's womb, acceptance would be born of rejection's pain. Again, the priest fought the man, asserting steady breaths in the clammy heat. His pulse slowed. Sweat trickled down his chest.

'Ruan, fetch another pallet. Quickly!' Yona's tense face disappeared back behind the drapes.

He stopped tying a cloth cover on the pot of lotion, went to the nearest chamber, hauled the blankets off and half dragged, half carried the mattress back.

'Can we get it under here?' Yona said as he pushed the curtain aside. She indicated the foot of Freya's bed. The new mother lay, weak but euphoric, suckling her newborn baby girl at her breast.

'What's wrong?' she asked, looking up from stroking the child's damp head.

'Nothing,' Yona lied. 'Bleeding,' she mouthed to Ruan.

He raised the bottom of Freya's bed with the weight of her on it. Yona wrestled the pallet underneath, doubling over the end to raise it highest. Apart from wait, it was all they could do. The heat in the roundhouse was oppressive. Yona folded her needles away in their cloth. Ruan fetched ale, held Freya's head up to help her drink. Lethra handed in a fresh, pulped liver to be fed to her. Slowly, the bedclothes stained, sodden with blood. Yona took the baby, gave it out to Kenna, who paced around the hearth. When the girl began to shiver, Ruan ran back to the next chamber for more covers to keep her warm. Freya's teeth chattered.

'Snow is falling in here,' she said, trembling. 'Where's Hanick?'

'Outside.' Ruan stretched on the floor to wrap his arms round her head and shoulders, holding her, trying to stop the tremors, to give her his body heat.

'With Skaaha?'

'I don't know.'

'She wants him,' she chittered, grasping the druid's tunic. 'Tell her it's all right.' Her eyes rolled.

'Hold on to me, Freya.' He shook her. 'Don't sleep. It will be Beltane soon. Stay with us till then. Your baby needs you.'

The shuddering stopped. 'That's better,' she sighed.

He took the baby to Erith while the women cleaned the body.

'Yona says if you put her to your breast the milk will come,' he said, passing the infant, carefully, to the forge-keeper, 'though it will take longer.'

Outside, women's voices sang, gathering in the furnace-keeper's house to celebrate the life gone to the otherworld.

He couldn't look at Skaaha, sitting by the hearth, head down. They'd spent no time together since his return. She hadn't joined him on the beach. Jiya took his place at Erith's mealtimes. As he walked to the door, Skaaha stood, stepping in front of him.

'How could you let that happen?' she accused. 'How could you?'

'Why do you fight me again, Skaaha? A life was exchanged for a life. Where is the sorrow in that?' His voice was bleak, hollow in his own ears. 'I have a message for you,' he said. 'Freya said to tell you it's all right.'

'What, that you let her die?'

'That you choose Hanick.'

Guilt wrote itself on her face. In it, Ruan saw the truth of Freya's words confirmed. He left then, going to join the men on the hill who'd begun to build the funeral pyre.

Skaaha sat alone on the rocks, watching waves crash into them. Strength wasn't inflexible but pliant, the ability to move. Just as fire consumed wood, the sea wore down stone. It was early. The crescent of old moon rose above glowering Alba hills. Already, dawn crept up towards it, to blot it out. The dark of the moon arrived, and still she didn't know who to choose. Erith had argued to go visiting. Several men from other villages had been championed. She refused, not wanting a stranger. Now it was too late.

The smallest sound, barely heard above the tide, made her look towards the druid huts. Ruan stood, paused in his doorway, looking at her. Her stomach contracted, as if he'd come to her, or she to him, but he didn't move. Her aunt's door opened, and she emerged, ungainly in her druid rags. Noticing Ruan, she glanced shoreward and saw Skaaha, but the man had already turned away, heading past the ancestral burial mound. With an exuberant wave to her niece, Jiya followed.

Skaaha folded her arms across her knees, rested her head. She was replaced, that precious time gone. Knowing he groomed rather than cared for her only increased the loss. Freya's wake deepened it. Hanick – perhaps she should choose Hanick. Her spirit sank lower. Near the water, a rock pipit hopped about. Behind her, the village stirred awake. People stumbled out to latrines, breakfast preparations started. The sky grew brighter, a misty blue-grey. She heard distant singing, male voices.

Puzzled, she stood, scouring the water. Out in the waves, seals turned, dived, rose again. The voices, louder, came from seaward. A low boat hove into view, oars working in unison. It was the Ardvasar warriors, Vass at the helm. Despondency and dignity forgotten, Skaaha scrambled across the rocks to reach the low shore first.

'Ho, Vass!' She raised a fist, calling the greeting to her uncle. She would, of course, ignore Fion, if she could keep the smile off her face. They spotted her. The rowing song rose to full pitch in her honour as they shipped oars and let the craft glide in. Vass was first off the boat, splashing through the waves, making mock play of shielding his testicles before he reached and enveloped her in a bear hug.

'A goddess calls us ashore,' he said, 'and we come to save her.'

'From what?' she giggled. 'Myself?'

'From grubby farm boys and charcoal burners,' he winked, 'and' – he let her go, stepping back with a wave towards the other approaching warriors – 'we bring a friend of yours.'

Automatically, her eye found Fion, standing four-square a few feet away. The plaited beard was gone, moustache trimmed. Grinning widely, he clamped an arm round the shoulder of a younger, slimmer man who stood beside him. Skaaha frowned. Then she saw who she looked at. Her face cleared.

'Thum!' Astonishment raised her voice. 'What are you doing here?'

The young man blushed, like the boy he had been. 'Vass apprenticed me when my training ended,' he said, and his face lit up with a smile. 'You've changed.'

'You too!' she exclaimed, throwing her arms round his neck. Below his ear, he bore the warrior mark of manhood. The passing suns had put muscle and strength in his limbs. 'It's so good to see you.'

Fion tapped her shoulder. 'It's good to see *me* too,' he

suggested, but when she turned to him, he held a hand up to stop her. 'Forbidden,' he reminded her. 'Look and lust only,' he preened, making her laugh as he thrust his broad chest out.

'Forbidden nothing,' she said, pushing her fist against it. 'I'm saying hello, not seducing you.'

His face fell, and all the warriors laughed. A few of them called out that they, too, were fit to honour the goddess at Beltane. To prevent their arrival turning into a beach auction of male prowess, Vass dispersed them and marched off to breakfast with Erith and Ard. Thum headed for the other houses to see his foster-mother and brother. Skaaha and Fion followed Vass. Around the hearth, the talk was all of Beltane. The warriors would be there, tribes from every island.

'Big magic,' Fion said, nudging Skaaha, 'needs a big man.'

'I heard about that,' Skaaha said quickly, in case he meant to illustrate. 'And one who'll practise restraint.'

'Ach, two weeks without a woman? This is nothing.' He rubbed his beardless chin, considering. 'Two nights till you choose me.' Delight dawned. 'For two nights, I make many women happy.'

Skaaha chuckled. The man was incorrigible, and fun. Yet she remembered his intensity, that brief flare of desire, their bodies close together in the dark. Her breath caught. Fion might be the one.

He bent his head down to hers. 'Do not look at me this way, little goddess,' he said, his voice husky, quiet. 'Or maybe we forget forbidden.'

Noisy altercations at the door announced Jiya's return, prompting pleasure, and disbelief at her druidic conversion, among her former fellow-warriors.

'I learn to use the gifts I'm given,' she retorted, 'and one of them is still knowing how to smack your heads for cheek!' Her high good humour made Skaaha wonder about the morning's activities on the beach. Her aunt was flushed, full of happiness and generosity.

'The warriors will take your mind off Ruan,' she told Skaaha when they got a moment alone. 'This is good. He's not what you think.'

'And what is he?' Skaaha asked, unable to prevent the tightness in her voice.

Jiya looked smug. 'More profane than sacred,' she said. 'Better you stay afraid of him.'

'Afraid?' Skaaha's hackles rose. 'Be glad you wear priest cloths or I would make you take that back. I fear no one.'

'Fine words, well said.' Jiya beamed. 'Ah, there's Thum coming. Now that's a nice boy.' She squeezed Skaaha's arm encouragingly and left to gossip with Vass and the others, seemingly oblivious to her niece's increased outrage.

'What's troubling you?' Thum asked Skaaha as soon as he reached her. 'This should be the time of your life.'

'Well, it's not!' she snapped, and was instantly sorry to see the joy of coming home fall from his face. 'Och, don't mind me.' She should be glad Ruan's vow was broken, his power gone. 'Too much has changed. I wish none of this was happening.'

He took hold of her hands, his angular young face vulnerably sombre. 'People forget there's a person in the middle of it all. They want it to go well, so they keep telling you things that are meant to help, instead of listening. When the time comes, you'll know the answer, and it won't be from someone else's mouth.'

'It'll be in my heart,' she agreed. Then, to shatter the unfamiliar intimacy, she gave him a playful push. 'How did you get so smart?'

He blushed again. 'Avoiding Mara.'

'Mara? Poor you,' she said. 'Come and tell me about it.' She ushered him inside. 'I must show you what Ard made with the silver you gave me.' Remembering the brooch reminded her of Bride. If being Danu was half as joyful, it would be good indeed. The fear she had just denied finally fled. What was in her heart could change.

After admiring the silver brooch, Thum sat on the edge of

her bed to tell of his adventures with the warrior queen. 'The strange thing is,' he said, 'she was more interested in you.'

'Me, while she was bedding you?' Skaaha pushed the repugnant picture of Mara seducing Thum out of her head. 'Why?'

The young warrior shrugged. 'I don't know, but I'm sure that's why she picked me out.' In the curtained chamber of the broch, while she brought him to manhood, Mara had questioned him repeatedly.

'Maybe she wants a new smith,' Skaaha surmised.

'She asked more about you teaching me, if Vass came often or taught you, and why the druids took Jiya away – that seemed to please her. Then she tired of me, fortunately.' He smiled and handed the brooch back. 'I didn't expect such beauty from those few nuggets. Ard is a fine smith.'

'As I am too,' Skaaha boasted. 'I'll make a torc for your master ceremony.'

'Two suns from now,' Thum reminded her. 'My beard will grow by then.'

She couldn't imagine his fresh face with growth, and stroked his cheek. 'I'll put an edge on your weapon now instead,' she offered.

He caught and held her wrist. 'Skaaha . . .' he began.

The half-closed curtain of the chamber was yanked aside. Erith, with Freya's baby suckling at her breast, glared in at them.

'You can't be in here, Thum,' she snapped. 'You should both know better.'

'We're only talking,' Skaaha protested.

'Talk is how it starts.' As Thum stood to leave, Erith's face softened. 'And what kind of son doesn't come see his mother,' she chided. 'Look at you, a man and a warrior.' Admiration got the better of her. 'Your foster-mother must be proud.'

That night, in Lethra's house, the stories and songs went on till late. Ruan, who ate there now, stayed on. Skaaha sneaked glances at him. He watched her, despite Jiya fawning over him.

To show she didn't care, Skaaha gave her full attention to the other men, and enjoyed theirs. Fion preened. Even Hanick responded to her teasing. Everyone drank too much. The warriors either found welcome beds with the village women or fell asleep round the hearth. Humming one of the drinking songs as she followed the others back to Erith's, Skaaha felt pleased with herself. To be desired was a fine thing. From behind, a hand caught her wrist.

'Wait!'

She spun round, stumbling on the cobbles. It was Ruan who held her. 'You touch me?' she objected.

He let go. 'You didn't hear or you ignored me, and you need some advice.'

'Not from you.'

'Do not play men against each other. There will be trouble.'

'Now it's you who doesn't hear. I'm not troubled, and you can keep your advice.' She continued home, unsteadily, even more pleased. He didn't like the attention she attracted. Good. Jiya might go to bed alone tonight. She hugged herself to sleep, more confident and excited than she'd been for some time.

The following day, despite Erith's disapproval, she joined the warriors in their morning routine. They all showed off, and though a few women watched, the exhibitionism was for her benefit. The power to make men strive was a joyful thing. How could she have forgotten something so recently discovered? In the water afterwards, splashing and fooling about in the spring sunshine, she saw Ruan come out of his lodge. So he hadn't gone to the beach. Better and better. The druid stopped at Jiya's door. When she emerged, they both went into Yona's hut. Plotting, no doubt, now their plans were destroyed. Grinning, Skaaha skelped water over Thum and Fion, ran out of the waves and went to dress.

In the forge that afternoon, Ard and Gern were pouring moulds when raised, angry voices intruded from outside. Skaaha laid the sword she was putting an edge to down on the anvil and hurried out. Warriors and village men crowded the outdoor anvil, where cold hammering was done. In the middle of them, Hanick crouched, facing Fion, a snatched sword in his hand. Skaaha pushed through the onlookers, half of whom called at the fisherman to put the weapon down, while the other half urged the warrior to take him on. Fion reached for the axe in his belt.

'Don't, Fion!' Skaaha yelled.

'This pup makes no coward of me,' he retorted. The axe was in his hand. The young fisherman was fit and strong, but he stood no chance against the warrior, who could split his skull with one throw.

'Hanick, stop this!' Skaaha urged.

'I'm not afraid of that bear,' he snarled.

Fion's arm drew back. A figure ran to stand in front of him. It was Ruan.

'Will you strike me, Fion?' he asked, calmly arms raised with his palms towards the warrior but poised to keep between them if either man tried to go around.

'Move,' the warrior said.

'Get out the way, Ruan,' Hanick shouted.

Panting, Yona arrived to stand with her fellow priest, but facing the fisherman.

'The blood you draw will be mine,' she told him, raising her hands.

Jiya bumped past Skaaha and stood on the other side of Ruan, not quite certain which way to face. 'Well, here we all are,' she said, jovially, palms up to repel, looking around at the watchers. 'So you're not needed. Go elsewhere.'

Lethra tugged her husband and young Calum away towards home. Vass put a hand briefly on Thum's back, and they walked off towards the shore. The others turned, in twos and threes, drifted away. Jiya caught Skaaha's eye and nodded to indicate she should return to the forge. Neither man could easily lose face in front of her. When she reached the doorway, Ard drew her back out of the sunlight, where they could see without being seen.

The standoff remained, but disempowered. To harm a druid meant eternal death. There was no escape. They would be hunted down. Capture, followed by scourging, ended with the ritual three killings of the body, before its preservation in a bog. Prevented from passing to the otherworld, it was an ignominious end which deprived them of a future for ever. The druids waited, chanting softly. The weapon in Hanick's hand wavered. Fion lowered his axe.

'I need beer,' he said, and holstered it. Jiya peeled off the line-up, looped her arm in his, and they headed for her lodge.

Hanick laid the sword on the anvil. 'The fish are waiting,' he said.

'I'll give you something for luck,' Yona offered. 'It's a good day for fishing.'

Ruan watched the two of them walk away towards Yona's hut. Women had ways to calm men that he lacked. Skaaha came out of the forge.

'Was that my fault?' she asked.

'Do you want it to be?'

'No,' she shook her head miserably. 'But you warned me and I didn't listen.'

'Then the fault must be mine,' he said, 'if Hanick and Fion are relieved of it.'

She frowned at the turnaround. 'I don't have to listen to you.'

'Indeed, but if I'd won your respect, or taught you wisely, you might have. If I'd thought faster, or acted sooner, their horns might never have locked. They're both good men, Skaaha. Choose tonight, before the drinking starts.'

He walked away and was half-way across the green before she realized he'd handed their rivalry to her to solve. Storming back into the forge, she grabbed the blade she'd abandoned, thrust it into the fire till it glowed then set about beating her frustrations out on it.

18

At nightfall, cloud rolled over the hills and hung low above them, promising rain. A new day began. The headwomen had joined the conspiracy. After dinner, instead of visiting in Kenna's, the other houses arrived at Erith's. The smiths and smelters, who'd worked shifts round the clock since the tin trader's visit, downed tools and joined them. Yona brought Skaaha a flask to drink from.

'To help you speak with ease,' she said. 'You'll feel better when it's done.'

Ruan told the first story, of a man who pulled a monster from the bog, and the girl who saved him by leading the creature, one of the eternally undead, away on a merry dance as she twirled and spun over moor and mountain, night and day till it begged for rest. It was a story Skaaha recognized, made into his own, but meant for her she was certain, and disconcerting. It ended when the girl skipped lightly over a bog, using clumps of grass as stepping stones. The clumsy creature slipped. Too exhausted to pull itself out, it slid back below the water, where it remained.

'Aye-yie-yaa!' Everyone cheered. Kaitlyn began a song, while the youngest children were put to bed. Ale was passed round. Skaaha continued to sip Yona's drink. Even though she knew the name she'd speak, the brew did nothing to loosen her tongue. Lamplight flickered on familiar faces round the crowded room. On either side of her, Ard and Erith seemed patient enough, unhurried. Perhaps it didn't need to be tonight. Fion reclined comfortably, his arm round Kaitlyn's back. Hanick, next to Yona, seemed content.

She looked for Thum. After his experience with Mara, he

would rise to this. It was him she cared for most. Let the druids make what they liked of that. The young warrior sat between his foster-mother and Vass, his hand resting lightly on the older man's thigh. So that was it. She smiled, heart-warmed. Opposite, on the far side of the hearth, Jiya put her hand against Ruan's chest, sliding her fingers inside the slit in his tunic to touch his skin. Skaaha shifted on the cushions. The druid gripped her aunt's wrist, spoke into her ear.

'I will speak now,' Skaaha announced.

Erith called for order. 'Skaaha, of the tribe of Danu, foster-child of . . .' the proudest pause, '. . . Erith, born of Kerrigen, queen of warriors, wishes to tell us who will be her consort, when she is brought to womanhood as the goddess Danu, at the sacred festival of Beltane.'

Skaaha stood, as was expected, so that she could see every face, and they hers. It seemed to take for ever, rising. The floor and roof opened out, growing wider away from her. Thum nodded encouragement, planting his fist against his chest. In the hush, she could hear rain pattering on the thatch, distant waves. The walls beat in and out, echoing her heart. She raised her arm.

'I choose Ruan,' she said, pointing at him, 'the druid.' Absolute silence drowned her ears, as if she'd fallen under water. Ruan looked back at her strangely. Had she spoken, or did she dream?

'Aye-yie-yaa!' Jiya jumped to her feet and punched the air, repeating the cry and dancing on the spot.

'Aye-yie-yaa! The cheer went up from all round the room, over and over. Skaaha swayed, bewildered by the betrayal of her tongue, puzzled by her aunt's joyful reaction, and sat down. Every face beamed with delight, even Fion's. He leaned over several people, stretching to shout to her above the din.

'You *are* a goddess,' he called. 'Smart.' He tapped his head.

'Inspired,' Erith said, hugging her. 'The only choice that offends no one.'

Ard raised his arms to quieten the noise. 'My daughter has spoken,' he said. 'Danu has made her choice. It is for Ruan to speak now.'

The druid appeared to be stunned, but collected himself and rose. There was only one thing he could say, but everyone strained to hear him say it. 'I am honoured to be chosen,' he said, 'and, with honour, I will serve.'

Hoots and cheers burst out again. Those closest reached over to clap him on the back or shake his hand. Mead was passed around to celebrate. Vass led the singing of a bawdy song. Skaaha stared into the fire. Words couldn't be unspoken. It was done.

When she woke in the morning, Jiya sat beside her bed. The druid clothes were gone. Instead, she wore the leggings, belts and tunic of a warrior.

'You're back,' Skaaha mumbled, sleepily.

'It was protection till I healed,' Jiya said. 'My head won't hold druid law. Where's the fun facing naked blades with empty hands?'

Skaaha sat up. 'Am I sick?'

'Shocked to be doing the right thing for a change,' Jiya answered dryly. 'We put you to bed.'

So they had. So she had. Truth had won. Yona was right. It felt easier done. Her brows came together in a puzzled frown. 'Then you're not angry that I took him from your bed?'

'Have you been cuffed by a bear?' Jiya scoffed. 'I never bedded him. He's celibate, remember?'

'Still?' That couldn't be. 'But you said . . .'

'What was true, mostly.'

'I saw you seducing him.'

'Jealousy sees what it needs to grow. Think again.'

Skaaha's frown deepened. 'You tricked me.'

'Helped you,' Jiya corrected. 'Thank me by taking the rust off my weapons.' She stood up to go. 'The warriors want training. They're leaving after breakfast.'

'Wait!' Skaaha hopped out of bed. Her head reeled, and she sat on the edge to steady herself. 'You sent me one of your weapons.' Reaching under the bed, she drew out a blue bundle. 'It's a broken spear.' She tipped the pieces on the bed.

'I don't know this,' Jiya said. Her face clouded. 'Hide it, hide it.' She raised a hand between her and the spear, couldn't look at it. 'You and Eefay,' she muttered, 'two pieces.' She clucked her tongue. 'Tluck-tluck-tluck. What is that?'

'I don't know.' Skaaha twisted the blue cloth back round the spear. Her aunt was becoming distressed.

'Tluck-tluck-tluck,' she repeated. 'Eefay has the answer.' Her fists clenched. 'Take it to Glenelg,' she urged. 'I don't know what I know.' She gripped her skull.

'All right, all right.' Skaaha bent forwards and pushed the bundle back under her bed. 'Look, it's gone.' So was Jiya.

She hadn't gone far. Putting the warriors through their paces calmed the agitation in her brain. After breakfast, when they prepared to leave, she stayed.

'I'll guard you,' she told Skaaha, who'd come to see them off. 'They'll be back to escort you to Torrin.'

Skaaha turned to Vass. 'You did save me from myself,' she said.

'Good,' her uncle said. 'You chose well, and I won't need to break some envious heads back in Ardvasar.'

Fion was still amused. 'The druid will make a fine show,' he approved. 'But you'll be half a woman,' he winked, undaunted, 'till you lie with me.'

For the rest of that day she worked. Beltane wasn't just a celebration. It was an opportunity for trade. Erith and Kenna made no concessions for drinking or goddesses. The afternoon was almost gone before she saw Ruan. He came to the forge to find her.

'We need to speak,' he said, and for reassurance, 'Jiya's here.'

Embarrassed, Skaaha glanced at Ard to check she could be spared.

He nodded. 'Bring water, and stay where you can be seen.'

His warning embarrassed her more. Her time alone with Ruan had never been questioned. Now it was forbidden. As they walked to the shore, with Jiya following as chaperone, the druid seemed amused.

'I thought Ard knew me better,' he said.

'You want to talk about my father?' she asked.

'No. You changed your mind. Tell me why.'

'I didn't change my mind.' She paused to roll up her leggings before going into the sea. 'I only changed what I said.'

'So you were saving Hanick from Fion.' As Jiya waited on the shore, he splashed behind her into the waves, caught her arm and turned her to face him. 'That was generous and wise of you, but now we have to do this.'

In the dying light of sunset, his eyes were grey with a concern she couldn't fathom. But it didn't matter any more what the druids hoped or planned for. She'd kept faith with herself.

'I changed what I said the first time, and spoke the truth. There was no one I wanted, except you.' He drew back, as if struck. The waves soaked her turned-up leggings. Barnacles jagged her feet. But the pain she felt was deep inside. He couldn't say he wanted her too. 'I hope it won't be too difficult.'

'Difficult?' He sounded surprised.

'For you to do.' Her voice almost broke. To avoid him seeing tears come to her eyes, she turned away and bent to fill the cauldron.

'Leave that, Skaaha,' he said, freeing the filled pot from her grasp so it sank beside their feet. From behind, he wrapped his arms round her, shifting them both to face the west. The sun was almost gone, a red curve on the horizon, sliding into the sea. Above, dusk crept over their heads, the next day about to begin.

'What is it?' she asked, though she knew what it was he wanted her to see.

'Just wait,' he said. His body curved round her back, the heat of him penetrating her clothes. Waves lapped around their knees. Leaning into her, he put his cheek against the left side of her face, stretching his right arm over her right shoulder, to point. 'There,' he said.

As the first shadow of night reached the spot he pointed to, brightness glowed in its grey-blue and the new crescent moon was born into the sky, the Seed moon of Beltane. From the village, voices called out as people saw it.

'Your moon,' Ruan murmured, his breath warm on her cheek, 'and by its light, with my body, I will worship you. There will be no difficulty.'

That much was true, she could tell. This close, with only clothes between them, a man's desire could not be hidden. Her body shifted of its own accord, moving against him.

His arms tightened round her, muscles clenching. 'We should go back,' he said. 'It seems Ard does know me better than I know myself.'

Thick fog blotted out the mountains as the procession wound through a world reduced to the length of forty strides. Vass led the way, Fion and Jiya behind him, the warriors in full honours and on horseback. Another four rode behind the cart in which Skaaha travelled, Thum among them. To Erith's annoyance, nursing Freya's baby meant her place as companion was forfeit. Kaitlyn accompanied Skaaha instead.

The remaining seven Ardvasar warriors would form Ruan's escort, but they would not leave Kylerhea for another three days. Travelling with them, the villagers would bring their stock and goods they hoped to trade. Between Skaaha's departure and theirs, treasured possessions were buried in small pits dug into the hillside. The larder could safely be left undefended. In spring, it was depleted, and passing strangers were not begrudged food or a bed, though none was expected during Beltane. The entire population of the island would soon be camped at Torrin.

On the rough tracks, the horse's hooves were almost silent. The mirk muffled all other sound. It was perfect weather. The delivery of the goddess to the festival site should be as secret as possible. The journey, timed to arrive at nightfall in case she might be seen, was almost over. Blinded by white fog and growing darkness, Skaaha huddled in a blanket. Dampness encroached.

'Ho,' Vass called, halting the group.

Up ahead, faint lights glowed through the fog. Peering into it, Skaaha saw tall, standing stones. Hooded, robed figures emerged from between them.

'Blessings on you, Vass,' an old woman's voice said. It was Suli, the high priest, more stooped than Skaaha remembered, her long staff prodding the ground before her as she walked. 'We'll take them from here. Go you on into the village with your men. A hearty Torrin welcome awaits you.'

Weapons jangled as Jiya dismounted. 'I'll stay with Skaaha,' she said.

Suli turned to the warrior visionary. 'Do you see need for a guard?' she asked.

'I can't see my feet in this fog,' Jiya retorted, 'but I'm staying.'

Wishing Skaaha luck, the warriors rode off, leading Jiya's horse. Other druids removed the bundles from the cart. Hands helped Kaitlyn and Skaaha down.

'So now you know how the body speaks,' a female voice said from below its hood, a voice that Skaaha had last heard calling farewell blessings in Kylerhea.

'Nechta!'

'Indeed, child, and we' – Nechta waved a hand at the group – 'are the keepers of Bride's sacred flame. Our cell oversees her festivals, and you are most welcome.' As the cart was driven away, the three women were conducted up a rugged slope. Suli, staff probing the ground, led the way. Night and fog made no difference to her. The others saw by the dim light of lamps they carried. The ground wasn't steep, but in the milky dark and dank, it seemed they might climb for ever.

Coming over a rise, Skaaha felt the ground level out. The smell of roast pig reached her, the crackle of burning. Low walls appeared. Behind them, on either side, low thatched roofs squatted on posts. The terrain underfoot changed to stone cobbles.

'Oh,' she said, 'it's the ring of fire.' The well of the sacred flame glowed.

'You've been before,' Kaitlyn said as they passed it.

'Not standing in it.' They skirted the altar, a flat, knee-high block of stone about two strides long. Aligned with the ever-burning fire, it lay pointing across the circle to a smaller ring of flat stones. Even when Kaitlyn, then Freya, had come of age here, Skaaha had paid little attention. Memories of Beltane's twin bonfires stretched back through childhood, but the ceremonies began late in the night. Children slept through most of it. Apart from chants, drums and writhing bodies in a darkness lit by leaping flames, it was daytime she recalled most, when there were more fun things to do than explore charred ashes.

'This will be the first time, since your mother, that the great theatre fulfils its proper purpose,' Nechta confided.

'There is always a goddess,' Skaaha corrected.

'Not of her blood,' Nechta said. 'We go down here.' She stepped into the ring of flat stones. Suli waited inside it.

'Mind your feet,' Suli warned. The faint light of Nechta's lamp illuminated an opening in the ground, stone steps leading down below it. Wooden doors that covered it had been pulled aside.

'We keep it shut,' Nechta explained, 'except when using it, or sheep fall in.'

One by one, they descended. There was light below, lamps guttering among rock formations. When they reached the floor, a sloping passage wound away from them. The sound of water trickled somewhere close.

'There are springs to drink from,' Suli said, 'and pools

further in for bathing, with a stream-sluiced latrine near by. But, if you turn in on the right, you'll find a dry chamber with ledges to sit on. Food is waiting.'

It was a feast that waited, on wicker flats, the chamber dressed with cushions. The druids, having stowed the packages, joined them to eat. Spirits were high, excitement over the impending festival released in jocularity and laughter. In good company, replete with food and drink, Skaaha began to relax, becoming eager to explore this mysterious place. The senior druid of the cell, whose long grey beard reminded her of Tosk, warned her of the hazards. In heavy rain, two of the deeper passages flooded.

'To the roof,' he said. But she'd be shown where, and how to move through the water if she had to. 'It's safe to wait either side, only you might get hungry.'

'And there are no bears?'

'No bears.' There were several ways in, or out, but all were kept secured. The greatest hazard was in narrow tunnels with jagged limestone walls so sharp they'd cut through clothes and flesh. 'So don't go squeezing into any,' he said, 'or there will be less of you coming back.'

'We're glad we came now,' Jiya commented dryly. 'You must be a welcome guest at every feast.' More laughter erupted.

19

When the meal ended, most of the priests took their leave. Only Suli and one of the younger men remained.

'Arin will stay tonight,' Suli said, 'to help and show you round.' She asked Skaaha to wait while Jiya and Kaitlyn were taken to their sleeping chambers.

'So you know the cave best?' Kaitlyn asked Arin as they left.

'No,' he smiled, 'but I'm the smallest, which helps if you get lost.'

Suli poured heather ale into Skaaha's cup. 'It's you who wants to speak,' she said, when the others were out of earshot.

'No.'

'Yet there is anger in you, at me.'

'You interfere in my life.'

'Do I?' Suli's calm scrutiny hadn't changed. Her voice revealed no surprise.

'It was you who ensured I went to my father.'

'Word was sent to Donal and to Ard. They came of their own accord, just as you went to the one you chose. I approved, yes. Ard is my son, and could be trusted.'

'With Skaaha, or with Danu's heir?'

'Both. Your line of warrior queens travels back, unbroken, to the first. There is no life-blood in the seed of men. The child's blood is from its mother. Your inheritance cannot be changed.'

'What blood? Danu is the earth, the second incarnation of Bride, the ever-burning sun, who forged the world then became the warrior who subdued it so that her children could be sustained. They're ideas shaped to seem like women.'

'Ruan is a good teacher.'

'It's a story, but there has to be a smith before it begins.'

'And you chose that. We go round in circles.' Suli smiled. 'Perhaps destiny finds us, Skaaha.'

'Ruan didn't find me, nor I him.'

'Ah, so now we have it. I gave you Ruan because he's wise, patient and was of an age to grow with you. His warrior childhood meant he'd understand yours.'

Skaaha faltered. Suli's replies made simple sense, except for one thing. 'It was you who made him celibate.'

'To protect you both – a young man and a growing girl, with all the closeness there can be between a pupil and her priest.'

'You make it all sound innocent.'

'Maybe that's because it is. Feel no shame, child. It's wise to know your enemy, and better to be wrong than right.' Suli's tone changed from considered to conversational. 'Ruan came to see me at Tokavaig, struggling with desire for you. Would you be happier if I'd relieved him of his post?'

Skaaha shook her head. 'No.'

'And he did nothing to coerce or persuade you?'

'Nothing.' It was hard to meet the druid's gaze. 'Quite the opposite.'

'Then everything is as it should be,' Suli said approvingly. She stood and stretched stiffness from her limbs. 'Arin is on his way back, and I must go. It's late, and these old legs grow too tired for climbing stairs.'

They walked from the chamber to the passageway. There was no sign of Arin. Suli paused at the foot of the steps.

'This is your passage to womanhood,' she said. 'It will be as you believe. But carnal pleasure enacts a spiritual truth, the seeding of life into this earth. The way things are cannot be changed.' She put her hand on Skaaha's shoulder. 'Blessings on you, child.'

As the old woman began to climb, Skaaha heard Arin's footsteps behind her. 'How does she do that?' she asked as he approached. 'Suli knew you were coming before I did.'

'Beats me,' he shrugged. 'Some day, I hope to learn. Come, I'll show you where you'll sleep.'

Outside, at the top of the steps, Nechta waited for Suli to emerge.

'I was beginning to think you'd died down there,' she said.

'If I had, you'd know,' Suli told her, stepping clear of the doorway so the other druid could close it. 'Skaaha had some questions.'

'Ah,' Nechta said. 'How did that go?'

'She asked the wrong ones.' The old woman paused, leaning on her staff. 'She is beautiful, isn't she?'

'Hair like night, the darkest eyes,' Nechta said. 'Slim and poised as a roe deer. Her father's nose, mother's mouth, the cheekbones and brow of a woman from the north, like her grandmother. She is extremely beautiful.'

Suli nodded thoughtfully. 'I knew that.'

'Maybe she also has the right to know,' Nechta said as they set off.

'Self-will must take her where she goes,' Suli answered. 'The living have one right only, to die.'

'And the dead, to live again.'

Suli glanced at Nechta, her blue eyes milky as the fog that surrounded them. 'How much heather ale did you drink?' she asked.

Skaaha woke in a gloomy cavern, surrounded by walls that looked like folded dough. Her bed, a mattress of straw and heather, smelled sweet and clean. It might have been midday or midnight. There was no way to tell. A lamp guttered on the wall, casting shadows that constantly crouched and leapt across roof and floor. The sound of splashing had wakened her. In sleep it seemed close. Now it was far away, barely discernible. Closer, she could hear breathing – Kaitlyn or Jiya asleep near by.

She closed her eyes again, remembering the feeling in her

skin, like tiny needles, when Ruan had put his arms round her in the sea. Since then it had been difficult to think of anything that didn't include his eyes, mouth, voice, his breath against her ear, the pressure of his body and its heat, the way he moved. The faint creak of wood interrupted, soft steps. She sat up.

'Who's there?'

A darker shadow appeared in the rock archway to the passage. It was Arin.

'I brought breakfast,' he said.

'It's still dark,' Kaitlyn's sleepy voice grumbled from behind a bulge in the wall of the chamber.

'I'll light more lamps now you're awake,' Arin said. 'Jiya's been bathing. She's coming back.'

'You can't have learned that from Suli since last night,' Skaaha said.

'No,' the druid grinned. 'Your aunt just came round the bend, with wet hair.'

Over breakfast of fish and bread, Jiya tried teasing him. 'You didn't join me in the pool, Arin.'

'Tomorrow, if you like,' he said seriously.

'I like,' the warrior agreed. 'We can practise for Beltane.'

'Fucking is forbidden in Bride's domain,' he said, 'though you may pleasure yourself, of course.'

Kaitlyn choked on her bread. 'Oh, wonderful,' she coughed.

'Or you may come to my lodge,' the druid continued, unperturbed. 'Both of you . . .' He indicated Jiya and Kaitlyn.

'*Both* of us,' Jiya interrupted. 'I'm a warrior. I eat druids for breakfast.'

'This might be very pleasant,' Arin said, with the hint of a smile, 'but I was about to say both of you may go above, but not Bride.'

'Skaaha,' Skaaha said.

'Bride till you become Danu,' Arin corrected, 'in practice, if not by name.'

He was going above once they'd eaten. Other druids would

be in and out, though only women from then on. None would stay at night again. 'If you need anything then,' he added, 'there is always someone' – he pointed upwards – 'tending the sacred fire.' When he left, Jiya went with him, to explore, see the warriors and find a place for her morning routines.

'And to wear out a druid, we hope,' Kaitlyn grumbled, as she and Skaaha followed the winding passage down to the round cavern to bathe in the pool.

'You spluttered bread everywhere,' Skaaha giggled.

'Well, has he got a hole in his head!' Kaitlyn was still astounded. 'Oh, thank you, druid Arin, we'll just go fuck ourselves now we know you approve!' She tested the water with her toe, wriggled out of her dress and stepped in. The water came up to her knees. 'I bet the best he can do is watch.'

'What he said' – Skaaha became serious, stepping in beside her – 'would you show me how to do it?'

'Pleasure yourself? Surely you know.'

The cave air was warm, and quite still. 'I don't think I do it right.'

Kaitlyn laughed. 'Can't see how you could do it wrong.' Moving to Skaaha, she put an arm round her waist, pulled their bodies close and ran her fingers down over her friend's stomach to probe gently through her pubic hair into the moist heat of her vulva. 'Right, there, you feel that, don't you?'

'I do that,' Skaaha said, drawing in a short breath, 'and get so tense it hurts so I stop. But I hear women cry out, and I know there's more.'

Kaitlyn gave her a quick hug and stepped back. 'I'd do it for you, but not now. Not in here.' Gingerly, she sat down in the pool. 'It might spoil you for Beltane.'

Skaaha sat too. The water was warmer than she expected. The surface rippled against her breasts. She was in the womb of the world, waiting to be born a woman. 'But if it doesn't work, I'll look a fool.'

'No, you won't,' Kaitlyn said. 'Ruan will, and that's not going to happen. The druids don't let anything go wrong.'

That day and the next passed quickly, the passage of time marked by the arrival of meals, visits from the priests who made the two-fold cloak, and regular reports of arrivals, whose tented lodges, flocks and herds, began to cover the hills. On the day the Kylerheans were expected, Skaaha could not keep still. A deep, unnerving excitement churned her stomach. She did not know if Ruan, on horseback and escorted by warriors, would be dressed as man or a priest. Ard and Erith, Gern and Kenna would follow in carts piled high with goods for the fair, with all the villagers and their stock bringing up the rear. It would be a fine sight, and she wouldn't see it.

'Are they here yet?' she kept asking. 'Are they here?' But it was always the strains of music and cheers to greet the other girls who would come of age, and their men. The young women were housed in a low tented dwelling on the left behind the fire theatre, men on the right. Finally, when she'd almost given up hope, she heard the great twin drums begin to beat out the arrival she'd been waiting for.

Kaitlyn and Jiya went above to watch, and were subjected to lengthy interrogations by Skaaha calling up the steps. Ruan wore the consort's fire colours – a red cloak over brown leggings and yellow tunic, with bronze and gold torc round his throat. The Ardvasar warriors, led again by Vass, who'd ridden his group out to meet them, flew red flags from their spears. Their helmets, swords and shields glistened in the afternoon sun. Drums thundered. The crowds roared. Other warrior chapters joined the procession. The druids of Bride marched in front, playing their pipes and hand drums. Cells from other charges brought up the rear. It was, indeed, a fine sight. Skaaha begged the details repeated over and over.

By nightfall, Jiya had disappeared. Kaitlyn fell asleep, her descriptive powers exhausted. Come morning, preparations for the ceremony would begin. When Skaaha finally slept, her dreams filled with colour, fire and fearsome creatures.

The sound that woke her might have been a rat scuttling. Half-asleep in the gloom, she sensed the otherworld loom. A shuffle that could be the silent Shee coming for her raised hairs on the back of her neck. Something cold touched her throat. Lamplight flickered. Shadows rose and fell like moving figures. The walls were melting stone. A long black line reached out to her bed from a sinister shape crouched not two strides distant. The squat was familiar, that dark line the shaft of a spear.

'Jiya,' she gasped, relieved.

'Guess again,' the figure hissed.

'What are you?' Fear tightened Skaaha's throat. The point of the spear pressed into it.

'Shhh,' the crouched figure warned. 'If you shout, or your friend wakes, I might jump. This' – the spearhead moved under Skaaha's chin – 'could slip.'

The voice echoed from past memories. As Skaaha became accustomed to the gloom, the shape assumed familiar lines, more chilling than any monster's.

'Mara,' she whispered.

'So you do remember old friends,' the warrior queen said, standing to look down on her. A scar scored the spiral on her cheek, but nothing else had changed. The spear remained at Skaaha's throat. From her bed, round the corner, Kaitlyn snored.

'If you harm me, you'll be caught,' Skaaha warned.

'Harm you? Tell me why I would do that.'

A metallic swish sounded from behind her, and Jiya stepped in from the passageway, sword drawn. 'We'll never know,' she said, beaming, 'because you're leaving.'

Mara's hand shook. The spear pricked Skaaha's throat, and steadied. 'Your aunt was never good at tactics,' she continued, ignoring the warrior. 'One thrust, you're dead, and she's mine. Tell her to sheathe the sword, or I'll take the challenge.'

'Touch Bride,' Jiya said, 'and the bog takes you.'

'A crazy warrior attacks while I pay my respects.' Mara played the spear tip under the curve of Skaaha's jaw. 'I kill her, and find our young goddess sustained . . .'

'Sheathe it, Jiya,' Skaaha begged. 'Please.'

Reluctantly, Jiya did, but stayed poised to draw again if there was need.

'Better,' Mara said. The spear rose. 'I came for a closer look. People say Danu returns.' She snorted. 'You've grown. Strong' – she nodded, glancing at Skaaha's arms – 'but no warrior. I saw your fear. Tomorrow changes nothing. Remember that, and this night.' She turned, stalked past Jiya and was gone, the clink of weapons fading round the passage, up the stairs, the door clattering shut.

A sob of relief shook Skaaha. 'Why did she do that?' she asked.

'Jealousy,' Jiya said. 'It's good I came. You should never be alone with her.'

'She fears you,' Skaaha said, rubbing her neck where the point had jabbed.

'So she should,' Jiya boasted, checking Skaaha's throat. 'There is no blood. I'll get the druids. They'll banish her from Beltane.'

'Then she'll think I'm afraid.'

'Her right to be here's forfeit.' Jiya turned to go. 'They'll send her home.'

'No!' Skaaha leapt from the bed to grab hold of her aunt's arm. 'I won't hide like a coward behind priests! Is that what Danu is? Is that what I become tomorrow?'

'No,' Jiya said slowly. 'That would not be good.' She stared at Skaaha's hand on her arm, the grip biting into flesh.

Skaaha let go. 'Look, Mara's like the bear: not wise to face her up, but wiser not to run away.'

Jiya rubbed her forearm. 'If you ever arm wrestle either, my bet's on you.'

Skaaha giggled. Spurred by the exhilaration of survival, laughter overtook them both. In the bed behind the bulge in the cavern wall, Kaitlyn woke. 'Whatever you're doing,' she grumbled, 'stop it and get to sleep.'

*

The smell of freshly cooked loch fish woke Skaaha. She shook Kaitlyn and Jiya awake. The warrior, still clothed and armed, had fallen asleep in the doorway, refusing to stand down in case they were visited again. Stripped and aching, she headed for the pool. Nechta brought breakfast, and a visitor. Erith had come with gifts. She laid the small bundle on Skaaha's lap. From inside, metal clinked on metal.

'Ard would have brought them, but men are not allowed,' she said.

'Open it, open it,' Kaitlyn urged as Skaaha's fingers tugged at the drawstring. The cloth fell aside to reveal bronze and gold jewellery. Even in dull lamplight, the pieces glowed like fire, shone like sun.

'Ard made all of this for me?' Skaaha gazed up at Erith in astonishment.

'Let's have a proper look then,' Kaitlyn urged again.

The largest piece was a flat torc like a crescent moon, the wide front becoming narrow as it curved to the back. Gold rope edged the bottom curve, the top row of filigree knot-work. Between them, at the front, was set a dark-red ruby and, from it, in each direction, flew a row of bronze eagles, each with a small red eye, diminishing in size to the end stops at the back. It was the finest work Ard had ever done, delicate and light but solid, so it sat perfectly round Skaaha's throat, resting on the clavicle bone, without shifting.

'Danu rubies come from the mountains in the north,' Nechta whispered. 'But I've never seen any set so fine.'

There were earrings with dangling gold feathers that encased a ruby stone; a wheel brooch with feathered arrow pin to hold her cloak, the quarters and cross-quarters marked with inlaid stones; three broad gold and bronze bracelets for ankle, wrist and upper arm; two rings for her fingers, one for her toes. And, finally, a bronze comb topped with a single red-eyed eagle, wings outstretched. From its talons hung fine rope chains, alternately gold and bronze, that would braid into her hair.

Ard had thought very carefully about dressing the goddess. Nothing would cut, dig in, obscure or impede the ceremony. Yet no matter how she moved, every limb would catch and reflect light.

'He said to tell you,' Erith began, swallowing to steady her voice, 'you're still the most beautiful thing he made.' With hugs and blessings, she left them to eat.

Jiya returned from bathing, scrubbing her hair dry, to find the others speechless, surrounded by treasure, and breakfast growing cold.

20

After the meal, Kaitlyn and Jiya were sent away to join the Kylerheans. Three women from Bride's cell arrived to help Nechta, full of chatter. Skaaha was stripped and rubbed with sheep fat mixed with wood ash before being sluiced off in the pool. Her nails were clipped, her hair washed under a water spout then rinsed with herbs. As the druids worked, they talked. It was an education. Older women taught young men the pleasures of the flesh. Two of the group had instructed Ruan.

'A duck to water,' one said. 'He learned fast' – grinning, – 'practised slow.'

'And repeatedly,' the other tutted. 'It took many moons before I could pass him on to other things.' Hearty chuckles echoed round the cavern.

Again, Skaaha's skin was scrubbed, with perfumed salts, and doused to remove them. Her ears were pierced, a quick, though painful, process. The third cleansing was with oils, rubbed off with rags. The druids' hands were thorough. Throughout it all, they gave a running commentary on the charms of her body, every curve and hollow praised. Ruan's tremendous luck was agreed, with conviction and more bawdy humour. By the time they were done, the shadow of Mara's nocturnal visit was erased.

Dishes of shellfish and roasted hazelnuts were brought for her to nibble on.

'Best you eat now,' Nechta advised. 'There will be no hunger later.'

'You haven't told me what I need to do.'

'We'll guide you,' Nechta said. 'All you have to do is walk to the foot of the altar stone. Ruan is being prepared in the sweat lodge. He'll do the rest.'

A ripple of nervous excitement ran through Skaaha. 'What if I run away?'

Nechta smiled. 'Hasn't happened yet,' she said. 'But we have much to do before you might get the chance.'

The braiding of her hair took longest. The eagle comb sat like a coronet, its fine chains worked into braids piled high, being wound around her head before they were pulled through to hang down behind into the nape of her neck. The bracelets were positioned, left wrist, right arm and ankle, the toe ring on her left foot. The rings and earrings were added, then the torc. The druids stood back to admire.

'Wonderful,' Nechta breathed. 'Perfectly wonderful.'

The others agreed: never had there been such a Bride. The two-fold cloak was placed round Skaaha's shoulders – red inside, white out. Threads of gold trimmed the white side, copper threads decorated the red. Nechta pushed the brooch's arrow pin through the fine wool to secure it.

Now that she was ready, Skaaha grew tense. Unanswered questions crowded, questions she might have asked Suli, but the old woman had not returned since that first night. Every moment took her closer to the ring of fire, and Ruan. Kylerhea was where she'd rather be, in the forge, beating iron. On the playing field, tumbling and leaping through the air at sunrise. Running, running to the sea.

'You're pacing, child,' Nechta said, pouring liquid into a cup. 'Here, drink this.' Beltane mead was brewed with honey and the bristly, tongued, bulbous female flowers of native hemp. 'It will calm you.' The druids were about to leave. They'd be back, in ceremonial robes, when the drums began. The entrance would be left open, so she could hear. 'Enjoy the solitude,' Nechta said, as she left. 'Your maid of honour will arrive soon.'

That meant it was almost dark. Skaaha sat on her bed, sipped the mead, and tried to feel moved by the birth of a bountiful earth from a sustaining sun, the guiding light of the moon. But the madness that had brought her here won. *Let*

nothing else persuade you, least of all some lovesick fool. She'd mis-
understood Nechta's warning. Her stomach churned. The
lovesick fool was herself.

Faintly, from above, came the clear notes of pipes, backed
by a marching beat on small drums. Distant cheers sounded.
A pebble rattled down the steps, feet descended. Skaaha stood.
Weapons clinked along the passageway. Fear shook her. Surely
they had not sent Mara. The warrior who approached turned
in the archway of the chamber, and paused. Fully armed, spear
planted at her side, her whitened hair jutted in thick spikes
from below a shining helmet that hooded her eyes. She raised
her free hand to lift it off her head.

'Ho,' she whispered, staring at Skaaha, awestruck, 'you even
look like a goddess.'

'Eefay!'

'Who else did you expect?' her sister asked. 'And don't
say, "You're too young." The druids asked me.' She grinned.
'I hardly had to shout and scream at all.'

Skaaha was too pleased to see her to care. They hugged
and admired each other. Skaaha checked the edge on Eefay's
weapons, the shine on her shield and helmet. Eefay studied
the torc and jewellery, the brooch in the waiting cloak.

'You really do get every honour handed to you,' she said.
'And this Ruan, is he something else I should envy you?'

Booom . . . the great twin drums interrupted from above.

Skaaha drew a deep breath. 'We'll both find that out soon,'
she said. Breathe, she told herself. Breathe the way you've
been taught.

Booboom . . . Outside, behind the cavern entrance, the twin
drums spoke again. Islanders crowded the slopes, cheering as
the massive orb of full moon rose over the horizon. Below
them, beside Bride's well, the senior druid raised his arms to
greet it. *Booboom* . . . The old priest added fuel to the ever-
burning fire. Flames leapt. The crowd yelled applause. *Booboom*
. . . Chanting, Bride's six women druids, in white robes, began

the parade up from the standing stones at the hill foot. They walked in pairs, swinging perfumed lamps. Between them, they carried a folded white cloth with which to drape the altar stone.

When that was done they turned towards the cavern entrance. Forming a single line as they walked, one by one, they vanished underground. *Booboom* . . . Picking up the chant, the cell's male druids, wearing Danu red, arrived in three pairs. Each one carried an unlit torch. *Booboom* . . . One by one, they lit their torches from the ever-burning flame, crossing to light twelve small fire stacks that edged the grassy circle. *Booboom* . . . A ring of thirteen fires blazed. Hundreds of excited islanders roared.

In the cavern, the procession of Bride assembled. Two of her priestess druids fetched six young women down the passageway, brought through another entrance that opened from their tented hut. The novices all wore fiery, beaded necklaces. Short cloths tied around their hips matched the creamy white, undyed woollen cloak worn by the goddess. Whispering excitedly, they lined up at the foot of the steps.

Shining from a darker sky, the moon's light waxed benignly. On the surrounding slopes, a hush swept through the watching islanders. The twin drums picked up to the pace of a heartbeat. *Boom* . . . *boom* . . . *boom* . . . Six men, strings of flame-coloured beads around their necks, short yellow loin cloths tied around their waists, marched into the ring of fire. The dance of ecstatic death began.

Below, the waiting girls giggled, nervous now their chosen men danced above. The leading druids murmured calming words, swung their perfumed lamps. Further back the line, Eefay coughed and glanced at Skaaha.

'You look terrified,' she observed. 'Did you remember to pee?'

Skaaha nodded. One day she'd pay her sister back. Right now, terror was precisely what she felt. 'How long does this go on,' she complained.

In front of her, a druid turned to answer. 'Till the fires are lit.'

Booboom . . . The dance ceased. Cheers burst from the crowded slopes. The senior druid raised two unlit torches to the moon for homage then turned to plunge both together into Bride's well of flame. *Boom* . . . *boom* . . . The drums picked up a slower beat. Two priests ran with the flaming torches to the twin fire stacks that stood north of the sacred circle. *Boom* . . . *boom* . . . the great Beltane fires were lit.

Waiting in the flickering shadows, the scent of oil mingling with the earthy smell of the cave, Skaaha turned to the priests behind her. 'Shouldn't we go now?'

'Listen to the drums,' Nechta said. 'Ruan's not there yet.'

'What if he doesn't come?' Her mouth spoke the thoughts without intention. 'Maybe he won't, maybe he'll change his mind.'

Nechta drew a small pot from her robes. 'Open your cloak,' she said, dipping her fingers in the pot. Skaaha held the fine wool aside. Nechta's hand parted her thighs. 'Hundreds of men out there would gladly take his place,' she murmured, gently massaging oily cream into the vulva of their goddess, 'but Ruan isn't one who'd run away from this. I promise you that.'

Boom . . . the drums ceased. Silence settled. Just as it hit the ground, a roll thundered from smaller drums.

Above, in the great theatre, Ruan strode out into the ring of fire. The great drums boomed again, another increased beat. *Boom* . . . *boom* . . . *boom* . . . *boom* . . . The dancers stamped and turned around the edges of the ring. Bride's consort walked to stand before the sacred flame, his red cloak flaring. His fair hair, part-tied in a pony's tail at the crown, hung to his jaw-line. Firelight gleamed on the torc at his throat. His bare chest and naked limbs gleamed with oils.

The drums thundered out a second roll. Ruan raised his arms to the Beltane fires, now blazing on the slope behind the well. Turning slowly to pay homage to the moon, he completed a full circle so that everyone on the surrounding pastures could see. A bronze armlet glowed on his right bicep. Low on his hips, a belt was slung. It carried a sparkling scabbard strapped to his thigh. In it, a bronze-handled knife glinted. He wore nothing else. The crowd went wild.

A hush descended. The ground-light of the moon crept towards the edge of the cavern. The drum beat slowed. Pipes and harps from the assembled druid cells began to play the haunting song of Bride. The master priest raised a goblet, passed it through the ever-burning flame, and gave it to Ruan. Turning towards the shadowed entrance of the cave, Ruan stepped forward to the altar. Moonlight illuminated the white cloth. The men who danced the ring of fire turned with him to face the cavern. Drums and pipes dropped to a whisper. The moon's light-shadow lit the steps. From underground, a chant began.

Boom . . . a women priest in long white robes rose up from the ground, followed by another. Both swung smoky lamps. *Boom* . . . each drumbeat sounded a stroke of Bride's hammer as she forged the world. Chanting the between-strokes as they came, the druids walked to the altar, to stand at either side. *Boom* . . . one by one, a line of young women appeared behind them. Cheered on by name from those who knew them, they peeled off to each side in turn, to stand before each man. *Boom* . . . seated outside the ring, at each alternate fire, the male druids in their red robes joined in the chant. The song of Bride swelled from pipes and harps once more.

Boom . . . two more priests, lamps swinging, came up from the cave, walked to the altar stone, took their places at each side. *Boom . . . boom . . . boom . . .* a thunderous roll began, building to a frenzy. *Boom . . .* the goddess rose slowly from the earth's womb, bronze eagle gleaming on her head, fire glowing in her dark, braided hair. *Boom . . .* the white cloak shone round her shoulders, sparks shimmered round her throat. *Boom . . .* lit ghostly by moonlight, the bringer of life stepped out from underground, and stopped.

'Aye-yia-yaa!' the islanders screamed from the surrounding slopes. 'Bride! Bride! Bride!'

Boom . . . the goddess stood on the rim of her domain, facing her consort. Between them lay the white-shrouded length of moon-bright altar. White-robed druids stood on either side. Behind the man, great twin fires blazed. Behind the woman, the twin drums thundered. Above them shone the full moon of Beltane. All around, firelight leapt and flickered.

'Aye-yie-yaa!' the audience shrieked, ecstatic. 'Aye-yie-yaa!'

Boom . . . the drum urged.

Skaaha didn't move. Ruan waited at that altar. A long red cloak fell from his shoulders. Light glowed on the torc around his neck, on the goblet he held. Shadows danced across his face and eyes. *I am Skaaha, of the tribe of . . .* she tried to run the words through her head, but they didn't fit. She was Bride, about to become Danu, and she couldn't move.

Boom . . . the drum urged again.

Leaning forwards, his long grey beard quivering, the master druid spoke in Ruan's ear. 'Go to her,' he said.

'You know I can't,' Ruan muttered.

'Shorten the distance.' The old man took the goblet from the consort's hands.

Boom . . . if a drumbeat could question, that one did.

From below Skaaha, on the steps of the cave, Eefay reached up and grabbed her sister's ankle. 'You have to walk towards him,' she hissed. Still Skaaha didn't move. 'Enough of this,' Eefay muttered, mounting the next few steps. As her head popped above ground, she saw Ruan come towards them, the red cloak flaring out as he strode. She ducked down. 'He's coming over,' she hissed to Nechta and the remaining druids still chanting at the foot of the steps below her. Two worried faces looked back. The goddess couldn't be compelled.

Boom . . . the drum warned.

Ruan stopped just before he reached Skaaha. Extending his left arm, he offered his hand for her to take, a question written on his face. Skaaha's brow furrowed.

'What's the knife for?' she asked.

He tilted his head a little to one side. 'To kill myself if you won't come to me,' he said.

The frown deepened. 'Would you do that?'

'If I fail.'

She stepped forwards, took his hand, began to walk. The drum boomed relief. The crowd shrieked, yelling with delight. Eefay rose from the cave to march behind, head held high, spear erect, helmet and weapons picking up the light. At her back, the last two druids emerged. Smoothly, without breaking their chant, they followed Eefay, swinging their lamps. The goddess and her consort stopped at the foot of the altar.

Boom . . .

'Stay beside her,' Nechta whispered to Ruan as she passed. 'Use this.' Turning to face across the white-draped stone, she sat the pot of oils in front of him. The chant ended. On harps and pipes, the final chords from the song of Bride faded, ceased. One final roll, and the drums fell silent. The crowd held its collective breath.

Raising the goblet to the moon, the senior priest spoke the blessing, gave the cup to the druid on his left, who passed it on till it reached Ruan, the only one who drank, a deep draught. Turning to Skaaha, he offered it.

'Drink,' he suggested, with half a smile. 'For luck.'

The sweet, narcotic liquid swallowed easy but lit a small fire in her throat. Murmurs rose as the crowd drew breath, the compact sealed. The druid on Skaaha's left took the goblet, passed it back. When it reached the senior priest, the others left to sit between their male colleagues, behind each small, alternate fire. The priest raised the goblet to the great Beltane fires. On the moonlit hillsides, murmuring ceased.

'Bride accepts her consort,' he called. 'It is time!'

'Aye-yie-yaaa!' yelled the islanders. 'Danu! Danu! Danu!'

Booboom . . . the drums began, beating out the rhythm of the fire dance. *Booboom . . . booboom . . . booboom . . .* the dancers stamped and turned around their partners, circling the ring of flame.

As the master druid arrived to take it, Ruan unpinned his cloak. Skaaha reached up, pulled feather pin and brooch apart to free her own. Behind her, Eefay drew the cloak from her sister's shoulders and draped it on her spear arm. Reaching round, she took brooch and pin from Skaaha's hands.

'Enjoy,' she whispered to her sister and, unable to resist, glanced at Ruan. 'Nice,' she said, cheekily. 'Hope you know how to use it.' She and the priest left the ring of fire to wait behind the well of Bride.

Skaaha gazed at Ruan. Apart from armlet and torc, the glow of fire on his skin, the scabbard that replaced his sling and pouch, he was as naked as he had been during all their sessions on the beach. Nothing had changed, yet everything was different. His eyes had not left her face since she stepped out from the cave.

Nor had the crowd ceased yelling. The drums held pace, the novices and their partners stamped the beat around the edge of the circle, forbidden, yet, to touch.

'Forget them,' Ruan said, putting his hands on Skaaha's shoulders. 'here is just you and me.' He had no idea what was wrong.

Skaaha stretched up, face against his cheek. 'Nechta put oil between my legs,' she whispered, 'and when I saw you, I couldn't walk.'

Ruan's face creased, a chuckle shook him, and he pulled her close, kissing her forehead, face, her mouth. Whatever she expected, it was not such tenderness, or the fire in her flesh that flared with his touch, cupping her face, stroking her throat. Longing surged like a flood-tide, stripping her strength again, body leaning into him. Her arms went round his waist, palms reading the shape of his back, the line of spine. New sensations rushed in – his blood heat, skin texture, taut muscles, chest brushing her breasts, their bellies touching, and their thighs. Against her abdomen, his cock moved, growing hard. She put her hand down to touch.

Ruan's breath drew in sharply. He stepped back beyond reach. For those close enough to see, his arousal was obvious. His eyes raked her hair, face, throat, breasts, belly – every detail, to her toes.

'You've seen me before,' she said, wriggling at the scrutiny.

'Not like this.' Firelight, reflected in his eyes, made them fierce. 'Not as a man who's about to fuck.' His cock jerked in response. Closing the gap between them, he touched the torc round her throat. 'Ard is a magician.'

'It's you who's different.'

His fingers lingered, tracing her breastbone with the back of his knuckles, over her breast. 'No.' Gripping her shoulders, he turned her around, spoke in her ear. 'It only seems that way.' He held her close with one arm, chest against her back, hips pressing into her buttocks, lips brushing the back of her neck, while he reached out to the pot Nechta had left.

'She did that, I told you.' *Boom* . . .

'There is more to do.' From behind, he stroked the swell of her breasts with small rhythmic circles. 'It will help.' Waves of pleasure washed through her limbs. Her head tipped back into the crook of his neck, eyelids flickering as if against bright light, mouth tasting his skin, brushing the rougher jaw-line, breathing in the scent of him. Touch became a continuous caress of arms, chest, ribs, belly and hips down to the inside of her thighs, gently rubbing in the oil. *Boom* . . .

'Danu! Danu! Danu!' yelled the islanders.

'Turn round,' he whispered. There was darkness in his tone, a foreign depth. The flexed muscles of his arms held her up. Her legs barely would.

'I might fall.' Her arms went round his neck.

'Only into me.' His kiss was fierce now, bruising, lips parted, tongue searching, touching hers – the surge of up-fire raised her hips towards him, belly moving against the swollen hardness of his erection. Keeping her tight to him, hand pressed between her shoulders, he stroked oil smoothly into her back, waist, buttocks, the rise and fall of his chest deeper with every breath. Something more should happen, and she ached for it, not certain what till his hand moved between their bellies, her thighs parting to allow the stroke of fingers into her vulva. *Boom* . . .

As if a fire was stoked, desire mounted like desperation, and she was kissing him, his face, neck and throat, his shoulders and his mouth again. 'Please,' she begged, 'please,' not knowing what she asked, except for mounting pleasure, except for release, except for the ache behind her clitoris that was an agonizing hunger.

'Soon,' he promised, voice deep and heavy in her ear. 'Soon.' Between her thighs, behind the tremor, his hand shifted towards that ache, pushing against and, his fingers, into . . . *Boom* . . .

'Aahh!' She cried out with pain, clung to him, burying her face into the crook of his neck, and cried out again as the next thrust of his finger jagged into her.

'Aye-yie-yaaa!' yelled the islanders.

Her thighs clamped together, trapping his hand, though she

still clung, bewildered, face buried in his neck, body quivering. 'That hurt.'

The crowd didn't seem to care. 'Danu! Danu!' they urged. Out on the fringes, some couples already fucked. High above, the moon sailed, skimming scattered clouds, half-way towards midnight. Inside the ring, several dancers looked perturbed. *Boom* . . .

'It won't last' – he kissed her hair, her ear – 'I promise.' His voice was ragged, rougher. He eased his hand back from between her thighs till it was free and gently teasing around her clitoris again. His erection surged. Eyes, darker than Ruan's ever were, gazed into hers. 'Don't be afraid.'

Her palms slapped into his chest . . . 'I' . . . pushing him back . . . 'am' . . . hard . . . 'Skaaha!'

On the mound below the twin fires, Suli rose to her feet. Something had changed; the tension in the crowd was charged with alarm. Opposite, on the slopes, Mara clenched her fists. It was going wrong. A thin smile curled her lip. *Boom* . . . the dancers dropped to a crouch. Something unexpected had happened. The rhythmic beat ceased.

Know your enemy. The words leapt in Skaaha's head, Kerrigen's. Words Suli had repeated. He dared to cause her pain. But she had seen his weakness. That made her strong. Let him be fearful. 'I will honour you,' she said, taking oil from the pot.

'Not with that.' His brows came down. 'I won't be able to . . .'

'You hurt me,' she cut in, sharply, 'so you're mine.'

He hesitated. Then his hands spread outwards in surrender. Skaaha smoothed the oil down over Ruan's cock. *Boom* . . . from his vantage point, the drummer was quick to pick up. The crowd caught on, roared, bellowing with delight and laughter. Copulating couples stopped and rose to watch. Skaaha gripped the whole erect length of her consort's penis, slippery now, and moved her hands slowly up and down. Again, his breath gasped inwards. His hands clutched her shoulders. *Boom . . . boom . . . boom . . .*

The seated druids exchanged puzzled looks. Nechta's oil helped arousal, made penetration easier for the goddess. On Ruan, who didn't need it, it would delay release. Smothered smiles travelled round the group.

Among the Ardvasar warriors, on the slope above the ring, Vass glanced at Fion. Both men grinned.

Fronting the Kylerheans, Ard looked down at Erith.

'You did warn her it would hurt?'

'Of course' – a pause – 'I think.' Erith shrugged. 'Somebody must have.'

When a man behind suggested Fion might have taught Skaaha more than they guessed, the blacksmith turned and floored the speaker with a single blow.

Moving forward beyond the bonfires' heat, Suli leaned on her staff, listening patiently. All the auspicious omens for this Beltane could not be wrong. Danu's sign, the warrior who strode the stars, was rising in the east. Since Kerrigen became the goddess nineteen suns had passed – the time it took the heavens to repeat the exact same pattern of stars. The same sky spread above them now as then.

Across the slopes, at the head of her warrior chapter, Mara craned to see. The old rivalry rose in her throat, threatening to choke her. It was like watching Kerrigen again down there – the same shape and form, the same dark, bewitching looks, the same arrogant confidence. She breathed deep, calming her rage. The daughter of her dead enemy might not become Danu after all, not if she kept this up.

In the ring of druids, Arin considered Ruan's stamina. If the consort failed to bring the goddess here, someone else must. The smallest druid's fingers crossed.

Around the now-seated novices inside the circle, girls grinned at boys, most of whom ducked shyly. One brave lad put his soon-to-be woman's hand under his loin cloth. Another tried to hide the premature patch of damp on his, and hoped for time.

Nuzzling into Ruan, kissing his ear, allowing his hands to trace her breasts and tease her nipples, Skaaha fought a rising passion. Using her body to raise his excitement was becoming dangerous. Guided by the drum, the increased rhythm of her strokes didn't work. Ruan was oblivious with ecstasy, but nothing more happened. Hanick would have been a stained heap on the cavern floor by now. Maybe she was doing something wrong. She dropped on to her knees. *Booboom* . . . The crowd roared.

Smiling, she chewed her lip. The drums spoke to her, egging her on, just as they'd spoken to him. Ruan's erection jumped in her hands. His hands cupped the crown of her head. Clearly, there was something to be done down here. She kissed the swollen tip of his cock. Even without the dancers' gasps, the drum roll or the islanders yelling themselves hoarse, the instant jerk was confirmation. Tentatively, she tasted it with her tongue. Ruan's fingers tightened in her hair. The oil had a smoky flavour, and a musky saltiness that might be man. She licked again, parted her lips around it, moving forward so the warm flesh filled her mouth. *Booboom* . . . *boom* . . . *boom* . . .

It was a mistake. Ruan groaned. Both of his hands gripped her head, his hips rocked, the smallest movement but enough. Power shifted back to him. He could hold her there, make her choke. Her oily fingers searched his scrotum, not to disable him but so she could if there was need. A shudder ran up his thigh muscle. Another groan came from above her. What he controlled was a desire to thrust, not her. All she need do was clench her teeth, close her fist round one testicle, squeeze, or draw that blade from the scabbard at his thigh.

How vulnerable he was, and trusting. Tenderness spread like light inside her. She wanted to go on, to be the giver of his pleasure. Her lips surrounded his flesh, tongue playing with the texture, moving so his cock rode in and out. Passion overtook desire, overwhelmed her.

'Skaaha, you're killing me,' he groaned. It was true. If his seed spilled on the ground, Beltane could not begin. If he was spent in her mouth, womanhood would not be reached. Danu would not become. His manhood would be forfeit. Shakily, she rose. His hands guided, steadying. *Booboom* . . . Her arms wound round his neck.

'We should fuck now,' she breathed.

He raised her body up, as if it weighed nothing, wrapped her thighs around his waist. With his hands under her buttocks, he shifted his hips till the swollen top of his erection pressed into the back of her vulva.

Skaaha clung on round his neck. There was nowhere it could go. This was not going to work. It was not going to work. Then he let her weight drop, and stopped it.

'Aahhh!' she shrieked. 'Aaahhh!'

'Danu, Danu, Danu!' the crowd roared. *Booboooom* . . . *Booboooom* . . .

'Breathe, my love,' he murmured against her shoulder, holding her so tight she couldn't move. 'It's all right.'

Nothing was all right. She had split open, something swelled inside her. 'Is it done?' she groaned. 'Is it?'

'Mmm.' He breathed deep. 'Almost.' And he let her drop further, rocking his pelvis, thrusting up.

'Aaahhh!' she yelled again, louder, before sinking her teeth into his neck.

'Aye-yie-yaaa!' the crowd went crazy. 'Danu, Danu, Danu.' They jumped around, hugged each other, cheered. Some had tears in their eyes, others screamed with joy. 'Aye-yie-yaaa!' *Booboom* . . . *boom* . . . *boom* . . . the drums thundered.

Ruan turned, still holding her tight to him, carefully lowering them both on to the altar, kissing her face, her mouth, her throat as he laid her down with him above, still joined. The woollen cloth cushioned the stone, softer than she expected. Nor did she expect to kiss him back, not after that, but she did and kept on doing it, her legs still wrapped around his waist as he began to rock, with slow, deep thrusts, into her. Every stroke made flames of fire dance on her skin. Inside her flesh pleasure mounted with intensity she could never have imagined or believed, and with each thrust desire grew, for more and more of him.

Led by the drums, the seated priests began the rhythmic chant for Danu, the rise and fall of ululation a wild celebration. For the waiting dancers in the ring of fire, prohibition lifted. Yellow loin cloths were discarded. White skirts, untied, were spread beside each fire. Among the crowd, festival mead was passed around, people danced, joined the chant, or let their own desire loose.

Suli settled again on her grassy mound, content. The air throbbed with excitement and the sound of coupling. Born in the dark of a thirteenth moon, Skaaha fulfilled all the prophecies. Legend, too, was relived, the goddess deflowered by her warrior priest. In the many generations since, history had not repeated so exactly. This Beltane, already late, would be worth the wait. Age wearied her body, but the high priest's mind remained sharp. Her instinct proved correct, her vision was confirmed.

When her consort guided Kerrigen's daughter round on top of him, Mara could stand it no longer. The druids knew, or guessed, to taunt her like this. Maturity was all they waited for. That consort was skilful, well trained. What people saw, they believed. The warning she'd given Skaaha in the cavern should have rendered the fearful blacksmith powerless and pitiful in that ring. Now the girl was led where she could not go, the crowds ecstatic. Cursing, Mara left the Bracadale warriors, working her way round the crowds, looking for the one man who could help.

She found him further up the hill, on the outskirts of the crowd. Her instruction barely caused a blink. He stared down at the copulating couple spread-eagled over the altar, the girl now upright astride the man.

'You'll know her again,' she said.

'Naked,' her companion grunted, slurping mead.

'Then get closer,' she snapped. 'There will be no mistake this time.'

'I lost half my men, trying to find what you wanted.' He paused, craned his neck. Another couple in the ring shuddered to a climax. His thick fingers scratched his crotch. 'She'll be easier to get, one thing in one place.'

'You should hope so. Fail again and this time I will hunt you with the druids' blessing.' Threatening him meant glaring at his fleshy face. He disgusted her enough to die for it, if she'd had no use for him. 'Go familiarize yourself with the place again while they're all here.'

'And miss Beltane? Outsiders don't get much welcome from women, except now, when they're full of this.' He waved the horn of mead, leering at her. 'A good fuck might work better than threats.'

Swallowing her distaste, Mara grabbed his hand and shoved it down her leggings. 'Feel that, Bartok,' she said, making sure he did. 'Bring me her head in a sack, and that' – she pushed her face as close to his stinking beard as she could bear – 'will fuck you to the grave and beyond.' She yanked his hand back up, slapping it away before he got ideas she'd have to kill him for.

'A man should die happy,' he said, sniffing her sex on his fingers. 'Yes, indeed, happy, happy.'

In front of the Kyerheans, chanting the ululation for Danu with her own cell, Yona found it difficult to keep the smile from her face. How much Ruan performed, how much was instinct, was impossible to tell. Moving Skaaha on top for a time was genius. It fulfilled the legend, a rare sight at the ceremony with inexperienced girls. The crowd loved it, as did the goddess – moving astride him as if born to subdue her mate, till he slid down to put his head between her thighs instead.

When he turned her again, on to her back, it was to hold them both in the state of bliss until the time came. Now, to cheers from the crowd for the last of the six novice couples to finish and leave the ring, he moved into the final act. Intended or not, he played out the mythic copulation – outlasting all the others, with all the tributes to the goddess made.

Around the ring of fire, leading the chant, Nechta and the druids of Bride felt excitement rise. *Boom . . . boom . . . Boom . . . boom . . .* the drummer beat the strokes to the rise and fall of the consort's naked backside. Next Beltane, someone else could drum. His own hips thrust the rhythm. He was developing a quite unnatural and misplaced passion for his instruments. With a nod towards them, the smaller drums came in, picking up the beat. The crowd began to shriek in time.

'Bel-tane! Bel-tane! Bel-tane!'

High above, the moon had long passed midnight. Ruan ran the tip of his tongue round Skaaha's parted lips then raised himself to watch her face while his fingers coaxed her clitoris to the point of no return. Just as it was about to tip, her breath a gasp, he entered her again, the firm warmth of wet, muscular flesh surrounding, gripping, drawing him in. Her feet moved from around his waist to between his knees, pressing down on stone, locking their legs together. She trembled, her whole body throbbing under and around him, uttering mindless sounds. Leaning on one arm, he raised her buttocks with the other till she was tight up against him.

He was losing himself. Her flesh clenched on his with every thrust. It must be now, for nothing in him could hold on. Orgiastic blindness darkened her eyes. Her head tipped back, fingers dug into his shoulders, and she cried out, over and over, as wave after wave broke around and through him, drawing him into her, over the edge into the shuddering oblivion of pure sensation. All sense of self was lost. Involuntarily, the name of his goddess uttered from his mouth as his seed was given into her womb, and he was absorbed into the bright source of ecstasy, beyond life or death or loneliness, at the end and beginning of time.

The crowd screamed with delirium. 'Aye-yie-yaaa! Aye-yie-yaaa!' The drums thundered on and on and on. Even the druids cheered, and wept. There had never been such a magnificent copulation. It would live for ever, as long as the great wheel turned, remembered in song and story and verse.

In front of the twin fires, Suli paced, stabbing the ground with her staff, clenching her fist. 'Yes,' she muttered. 'Yes!' It was done, magnificently done. Reborn clinging to her consort, the young goddess would find her way forward when the time came. Tears spilled down the old woman's age-softened cheeks.

22

Skaaha's eyelids flickered, blinking as sight returned. In the blackness, the net of sharp stars she had fallen from pinned itself back into place. Above, Danu the Warrior strode the heavens, sword sparkling from her belt. Beyond, the moon stared, amazed. The weight of man began to tell. Tentatively, Skaaha caressed his shoulders. He raised himself up to look at her. Awed, she stared back, scanning his features in wonder, touching her fingertips against his mouth, tracing the shape of it. He tilted his head, in that familiar serious way, as if considering a question.

'The adoration is the wrong way round,' he said softly. 'You're beautiful, woman and goddess.'

'I am a woman now,' she grinned.

'Oh yes.' He eased himself up, reached to his waist. The warmth of him slid wetly out of her, making her gasp, soundless with disappointment.

'What are you doing?'

His fingers unbelted the scabbard. 'There needs to be blood . . .'

'It will be your own,' she interrupted, quickly.

He started to laugh. 'And there is,' he chuckled, standing up beside the stone. 'So the blade is yours.' He helped her rise. 'Do you ever let me finish?'

'I thought you did,' she said, smiling again, 'and very fine.'

'Then you'll have no use for this.' On his knees, still chuckling, he fastened belt and scabbard round her hips.

Eefay and the old priest returned with their cloaks, Skaaha's reversed, red side out. The crowd kept yelling, though the drummer was beyond help, a quivering heap behind his instruments. Arin rose from the ring of druids and took his place.

Boom . . . Cloaked in red, Danu and her consort left the ring to wild applause. Hawthorn blossom showered them as they headed downhill to the tented hut inside the standing stones, beside the grove. Eefay followed behind, carrying the goblet of mead.

Boom . . . In the ring of fire, the senior priest held up the altar cloth, stretched between his hands, to show the people. 'Witness the blood of Danu,' he called, at all four corners of the circle. *Booboom* . . . the cloth of Bride was ceremonially burned in the well of her sacred flame. 'Beltane is begun!'

Inside the ring of stones, Ruan took the goblet from Eefay's hands. 'Thank you.' He barred her entrance to the tent. 'This is for Skaaha alone to do,' he said.

'But I have questions.'

'Which will keep. Live the day well.' He stepped inside, closed the flap.

Outside, on the slopes, the party raged, with food, drink, songs and dancing round the great fires. As the warrior chapters broke up, looking for friends and relatives, Mara stood on the rim of a rise, alone, looking towards the shadowed trees of the grove. That druid consort might be worth attention. Danu was legendary, but the girl he mounted would be no more than that now, a blacksmith whose time had just run out. The warrior queen's eye found Eefay, shield and helmet glittering in the firelight as she marched back to Donal's school. That one could be the greater threat, but easier, far easier, to reel in.

In the tented hut, even after Ruan and Skaaha had eaten their fill from the waiting feast, he still chuckled.

'Will you tell me what is funny?' she asked.

'You, so quick to rise in anger, so languid in your pleasuring.' He kissed her nose. 'It would have been my own blood shed. The sign of Danu should be seen, but I could not have cut you.'

'This is good, because I would have killed you.'

He chuckled again, going over to the hearth, where a cauldron of water steamed. Skaaha stretched luxuriously on the cushions, sprawling on her stomach to watch him. Tiny white blossoms still stuck to her skin.

'Who was Bride?'

'*Is* Bride,' he corrected. '*Is* Danu, *is* Carlin.' He was washing himself, all over. 'What do you learn from that?'

'You forgot Telsha?' she said brightly. She could tell he smiled by the half-turn of his head, the brief hesitation before deciding not to rise to her cheek.

'Telsha's part of Danu, when she's a foster-mother. The goddess is the sacred three, the tri-unity of sun, earth and moon. So what do her festivals say?'

'That she grows old and new again, as they do.' She threw the shell of an oyster at him. 'Don't tell me stories. I'm grown up now.'

He glanced over his shoulder. 'Time,' he said. 'She's time, the beginning and end of all things, the bringer of life, without whom nothing is, before whom nothing was. Unless she passes, nothing lives.'

'So she never was a person and can't be reborn. Why say she is?'

'Every moment dies and is reborn, yet time is. Bride gave birth to the sun, forged the world from a ball of flame then fashioned the moon. They speak her truth.' He turned to her, began to wash her feet and legs with a warm, wet cloth. 'But what you ask can only be told through stories. There are many Brides – Gaia, Isis, Ishtar, Kali, Amaterasu, Inanna, Toci.' He wrung out the cloth, and continued to wash her bottom, back and shoulders. 'Annait, whose stones stand outside, came with the ancients, the winged warrior of time. Her spirit enters Bride when she becomes Danu.' A kiss dropped between her shoulderblades. 'Turn over.'

She rolled over. The cloth washed around her throat and breasts, down her arms. 'But Danu was the first warrior.'

'*Is* the warrior,' he corrected again, 'who first became after women began to farm and keep herds so their children would never starve. While men hunted, another tribe tried to take cattle from the mothers.' The cloth was wrung again in warm water, washed over her belly. 'Bride turned the blade which had been used to cut corn against these raiders, becoming Danu, the warrior who protected her clan from loss and harm.' The wet, warm cloth washed between her thighs.

'What are you doing?'

'Removing Nechta's oil.' The cloth dropped in the bowl. 'Out there was for them, for show.' The bowl returned to the hearth. 'In here is for you.' On his knees, he came over to recline at her side. 'For us.'

'You mean we can do it again?'

'Oh yes.' Flickering lamplight reflected in his eyes as he looked down at her. A grin that was truly wicked lit his face. 'There is always more to learn.'

When day broke, Yona arrived with her needles to tattoo the mark of maturity on Skaaha's neck, the thumbnail design applied below the left ear. Ruan squatted beside her so that she could rest her head on his thigh.

'You must keep still,' he warned, 'and it will hurt a little.'

It hurt less than she expected; a cool, soothing cream was applied before the repeat short jabs from the bone needle. All adults wore the sign of maturity, according to their trade. Farm women bore the triple spiral triskele, their men the cord of life. Priests, blacksmiths and warriors all had different designs. But when Yona had finished and handed Skaaha a mirror, the pattern inside the blue ring on her neck was the triquetra of druid faith. It represented the triple nature of all things: mind, body and spirit; earth, sea and sky; sun, moon and earth. It was the same mark worn by her mother, the sign of the goddess: maiden, mother and crone.

'I can't have this,' she said. 'It's Bride's.'

'Danu's,' Ruan corrected, splitting hairs. 'And you earned it.'

'It's yours by right,' Yona said. 'Only one living person can wear it. If you disagree, argue with Suli. But you have work to do now, and should get dressed.'

Outside, the twin bonfires were stoked up to begin the blessing of the beasts. Skaaha, dressed in red, drove the first cow between the fires, slapping its hindquarters with a birch switch to bless it with fertility. Long lines of beasts followed, ceremonially whacked through by druids bearing similar switches while the smoky heat and crackling flame cleansed the animals of pests.

The goddess and her consort were in great demand, hailed and congratulated in turn wherever they went, Danu's blessing sought for every activity. Skaaha bound the wrists of couples wanting to leap the broomstick between the fires. Those hand-fasting till next Beltane went first, then marriages. Ruan untied those already coupled who jumped to separate. Cows in milk were put to bulls for next spring's calves, the shaggy island ponies bred. Deals were struck for the services of boars, rams, bucks and cockerels, the coarse wool stripped by hand from native sheep, young stock traded. Beltane ensured the healthy cross-fertilization of the island herds.

Stirred with smells of dung and cooking, the wood-smoked air filled with calls of beasts, birds and, as artisans set out their stalls, of barter. Pots, cloth, implements of bone or horn, and ironware were laid out on grassy plots alongside stalls with dripping honeycombs, cod and salmon roe, lobsters and sea kelp, birch wine, skins, fleeces and spare wool. Everybody worked, but it was different work from usual. Jugglers, tumblers and fire-eaters entertained. The warriors put on fierce displays. There were games of chance and skill, and when darkness fell, opportunities for exchanges of other kinds: to hear stories, old and new, from less familiar tellers; listen to the legends and tales of heroism sung by the druid bards; drink, or dance or sleep.

*

By the sixth day, the Kylerheans had exchanged most of their goods for produce, clay pots and the services of bulls, with credit accrued towards new thatch and future matings. But Skaaha's best piece, a dagger with bronze hilt and decorated leather scabbard, still lay in the centre of the remaining display.

'Because your father refuses every offer,' Erith explained. 'We've had double for everything made by Danu, and could have had three times what that is worth.'

'I'll trade it next Beltane,' Ard excused himself to his daughter. 'You'll have made something finer to replace it by then.'

Even as they spoke, a man crouched beside Skaaha, examining the knife. Thick-set, with lank hair and greasy beard, he stood to draw it from the sheath.

'Sharp,' he said, testing with his thumb. He began to slide the blade slowly into then out from its scabbard. 'Goes in and out easy.' His eyes watched Skaaha as he spoke. 'Nice work for a goddess.'

'And it's not for trade,' Ard said, standing to take it.

Ruan steered Skaaha away to her next blessing, of the hunting dogs.

'Pity.' The man reached out, handed the dagger back, though he still gazed after the festival couple.

'You from round here?' Ard asked. Something about him was familiar.

The man shook his head. 'Raasay.' Having given the name of a small island between them and the mainland, he turned away, going in the opposite direction.

'That wasn't a Raasay voice,' Erith said at Ard's elbow.

Ard still watched the head bobbing away in the crowds. 'Might have married to it.' He knew the man from somewhere.

'That's never married,' Erith snorted. 'He stinks, and that's never Raasay cloth he's wearing either, even under the dirt.'

'The tattoo.' Ard finally got it. 'I know that design.' He'd seen it before, but couldn't recall from where.

*

Skaaha petted the huge bitch, fondling its ears before guiding it into the mating pen. The owner was a warrior from the north. He'd chosen three good dogs from other chapters to mate with his bitch. He and Ruan each held one back while the first was engaged. Unlike cows, which came into heat within days of scenting bull, the bitch's season coinciding with Beltane was luck. The warrior expected great pups.

'And many of them,' he added. 'If she's two or three by each in her, I can breed new lines into the others back home.'

'So one dog won't be the only father?' Skaaha asked.

'Nah,' the man said, giving the dog he held to her to hang on to while he went to turn the one with the bitch, to tie them back to back. 'It's not like women, where the best seed wins out however many you mate with. Hounds can give out young to all of them.' He held the bitch to stop her wandering off, dragging the poor dog behind her, still tied. 'Can't you, my beauty?' He crouched, face level with the massive beast, petting it.

'Doesn't mean she will, though,' Ruan added, nodding to Skaaha as the mounted dog released himself. 'You can let that one go in now.'

She was glad to. It had taken all her strength to hold the struggling dog from leaping the flimsy fence to get to the bitch.

Gern returned to the Kylerhean stand from carrying salted pork back to the cart for Lethra. Ard was crouched, scratching in the dirt with his knife.

'You're not thinking of using that on something?' Gern asked, peering down at the pattern; a row of six slithering snakes, their ascending and descending sizes forming a rough circle.

'Trying to jog my memory,' Ard said. 'I've seen it somewhere.'

'Other than in the forge?'

Ard looked up at the older man. 'The forge?'

'It was you hung it there,' Gern said. 'About four suns ago.'

'The outsiders.' Ard got slowly to his feet, remembering.

'Aye,' Gern agreed. 'You copied it on a disc off a tattoo one of them had. If you ever worked on fish hooks, you'd see it hanging next them still.'

But Ard was gone, running. 'Tell Erith,' he shouted back. He ran part-way in the direction the man had gone but, seeing no sign, veered off to find Vass. The man might be anywhere by now. His brother was easier to spot, arm round Thum's shoulders but flirting with the women who watched the wrestling bouts.

Alerted, the Ardvasar warriors fanned out, searching the crowds. Nechta sent the attendant druids to marshal the others. Outsiders, exiles from society, had no right to be here. Permanent banishment was rare – for serial offenders – and severe. Those banished lived rough, often committing other crimes. If this man was an exile, there would be more crimes in his past, and to come.

Mara became awkward when asked to suspend the games and detail the other chapters to join the hunt. 'Is there a point to this,' she challenged Ard, 'if they took little and had half their number killed?'

'Half their number?' Ard queried. No one knew how many had escaped.

'However many,' Mara snapped. 'It was theft, and so long ago it's hardly worth drawing a blade over.'

'Let it grow dark,' Jiya suggested. 'When he sleeps, your sword might leap courageously to hand.'

'Tread carefully,' Mara warned.

'The law will be applied,' Nechta interrupted hurriedly, to save the peace. 'The Kylerheans were offended against, and now Beltane.' The druid cells encircled the festival area to ensure no one left till the search was done. 'Describe him to me,' she asked Ard, 'and I'll pass it round.'

'You'll smell him,' Ard said, sketching in the details of the man's appearance and ending with the tattoo. 'On his right forearm, a moon of six crawling snakes, like this.' He put his four fingers against his palm to demonstrate.

Grimly, Mara quartered the site between her women and the other chapters. If Bartok was caught, he had better talk his way out of this, or she would have to silence him. Either way, her plans were jeopardized.

High above Loch Slapin, Skaaha collapsed on her stomach in the long grass as Ruan rolled over to lie beside her. Soft groans of subsiding pleasure purred in the back of her throat. The heady scent of hawthorn, Bride's blossom, filled the air.

'You make a fine, contented cat,' he said, drawing the back of her skirt down to cover her against the growing chill. After the dogs, they'd climbed the slope to enjoy stolen time alone outside, away from the crowds.

'Did you know it would be like this?' she asked, turning to look at him. 'My skin wants to be against yours always, and my eyes won't close in sleep for wanting to look at you.' Her dark eyes were luminous. 'And when we're joined, sometimes I can't tell which or what is me or you.'

'As if we become each other,' he completed, 'or one being made whole again.' He tucked a strand of hair behind her ear. 'No, I didn't know. It's always pleasurable, but the stars don't always spin.' Nor did it always engage the heart.

A thought registered in her eyes before she spoke, chuckling first. 'And Fion said I'd be half a woman till I lay with him.'

He smiled. 'That sounds like Fion.' The wheel took no time at all to turn, the future announcing its coming to the present moment.

'How can I be more woman than I am now?'

'Lie with him and find out.'

'I will not,' she said, rising up on to her elbows to look out over the loch below. The setting sun gilded her hair. Her eyes found his again. 'It's you I want.'

He turned over, resting on his stomach in the grass alongside her, to watch the day go. 'That won't always be.' Against intense blue, pink clouds edged with gold painted their reflections in the sea. Dark on the water, a small boat rowed out of the estuary, heading south around the coast. Lobster fishers, maybe.

'It will,' she said, earnestly. 'The way things are cannot be changed.'

The quote made him smile again, having the teachings given back stripped of the wisdom behind the words. 'No, they can't,' he said, though he could have wished it otherwise. 'But you're right.' A terrible tenderness at her belief in the simplicity of love was tearing up his heart. 'This time will always be.'

Darkness fell. The warriors reported back to Mara. None had seen any man resembling the description. If he'd been among them, then he'd gone.

'You can rest easy, Ard,' she said. 'I'd help you out, but younger men suit me best these days. One of Nechta's potions might better cure your nightmares.'

Ard bit back a retort. Mara never forgot a slight, real or imagined, had never forgiven him for leaving her bed in favour of Kerrigen's. She'd have killed him then, for sure, except she feared the warrior queen.

'Don't mind her,' Nechta said, as the warriors left to join the evening feast. 'They'll be alert now, as will we. If he returns, he'll be seen.'

'He's rash enough,' Ard said, grimly, 'to cross water and trespass Beltane.'

'What is there to deter his like?' Jiya asked. 'Mara mistakes spite for strength. Bracadale is grown soft since Kerrigen died.'

'There's truth in that,' Nechta agreed. The Islands of Bride suffered from weaker leadership and lost reputation. Raids and lawlessness increased. Now an outsider felt safe enough to transgress the festival. 'But warriors must have a queen – and who will challenge her: you?'

Jiya chuckled, rubbing the trepanned indentation on her crown. 'Aye,' she said, 'when I need another hole in my head.'

23

It was early morning when the small boat rounded the spur and hove into view of Kylerhea. A mist hung round the hilltops and, in the half-light on the hazy shore, the only witness was a reindeer snuffling the edges of the abandoned playing field.

'My arms is near off, Bartok,' one of the three men in the boat complained. 'We better be getting sleep soon as we makes land.'

'You're never anything but asleep,' Bartok answered. 'I could've rowed here quicker with one hand than you pair with four of them.'

As they approached the jetty, keeping close to shore so the current wouldn't pull them past, the other man scoured the misty slopes.

'You sure there's no crazy folk about?' he asked. Nightmares of flaming arrows and fiendish shrieks still haunted him. A movement on the hillside made him jump, clattering the oars. It was a fox, leaping on some prey too small, at this distance and low-level light, to see. In his past, he'd found cause to fear. A slash cut across his left eye, causing it to droop, the bulb of it unseeing white. Behind his droopy moustache lay a mouthful of broken teeth.

'We'll soon see.' Bartok stood to loop the rope around the post. 'Might be one of them left behind, forbidden to attend for fighting or not repaying a debt in time.' He climbed the step up to the jetty. 'If there is, we're just passing.'

The first man, the youngest and only clean-shaven one of the three, stepped on to the jetty behind him. Tall and lean next Bartok's bulk, dull eyes unblinking like a shark's, he played his thumb on the blade of a dagger pulled from inside his coat.

'Innocent travellers,' he agreed. 'Till I gets close enough to stick them.'

The murmur of voices woke Skaaha. Early sun glowed yellow through the tented skins. She stretched, but there was no warmth of Ruan's body beside her, just empty space. Thin shafts of light carried columns of drifting dust. She raised her head, looked around, but he wasn't at the hearth, shaving or dressing. Her head dropped on the pillow. He'd be back soon. A shiver of delight, which had become a feature of her life, wriggled through her flesh, making her shoulders circle in their sockets, her skin tingle. A smile, which had also become an habitual expression, spread across her face. She closed her eyes, and could see every detail of his face, the look he wore when gazing at her. Another shiver shifted her shoulders.

'I can't do this,' Ruan said. 'You ask too much of me.'

Skahaa's eyes flew open. It was Ruan, but he spoke outside the hut.

'It's you who asks it of yourself.' A quiet, softer voice – Suli.

'Then I'll ask no more.' He was pacing, quite unlike him. Now Skaaha strained to hear. Words drifted, becoming lost. 'Let me go. I fulfilled my task.' Fear scrambled Skaaha to her knees, crouched close to the skins, listening. 'I can't be with Skaaha, not like that, not any more.' A pain like a blade twisted in Skaaha's gut, doubling her over.

'Then what will you be?'

'I don't know,' Ruan groaned. 'Send me away. Send me to Cul Bhuirg, or anywhere, but don't send me back to that.'

'A sabbatical might help,' Suli mused. 'Walk with me.' Feet moved away, rustling grass and leaves. Their presence just beyond the skins faded.

Skaaha clutched a cushion to her belly, biting her other fist, rocking back and forth. She could not have heard what she did. Yet she had. It was a wounding worse than one that bled. Tears stung but did not fall. Life should end now, if it could hold such pain. Summer had filled her heart, warmth had reached her bones, light – her head had filled with brightness – and all of it was gone, was not real, had never been. They'd used her. *He* had used her, just as she first suspected. It was lies – his words, mouth, touch, even his body – all lies. With a great howl of agony, she tore the cushion apart with her hands, slapping feathers everywhere. Standing, with down drifting on to her naked back, she bent, grabbed and tore another, then another one.

Suli and Ruan walked below the twisted elder trees for some time without speaking, without sound except the crack of twigs underfoot, the peep of birds. When they reached the small stream that sprang from the well of Annait, Suli rested on a bent branch, its shape telling of its frequent use as seating.

'In this world or the next, there is pain,' she said. 'It can help us grow.'

'And sometimes it tells us to move to a place beyond its reach.'

'You know this place?'

Miserably, he shook his head. 'But it's not in Skaaha's life, advising on her lovers, ministering to her marriages, trying to help her live through childbirth.'

'You're a priest.'

'I'm a man.' The words were torn out of him. 'A man who loves her.'

'A man discovering the desire to possess another.' Suli's voice was firm, hard. 'Love doesn't seek to own.'

'That's unfair. I'm asking to leave, to let her go.'

'And this will help who?'

Eefay groomed her horse, preparing it for the warriors' parade that afternoon. She had been wakened by news from Glenelg. Donal's elderly, sick mother had died. They returned tomorrow to a wake. For Eefay, the celebration would be two-fold. The school passed to her keeping now. She would ride at its head in the parade, mistress of Glenelg, her father relegated as tutor to second place.

There were few other grooms about this early. It was her favourite time, the grey mare nuzzling her face, dunting her shoulder if she went too hard or slow, quivers rippling through its muscle when pleased.

'If you're very good,' she told it, 'I might braid your mane.' The mare flared its nostrils, began to chew on her hair. 'And if you don't behave,' Eefay said, jerking her head away, 'I'll braid your tail. Make you feel a right nonce.'

In the far corner of the paddock, there was a disturbance. A saddle was slung over a Kylerhean pony. Eefay pushed through the other horses, crossing the paddock. It was Skaaha, mounting up, dressed in ordinary clothes. A few white, goose-down feathers wafted in her dark hair.

'Have you been plucking birds?' Eefay asked. It was hardly goddess work.

Without a word, Skaaha snatched up the reins, nudged the horse forward with her knees. Her face was set, teeth clenched.

'Where are you going?' Eefay asked.

'Home,' her sister said, easing the horse through the stock towards the gate.

'But why, what about tonight, the end-of-festival eat-drink-fuck till you drop party?' Eefay walked alongside, without thinking, even opening the gate. 'Don't tell me you wore out the lusty priest. There's a cart-load more up on the rise if . . .'

'Shut up, Eefay.' Skaaha's eyes glinted. 'Tell Ard and Erith, so they don't worry.' Her voice choked up. 'I'll see you tomorrow before you cross the kyle.' She kicked the horse away over the grass.

'Hey, I've something to tell you,' Eefay called, but Skaaha, quickly out of earshot, didn't stop. 'Maybe not,' she muttered, and went back to her mare.

Suli let a few moments pass so the stream could speak. 'This fire between you may burn out. Or it may burn through the ages, and have done so. Skaaha will know many men. How does that diminish you?'

'It doesn't,' he admitted.

'As her priest, you might be with her till her last breath in this life, if hers comes first. You can help her grow and learn and become all she might. You will ease her pain, tend her sickness, calm her fears, soothe her sorrows and guide when she is going wrong. Is that not love?'

He hung his head. 'My fears seem small indeed.'

'Not so small when even gods are jealous.' She put a hand on Ruan's shoulder. 'I've lived almost three times your five and twenty suns. Desire burns less brightly, but Beltane's message is the same. It's in acts of love that we learn what it is to be, by not being.'

'Put self aside,' he murmured, 'if you would know the way.'

Suli nodded, not necessarily to agree, but as if she listened to another voice, from elsewhere. 'Come,' she stood, gripping her staff, 'we should walk back.'

At the hut, they stopped outside. 'Love is the law,' Suli said. 'It's not gentle in its demands. If you can't fulfil it, you're not druid. So ask yourself what love demands from you, but don't seek tomorrow in today.'

'Blessings on you, Suli,' Ruan said. That was exactly what he'd done, conjured tomorrow to torment himself. With or without him by her side, Skaaha would love other men. It was the way of things. If he couldn't, yet, let go, he could at least set it aside. This day, Skaaha was alive with questions and spirited enough to argue or disbelieve. They tested and nourished one another. This day, when she woke, she would wrap arms and legs around him, her bed-warm body drawing him in. Lifting the flap, he stepped into the hut.

'Thought we was getting some sleep.' Stick sat astride Kylerhea's outdoor anvil putting an edge on his dagger with a rubber. They'd found the larder first, ate salted herring and cheese while checking out the houses. But day was normally for sleeping through. Stick paused from sharpening to gulp ale from the jug beside him. The night's rowing began to tell. 'What is we here for?'

'To get a woman.' Bartok stood with his thumbs in his belt, looking round.

The younger man glanced around the deserted village. 'Should've stayed at Torrin then. They's all there.'

'They'll be back.' He kept his plans close, telling only what the other two needed to know. They'd learn the rest soon enough, except who the hirer was. He'd keep that to himself. No point risking double-cross. 'She'll be with them.'

'Do I gets to stick it?' The blade flashed in the sunlight as Stick turned it.

'When I say. We have to get her first.' Bartok scratched his ear. 'We'll camp over there.' He pointed to Alba, to the other side of the crossing. 'Close enough to watch.' They'd have to learn her habits, when she'd be alone. It wouldn't be easy. Blacksmith, Mara had said. Pity. A herder or charcoal burner was easier to get at. 'What you got there, Cut-eye?' he called.

Cut-eye was on his bony knees at the foot of the slope, digging earth with his bare hands. 'Stuff,' he shouted back. 'Stuff they hid before they left.'

Bartok hurried over. 'Leave it be,' he said. 'We don't want them knowing we've been here.'

'We just ate,' Cut-eye said, pulling up a pair of iron fire-dogs. He nodded his blind eye towards the open larder door. 'They'll know somebody was, and we can trade these.'

Bartok wondered. Beds and ready food appealed more than sleeping rough. They were safe here till late tomorrow, could take food when they left. The contents of the larder would last the three of them a whole moon casy, and there was ale. Life was tough for outsiders. They could hunt or fish, but tools and clothes were easier got by theft. So they island-hopped between the uninhabited and those they could steal from. Warriors were often on their trail. The only respite was to travel the mainland as traders, goods provided by robbing festival-emptied homes.

Bartok had several caches hidden away. No reason why this job shouldn't add to those. Evidence of robbery wouldn't interfere. The villagers would think them been and gone. Thieves didn't hang about waiting to be caught. The warriors would search, but not in the vicinity or just across the water. No, they'd scour deserted hideaways, all well away from here, leaving a safer, clearer coast to get the girl and be gone.

'You're more than a pretty face, Cut-eye,' he said. 'We just got ourselves a nice place to be at home in.' He turned, called back to Stick. 'Go find a bed. We're stopping here for the night.'

'And I can have these?' Cut-eye asked, wielding the fire-dogs.

'Yes, indeed,' Bartok agreed. 'I'm for more of that fine ale, and sleep. Put them in the boat, and anything else you find. We'll ship everything across the kyle before they get back tomorrow.' It would mean finding a good place on the mainland to hide the bounty for collection later. But, with that part of a plan in place, there was only the girl to worry about. He'd do that when he woke.

Ruan ran towards the Kylerhean tents, a blur of brown leggings and yellow shirt, sling strapped to his thigh. No red cloak. Ard was at the cart, packing it for travel next morning. The druid veered towards him.

'Is Skaaha there?' he called as soon as he was close enough.

'Not with us,' Ard said. 'Might be with some of the others. Is she wanted?'

'Something's wrong.' Ruan glanced around, hoping to spot her. 'She wrecked the tent. I thought she'd come here.'

Now he had Ard's full attention. 'Why would she wreck your tent?'

'I don't know.' Ruan ran his fingers through his hair. 'I wasn't there. When I came back, she was gone, things broken and scattered, feathers everywhere.' It had looked like snow, and as chilling.

'It's not like Skaaha to destroy things,' Ard said. 'She knows the value of work.' He frowned, puzzled. 'You're sure she left of her own accord?'

Ruan nodded. 'One of the druids saw her leave the grove, running.'

'Then she's fine,' Ard said. 'Annoyed, but fine.' He paused. 'Did you go with another woman?'

'Only Suli.' Ruan couldn't recall exactly what he'd said outside the hut, but knew what he had asked. 'Maybe she overheard us talking.'

'Don't try to work it out,' Ard warned. 'Sure as the sun sets, you'll be wrong.' He swung the last sack into the cart. 'She'll be back soon, to tell you that and put you right.'

'You think?'

'No woman lets such an opportunity pass. It's the way of things.' Ard raised the tent flap. 'Come and eat breakfast. If she hasn't cooled off and come back by then, we'll go look.' He ushered Ruan into the tent.

Skaaha trotted the horse half-way home before letting it slow to a walk. Overhead, a pair of eagles soared. *Rau . . . rau . . .* She didn't look up. *Yip – yip – yipp.* The sound twisted in her heart. She rode on past the green valley, past the three lochs where she'd sacrificed Kerrigen's armour and weapons. The scent of hawthorn mocked her. If the white-tails barking above brought her mother's voice, it too was mockery. *Pain is the teacher.* It taught her to run. Yet it couldn't be outrun. Kerrigen would have confronted him. She would not have run, not from any man.

Perhaps she should turn round, go back, face him. *Yip – yip – yipp.* And hear those words again. *I can't be with Skaaha, not like that, not any more.* She doubled forward over the horse's neck. Jiya had warned her, before the druids opened the warrior's skull. *Don't be fooled.* 'Aha!' The agony cried out of her, shaking her chest, repeating over and over. She wasn't running anywhere. If she hadn't been on horseback, she would have collapsed to the ground, hugging the grass, prostrate with grief, body heaving. Without the horse, she could not have got beyond the camp. The shaggy pony jerked its head, ears twitching, but its stride didn't falter. It was going home.

By the time Skaaha reached the stream where, so long ago, she and Ruan had broken the fast of sacrifice with water, her howls of grief had run out. Dismounting, she washed, drank. While the horse did the same, she scoured the sky. It was almost midday. Raincloud glowered above Kylerhea, black and brooding. The eagles were gone. Kerrigen didn't always attack. The first rule of war: the foolish run into trouble, the wise run away. *Don't send me back to that.* The blade twisted again. She wanted home, the cradling of familiar walls, the safety of her bed, the oblivion of sleep. Mounting up, she trotted the pony on. Heavy gobs of rain began to fall.

In Erith's roundhouse, sprawled on the biggest bed he could find, Bartok shifted in his sleep. Caves and heather were his usual sleeping arrangements. Discomfort disturbed him. He stirred, scratched, woke. The ale he'd drunk had filled his bladder. Rolling off the bed, he stood, loosed the flap of his leggings and relieved himself into the corner of the bedchamber. The stream hissed against the hard earth floor, trickling under the wicker screen. He heard rain. Glancing through the chamber entrance towards the open door, he saw that grey light had replaced sunshine.

Not long begun, the rain already puddled the cobbled path, bent blades of grass beyond. They were lucky not to be out in it, or in the boat. It was storm rain, the kind that soaked through to skin but passed as quickly as it came. Bartok was tying his trouser flap when another sound reached him – the beat of galloping hooves. Without a word to alert his two companions asleep in other chambers, he snatched up the long knife he normally kept hidden under his coat and slipped out of the house.

24

Creeping round the stone building, Bartok cursed his luck. His ears told him that horse and rider had galloped down the slope, slowed and cantered past the forge, heading for the animal pens. If there were more of them, if this was just the first, he might not make it to the boat. His only hope, when this rider got indoors, was to make a run for it. He rehearsed the story, of passing travellers from the mainland, in case he was caught. His friends were on their own.

Shifting along the side of the roundhouse, he squinted up the hill. Rain soaked his hair and beard, dripped from his eyebrows. There was no sign of anyone else. No sound, now the first horse made none, of other horses, carts or folk. Running feet splashed across the grass, coming to the house he hid behind, where his companions lay asleep. They were lighter feet than he expected, a youth maybe. His sleeping friends stood a fighting chance. Bartok waited, with no intention of helping, till the running rider reached the path, ran indoors.

'Fool,' a voice complained, with that shudder of someone shaking their head. 'Such a fool.' It was a female voice. Bartok hesitated. Unless she was that warrior from last time, this could get interesting. He'd heard no clink of weapons as she ran. Maybe his luck was not so bad. As soon as the woman realized she wasn't alone, he'd know. First sound of a sword drawn, or a squeal from either of his friends, he'd be off for the boat. Balancing the knife in his hand, he waited, rain soaking through his coat, watching the hill.

Rain in the south-west headed towards Torrin as Ruan and Ard returned from a fruitless search of Loch Slapin shore, deeply worried. There was nowhere left to look. The lochside had been their final hope. It was also where an outsider's boat would have tied up. Ard was still troubled by that presence at Beltane, sensing connections where there could be none.

'He watched her' – he remembered the dagger in the man's hands, his eyes on Skaaha's face, the rising urge to hit him – 'and I didn't like it.'

'But if he'd gone . . .' Ruan paused. 'We saw a boat leave the loch, going south. Looked like lobster fishers, but they'd all be here to trade.'

'All maybes,' Ard said. 'Safe to come is safe to go. He risked being here. Skaaha can't have vanished into thin air.' Ahead of them, marshalled for the parade, the warriors waited, assembled behind druid pipes and drums.

At their head, Mara sat erect on her mount, hair spiked white, inscrutable. In front of her, two decorated ponies stood, riderless. Skahaa's consort approached the druids. Of the goddess who'd lead the parade, there was no sign. Perhaps that late-night visit to Skaaha in the cave meant the girl wasn't keen to ride in front of her warrior queen. Or, if her absence had anything to do with Bartok, she might never turn up at all.

Fronting the Glenelg school, Eefay strained on her mount to see what the hold-up was. The approaching rain promised to douse the twin fires. Instead of the evening party, Beltane would end with the parade. Islanders lined the sunwise route, all packed up, ready for their journeys home. Joining the parade was an honour for the school of warriors, and Eefay's first chance to show off her new authority. Itching for it to start, she twisted round in the saddle to face her father.

'What are we waiting for?' she complained.

Donal rode out of line, craning to see past the chapters from the north. 'Your sister,' he called. 'Her consort just arrived to speak with Suli, but I don't see her.'

'You mean she's supposed to lead? For Danu's sake!' Eefay kicked her horse out of the line, rode to the front. Pulling up next Ard and Ruan, she leant down to speak. 'Skaaha's gone,' she said. 'I was to tell Ard and Erith, but I forgot. So we better just get on. She isn't coming.'

'Then where is she?' Ruan asked. 'We've looked everywhere. The Kylerheans are still searching.'

'She isn't lost.' Eefay sat back in the saddle. 'She went home. Took a horse and rode off, not long after daybreak.'

'And you didn't say?' Ard accused.

'It's not my fault,' Eefay protested. She pointed at Ruan. 'It's his.'

Suli handed Ruan a cloak borrowed from another druid. 'For the rain,' she said. 'Go. We'll conduct the parade.'

As drums and pipes struck up, Ard pulled the two horses from the parade, holding Ruan's so the druid could mount. 'She'll be safe home by this time,' he said. 'But she shouldn't be alone, not with outsiders about. You get off. We'll follow when we can.'

Quelling the urge to gallop, which would quickly tire the horse, Ruan set off at a trot. He wanted speed, but cantering meant letting the horse walk half the road. A steady trot would get him there more quickly. If that boat was outsiders, they headed south. But there were many empty homes to tempt them ashore long before they reached Kylerhea. On foot, the man might have headed anywhere. Thieves, unless disturbed, were not the greatest threat. Penalties for harming people were greater than those for theft. But anything might startle a horse, throw a rider, leave them vulnerable to lynx or wolves. His fingers found his sling, wild beasts the reason why he always wore it.

He stopped himself. Love made him afraid again, afraid to lose what could be given or received but never owned. His fault, Eefay had said. That's where his real concern lay, not with other men or beasts. He'd let manhood displace priesthood, allowed fear to tarnish what was deep and strong and passionate, but it wasn't broken. No, it wasn't broken yet. Not if they talked. Not if he could reach her.

*

About to haul her wet dress off as she walked to her chamber, Skaaha paused. Adjusting from the sound of falling rain, her ears picked up another – gentle snorts from inside. A warning shiver crept up her back. The door had stood open. Still did, for light. But it wouldn't have been left that way, in case wild animals wandered in. If that breathing was a bear snuffling or snoring in one of the far chambers, she was in danger. A cornered beast was not forgiving. She backed towards the door, eyes straining as they adjusted to the gloom. Half-eaten food and jugs of ale lay around the hearth. Erith would not have left that mess. No bear then, but human.

'Who's there?' she asked.

A snort came from one chamber round the left side, but it was three stalls from where she stood that a half-drawn curtain shifted. A young man's head poked out. Relieved, Skaaha automatically raised and dropped her sodden skirt, asserting her femininity and right of occupation.

'Welcome to my home,' she said. 'I am Skaaha, and this the house of Erith, forge-keeper of Kylerhea.' Her nose wrinkled. She could smell urine. 'It should be treated with respect.'

A grin spread over the young man's face but didn't reach his lifeless eyes. 'We'll be sure we does that,' he said. As he rose, pushing the curtain aside, a smaller man appeared from the chamber on the left. One of his eyes drooped, glowing white.

'Begging your pardon,' he said. 'You people got nothing to worry about. We took the chance to rest but we'll get on our way now. Come on, Stick.'

The young man didn't move. His cold stare had not left Skaaha. 'I hears no people,' he said.

Behind Skaaha, the sound of rain changed. She turned. The bulk of a big man, water dripping from hair and beard, filled the doorway. There was a long knife in his hand.

'There are no other people,' he said. He looked her up and down, his eyes coming to rest on her face. 'Sweet Bride,' he swore. 'We're in the presence of a goddess, lads. It's our lucky day. Yes, indeed, lucky, lucky.'

Skahaa spun round, grabbed an iron spar from the fire-dogs on the hearth, turned back and swung. The metal bar whacked the man's arm. He yelled, crumpled. The knife spun away. She leapt, high, for the gap between him and the door. Her skirt was grabbed from behind, pulling her over backwards. As she landed, half on top of the young man who caught her, she threw her feet up, somersaulting backwards, tearing free. The young man stumbled, but was quickly on his feet again. Now two of them stood between her and the door, the one-eyed man to her side.

'Shut the door,' he shouted, grabbing the other fire-dog spar. His companions hesitated. If they did that then they wouldn't see. There was no fire, no lamplight. She knew the house in dark or light, might slip past. To persuade them to move, Skaaha swung again. The iron rod smacked into the little man's head. Squealing, he fell on to the hearth. The young man, dagger in hand, lunged but the first man grabbed his coat, grunting with pain from his arm.

'Don't be a fool, Stick,' he growled. 'That's what she wants. Go to her, and she gets past you. There is only one way out.' The little man groaned from the hearth. Skaaha brought the bar down again, across his legs. He howled, scrambled away on his knees towards his friends. Neither of the others moved to protect him. Now she was out of options. Balancing the rod in her hands, she waited, the next move theirs.

'Stop whimpering, Cut-eye,' the big man said, flexing his hurt arm. 'Get my blade.' Still on his knees, the little man scrambled to the knife, took it back.

Skaaha breathed deep and steady, expecting attack. Instead, hauling Cut-eye to his feet, the big man stepped away from them, ripped down the curtain from the nearest bedchamber and tore a strip off it. Looping it round the door post, he pulled the door almost closed, passing the strip through the metal door ring before tying the ends. The gap he left let in some light but wasn't big enough to squeeze through.

'Now can I stick it?' the young man asked, playing his dagger.

'Put that away,' the big man said, tucking his own blade inside his coat. 'She's had her fun. Now she owes us some.' All three of them leant forward, ready. 'Now!' In a body, they rushed towards her, ragged clothes flapping.

Skaaha raised the metal spar in both hands and threw it at Stick's head. He ducked. She leapt, using his shoulders to propel her over in another somersault and past, running for the door as soon as she landed. With all her weight shouldered into it, the cloth stretched, the gap widened. Not enough. Hands grabbed her clothes and hair from behind. Dragged away over the floor, she punched, kicked, bit what was nearest. The musty stench of sweat and dirt filled her nose and mouth. An arm gripped round her throat, squeezing. Her work in the forge had made her strong, but they were stronger, frighteningly so. Weight landed on her chest, crushing. Ill fed and unfit though they were, still the sheer physical power and weight overwhelmed her.

Cut-eye lay across her legs. 'I got her, I got her, Bartok,' he yelled. Cloth tore. Her arms were yanked, wrists bound together with a strip torn from the ruined curtain, and tied again to the bottom of a bedchamber post.

'There,' Bartok said, sitting up, panting through his beard. 'Now we'll see what we got.' He walked to the door, untied and opened it, letting in more light.

Fighting to control panic, Skaaha steadied her breathing. Raiders took women. These were thieves. She was of no use to them, without value. Crouched beside her, Stick played again with his dagger.

'Hurt me and you'll be in trouble,' she said, though they must know that.

A sound that might have been a laugh snorted in Stick's throat. 'Like we's in trouble,' he said, tucking his knife away.

Bartok loomed over her. 'Shift, Cut-eye,' he said. 'Hold her legs.'

The weight on her knees shifted. Skahaa kicked out, but

Cut-eye had already wrapped his arms round her thigh. Stick hooked his around her other knee.

'You sure it's not bad magic, Bartok,' Cut-eye worried, but hanging on, helping pull her legs apart, 'her being Danu? The druids –'

'Can't touch us,' Bartok cut in. Kneeling between her legs, he grabbed her skirt, tore the dress all the way up to her throat. 'Nice, he said, running his eyes down her body. 'Very nice.' Rough fingers probed her vulva.

Skaaha gasped, shocked. 'You can't do that!' She writhed, struggling to stop the invasion. Cloth tightened round her wrists. Arms tightened round her legs, bone against her bone.

'Easy, girlie,' Bartok muttered as she bucked, pointlessly trying to free herself. 'We not good enough for the likes of you, is that it?' His head bent, fingers fumbling with his trouser flap. 'Well, we'll see. Yes, indeed, we'll see about that.'

'No,' she said. 'No, you can't. I do not allow. I won't allow . . .' She clenched her pelvic muscles to keep him out. There was pressure against her cunt, a snort, and . . . 'No-o,' she shrieked . . . as he jerked forward, grunting obscenely, her vagina filled with brute flesh . . . 'No-o,' she wailed . . . rammed in and out, his body weight pressing down. This could not be.

Skaaha's eyes clenched shut against the sudden sting of tears. A stinking beard brushed her face, with every cold, degrading thrust, killing who she was. Why didn't death take her now . . . that should surely happen . . . her person dying . . . but it kept on, shoved and shoved and shoved into her, fouling intimate places that were no longer . . . and in her ears the slap, slap, slap of filthy flesh against her. Despoiled, she was beyond disbelief, that man could do this to woman, and how easily, so easily that she could not prevent, before the man shuddered, grunting, to a stop and the shrivelling contact of his body slithered out, over her thigh, was gone.

A hand clasped her chin. 'I think it likes that, Bartok,' Stick said.

Skaaha snapped, teeth closing on bony flesh, sinking in, shaking it like a dog, with the scream that came, drawing blood. A fist smashed like stone into her jaw.

'Don't waste the head,' Bartok warned.

Dazed, numb with pain, brain and body fogged, she lay like the dead thing she was as another fouling repeated the first. Dead limbs, dead mind, dead heart. There was no fight, nothing to prevent. All she was had gone, finished, her inviolable self that centred in her womanhood ended. Fetid breath panted in her face. Semen ejaculated into her vagina. No name existed now that she could own. She was a thing used, knowing every stab into the nothing she became. Her mouth hung open, saliva dribbling. Abandoned by the world she knew, no otherworld claimed the husk of her. No blessing of oblivion came.

The half-blind man, his fear of druids forgotten, swapped places with the young one. Flopping out of his clothes, the lump of his cock nudged her thigh, fingers scraping her flesh, his gasp as it slid into her. Unlike the other two, he talked.

'Bet you'd like' – squeezing her breast – 'me, how you did' – puffing out his long moustache – 'him, in your' – twisting her nipple – 'mouth' – moaning.

'Like in the fire ring?' Bartok asked. He was at the hearth, supping ale. 'Aye, sweet stuff, that was. Go on then, Cut-eye, give us a show.'

'Better you knocks its teeth out first,' Stick advised.

'I said don't break the head,' Bartok reminded. 'It's wanted.'

The jerking into her stopped. Fingers touched her face, moved her chin. 'It's a bit broke already,' Cut-eye said. 'Half her mouth don't shut.'

'Then it can't bite,' Stick said. 'Go on, gives it some meat to chew on.'

'Naw' – the little man began thrusting again, faster – 'this'll do it, this'll do it' – but the idea was in his head, irresistible. Bartok called encouragement as he withdrew, shuffled on his knees, leggings round his ankles, up to Skaaha's side. 'Pull her down a bit then,' he panted. 'She's too near the post.'

Stick obliged, grabbing her ankles while she thrashed again, yanking, pressing down to hold them as he watched, grinning, while Skaaha gagged, slavered, choked, accompanied by Cut-eye's grunts and moans and deeper, louder cries of ejaculation.

The rain was passing north. Soaked through, Ruan rode out of it just before rounding the bend on the hilltop above Kylerhea. The warmth of fire, dry clothes and hot food waited below, and Skaaha, and talk. Light lifted the sky. He slowed the horse to let it walk the slope, shook back his hood. There was no drift of smoke through the thatch of Erith's or any other house. He stopped the horse. The first thing Skaaha would have done was light a fire. Her horse was in the paddock next Lethra's house.

He scanned the village. In odd out-of-the-way spots, several small holes were dug. The wet cloak on his back clung tighter. Those puddled earth heaps were where the villagers had buried valued goods. Casting along the shore to the crossing jetty, he saw the boat, bumping level with it now the tide was up. A boat too big for one man to handle, it could carry half a dozen, less with goods.

2 5

Trying to calm the thunder of his heart, Ruan turned the horse, walked it back around the corner. Once out of sight of anyone below, he tied it loosely to a tree. Its presence would, at least, warn the homecoming Kylerheans if he did not return to release it first. He had no plan, other than to find out what awaited him below. Skaaha was fast, faster than outsiders. She might have run away. Smart, too, she may have bargained with them. Unless by accident, it was unlikely they would kill. He stilled his racing mind into the present moment. Pulling the sodden cloak to cover the yellow of his shirt, he climbed off the road into the scrub and began to make his way down the hill through the covering trees and shrubs.

'Fire,' Bartok said. Now the rain was off, he could get his coat dried out. 'Fire, food, and more ale.'

Cut-eye scurried to the door then stopped. 'Don't let Stick waste her,' he said. 'We could take her with us, all of a piece.'

Bartok glanced over at the girl, tied and crumpled next the post. 'Aye, we could, for a bit.' The left side of her face was bruised and swollen. On each breath, a bubble of spit blew and shrank from the corner of her drooping mouth. Body looked a bit battered, but it was the head he wanted nice. Time would fix that. They could all use a woman for a while yet. 'Peat.' He glared at Cut-eye. 'I'll light the kindling.'

Cut-eye darted off outside. Bartok took the makings from the dry box next the hearth and struck the flint. There was shuffling from the girl. He looked round. Stick sat astride her body, playing the tip of his dagger round her bare breast.

'I told you no,' Bartok growled. 'Stick her all you like, but not with that.'

'Not killing,' Stick muttered. 'I just needs to see it bleed.'

The tinder flared. Bartok piled on chips of wood. Cut-eye was taking his time. He stood, walked over to look down on Stick's handiwork. In the girl's swollen face, a puffy red eye stared back. The tip of the blade circled her left breast, scoring it. Drops of blood oozed. Stick's free hand went to his crotch.

'You're sick,' Bartok said. Cut-eye had obviously found something else to dig up. He'd best go get the peat himself. As he left, Stick pocketed his blade, smeared blood on his hand and rubbed it on his swollen penis, groaning softly as he did.

Outside, Bartok walked to the peat stack at the side of the house. There was no sign of the little man. 'You're asking for a slap, Cut-eye,' he bellowed. For answer, the corner of his eye caught a yellow blur from behind the building, quickly followed by a crack he never heard. His unconscious body dropped on to the peat stack.

Inside, Stick scuffled with Skaaha's resistance, tearing away the remnant of her tattered dress as he turned her over. 'Better you fights,' he muttered. 'I likes that. I likes that best.'

His grip round her gut was like a band of iron. His knees, between hers, spread her thighs, phallus poking the crack between her buttocks. She kicked out, tried to draw away, hanging on to the bedchamber post.

Outside, Ruan roped Bartok's wrists to his ankles. He couldn't easily carry this one to the forge. Dragging him would leave a track across the grass. On the cobbled path the noise might be heard. Grunts and scuffling came from inside the house. Ruan forced his breathing to stay deep and steady, to keep at bay the knots that tried to tie themselves in his inside. Rushing in, when he had no idea how many he'd face, would not help Skaaha – if she was even in there. Lacking a staff, he'd fetched a rod of iron from the forge, thrust Bartok's knife into his belt. The sling that downed the first two was useless as an indoor weapon. He yanked the tie tight.

Inside, Stick jerked his hips. Burning, hard and fierce, tore into Skaaha's backside. 'Now you,' Stick hissed, 'gets it,' as a howl issued, involuntary, from the girl's throat. 'Now you' – ramming in – 'knows what' – repeatedly – 'you's for.'

Outside, the animalistic yowl ripped through Ruan's ears. He grabbed the bar of metal, ran for the roundhouse door. Let him not be too late. *Bride, let her live*, the words begged in his head. All he had, however many waited, was surprise and speed. Bursting through the doorway into the gloomy interior, the flickering flame in the hearth lit only one crouching, shadowy figure, back towards him. As its head turned, hearing feet, he saw the second body held in front. Ruan leapt, swung the iron bar. The man keeled over, writhing on the floor. The other body slumped, curled foetal. Ruan side-stepped as the man tried to rise, cracked the metal against his skull again.

Dropping to his knees, Ruan put his hand on Skahaa's back. Her skin flinched. He laid his forehead against the grime ground into her shoulders.

'It's me,' he said, 'Ruan,' slicing through the tie with Bartok's blade. Her head, against the post, was in shadow. 'Skahaa' – gritting his teeth – 'tell me how many there are.'

Slowly, her arm extended from underneath. Painfully, she uncoiled her fist, showed him three fingers.

'Three.' Ruan let his breath out. Gently, heart burning with rage and grief at her broken face and body, he gathered her into his arms. 'Then it's over.'

She was heavier in his arms than she'd ever been. The curtain from her chamber had gone. Carefully, he laid her down, checked her limbs, the bruising and swellings – all the time aware that the greatest hurt could not be seen.

'Don't turn away,' he said, cupping her head. She closed her eyes. Steeling himself to look at her battered face, he tracked her jaw-line with his thumbs. It was unhinged on the swollen side, not broken. 'Sit up,' he said to her shuttered face. 'We can fix this.' He took the remnant of cloth from her wrists, tore it, bound his thumbs. 'It might hurt.' Putting his padded thumbs in her mouth, he pressed down hard on her back teeth, felt the jaw pop into place, biting into him. Released, her mouth closed, head lowered, and she rolled over on to the bed, curled up, hugging herself.

Leaving her, he tied the man whose skull he'd cracked, dragged him outside, brought peats, built the fire, set a cauldron of water on the fire-dog spars. Then he carried Skaaha, silent and unresisting, to the sea. Sitting, chest deep in the waves, he bathed her bruised body and face, let the water wash her hair. Spiral scars scored one breast. Small crescent cuts bled in her palms, made by her own nails in clenched fists.

When the salt had done its work, he carried her back inside, laid her on sheepskins by the fire, washed her skin and hair with warm water, dried it and put her into bed. Again, she turned away, unable or unwilling to look at him or speak. He had no words now, and went outside, running back to the shore. Guilt hugged him like a shroud. Skaaha was here because of him. As if in mockery, the low afternoon sun cast a golden path across the water. Without stopping, he plunged back into the waves, cursing, slapping at the sea with his hands. When the tide reached his waist, he raised clenched fists, shaking them at the first pale stars, the rising moon, bellowing out his anguish to a disinterested sky.

Behind him, on the hill, hooves beat as the Ardvasar warriors rode down the slope, followed by the Glenelg school. Above them, the first Kylerheans rounded the corner, coming home.

Only the condition of the three outsiders saved them from the warriors. Bound by honour codes, unable to attack unarmed, constrained, unconscious bodies, they raged instead.

'Let them loose,' Fion roared at a sodden, dripping Ruan. 'I'll feed them to the fish, gut first, piece by piece!'

'Give them weapons,' Jiya shrieked, 'then go indoors!'

'We'll deliver justice,' Thum swore.

'I want them,' Eefay insisted. 'They'll wish they'd not been born.'

Yona, shaken, stood side by side with the white-faced young druid, defending the indefensible until the law could take its course. Ard went straight to his daughter. Returning only moments later, he had to be restrained from tearing the intruders apart with his bare hands. Jiya couldn't look at Skaaha. Eefay tried to sit with her but had to leave, to move. Erith, struck silent, cleaned up her house around the broken girl then cleaned it again. Lethra wandered back and forth at the foot of the ridge, her old face haggard, wailing. Other women lamented with her. Inconceivable, this offence struck at them all. They wept and cursed wordlessly till it seemed the world went mad.

A new druid had come with them, sent by Suli to complete the Kylerhean cell. An older man, beard on to his chest, who would take Ruan's training to the next stage, he also insisted the law would operate. A court was called. Digging posts into the playing ground gave the men something to do. Warriors carted the outsiders to the stakes, roped them upright. Stick's head hung, still unconscious. The other two, floored by stones from Ruan's sling, came round. Bartok and Cut-eye, terrified, began protesting. They had just been passing, belonged on the mainland, had only meant to eat and sleep. Ard's claim that they'd robbed Kylerhea before was hurriedly denied.

'So somebody has the same tattoo,' Bartok blustered. 'I never met him. Thieves got brands, hands missing.'

'We didn't know it was stealing' – Cut-eye's voice shook – 'digging out that stuff.' The boat loaded with Kylerhean goods was damning evidence of theft. 'We thought it was a trash pit, stuff you didn't want.'

'That girl came from nowhere.' Bartok picked up the innocent plea. 'She attacked us.' Threats rose from the watching crowd encircling the court. 'You can see the bruise on my arm,' he protested, 'the bite on Stick's hand.'

Vass, in charge of the captives, checked, nodded.

'And she broke Cut-eye's head,' Bartok elaborated.

'Ow,' the little man yelped as Vass looked for it. 'Not that one. That was him,' he nodded at Ruan, 'and she got the back of my legs. Mad crazy, she was.'

Doubt rippled through the crowd. Skaaha was strong and fast. If she thought she disturbed robbers, there could be truth in the story. Her aunt had killed three of the last intruders.

'We only tried to stop her,' Bartok wheedled. 'We're right sorry she got hurt.'

'You used her,' Ruan accused. 'I saw him.' He indicated Stick.

Bartok glanced sideways. The young man's head still drooped, saliva trickling. 'We don't know what he was doing. We were outside.'

Stick groaned. His head rolled to the side. 'You's a rat, Bartok,' he muttered. His eyes, devoid of emotion, found Ruan. 'We all fucks it,' he drawled. 'Him first.' He nodded at Bartok. Grunting, he rested his head back against the post, still holding Ruan's gaze. 'You asks Cut-eye what it eats.' His mouth smiled. 'I's the only one' – he spat blood and saliva – 'gets more'n you did.'

Bartok cursed him, screaming that they did nothing the girl didn't want, how she'd asked them to, went on about Beltane, how she was hungry now for other men and, name of Bride, they were only flesh and blood. Where was the harm in a bit of pleasure? Everybody knew the insatiable appetite of women. Any man would oblige. Ard already strode to the forge to fetch the tongs.

Skaaha lay, face to the wall, not responding to anyone, refusing food or drink as the village seethed and argued around her. Eefay came, and left. So, too, perhaps, did Jiya. Kaitlyn brought a fine wool shift to put on her. A new curtain screened her chamber. Sometimes she dragged herself to the pot Erith had left to save her visiting latrines. Yona put balm on her bruises and cuts. Ard, and others, raged outside. It meant nothing, none of it. Words rose and fell like tides against the house, meaningless.

Even the tortured screams of men, savage and high-pitched like crazed beasts, did nothing to shift the deadness, so deep it wasn't grief but the denial of living. Weeping, she heard weeping, and monumental moans that rose like walls before subsiding into bleating whimpers. The smell of the lit forge drifted to her, but no work was happening. Unnaturally quiet, mealtimes came and went. The warriors remained, like warrior ghosts. The village paused, waiting.

On the morning of the third day, Ruan came to her again. Kneeling by her bed, he offered water. 'Please drink, Skaaha,' he said. 'There is something you must do. We can't let these men go till it's done.'

The puzzle of his words prompted her voice, a croak. 'They're not dead?'

'Worse than dead. They were punished according to the law. But you were wronged. The court must tell you its judgement before they can go.' Silence filled the space he left. 'You needn't see them. The priests will come to you, if that's easier.'

Skaaha's voice stuck in her throat. She turned in the bed, grabbed the cup of water, drank it down.

'That won't be,' she vowed. Pushing the covers aside, she rose and immediately toppled. Ruan caught her.

'Careful,' he said. 'That knee's still swollen.'

'Don't' – she emphasized each word – 'touch' – avoiding his eyes – 'me.' He let go. She wavered, got her balance, limped to the door and out. A rush of light hit her, the sound of sea and birds.

On the playing field, the court awaited Ruan's return. No one expected Skaaha. When she appeared, hobbling over the grass, a frisson ran through the villagers, assembled again for the final act of this horrific affair. Those who were slow hurried back. All of them pocketed stones to see these men on their way in their emptied boat.

Eyes, Skaaha felt eyes on her every limping step of the way. Head bowed, she stared at the grass passing underfoot until she stopped in front of the druids. Ruan took his place next Yona. The new priest gave their judgement.

Lawbreakers were punished swiftly and released. It was the

way of things. The law determined punishment to fit the crime, and prevent repetition. All three outsiders had dishonoured manhood, so it was removed by crushing their testicles. That painful castration caused the first screams she heard. Like geldings, they would never mate again or breed. With no certain evidence of previous theft, their foreheads had been branded. Further offences anywhere in druid lands would lose them each a hand. Bartok suffered first, and most. For his claims about Skaaha's willingness, Ard had torn out his tongue.

'So he will not speak of you again,' the unfamiliar, bearded druid assured her. 'If your honour is satisfied, justice is done.'

All she need do was nod or go, and it was over. A light breeze tugged her hair, played with the hem of her shift. White clouds streaked the sky over Alba's hills. Behind her, beasts lowed and bleated in their pens. But it was not her world. Not now. The sanctity of womanhood was a myth. Men could destroy it. All around, villagers strained to hear her response. Ard, her father, couldn't look at her. Nor did Lethra. The others did, even Ruan, but with sorrow in their eyes. Just as she stood apart from what was natural, so they were apart from her. She was a source of guilt, an object of their pity. *Never mate again.* Not one among them understood what had been done.

'My honour,' she said, 'is not satisfied.' The master druid leaned forward to pick up her words. 'They hurt *me*,' she stressed, 'so they're mine.'

'Any wrong that is not addressed will be righted,' the priest advised, 'within the law.' His voice, a stranger's, was moderate, balanced. 'Tell us.'

Steeling herself, Skaaha turned. The three men, their hands and feet tied, had been fed and watered, Bartok in the middle between the other two. They were tethered to the posts, the ropes round their chests loosed to let them lie to sleep. Raw brands burned on their foreheads. They still had pain, but that would pass. A sense of loathing filled her, so strong it made them difficult to look upon.

'They are clothed,' she said.

A lightness rippled through the crowd. The Glenelg women warriors, grouped behind the captives, were first to move. Happy to add humiliation to the men's distress, the young novices tore and cut off their clothes, issuing cheerful catcalls and disparaging lewd remarks as they did. Great play was made of the captives' bruised, empty scrotums. Insults hurled from the villagers targeted their shrivelled phalluses. When the fun was over, the new priest raised his hands. Silence fell.

'The rags will be taken to your boat,' he told the men.

'I'm not done,' Skaaha said, her voice stronger. Fighting down the disgust heaving in her gut, she walked the line of posts, staring at each man in turn. Stick's blank eyes stared back. Bartok slobbered, trying to speak. Cut-eye was the only one who looked afraid. It was unbearable that they should walk the same earth she did, breathe the same air. 'I want their heads,' she said.

A gasp rose from the villagers. Standing together next the posts, both Eefay and Jiya punched the air.

'Aye-yaa!' Jiya shouted.

'Aye-yaa!' Eefay echoed.

Murmurs arose. Some sided with Skaaha, some not. The consequences of punishment should be lived with. Death gave these men an easy way out.

Ruan went to Skaaha's side. 'If they killed,' he cautioned, 'the law would give them death. Their crime is greater, the punishment more severe. There is no justice in their escape to the otherworld. We don't send such offenders there.'

She faced him. 'They killed me,' she said, quietly, 'because I am not Skaaha.' She walked to the centre of the court, hauled the shift off over her head. 'Look at me.' Like the bruises on her misshapen face, great black and blue stains patched her body, turning yellow. Scars crusted her left breast, swellings on her limbs distorted her shape. 'This is what the law addresses, as if I am a piece of meat.

'Does it live, does it not? What lives in me, isn't that what justice ought to ask? Druid teaching speaks of body, mind and spirit. The punishment does not address what lives here' – she gripped her head – 'what dies here' – she punched her heart. 'He can't speak,' she spat towards Bartok, 'but he can think of me in ways he should not know. All of them stole knowledge of me, taken by force. I claim it back, and my right to remove it from them as they took from me. Their heads are mine.'

26

It was inarguable. Offenders could keep nothing obtained by criminal act. Skaaha had clarified the law. What was taken from her must be given up. The three druids searched their combined learning but found no method of removing memory that wouldn't, inevitably, cause death. The captives' heads were forfeit. Already convinced, the villagers roared agreement. Vass put his sword into Skaaha's hand.

'It still has the edge you put on it,' he said. 'Aim through, like chopping wood, and if you flinch, I'll gladly finish the job.'

But it was to her sister Skaaha turned. 'Haul him up, Eefay,' she said, nodding at the blubbering Bartok, who'd slid on to his knees. Eefay yanked the tether, pulling the man back against the post. Jiya added weight to the rope.

'Higher,' Skaaha said. He was yanked again, till his face was at the level of hers. Holding the sword with two hands, Skaaha put the point of the blade against his solar plexus, pressing it into the soft flesh below his ribs, aiming upwards. She pushed her face into his, the greasy beard brushing her skin again. 'This is what you put in me,' she said, and thrust with all her strength behind it, up into his heart.

To assist, Eefay and Jiya let the tether slacken just enough. Tongueless, the man could still howl, and did. His body shuddered, jerking. Blood gushed over Skaaha's hands.

'Let him drop,' she said, stepping back. Juddering, he was dropped to his knees, the body weight taken by the rope. He swayed out from the post, head falling forwards. Skaaha raised the sword, drew deep for breath and strength. 'Haa-yaaaa!' she shrieked, bringing it down across his neck, aiming beyond, as Vass had said. The head thumped on the grass, rolling over.

'Aye-yie-yaaa!' the cheer went up. Jiya released the rope. Eefay let the twitching body drop.

'Yes!' The young warrior danced a little jig. The other women warriors joined in, chanting a victory. Skaaha was doing just as they would have, if they'd met these men as armed enemies on the field. This was warrior justice, and they sang the dance in praise of it.

Cut-eye was a snivelling wreck. Skaaha turned her attention to him.

'I do not want your head,' she told him. His one eye swivelled skywards. 'My sister can have it.'

Eefay, dancing, flung both arms in the air with delight then drew her sword.

'When I have given back what he gave me,' Skaaha said, directing Jiya to drag the man to his knees and haul his head back by the hair. Blade pointing downwards, Skaaha gripped with hilt again with both hands, forcing the tip between Cut-eye's rotted teeth.

'G-no-o.' He gagged on the blade, trembling.

'But you like this,' Skaaha told him, and thrust down, ramming the shaft deep into his gullet, her weight leaning behind it. When she yanked it up, stepping clear, blood frothed, bubbling over his face.

Eefay shrieked, and swung her blade. Without the strength of Skaaha's arms, won from the forge, the young warrior had to take a second swing before the head was off clean. Another wild yell went up from the villagers. Skaaha was telling them a story, the story of her pain. They hadn't understood. Now they did, were with her and, like her, wanted the brutality avenged. All the warriors danced, stamping the rhythm with their feet, howling the victorious chant for the blood of vengeance.

Stick's expression hadn't changed, but his limbs shook. Following Skaaha's requests, Jiya dropped him to his knees, wound the tether so he remained crouched, unable to prostrate himself, put her foot on his neck.

'His head is yours,' Skaaha told her aunt. Feet apart, straddling Stick's calves, she took her two-handed grip of Vass's sword, pressed the point into the man's exposed backside. 'Now you gets it,' she said, loud enough to reach his terrified ears, and thrust the weapon home, driving deep. 'Now you know.'

With screams, yells and cheers battering her ears, Skaaha twisted the sword, withdrew it and plunged it into the earth, cleaning it for return to Vass. Jiya had the head off in one stroke. She and Eefay danced around the cheering circle of villagers, showing off their trophies. Skaaha retrieved Bartok's head, gripping it by the hair, and limped off up the slope, following the river course, its filthy beard sweeping the ground.

'Suli was right,' the master druid murmured. 'Danu is among us once more.'

Ruan lifted Skaaha's discarded shift and followed his charge. There would be no escape into the otherworld for the spirits of the men who harmed her. The warriors would preserve and keep the heads they'd taken off. Skaaha took the other to the bog. She had kept the law, using it to resolve its own difficulty. Now he understood the barbarity she'd undergone. The death she delivered spoke more clearly than what he'd seen, or what he heard from the outsider's silenced tongue. It showed the body of man used as a weapon. Shamed that masculinity could be so debased, a stone settled where his heart should be, a stone like the world with a furnace in its heart. Justice was done, but would not erase the wrong. One mind still held those memories – Skaaha's. There had been no joy or sorrow in her eyes, and no relief.

He followed her up river, the gory trophy in her hand snagging sometimes on gorse or bramble, swivelling its dead face towards him. Driven by her intent, she limped on, hobbling round obstructions. When she reached the furthest bog, where the sleeper slept through its eternity, she found a rock, rammed it into Bartok's gaping maw. Her arm drew back, swung. The head sailed out, splashed down into the murky water, and sank. She sank too, as if her strength gave out, on to hands and knees, as if everything she could do was done. He was beside her then, her shift thrown over his shoulder, raising her up, feet sinking in the marsh.

'Don't give up now. You have more courage than you know.'

Trembling, she spread her arms, gazed down at her bruised, naked body. 'Their blood is on me.'

'Come.' He took her to the stream, a stream where he had washed her once before. As tenderly as then, he washed her clean. 'Skaaha' – he didn't know what to explain – 'what you heard, it wasn't you I wanted to escape from. It was my own fear of a time when . . .' his voice broke '. . . of the future.'

Her wet, cold hands cupped his face. 'You saved me from more of it.' Dark eyes, bleak as storm-washed moorland, looked at him as if she knew why a man might cry. 'Don't be sad,' she said. 'It's done.' Her lips brushed a kiss against his mouth, soft and fleeting as the velvet wings of a moth. Then she stood, pulled on the shift and set off, still limping, back down the hill.

It wasn't done. Skaaha returned from the bog empty-handed and emptied out. Eefay returned to Glenelg. Jiya left with the men of Ardvasar. With all the warriors gone, work resumed. The presence of intruders was erased, their blood washed into the soil with river water. Seed moon passed. But each night Skaaha sat from dusk to dawn on rocks above the sea. Each day she slept, shut away in her chamber. Before and after sleep, she walked the perimeter of the village thirteen times, sunwise. She ate, but little. She talked to no one. Her body healed. So did the village. A baby was born in Lethra's house, a boy. Mother and child both survived. Kaitlyn would be its foster-mother when it was weaned. She had inherited an inland farm from an aunt. Falling into step with Skaaha, she told her this.

'Come visit,' she said, 'when you're fed up being crazy.' They passed behind the druid huts, past the mound of the ancestors. Skaaha's stride was steady, the rhythm never breaking. 'Even if you're still crazy, you'd be better company than them.' Kaitlyn's husbands stood waiting, ready to shoulder the packs of her few belongings. 'I meant to divorce that one, but the extra pair of hands will be useful. Half the land is bog. He can farm the ore.' Her aunt had left husbands too, men to show them the ropes. They walked on, below the cavern where their friendship had begun. Time changed everything. 'I'll be back to see my foster-son, and to fetch him when he's big enough. I'll see you then.'

Following the curve of the rise, they approached the rear of the forge.

'Don't come back.' Skaaha's voice was so quiet, Kaitlyn wasn't certain that she spoke. 'It's not safe where I am.' Her stride didn't falter.

'Not safe?' Kaitlyn stopped walking. 'Of course it is.'

Skaaha strode on.

Ard beat out his days in the forge, stripped in the heat except for his leathers. The boy Calum was apprenticed to a woman smith. Men didn't learn from men. The lad talked enough for all of them.

'Is Skaaha coming back to work? She was going to show me how to bend a hook. Why is she the only one who doesn't work? Is that because she's a goddess?'

Ard plunged the red-hot iron in the cauldron, sending up clouds of steam.

'Leave off talking about Skaaha.'

'Why, is she not a goddess any more?'

He took the boy by the scruff back to Lethra. 'When his foster-mother comes in from milking, tell her he talks too much.'

The old chief sat the lad on a stool. 'Hand, mouth,' she said.

Calum dutifully clamped his hand in place. Lethra followed Ard to the door.

'Do the opposite for your own,' she said. 'Loosen her tongue. She holds it all in. That's the real trouble now.'

It was day. Skaaha slept. Soon, when night came, she would sit on the rocks, cradled till dawn by the sound of sea. How could he, father or man, give back what was gone? He went to the dresser in Erith's roundhouse, took out a bundle wrapped in white cloth. It clinked as he walked with it to Skaaha's chamber. Awake, she sat up, long hair tangled like black seaweed adrift. He put the bundle in her lap.

'This is who you are,' he said, his voice rough, abrasive as the rasp from the forge. Metal jangled behind him as he left. Erith reclined on cushions by the hearth, nursing Freya's baby.

'What did you do?' she asked.

An ear-splitting howl tore the air in two, chilling his blood. He ran back to his daughter's bed. She crouched over the gold and bronze jewellery, clutching her hair, rocking on her knees. Issuing from deep in her throat, unbroken except for quick intakes of breath, a long, mournful note rose and fell, like the howl of a hound bereaved. Her grief beat in his ears, battered his chest. All he could do was hold her. All he could do.

Ruan took her to Tokavaig, to the healing centre at the sacred grove on the west coast of the southern peninsula. Howling hung in his ears, the animalistic sound that had ripped through Kylerhea only days before. Now she rode at his side like an empty shell that held only an echo of the self. Suli waited for them, with the master druids of the cell. The old woman had aged more since Beltane than in the previous ten suns, her face lined, her stoop pronounced.

'It's a hard fate that works through her,' she said, 'harder than we . . .' She stopped, controlling a tremor in her voice. 'It will temper her for what she'll face.'

'How can you believe that?'

'Because I must,' Suli snapped back. 'Danu is always born of pain!'

It was the first time he'd felt anger with his high priest. 'She dies of grief!'

'If you've lost hope, find your faith. Trust the world to do its work.' Her tone was harsh, breaking. 'Do not ever think you know better than Bride!'

Skaaha's bed was in his lodge. At night he lay, hearing her breathe, knowing if she also lay awake in the dark. Day broke early, with the dawn chants, and the first visit from the priests. They brought food, ate with them, Skaaha's meals specially prepared. Bathing took place in the pool, deep in the centre of the grove. Fed by sacred springs, its water was clear and fresh. The air was warm, though night fogs rolled in, forming first on the peaks of the black mountains across the bay before snaking down to roll across the water, throw a blanket over Tokavaig.

When Suli insisted he apply the healing oils, he objected. 'Why me? Won't she see a woman's hands as kinder now?'

'She trusts you.'

'It's possible,' he countered, 'that the high priest could be wrong.'

'Possible,' Suli agreed, 'but unlikely. You saved Skaaha's life.'

He snorted. 'I brought her to that place and time. Every step. You know that.'

'I don't believe she thinks so.' Suli put the pot of oil in his hands. 'There is more than the rape of her body in her mind. I see a darker shadow, one she struggles to comprehend. Help her speak of that.'

Skaaha could tell no one. The enemy wasn't dead. It froze her mind. Her own kind had broken her. Not those warped dregs of humanity, but a warrior. All she trusted, all she ever trusted. The honour code meaningless, breached to hunt her with hatred so foul it sought her head by stealth, meant to vilify her with perpetual torment, erased from eternity, as if she were filth. Her life was not saved, nor safe, nor was anyone. She drowned in that hate, her spirit dying every moment of every day.

Ruan laid her down on cushions in their lodge, worked oil into her skin, his hands renewing their knowledge of the curves and hollows of her form, and she allowed it, until that morning. As he worked over her breasts, trying to ignore the red, angry scars, he talked. 'Tomorrow, we'll try the warrior steps.' Her spine arched. 'The routine will do us good.' In her eyes there was the briefest flare of life before she pushed away his hands, rose and dressed.

They spent the afternoon under the trees, as they had every day since they arrived. It was the place where knowledge was shared. Every tree had its own lessons: medicine, law, history. For the oak, it was time, the sacred mysteries of the universe. Learning followed each strong limb, branching out to different aspects. Recollection did the same. Go to the oak, look, touch, and the voice of the teacher returned, with the lesson. Today, the bards taught, singing ballads of their origins, telling stories of the goddess, speaking the poetry of their beliefs. It was late when the last one finished, fog already creeping white through the ancient trees.

'Keep close,' he told Skaaha as they walked back. 'It's easy to be lost in the wood.' Stones ringed the roots of each tree. Leading the way, he began to tell her why, why the groves were sacred, each tree nourished as a sapling by the ashes of a past druid at its roots. The type of tree told of each master's knowledge, by which, beside which and under which it was passed on. 'So we remember,' he said. There was no sound behind him, her footsteps silent, her presence gone. He turned, but saw only wizened trunks, twisted branches fingering the mist. His ears picked up the crack of branches, the distant snap of twigs, the fading sound of running feet.

Fog, white as frosted breath, and she was running through it. Turn by rapid turn, each foot thumped down on cushioning grass and sprang away again. A spider's web of water-drops dragged against her face. Her hair dripped, nostrils clogged. Beads formed on her eyelashes. Drawing dank air in, her chest burned, breath came fast. Some way behind, heavier footsteps followed, closing the gap.

'Skaa-haaa! Wait!'

Skaaha was done waiting. She ran, feet skelping through thick fog, racing over unfamiliar ground, running towards the sea. Blind in the whiteness, she heard waves crash on to rock. The sound spoke of cliffs, sea below. She ran faster, running till the ground ran out. Then she would leap. Falling from sky into water, brine would fill her mouth, flood her ears. The sea would solve her, washing everything away.

'Skaa-haaa!' A roar of warning lost in another roar. 'Stop!'

The edge came, the end of earth. The otherworld waited, a new life. Every muscle burned with effort as she threw her body forwards, leapt up and out. Below her, a great slap of sea flung upwards against a jagged spur of rock. Spume frothed.

Ruan's feet padded to a stop. His hands grasped his knees, breath gasped. 'Skaaha,' he groaned. She had jumped or fallen. Only the incoming tide knew which. The smash of breakers against the cliff stole any other sound. The fog closed in, blinding him. 'Skaa-haaa!' he roared. 'Skaa-haaaaa!'

Dancing up the Sun

27

It's done. They were the last words she'd spoken to him. He sat, cross-legged, on the grass edge above the cliff, embalmed by fog. It was done now. They had lost ... *he* had lost her. Just when she might awaken, begin the slow return to life, she was gone. Night rose, darkening the mist. He sat on, in penance, releasing all the sorrow that had gone before, remembering her brightness. Sometimes he thought he saw her, floating in front of him, a trick of moonlight making shadows in the thick, white mirk. Below him, the sea sucked and crashed, drawing out. The shore was rocky here, jagged pinnacles of stone that would trap flotsam from retreating waves. He could hear seals resting on them. *Rrrawww ... rrrawww ...* The bulls bellowed, cows bleated. *Rrrreh ... rrreh ... rrreh.* When morning came, he would seek her body, take her home.

That night seemed endless. Stiff, cold, squatting on damp grass on the promontory above the sea, Ruan saw the moon rise in the east, a flat white disc behind fog. Only when its rays began to burn through did he realize it was the morning sun. In front of him, in thinning mist, the growing light gilded a shape suspended in the air. Perched on cloud, not forty strides away, the faint figure of a woman sat, long black hair tumbling down her back. Riveted, struck with awe, he rose slowly to his feet.

'Bride?' Or did he see Danu? It was a vision, surely. He stepped forwards to the edge, straining to see more clearly. Below, jagged rocks thrust upwards, washed by the last of the retreating tide. Beyond this gully rose a cliff face, still wreathed in fog, a great stack of rock separated from the land he stood on by a deep ravine. Threads of mist drifted and dispersed. It was no vision he saw. On a grassy mound across what was a narrow strait, Skaaha sat looking north towards the black hills.

The last fog rolled itself up. Morning sun sparkled the water where Loch Eishort and Loch Slapin opened to the sea. Across the bay, beyond the next peninsula, craggy mountain peaks etched charcoal-black. Behind them lay Ullinish, Loch Bracadale, and her childhood homes, Doon Beck and Doon Mor – Mara's domain. *Leap only if you trust your wings.* Jiya's words, last time they were in the broch. When her feet hit solid ground where she expected air, she landed hard. The smell of soil filled her lungs, not brine. Dazed and winded, she lay a long time on the thick, coarse grass, certain she arrived in the otherworld. Voices echoed from the world she left, calling a name she no longer owned. Who was she now? She had leapt in the dark, trusting only death and the fall into water, and landed in this life, on the earth.

Stones fell. Ruan scrambled over the edge of the rock. 'No one could make that leap,' he said, coming towards her across the grass. 'The gap is easily seven strides. You should be in the sea, with your head broken.'

'Bride caught me,' she answered. It was simple, faith, less complicated than despair. Her voice, unused for so long, sounded distant in her ears. 'She threw this landing up from her forge.'

His eyes shone like that sun on water. 'Then it's yours.' He spread his arms to encompass the expanse of it. 'Doon Skaa, Fort of Shadows. It was right there, in front of me. You were right here. I couldn't see it, or you.'

The rock was imposing enough, with a clear view west across Bride's sea to the outer chain of islands. As a fort, it could watch over the mouths of two sea lochs, guard access by boat to Torrin, protect the sacred grove of Tokavaig nestled behind it. She had leapt into death and landed here.

'I have something to do,' she said, rising. 'We must go.'

*

'You have a visitor,' Donal said, poking his head around the curtain of Eefay's chamber.

'What, this early?' Eefay struggled in the gloom to come awake. 'Who?'

'Go see. They wouldn't come in.'

'They?' Eefay muttered. Pushing aside the girl's leg that covered hers, she kicked off the cover, grabbed her shift and staggered out into the great room pulling it on. 'Now it's "they".' Her bare feet slapped down the stone steps between the walls, crossed the earth and rock floor of the stockroom, squelching as she stepped in horse dung. 'Oh, yes, lucky day,' she grunted, going through the hall of the great stone doorway of Doon Telve. Blinking in bright morning sun, she stared at the figure standing beyond the outside wall dressed in leggings and tunic, black hair tied in braids down her back. 'Skaaha!'

'Blessings on your house, Eefay,' her sister said. She looked pale and serious.

'What are you standing out here for?' Awake now, Eefay saw the druid waiting further back the path. Two travel packs lay at his feet. That explained 'they'. 'Why didn't you come in?'

'I might not be welcome.'

'Why, do you bring bad news?'

'I have something to ask.'

'Anything,' Eefay offered.

'Teach me to fight,' Skaaha said.

There was a hair's breadth of hesitation then Eefay swung her arm. The flat of her hand hit a stinging slap against Skaaha's face, jerking her head to one side.

Skaaha drew breath. Her brown eyes turned to look into Eefay's again. 'Is that your answer?'

Eefay swung her other arm. Skaaha caught her wrist, held it. The grip was like a vice.

'Hit me again,' she said, 'and I will kill you.'

'Ha!' Eefay let out a shriek of joy. 'So there is some fight left in you.' She dropped her other hand to grip her sister's wrist, swung their arms up and turned. Skaaha shot over her shoulder. As she slammed on to the ground, Eefay knelt over her. 'Yield,' she said, twisting Skaaha's straightened arm, 'or I'll break it.'

Skaaha's legs swung up, her ankles crossed behind Eefay's neck, yanking her down. 'Not to you,' she swore. 'Never to you.'

As she toppled, Eefay tucked her chin into her chest, drawing her head free. At the same time, hands against Skaaha's backside to help momentum, she rolled her sister over and leapt to sit on Skaaha's back facing her feet. Yanking one ankle up across the back of Skaaha's knee, she pulled the other leg up to trap it there.

'Now yield,' she grunted, leaning back and working the leg she held by the ankle like a lever to create pain in her sister's knee.

'Aaah!' Skaaha's hands slapped the grass. 'I yield,' she yelled.

Eefay released her immediately, rolled over and lay on the grass, looking into Skaaha's face. 'Took you long enough,' she said, grinning.

'So you will teach me?'

''Course, can't have my sister defeated by men.'

The girls from the school's second broch arrived. Doon Trodden sat further into the valley, on the lower slope among the trees. Far enough from the sea to be safe from coastal raiders, Doon Telve stood in the river plain, surrounded by vast circles of flat ground suitable for training. Despite excitement about the new arrivals, when Donal appeared lines formed up immediately. The morning routines began. Skaaha and Ruan stripped and joined in. Although discipline didn't falter, it was soon obvious that he attracted more attention than she did.

Warriors began training in their thirteenth sun. Three suns later, they were apprenticed to a warrior chapter, where they matured as full masters of the martial art. The school heaved with pubescent fancies, most of which now targeted the druid. When they jumped in the river after the exercise period, the half-dozen oldest girls gravitated towards him, splashing, giggling and wrestling playfully with him and each other. A redhead with the warrior tattoo of maturity below her ear dived under the water and emerged in front of Skaaha, spouting water.

'Is he your man?' she asked, nodding towards the beleaguered Ruan.

'No.' Skaaha shook her head. 'He's my priest.'

'Then we won't fight over him,' the girl said. She smiled brightly, reminding Skaaha of Jiya. 'Luckily for you.' She began to wade away then turned back, touching the mark of the goddess on Skaaha's neck. 'Is this why you have a priest of your own?' she asked.

'I'm here to find that out,' Skaaha said. Among so many girls, mostly younger than herself, she was already wondering if she'd made a mistake. They were like puppies, constantly playing, leaping on anyone in reach, man or woman. Even when they talked or lazed around, they lay across each other, held hands, traded punches, linked arms, hugged. Their ease with physical proximity froze her.

At breakfast, the school's druids joined them to eat. Afterwards, Ruan left with them to be given a lodge. Weapon training began. She was handed a wooden shield. The smallest girl in the school opposed her, brandishing a wooden sword.

'Is this a game?' Skaaha snapped, annoyed.

'First you learn to keep that between you and your opponent's weapon,' Donal said. 'Then you learn to strike back.'

'I mean to strike first.' Skaaha threw down the shield. 'Give me a sword.'

'No,' Donal said.

Skaaha snatched at her opponent's. The girl swung. The wooden blade smacked the back of Skaaha's hand. The girl spun round behind her. The flat skelped across Skaaha's backside.

'Pick up your shield,' Donal said. 'Misha will keep hitting till you do.'

Skaaha grabbed the shield. She was faster than Misha, but to jump or somersault out of range would look as if she were running away, especially when the little minx was bound to follow. The shield was at least response. Misha landed one more blow, but it was the last. Skaaha parried every stroke and thrust.

'You're good,' Misha said, when they broke for midday dinner. 'Tomorrow you'll get someone better than me.'

'And a sword?'

'No,' Misha giggled. 'You work up, through everybody, till you can protect against spears and proper swords. Then you get a weapon, with a wooden blade.'

At dinner in the great room of the broch, Skaaha took Eefay aside. 'I asked you to teach me, not Donal.'

'Women don't teach women.'

'It's you I trust.' She gazed into Eefay's green eyes. If she was wrong, and her sister was the enemy, her life would end here in Glenelg.

'Donal does what I say now.' Eefay frowned. 'I thought you asked admission to the school.'

'It's yours?' Something shifted, but Skaaha wasn't sure what. She'd known Eefay was the heir. There were no surviving women on the Glenelg maternal blood-line, only Donal who, being a man, couldn't inherit. 'Since when?'

'Beltane.' Eefay glared at her. 'Of course, you wouldn't know because everything's about you. Well, not here. I'll train with you *if* you ever reach my grade. This is a school for warriors. There is no special treatment.' She went back to join the others round the low table.

Skaaha leant against the warm stone wall, watching her sister recline on furs and cushions to eat. The girl beside her, one of the seniors, stroked her arm in a gesture that spoke of closeness, a touch that Eefay allowed. One thing seemed more certain: her sister was not the enemy. Eefay was too honest in her joys, too open in her hostility. Misha came over with a horn of ale.

'Don't mind Eefay,' she said. 'I like you.'

Frustratingly, the afternoon was spent in lessons from the druids. There were three in the Glenelg cell, one of whom would now move to Kylerhea to take up Ruan's empty post, unless Suli moved them all around again. The students divided into groups, Skahaa again with the youngest, outside under trees, learning to recite.

'What is the point of this?' she railed.

The druid, another older, bearded one, had infinite patience. 'Discipline,' he said. 'A warrior must know thirteen books of poetry. It trains the mind.'

Thirteen? It would take for ever, when she must learn fast how to fight. But she did as instructed, choosing a branch of the tree, an ash, repeating the lines after the druid, in paired couplets like the leaves. The music of the words was like the rhythm of movement, smooth and flowing, while the meaning told of battles and heroism. They learned stanza by stanza, reciting together then individually. It was a long work, but when they finished, each of them could speak it faultlessly.

'I'll never see an ash tree again without that poem running through my head,' she complained to Ruan as they walked across the field going back to the broch.

'Not in this season,' he said.

'And you are smiling why?' she asked.

'Because that's the point,' he said. 'But there are four seasons, and more poems than trees.'

'Oh no,' she groaned. There was new leaf, summer leaf, autumn leaf, no leaf, maybe even flower and fruit, and the possibility of learning a poem with each, for every kind of tree. 'Don't even think of telling me how many poems make a book,' she warned. 'And I bet you know them all.'

He said nothing, but his smile deepened.

'All right,' she said, 'the sixth poem of the third book.'

'Out from the land of ice and snow,' he began, 'where the white bear stalks when chill winds blow . . .'

'You're making it up,' she interrupted. 'That's about winter, and I saw you look at that beech tree.'

'So I imagined it naked.' He grinned.

She leapt on him, wrapping her legs round his waist, grabbing his hair. 'You imagined a white bear too.' She shook his head from side to side. 'They're brown!'

'Or red, or black,' Ruan said. His arms had caught her, one wrapped around her waist, one under her buttocks. She stopped shaking his head. 'But the bard said white and so must I.' His voice had changed, quiet, deeper.

'Let me down,' she said, realizing what she'd done. He did, at once, her body sliding down his to stand before him. She looked into the darkening blue of his eyes. 'Don't hope for me to live.' Turning away, she went in alone to the evening meal.

When he followed, some time later and only after the woman druid went to fetch him, he sat with the other priests. Lana, the woman, sat beside him, talking. She was young, younger than he was, and good to look at. That's where he should go if he needed comfort, if he wanted sex.

'So you lied.' It was the redhead from the river, sitting next her.

'What?'

'You act like he's your man.' She carved a chunk of lamb, offering it.

'No,' Skaaha refused. 'And, no, I've no interest in men.'

The girl chuckled. 'Then you're in the right glen.' She put the lamb on Skaaha's server just the same, began to cut her own. 'We're the only place in Alba with too many women. Take your pick. Misha likes you.'

'She's not of age.'

'Not for men. But she's a warrior, first sun, so she'll do what she's told. After that, depends, you might have to fight for, or against.' She chuckled again, began to chew. 'I'm Terra, by the way, short for terror, because of my temper.'

Skaaha finished her food and ale. It seemed there might be

many reasons to keep her strength up. A short rest period followed the meal. Everyone sprawled, chattering or playing board games. Collecting one of the blind iron swords from the door-keeper, Skaaha went outside, practising against trees and shadows till the others came out. Weaponless hand-to-hand followed, so they stripped again. This time she was put with the middle grade, but only due to her height. The other girls complained at having to step out the moves so she could follow.

'It's good for all of you,' Donal silenced them, 'to have to think again about how you move and why.' To Skaaha, he explained. 'We fight naked because there's little to grip, apart from hair, and lime paste solves that.' The advantage of women over men was clear, even before he detailed it. Throwing opponents meant catching by the narrow parts, wrist, ankle, throat, where even oiled skin would not allow slip.

Already confident about rolling as she fell, Skaaha learned fast, blows coming at her from her opponent in slow motion so she could work out the throw. But when Donal upped the speed, she was lost, often winded by a kick or punch, more often slammed down on her back or belly, and trapped there, than on her feet.

'No contact blows,' Donal shouted. 'It's practice not contest.' Eventually, he intervened, calling her out while the others continued. 'Work with me,' he said, miming a punch, which she blocked and returned. 'Not even close,' he said. 'You don't move in. Try the throw.' He put his hand on her shoulder. 'Right, I've pushed you round to slice your head off. Catch my wrist. Turn your back into me. Into me, Skaaha.' His other arm pulled her in, buttocks tucked against his groin. 'Fighting or fucking,' he said in her ear, 'you must get close to do it. Bend your knees.'

She froze. 'I can't.' His genitals were not strapped, and already reacting.

'The longer you're tucked against me the more I'm going to like it.'

She bent her knees, pushed her other arm up through his and heaved. Nothing happened. He slapped her shoulder to let go then turned her body through the moves.

'Knees bend to get in, straighten to tuck your backside into my gut and lift my weight off the ground, roll forwards as you pull.' She tried again. Still he didn't pitch over. 'Again, faster.' And he was over her back, down in front, rolling and up on his feet because she forgot to follow through. 'Much better,' he said.

'You let me do it.'

'Again.' He grabbed her shoulder. She caught his wrist, turned, tucking into him, arm up behind, heaved, and he was down, and back on his feet. 'Again.' After six or seven, he stopped. 'How does that feel?'

'Better.'

'Strong men are slow,' he said. 'Speed, dexterity and deviousness are your best weapons. You've got the first two. The deviousness will come. But you won't rip a man's testicles off if you can't put your hands on them. Do something about that.'

Bruised and sore, Skaaha was glad of a final dip in the river. A round of ale and storytelling in the broch ended the day. The students returned to Doon Trodden. Skaaha settled into the chamber she'd been given in Doon Telve.

Too exhausted to unpack, she lay in the warm, smoky air staring at flickering shadows cast by the fire and stairwell lamps. She could hear snoring, murmured words, cries of pleasure, a cough, the sounds of love. It was like coming home, the great stone edifice with its familiar, near-forgotten curves. Her mother trained in this school, before Donal, under – she didn't know who, whoever his mother had engaged.

So much she didn't know, even about Kerrigen, who left Kylerhea to spend her youth in this broch, might even have lain in this chamber. Kerrigen, and Jiya, and . . . Mara. Someone wanted her dead, for eternity. Was it Mara? Childhood fears were not enough to justify the charge. The warrior queen could have killed her with impunity, asleep in Bride's cavern, and didn't. It might be anyone, for reasons she couldn't guess – someone she crossed or let down, a stranger wanting a trophy. Only one thing was certain, her enemy was a warrior. No one else would ask for the head.

28

Lunasa approached. The sun burned a hole in the sky. The Island of Wings sweltered in heat. Inside the squat fort, in the cooler shade of his quarters, Vass handed his newly arrived guest a horn of ale.

'This is a rare honour,' he said. 'The first time since Kerrigen that Ardvasar has been favoured by its queen.'

Mara swallowed a mouthful of the drink before she answered. 'Your tongue and tone don't please me, Vass,' she said. 'If you lose the first, the second might change.' While he apologized, she walked to the cold hearth, staring into dead ashes. A boy scurried in with a tray of food. 'I heard Kylerhea had a problem with intruders, again.' Her eyes rose to meet his. 'Maybe the great warrior, Vass, grows too old and slow to defend this corner.' She held his gaze as the threat struck home. The placement of warriors, and their command, was for her to dictate. 'Explain.'

So he told her, including what she already knew, that robbers had come during Beltane, the harm done was to Skaaha, everything taken was retrieved, the men killed. She made him repeat every detail of the court, the punishment, every word he could recall that the men had said in their defence, the manner of their dying.

'So Ard pulled the leader's tongue before the branding?'

'First, before castration. I held the man's head myself.'

Mara chewed on a piece of fruit. The agony of crushing was great. Bartok would have bartered her for a quick death if he'd been able to speak. 'That was unduly hasty. Pain loosens tongues. You might have learned more than you did.'

'I doubt there was more.' Vass shrugged. 'They were outsiders, taking advantage of empty homes. The other two said nothing different.'

'Then they deserved every pain-filled moment of their deaths,' she said, settling on the cushions, 'for their stupidity in being caught, if nothing else.' She'd cursed herself for carelessness since word had come to Doon Beck. The druids would have ordered her head if Bartok had breathed one word of her involvement. 'Come, sit.' She patted the goatskin next her, waited till he settled. 'I take it our little blacksmith is none the worse for her ordeal.'

'I don't know.' Vass wiped ale from his long moustache with the back of his hand. 'She's gone.'

'Gone!' The exclamation was too sharp, so she took a breath, lowered her pitch to normal. 'From Kylerhea? Gone where?'

Again, Vass shrugged. 'The druid took her. To Tokavaig, I think.'

Mara quelled her reaction. Beads of sweat prickled on her upper lip. The sanctuary was not a place she could go, nor one she could easily gain information from. But Skaaha's presence there meant she did not recover. Like her moon-crazed aunt, perhaps her mind had gone. 'Good,' she said, letting her mouth curve in a smile. 'At least she'll get the best of care.' The girl had distracted her long enough. The younger one, the warrior, was now the greater threat. But, as each sun passed, she grew easier to reach. Patience was all that was required. Mara stood to go.

'Stay the night,' Vass offered. 'The ride home will be cooler come morning. Give my men and your women the chance to be reacquainted.'

'Better your warriors spend time training,' Mara said, as he followed her out to the sunny forecourt. Brightness narrowed her eyes, the midday heat intense. 'The standards of this chapter have slipped. Be careful they don't slip further.' She mounted her waiting horse, called the women to order and rode off, hooves clattering over cobbles and out through the gates.

Vass shrugged sympathy to his bewildered men and went back inside. Jiya had emerged from the room she'd vanished into to avoid the warrior queen. She stood by the hearth, staring down at the half-drunk ale, the barely touched food. Her head came up when he entered.

'Touching,' she snorted, 'her concern for Skaaha.'

'It's a first,' he agreed. Long ago, as Glenelg tutor, he'd trained both Mara and Kerrigen, and later, Jiya. 'Cunning and jealous, that's Mara. I brought her to womanhood, but even in the ring of fire it was Kerrigen's reception the previous Beltane that consumed her.' He'd felt sorry for the young warrior, unable to enjoy her triumphs, always watching her rival, while Kerrigen, focused on the task, streaked ahead. In the end, despite considerable talent, Mara had defeated herself. Now, by force of accident, her desire was achieved. 'I doubt she cares for Kerrigen's daughter, but that rivalry is dead and gone.'

'Until she threatened Skaaha in Bride's cavern. And there's something else, something more.' Jiya gripped her head. 'When the druids put this hole in my skull they took it from me.'

'Don't push, Jiya.' Rebellion against the chain of command couldn't be countenanced. 'Bracadale upholds Mara. No man can lead against the queen.'

'Yet you didn't tell her Skaaha was at Glenelg.'

'Must've slipped my mind.' Vass stroked his moustache. 'Put it down to being old and slow. Everything goes, like my standards.' He tipped the tray of food into the dead hearth. 'She'll find out soon enough.'

At Glenelg, the final night of Lunasa was dedicated to gambling and drink. Around the low table in Doon Telve's great room, Donal raised the last drinking horn of the night.

'Who lives for ever?' he shouted.

'We do!' the students roared back, raising their drinks.

'What do you seek?' Donald called again.

'Death in glory!' The toast was drunk by draining the horns. Everybody struggled to their feet and set off for their respective quarters.

In her chamber, Skaaha stripped for bed. She'd done well in the festival games, except for riding chariots. The school had four, one of which was Eefay's, inherited from Kerrigen, and four charioteers – strong young men who drove while the girls took turns on board, throwing javelins at straw targets. Skaaha's inexperience had gone against her, the difficulty of working with a partner. The curtain on her chamber shifted. Terra came in.

'Shouldn't you be back in Doon Trodden?' Skaaha asked.

'Donal sent me.' The redhead pulled off her tunic. In the gloom her breasts looked even whiter than they did outdoors. 'To teach you the rules.'

'What rules? I'm going to bed.'

'Those rules.' Terra wriggled out of her leggings. 'The rules of fucking for warriors.' She paused to grin widely up at Skaaha. 'He said you shied away from the charioteers, even while drinking, so I should work my magic instead.' She stood up, ran her hands over her bosom and down her belly. 'Nice, huh?'

'Your body's beautiful, Terra, but I don't want pleasure. I'm here to work.'

'Ah, but that's the first rule. Warriors drink and fuck as hard as they fight. We don't live long. There's a lot to fit in.' She sat down on the bed, rolling over to leave space for Skahaa beside her. 'Don't worry. I won't force you. We can just sleep. It's not like you owe me a forfeit.'

'What, then I'd have to?' Skaaha eased herself on to the edge of the bed, stretching out, the girl's arm a ridge behind her neck.

''Course. Is there some kind of forfeit you don't have to pay?' She put her hand round Skaaha's waist, yanked her properly on to the bed. 'You'll fall out.'

Their skin touched all the way down the length of their bodies. The redhead's breast lay on Skaaha's arm. The still air stifled, the broch too warm.

'Go home,' Skaaha said. 'It's too hot.'

Terra's head tucked on to her shoulder. 'Hot's good,' she said. 'Donal wants you warmed up. Cuddling would be a start.' Her fingers traced the pale white scars on Skaaha's left breast, round and round. 'That's pretty, you know.'

'The scar?' Skaaha gazed down at Terra's hand. Anger grew in her. 'Don't you know how I got it?'

'Mostly. I was there when you had their heads off. We all were.' Between comments, she kissed Skaaha's other breast, playing the nipple with her tongue. 'You're our hero, don't you know?' Her hand caressed Skaaha's ribs, her belly. 'There isn't anything we wouldn't do for you.'

'Except stop touching me?' It was strange, because she didn't really care. Her body was just that – a body, not her, nothing to do with her.

'All right.' Terra wriggled up the bed a little, reached over and pulled Skaaha's arm around her. 'You touch me then.' It was their noses that touched, bodies pressed together, the heat creating beads of perspiration between them.

'I can't.' The words came out like a cry for help. She couldn't move away either. Breasts pressed against hers. Hands stroked her shoulders, spine. Another heart beat on her ribs. The soft skin of their bellies touched, rising and falling with each breath, sticking together then peeling away. Her arms went round the other girl's neck. Their faces touched. Cheeks rubbed together. Her mouth made little kisses on Terra's, wanting something human to happen, to reach her.

'You can't die either,' Terra whispered, meeting each small kiss, 'with your body remembering those men. Make better memories for it.'

A groan that might have been despair welled up from Skaaha's throat as she rose above the girl, deepening the kiss, lips parting, pressing into, tongues touching, tasting. Her body

262

covered Terra's. Under her, the redhead eased on to her back. It became the most urgent need to touch and stroke and kiss, to explore the smooth, warm skin of this excited and exciting lover, to spread those pale thighs and let her fingers discover how the flesh of a woman felt to touch, to enter and be enveloped by.

'Am I like this?' Amazement filled her, feeling moist muscled strength, the clenching tremor. The need to give of herself into this woman rose, irresistible.

'You bet,' Terra murmured. Threading her fingers through Skaaha's, she moved their two hands, linked, between Skaaha's thighs, parting the lips of her vulva, playing around the damp, swollen clitoris. 'See,' she breathed, and eased their joined hands back till both middle fingers pushed gently into the firm wet warmth of Skaaha's cunt. 'Feel for yourself. As beautiful as I am.'

In his chamber on the other side of the broch, Donal lay uncomfortably awake, aroused and wishing he'd had the foresight to fill his own bed for the night. Skaaha promised to be the most talented student he'd ever taught. She'd come with physical strength honed from long hours in the forge and, like Eefay, a lifetime's practice in dexterity of movement on the ground and in the air. All he need do was translate those into battle skills. But tension made her rigid, not caring who touched her but not participating, not freely, fully engaging her body. From the sounds he couldn't help but hear, Terra was making the first steps towards loosening that grip.

Skaaha woke at dawn, legs tangled with the other girl's, the taste of sex still on her lips. A lover's sense of power lifted her spirit. She, with her hands, mouth and body, had brought a woman to the peak of ecstasy, holding her through that extraordinary intimacy. In the gloom of the broch, she stared at the sleeping face beside her. Wonder lit her mind. Her body had felt pleasure, and survived. There was nothing ugly inside her. The shame of being female was gone. Sliding out of bed, she grabbed her shift, tiptoed downstairs and ran outside to tumble and cartwheel over dew-wet grass. The mauve mist of morning rang with birdsong. She was a woman in a woman's body, beautiful and alive.

As the students began to arrive, Terra appeared. Skaaha hurried to her side.

'Will you come back tonight?' she asked.

'Can't.' Terra yawned. 'I promised to fuck with Donal. My reward, or his, I'm not sure which.' She grinned. 'Good, weren't we? Now get yourself a man. Rub out all that stuff you didn't want. Oh' – about to cross to the park, she turned back – 'except in the middle of your moon, when you're truly desperate. That's when women are best. You don't get with child then.'

Skaaha stared after her as the redhead went to warm up for the morning routines. Then she ran back to snatch up her shift from the grass, hauling it over her head, all fingers and thumbs. Donal called as she ran away from the broch. He could wait. She needed Ruan. He might be up and gone, and she didn't know where he did his morning practice now. He hadn't joined the school again since their first day. Running towards the druid huts among the trees, she shouted his name, repeatedly.

The door of the middle lodge opened, and he stood looking at her, tousle-haired from sleep.

'Ruan,' she gasped, running up to him. 'You need to do something for me.' She pulled him back inside, and stopped. There was someone in his bed.

'What is it?' Ruan asked.

It was Lana, the female druid, awake, beginning to rise.

'I didn't know you were busy.' Skaaha turned to go. 'I'll come back.'

'It's all right.' He was quite unperturbed. 'What's wrong?'

Lana, equally unperturbed, pulled her robe on. She was very pretty, more rounded than a warrior. 'I'm going anyway,' she

264

said pleasantly. 'You'll have peace to talk.' She smiled at Skaaha. 'We're honoured to have you with us.' Her hand squeezed Ruan's arm as she walked past. The door closed behind her.

'Skaaha?' Ruan prompted.

'What was she doing here?' Skaaha's thumb jerked towards the door. 'Is this your morning practice now?' Fury, real, burning fury, raged in her gut.

'So that's what you're here for.' He went to the hearth, and ladled hot liquid into two cups. 'To discuss who shares my bed?' He offered one of the cups. 'I stopped being celibate when you came of age.'

Skaaha smacked the cup away. Steaming liquid arched through the air. The cup clattered into shelves of potted herbs. It wasn't allowed to rip the head off a druid. Not his, and not hers. 'I came because I haven't bled since before Beltane.' Her teeth grated together. Fists clenched, her breath came hard.

'You're certain?' He looked puzzled, as if he couldn't understand the terror of that. 'You were given something at Tokavaig to make sure you did.'

'Then it didn't work! What kind of fool do you think I am?'

'Not any kind.' He was smiling, tried to hide it by taking up his own cup. As he turned with it in his hand, she swatted it away to join the other.

'Three moons,' she said. 'Be grateful I'm not allowed to kill you!'

'Your restraint is remarkable,' he said, but his grin widened and he began to chuckle then to laugh. 'If I'm to help you,' he got out, 'we'll need cups.'

She spun round him, pushed her foot into the back of his knee then raised it to stamp his back as he dropped, but he turned as he fell, caught her ankle and brought her down. Her weight landed on top of him. Throwing her leg across him, she lunged to grab his head. Her teeth grazed his cheek as he rolled them over, bodyweight heavy on her chest, his legs between hers, hands pinned either side of her head.

'How did you ever think you were not a warrior?' he asked. Risking being bitten, he dropped a kiss on her nose, then her mouth. 'You were with a woman yourself last night.'

'How do you know?' she snapped, moving her hips to shift the clothes that were between them, the skin of his thigh touching hers.

'I can taste her.'

How easily she might throw him off. 'I don't want to hurt you!' she yelled. Her body writhed, arching against his.

'If there's something you do want' – he struggled to hold her – 'ask.'

'I want to fuck!' she screamed into his face.

His mouth came down on hers. Hands released, she grabbed his head, meeting the brutality of his kiss as if starved for it. Fire surged through her, flaring, hot waves. Hungry to be filled, her cunt swelled, ached, body urging him into, breath gasping at the ferocity of the thrust.

'This won't help,' she groaned, her voice cracking, arms holding tight in case he should go, or stop, rocking to draw him deeper, deeper, deeper in.

'It will' – his voice hard – 'help us both' – husky, at her ear – 'a lot.'

When the wildness subsided, they lay, wrung out, on cushions by the hearth, hands still finding skin to speak through touch, murmuring nonsense words till they returned to themselves.

'You see?' he asked. Some moments were for ever, and this was one, already passing. 'We can feel too much.' The weight of her head lay on his shoulder. 'Now the balance is restored.' Her fingers pressed into the grooves of his ribs.

'There's more, Ruan.' Her head shifted against his arm to look at him. 'I'm not safe.'

'Here' – he frowned – 'or with me?'

Her eyes searched his, as if she looked for an answer in him. 'With myself.' She moved her head to rest her cheek against his chest, listening to his heartbeat.

He kissed the crown of her head. The distance between them returned. Some part of her, unreachable, closed off. 'Good or bad, we make our own feelings. It's our spirit speaking, to guide us.'

'Mine belongs to Bride.' Her voice was muffled, sorrowful. 'I trust no one.'

'That will change. Go on with your training' – this was the moment of dread, where his priesthood was affirmed or abandoned – 'and take other lovers.'

She raised herself, looking down at him. 'Terra said that too.'

'Warrior wisdom.' There was a deal of truth in it. 'Slay your ghosts or they slay you.' Time, the flow of stillness, was the true gift. 'Embrace it.' He shifted a strand of hair that had fallen across her eyes. 'Loving should come as easily as breath, and be as sweet.'

'I know.' She rose, pulling down the crumpled shift. 'Will you give me something to make me bleed?'

'If you're certain.'

'Three moons, what else could it be?'

He stood, went to his shelves, keeping his back to her so his distress would not be seen. 'The child might be mine, from the ring of fire.'

'Or not,' she said. 'The odds are against it.' It was said matter-of-fact, the die already cast. 'I need my body fit to fight.' Her thoughts had moved on.

'It's better fresh,' he said, assembling dried feverfew and pennyroyal, juniper oil. 'I'll find some, and prepare it.' He turned, walked with her to the door. 'Come back this evening. You'll need to stay till it works. There will be pain, maybe vomiting. Better if I'm with you.'

She nodded, put her hand on his chest, over his heart. 'I'll have a child for you some day,' she vowed, 'when the time is right.' Then she left, swinging down the track through the trees, heading back to Doon Telve and the training ground.

He watched her go, a shifting shadow among silver-birch

trunks and backlit leaves of translucent green, caught now and again in shafts of sun. 'Live the day well, Skaaha.' He called the warrior farewell.

Reaching the edge of the treeline, she turned and waved.

29

It was Sowen, blood harvest and festival of the dead. Kylerhea was crowded with guisers in strange attire. Up on Carlin's Loup, the bonfire blazed. On hills around the islands, across and down through Alba, chains of fire linked the whole druid world in celebration.

'Look at you!' Jiya hollered, jumping off her horse and striding to grab Skaaha by the shoulders. 'Quite the woman.'

'For some time.' Skaaha grinned, throwing her arms round her aunt. She had been home for several days, working in the forge. It felt good to be back among the loved and familiar, doing what she did best. 'I moved up to second sun training.'

'Already?' Jiya shrieked, dancing her round in a jig. 'Ho, Ard,' she shouted over her shoulder, 'we need drink, some of Lethra's finest mead, to celebrate.'

They went inside to talk. It was late. Only the young still jigged around the flames. Most revellers staggered or dragged themselves to bed. Determined to catch Skaaha on this rare visit home, Jiya had abandoned the Ardvasar warriors.

'We're patrolling Loch Eishort and Loch Slapin coasts,' she explained, as they settled round the glowing hearth. 'The sails of raider ships were seen.'

'Mara should set up a chapter there,' Skaaha said. 'The north is well protected, but she leaves Torrin undefended. They could strike right to the island's heart.'

'Tactical defences too?' Jiya queried, impressed. 'Vass grumbles plenty, but it's a brave man who'd give the spiteful one advice. Oh' – she spluttered mead – 'she hopes you're well.'

'Mara does?'

'With her tongue slit,' Ard said. 'Does she know about Glenelg?'

Jiya shook her head. 'Thinks our little goddess languishes at Tokavaig.'

'No one here knew,' Erith added, joining them, 'till today. But word travels. People go home from festivals and gossip.'

'It's not a secret,' Skaaha objected. 'If she doesn't like it, what can she do?'

'Tell Donal not to train you!' Jiya yelped.

Skaaha gazed at her aunt. Jiya was loud, eyes huge, staring, wilder than she'd been for some time, since before the druids opened her skull. 'Can she do that?' The students were mostly mainland.

'Donal's warrior allegiance is to the island,' Jiya assured her, 'or the school wouldn't stand where it does.'

'Most things are best kept secret from Mara,' Ard said, topping up their drinking horns. 'She knew more about those outsiders than she should.' A blast of questions greeted this. 'At Beltane, she said half of them were killed here,' he explained. 'By you' – he nodded at Jiya – 'that Sowen. *Half*,' he repeated.

'Three of them in one attack.' Jiya thumped her chest. 'I should've got the rest then too.' She banged her fist on the hearthstone.

'Did you know there were three more?' Skaaha asked, staring at Ard.

'Not till' – he dropped his gaze – 'not till we returned from Beltane.' He stirred the fire for no apparent reason then his eyes met hers again. 'But Mara did.'

Erith glanced uneasily from one to the other. 'It means nothing. One word? There could be more of them, another two, three, five, somewhere else.' She got up, agitated. 'Don't make trouble where there is none, Ard. Let it go. I'll fetch food.' She left for the larder.

'Are we in trouble?' Jiya asked. 'Is that what's flapping her skirts?'

'She's fretful.' Ard put an arm round Skaaha's shoulders. 'We're expecting another baby, before next Beltane.' He squeezed his daughter reassuringly. 'Erith will be right. There's nothing to fear.'

Yet Erith, like Jiya and Ard, didn't want Mara to know she was at Glenelg. 'Why do you think they were the same men? The court didn't' – Skaaha clutched at straws while, out of the bog, a sleeper rose, face leering into hers, a face she knew – 'or they'd have lost a hand each instead of being branded.'

Ard took her to the forge to see the pattern of the tattoo. 'Don't know why I keep it,' he said. 'Maybe in case there are more.' He put it down in front of her. 'I copied it from one of their bodies the first time,' he said. 'And the ringleader –'

'Had the same one,' Skaaha interrupted. She'd forgotten the first tattoo, if she'd even noticed as a child what Ard did and why, but she'd never forget Bartok's.

Ard nodded. 'I saw him at Torrin, looking at that dagger you made, but staring at you. When Gern remembered the design, we searched for him. Mara didn't want to look for petty thieves. That's when she said we had already killed half their number. But they'd gone, come here, only we didn't know that then.' He bowed his head.

'I didn't know any of this.' Shadows leapt in the forge. Cut-eye had talked about Beltane. *Half their number.* 'Why didn't you tell me?'

He turned away. 'You were in no fit state.'

'Hey.' Seeing his broad shoulders heave, she wrapped her arms round him, rested her cheek on his back. 'Don't, Dad. It's all right.'

'It's not all right, Skaaha.' Sobs shook him. 'It will never be all right.'

'No, it won't be,' she said, holding him. They had made her father ashamed of masculinity, reducing him and every man, just as they'd made her nothing, of no account, a thing to vent hatred on, to despise. It was an illusion that she lived again. Loving others didn't warm the cold, hard knot inside. Her purpose was to wreak revenge. She couldn't let Ard know he'd named the cause of it. He suspected, but she held the final piece – *Don't waste the head* – the danger too great to share it. *It's wanted.* Bartok and his men were at Beltane. They sailed straight from Torrin to Kylerhea to lie in wait, thinking they had a protector. *Druids – can't touch us.* The warrior queen had sent them to bring back her head. Her enemy was Mara.

Unable to keep still, Jiya had gone by morning, back to rejoin the Ardvasar men. The smell of roasting pork from blood harvest wafted round the village. Skaaha was also leaving. The sword she'd come there to make hung at her side, perfectly balanced in weight, length and grip so that it felt like an extension of her arm. Gern had decorated the scabbard with the ruby-studded triquetra of Danu.

'Stay for the feast,' Kaitlyn begged. 'Help me jump the fire.' She'd come to trade iron from her bog for tools and spend the festival with her foster-son, her own belly finally swollen with pregnancy.

'Can't,' Skaaha said. Nor could she speak the truth. It endangered anyone who knew it. 'I've training to do. Have to make my own luck.'

'And you're not crazed?'

'No.' She hugged her friend tightly. They might not meet again.

'Who'd have thought,' Kaitlyn said, 'after all our nonsense up in the cavern, we'd become responsible adults.' They were both transformed – Kaitlyn to farmer, Skaaha to warrior.

'Speak for yourself,' Skaaha corrected. 'Erith thinks I'm less respectable.' She turned to Lethra, too old and stiff now for leaping bonfires. 'Kenna is only half the Carlin you made,' she told her. The noman's love of sparkling jewellery spoiled the stern illusion.

'Away with your bone-crushing,' Lethra grumbled, pushing off her embrace, though only after she squeezed the warrior within an inch of her life.

Young Calum danced around. 'Are you still a goddess?' he

asked, and when Skaaha assured him she was, he grabbed her wrist. 'Can I tell you a secret?' She bent down to hear it. 'I saw Bride once,' he whispered, his breath making her ear moist. 'She's real, real as you are.'

'I know,' she whispered back. 'Blessings on your house.'

'That's what she said,' he squeaked. 'That's just what she said.'

Outside the house, Ard waited to walk with her to the jetty. 'There is a place for heroes,' he said. In his hands he held a bronze, oval shield. 'A gift.'

It was beautifully ornamented, with three embossed circles, the basis for the triquetra, studded with ruby stones, the circle of the central boss larger than those at each end. It was also beautifully made, the precise thickness of metal to provide protection, lined with hide – strong but not heavy. It was a shield that might be given to a warrior on maturation, but not while training. He had worked on it a long time. She met his eyes, dark as hers, unable to speak.

Erith, busy directing the seasonal cleaning of the house, bustled out to say goodbye. 'You're laden already,' she tutted. 'Do you want this?' She held out a slim bundle wrapped in tattered blue cloth. 'It was under your bed.'

'Ach,' Skaaha swore. 'I could've asked Jiya about that again.' She tucked it into her pack. 'It's for Eefay.' They exchanged hugs. 'Blessings for the baby.'

'Come back and be a smith,' Erith said. 'You're far too talented to waste it on the rough life of a warrior.'

'Some day.' Waving to the others, she walked with Ard to the crossing. He was quiet, sombre. 'There's a small forge at the school I can use,' she said, hoping to cheer him.

'To sharpen blades is all,' he said. 'You're more gifted than that. Will you come home for Imbolc?'

'I'll be back when I can fight.' They stopped on the jetty, held each other for the longest time. Waves washed the rocks. Eagles called in the skies above. 'Don't worry for me. When I've done what I have to do, I'll be a smith again.'

'In this world, or the next?'

'You look forward to that baby.' She stepped into the coracle, sitting quickly to grip the sides so it didn't pitch her out. 'A brother would be nice.'

All the way across, she watched him standing watching her as they both shrank away from each other. He knew, of course he knew, and that she'd need shield, goddess and more on her side. Mara was a master warrior, unbeatable by a novice, and in her prime. Even when she thanked the boatman and collected her horse from the stable on the opposite shore, her father still stood, watching till she disappeared into the Alba hills.

Riding up to Doon Telve in the autumn sunshine, Skaaha saw Eefay perched on the surrounding wall outside the broch, rubbing cedar oil into Cut-eye's head. There was relief in the safety of Glenelg, at her sister's easy approach to life.

'That looks good,' she called, dismounting and slapping the horse on through the doorway. The empty eye-sockets stared. The scar added an air of menace.

'Better looking dead than alive,' Eefay agreed. 'You're back early. Come to jump our fire?' She leapt down from the wall to admire her sister's sword and shield.

'No.' She had no future to jump into. Shaking off her pack, she crouched and pulled out the cloth-wrapped bundle. 'I brought something for you.'

Eefay squatted beside her. 'A broken spear?' she queried as Skaaha unrolled the bundle. 'What do I want with that?' She picked up the two pieces, held them, useless, one in each hand.

'I don't know,' Skaaha admitted. She'd kept them for so many suns, waiting for Jiya to explain, and when she did it made no sense. 'Jiya wanted us to have them. She said we were two pieces, and you had the answer.'

The sound of hooves clattered through the paved hallway behind them.

'To one of Jiya's riddles? I don't think so.' Eefay rose, looking at the broken weapon, perplexed. 'Did she say anything else?'

Donal, dressed for travel, led a saddled horse out of the broch. 'How did you manage that?' he asked, mounting up.

'I didn't break it,' his daughter protested. 'Jiya sent it, broken already.'

'Why would she do that?' he said, taking the spearhead half of the shaft from Eefay's hands to look at it. 'Especially when it's not hers. She likes a longer point.'

Skaaha got to her feet. 'Then who did it belong to?' She had sacrificed Kerrigen's in the loch.

'See that spiralling running down the rib?' Donald showed them. It was hard to discern under the rust. 'Only one of them has that design. It's Mara's, or was.' He gave it back to Eefay. 'Useless now, unless you sharpen it and fix a new shaft.' Reminding his daughter he'd be gone till the quarter-moon, he heeled the horse and rode off, cantering away towards the coast.

The air beat in Skaaha's ears. She'd brought a haunting with her.

'It's good Jiya's crazy,' Eefay said, 'or Mara would kill her for breaking her spear. No wonder she hid it.' She handed the pieces back. 'If I were you, I'd throw it in the pit.' Stooping, she scooped up the tattered blue cloth. 'And this with it.'

Kya . . . Kya . . . Kya . . . a golden eagle shrieked overhead.

'I can't.' The shadow of the bird crossed the grass. 'Not now.'

Holding it with both hands, Eefay shook the material out. 'Is this Kerrigen's?' she asked. Puzzled green eyes looked at Skaaha. 'It's from a sash cloak.' She held it, crumpled, to her face. Any smell of their mother was long gone. Her eyes filled with tears. 'What's going on? Why are you here? Why' – her voice broke, fingers clenching the torn strip – 'is *this* here?'

'I don't know. I didn't know the spear was Mara's.' Dread had followed her. Mara's reach was long, her power unassailable.

Skaaha hunkered down beside her pack. 'We better talk,' she said, patting the grass for Eefay to join her.

'You're scaring me,' her sister said, clutching the cloth, 'with ghosts.'

'Not ghosts,' Skaaha said, 'the living. It's not Jiya that Mara wants dead.' She paused. Trust did not come easily. Blood might not prove thicker than the danger she asked Eefay to embrace. 'It's me.'

'What!' Eefay exclaimed. 'Are you crazed?'

Sitting on the grass at the foot of the wall while, above them, Cut-eye's oiled head browned slowly in the sunshine, Skaaha told her sister what she'd learned at Kylerhea. 'Someone sent them for my head,' she concluded. 'Now I know who.'

'Blessed Bride,' Eefay swore. 'Mara?' She began to rise. 'We better get the druids. You have to tell them this.'

'It's not enough!' Skaaha said, forcefully pulling her down again. 'She'd deny it then claim my life as forfeit.'

'But why kill you and not me? We're both' – Eefay clutched the strip of blue cloth – 'Kerrigen's daughters . . .' Her voice tailed away.

'Two pieces.' Skaaha picked up the broken spear. 'Maybe Jiya meant to warn us.' The threat to Eefay steadied her courage, just as it had that day on the shore when the warriors came out of the fog, while the dogs howled in it, and Mara sat high on her horse, looking down on them. It was easier to be strong for someone else.

Eefay played the tattered fabric between her fingers. 'Kerrigen wasn't killed with a spear.'

'No, she raced Mara in their chariots. It was an accident.' The image of Kerrigen's chamber at Doon Beck returned to remind her. The guttering lamplight, her mother reaching out – *Skaa-haa*. 'Her skull was broken.'

'And Jiya said nothing else about this?' Eefay held out the stained blue rag.

Taking it, re-wrapping the broken spear, Skaaha struggled to recall. 'Just clucked her tongue, over and over, and got very agitated.' There was more though. She knew there was more, but it was buried in Jiya's distressed brain.

'So what should we do?'

'You can teach me,' Skaaha said. There was only one course, one way forward. 'The right of vengeance is mine. When I'm ready, I'll challenge her.'

'This is Mara you have to fight!' Eefay exclaimed. 'She'll take the head off you without breaking sweat.'

'Then you can avenge me.' It wasn't said in jest, but the bald temerity of her assumption made them both smile.

'If it takes a hundred circles of the sun,' Eefay promised. She leapt to her feet, held out a hand to haul her sister up. 'We better work.'

'She doesn't know where I am.' It was the one thing in her favour. 'We've got time.'

'Not now, we haven't,' Eefay said, her green eyes clouded with concern. 'It's Sowen. Donal went to Doon Beck to train the Bracadale warriors. He'll tell Mara you're here. He's got no reason not to.'

30

'This is why I like you, Donal,' Mara groaned. 'Always ready to please a queen.' She was astride him, naked, in her chamber at Doon Beck, pitched forward so his hands could reach her breasts. His brief marriage to Kerrigen was the reason she bedded him. It excited her, deeply, to mount and master this man whose body once pleasured the great, and long dead, warrior. Covering his mouth with hers, she rocked her hips, biting his lip, drawing blood.

'Honouring you,' he muttered, 'is why I live.'

'Believe it,' she agreed, rolling over and guiding him down till his head was between her thighs, his tongue pleasuring her. Blessed goddess, he was good at this. She grabbed his hair, moaning and panting. Donal moved her in ways no other man or woman ever did. His skin and touch and flesh and hands and mouth spoke achingly to hers. If he'd never been Kerrigen's she might have made a husband of him, for a time. Since he had, it pleased her more to make him serve without reward.

'Now,' she breathed, 'come into me now,' feeling the bed dip as he moved, her flesh shuddering as he did.

She roared, bit his shoulder, clinging on, nails raking his back. The agonizing loss of self, and control, shook out through her, going on and on as he drove for his own climax, his seed spurting into her, giving her everything he'd ever given Kerrigen – except a child. Weakness, her own neediness, wanted to howl out of her, wanted to rest in his arms, held and comforted. But the fleeting moment of trust had already passed. He'd dallied on his way here, spent the last night of Sowen with his foster-mother at Doon Torvaig rather than with her.

'Get off.' She pushed him over. 'You're heavy.'

'Sorry.' He lay beside her on the bed, limp, damp. The smell of sex rose between them. 'I missed seeing you at Lunasa,' he said. It sounded rehearsed, unconvincing, like everything else he said, like his reason for arriving for the morning session instead of with the new moon last night.

'We were out on patrol, down at Ardvasar.' She got up, drank some ale, began to dress. She'd taken him into her chamber half-way through the midday meal. Fucking Donal didn't take long. There would be time for afternoon training before dark. 'Tell me about Eefay,' she said. 'Her training must be complete. You've had her with you long enough.'

'She's good – very,' he agreed. 'Wants to start training boys soon.'

'I bet she does,' Mara said. Over recent suns, fewer boys came to train with her at Doon Beck. Yet they had flocked to Kerrigen.

'We'll house them in Doon Trodden, bring the girls into Doon Telve.'

'Then she had better do her maturation first.' Mara strapped on her sword. He made it easy, setting it up. 'Send her to me, when you go back.'

'What?' Donal sat up. 'You'll apprentice Eefay to Bracadale?' For once, his pleasure seemed genuine.

'That's what I said.' She slapped his shoulder. 'Did you come to train warriors or lie in bed?'

'She's advanced enough.' Donal grabbed his leggings, pulling them on hurriedly. 'And the honour is great. But she's not come of age yet.'

'With you as her father?' Mara hooted with derision. 'I expect she's had every farmer's son in Glenelg, after she tired of girls and charioteers.' The insult to the men of Alba, that they fucked with children, stopped Donal, swaying, in mid-dress. Mara swept aside the curtain, crossing to the stairs.

'She wants to do it properly.' He caught up with her halfway down the stone steps. 'At Beltane, in the ring of fire.' They crossed the stockroom, heading for the doorway. 'She wants to be the goddess.'

'Of course she does.' Outside, the women were assembled, waiting. 'She can do that from here.' There would be no discussion. Eefay would come under her command, where any ambition the girl might harbour could be controlled, or ended. 'My numbers are still short from losing those two in the spring.'

'Then you might have Skaaha too, given another sun.' Donal clapped his hands to bring the women to attention. 'Sword work, dressed,' he shouted, 'with shields.' On the field, the ten warriors paired off. 'Let me see what you can do then we'll pick up the slack.'

Ice flooded Mara's veins. Her hand, resting on the hilt of her sheathed sword, tightened round it. Cold metal dug into her fingers. 'Skaaha?' Bartok was sent to prevent this. Swords and shields clashed, clattering. The air rung, iron on steel.

Donal glanced at her, nodded. 'She came to us before High Sun. Works like one demented, learns fast, the best novice I ever had. Might even outstrip Eefay, given time.' He turned back to the field, raising his voice. 'You're playing,' he yelled. 'Take more space. Show me some blood lust!'

Behind him, Mara drew her sword.

Swords rung on the field at Glenelg. Skaaha's spun out of her hand.

'Shield,' Eefay shouted, chopping towards her neck. The shield came up, just, the blow on it dropping Skaaha to one knee. Eefay stopped. 'Now you're dead, because I won't let you up again.'

'So what do I do?'

'Stay down.' Eefay stopped her rising. 'You tell me – what can you do?'

'Keep the shield covering my neck and torso. Stay close so you can't get a good swing.'

'Good, because instinct will try to make you move away. What else?'

'Draw my dagger, stab your leg.'

'If you're fast. I won't be standing still.'

'Yank your ankle first?'

'Only if my weight's not balanced on it, and if you stretch any distance your hand's off.'

Skaaha straightened up. 'I don't like those choices.' She walked to pick up her sword. 'What would you do?'

'Maybe this.' Eefay sheathed her sword, raised her shield, copying Skaaha's movement, but as she dropped to one knee she brought her shield arm down on to the ground, tumbling over it and leaping to her feet again. 'Then you're out of range before your opponent can swing again. You can run away or get your sword.'

'I like that better,' Skaaha said, trying the move. It was awkward with the shield, like tumbling with a server plate, easy to break that arm for want of practice.

'Speed,' Eefay encouraged. 'Be faster than your opponent or be dead. Or' – she wasn't finished – 'if it's close fighting, too many others around, don't go down in the first place. I'll show you.' She drew her sword, threw it down. 'Swing at me.'

Skaaha swung her sword, aiming for Eefay's throat. Her sister's shield came up, swept the blow aside. An arm grabbed round her neck. A knee thumped her groin.

'A man drops,' Eefay said as Skaaha grunted. 'I'd have my sword back and his head off before he stopped squealing. Get right in close where their sword is useless. Rip their nose off with your teeth. Poke their eyes out. Use your knees, teeth, hands and dagger. Don't linger, they might be stronger than you. Go in fast, do what damage you can, throw them if possible, then go for your sword.'

They tried again. This time, as Eefay's shield swept the swordstroke aside, her fist crashed into Skaaha's jaw. Before she'd time to collect her wits, Eefay's sword was recovered and at her throat.

Eefay threw it down again. 'Now swing again.'

Skaaha swung, this time slicing downwards. Her sister stopped the blow, but the force made her duck. The ball of her foot thumped into Skaaha's gut, then she was gone. Skaaha straightened up, breathless. Solid metal clattered off the back of her skull. Ears ringing, Skaaha staggered. Eefay had spun round behind to whack her with the shield.

'All right already,' she groaned when Eefay reappeared in front of her, sword poised. 'I get the point.'

'So next time, do something and do it fast. Attack, don't expect mercy. You won't get any from Mara.'

Donal turned from watching the warriors as he heard the swish of Mara's sword leaving its sheath. He saw his death in her eyes before she swung the blade, heard the air whoop as it slashed.

'What are you doing?' he gasped, the words chopped off as the weapon sliced into his neck, severing windpipe through to the spine.

'Closing your school,' Mara snarled, yanking the sword back. Blood spurted, pumping from the gash.

Donal's body dropped, head tilted, dangling from white tendons and pink flesh, to the grass. His dead limbs writhed, twitching. The clash of swords on shields rippled to silence like a pot breaking into scattered shards over cobbled stones. Ten women stared as their queen thrust her sword into the earth before returning it, clean, to the scabbard.

'War council, now!' Mara ordered. Marching down the slope to Doon Beck, she pushed past beasts and herders returning for the night. 'We've had a death,' she snapped at the door-keeper. 'Send someone to deal with it.'

'Weapons,' the man reminded her, holding out his hand to take hers.

'Don't annoy me,' she warned. 'But see the others leave theirs.'

Upstairs, she snapped her fingers at the pot-boy for ale and tossed back a full horn before the first of her warriors arrived. It was Corchen, second-in-command, older and slower than the others.

'What happened?' she asked as soon as she came in.

Turning her back, Mara walked to the opposite doorway, the steps leading to the roof. Corchen's presence meant some discussion kept the others on the field. Donal had trained them since Kerrigen had been queen. He was liked and would be missed.

'Mara?' Corchen prompted. 'The druids will be here soon.'

'Only Kirt is to come up,' Mara muttered. Her mind raced. 'The others can see to the pyre.' How could Donal do this to her? Training Skaaha wasn't just stupidity. Did he understand nothing of his queen? Even without express orders to the contrary, it was disobedience. More, it was open rebellion. Feet clattered into the room behind her.

'They'll want an explanation,' Corchen urged.

Mara banged both her fists into the lintel above her head. 'He conspired against me!' she howled.

'No.' It was said softly, sadly. Corchen's hand touched her shoulder. Was it sympathy or denial?

'Yes, yes, yes!' Mara thumped the stone with each word.

'Hey.' Arms came round her, Gila's arms. The younger warrior was their best archer, an aspirant to promotion, and Mara's sometime lover. She'd never known Kerrigen. 'Nobody doubts you.'

The queen spun round, buried her face in the younger woman's neck. 'But I'll miss him, from the field and from my bed. How could he do this to me, Gila, how could he?' Now the sting of tears came. She raised her head, eyes glittering, wiped the back of her hand across her nose and turned to the crowding warriors. 'I, too, feel disbelief.' She excused the display of emotion. 'Sit, sit.'

As they settled round the hearth, Mara assessed them. Despite Gila's assertion, there were some doubters. None was strong enough to challenge her. Corchen was slippery, Gila easily led. Both would side with her. The others withheld judgement till the facts were known. Kirt, the druid, inscrutable as all druids, had a soft heart which made him pliable. She sat between them, squeezing the older man's arm for support as she did. The pot-boy filled the last horn with ale.

'We have trouble at Glenelg,' she said, pausing to let the ripple of shock run around the circle and fade. 'Donal has fomented rebellion against us.'

'In what way?' Kirt asked, puzzled.

'He was training Kerrigen's daughter, Skaaha, in the art of war.' The peat flickered in a draught from the open skylight. 'She and her sister plot to usurp me.'

'That won't happen,' Gila burst out, stoutly. 'Let them come.'

Jolted, the others would take more persuasion. The dead queen lived in their hearts. They held fond memories of two little girls who played around their feet.

'Did Donal tell you this?' Corchen asked.

'The first part,' Mara confirmed. 'Their intention, though, is clear.' The right lie would make it so. 'At Beltane, I refused permission for Donal to train Skaaha.' The obvious justification leapt to mind. 'The island needs blacksmiths, *we* need blacksmiths and, by all accounts, she showed great promise.'

This was true. They all knew of Skaaha's talents, talents that raised tribal pride in one of their own. They had also raged at the attack on her, a child of Danu. An assault on womanhood violated them all. Skaaha's execution of warrior justice on her attackers was celebrated in Doon Mor, away from Mara's ears.

'Perhaps she only seeks to protect herself,' one of the doubters suggested.

'Is this not *our* purpose?' Mara asked. 'Does she doubt your ability, the ability of the Ardvasar chapter, *my* ability to ensure her safety?' This was better received. Warriors were quick to rise to any potential insult. 'Did she come to me, to seek my blessing? No, she did not.'

'Didn't she send Donal to ask on her behalf?' Kirt asked.

'No,' Mara replied. 'Donal confided her wish out of loyalty to me, in keeping with his oath, or so I thought, and I refused. But their deception was revealed' – she faltered, hardly able to believe her own naivety, sipped ale, cleared her throat – 'when I offered to take his daughter, Eefay, into this chapter.'

Now the murmur was of anger. For Mara to bend enough to offer her old rival's daughter a place was a triumph of honour over pride. It should have been met with gratitude not deception.

'But she trains with Skaaha, that was his response' – Mara stoked the flames of wrath – 'and then, realizing he'd slipped up, fear in his eyes.' She allowed a moment for expressions of rage. 'They work together – those were his last words, a truth too late to be apology.' She glanced at Kirt. He couldn't argue her authority on this. 'I did what was necessary to maintain warrior discipline. Donal paid rightly for his disobedience with his life. Glenelg school is closed.'

Heads nodded around the circle, the action fair. There were no dissenters.

'Now I will hear your advice,' Mara said. Across the fire, her eyes met Gila's. Was more prompting needed?

'We must hunt down the plotters,' the archer announced. 'Skaaha and Eefay should be brought to justice.'

Mara nodded, careful to keep her expression one of consideration rather than approval. A few voices sided with Gila, including Corchen's.

'Can we do that?' the older woman asked the druid.

'If they return to the island,' Kirt answered. 'But since neither has taken warrior vows, they're not subject to the queen's justice and must be brought to a druid court – with the necessary proofs.'

Mara's plans did not involve courts where truth might prevail. The sisters would die resisting capture. She would ensure it. 'My word against theirs?' she queried, playing along.

'The Glenelg druids will know if Skaaha trains,' he assured her.

'And if they don't return to the island?' Gila asked.

'Self-banishment is adequate punishment,' the druid said. 'What you can't do is ride on Glenelg. That would cause war with the tribes of Alba whose daughters also train there.'

'Not without Donal,' Mara corrected.

'No,' he conceded. 'Unless you replace him, they will leave. But Eefay is keeper of the school. She will stay, and might keep her sister with her.'

Mara dropped her eyes to the hissing peat. Surely she hadn't killed Donal for nothing? He was at least under her jurisdiction. Alive, she could have sent him back under orders to cease training Skaaha and send both sisters to her. To hide her frustration, she buried her face in her hands. The gesture, interpreted as defeat, spurred the others.

'We can't let them continue training to attack us,' Gila protested.

'There must be something we can do,' Corchen added, 'within the law.'

Kirt nodded. 'We can seek an order from the druid elders. If it's granted you can cross to Alba under licence, providing you harm none but the offenders.'

Mara's head came up. 'Then seek the order,' she snapped. 'Go now!'

'They won't meet again till Low Sun,' Kirt explained. 'But I'll go early to Tokavaig and present your case.'

Mara drew deep for control, blanking her impatience. 'Do it well, Kirt,' she said. 'We depend on you.' She glanced up at the open skylight, the patch of clouded sky. The solstice was barely two moons away. This matter could end then – two threats erased in one stroke. Killing Donal might well prove the wiser move. With the order granted, explanation of the deaths of Kerrigen's daughters would be simple.

She studied her warriors. Those who had served under the dead queen considered themselves foster-mothers to her girls. Yet she'd won them over. There was much to celebrate. It would cost her stock – the tribe became parsimonious with provision – but a feast would confirm her munificence.

'A brave warrior travels to the otherworld,' she said. 'Donal's crime was love for his kin, but he served us well for many suns and deserves the finest wake. It shall be done.' She raised her drinking horn. 'For our fellow, Donal. Death in glory!'

Raising their horns, charged with ale and their queen's magnanimity, the warriors roared the toast. 'Death in glory!'

31

On top of the broad wall that surrounded Doon Telve, Skaaha danced. Eefay was at Doon Trodden, greeting students returning after Sowen. She'd put the watch-keepers on alert. Her father would soon be home. If he told Mara, the warrior queen was unlikely to show her hand, but strangers remained suspect until Donal returned to warn, or reassure, them.

Unwilling to waste time, Skaaha had etched the platform, spar and pole of a chariot on the flat stone with charcoal. A pile of peats represented the charioteer. It was her footwork she concentrated on, though she held a spear. Singing mouth music, she danced in time from box to strut to pole, sometimes hopping nimbly, sometimes a leap, the spear used to propel or balance her. Throwing at imagined enemies could wait, since she hoped to stay on the wall.

Unaware that she was being watched, she tested herself. The pile of peats irritated, often in her way. Perhaps she should dispense with a charioteer; the real test was to keep her feet inside the lines while hopping at speed from one part to the other. Her dance resembled the warriors' battle celebration, theirs over sword and scabbard crossed on the ground, fast and nimble to avoid cuts.

'You're watching your feet,' a voice called. At the far side of the broch, one of the charioteers stood watching her. They were smaller men, muscular, and the girls joked that they loved their shaggy ponies more than folk. This one was taller than the others, his normally tousled brown hair tied like a pony's tail in the nape of his neck. 'I'll hitch up a chariot if you want to work,' he offered.

Skaaha somersaulted off the wall, turning in the air to land neatly on the path. 'Great,' she enthused, following the man to the circular field behind the broch, between it and the river. While he vanished to the stable, she stripped off to belt and scabbard. The air was chilly. Cold fingers of wind trickled over her skin. A hare scooted across the park, a good sign. Winter was slow in coming but would bite deeper here when it did. Everything that bought her time was welcomed.

The charioteer returned, leading the ponies and undressed now for work, leather genital-pouch strapped round his waist. Leather bands belted to it sat over his shoulders, crossing chest and back. His only weapon was a dirk. Charioteers relied on warriors for protection.

'And you rely on me,' he said. 'I'm not a stack of peat.'

He proved it too, standing on the flat platform, trotting the ponies around the field while she repeated the exercises she'd tried perfecting on the wall. There was a world of difference. The platform, sprung on its straps, was stable as the chariot bounced over ruts and clumps of grass, but her footing shook if she moved on to strut or pole. Automatically, she gripped the horses' harness or charioteer's straps to keep her balance. He sat, as he would in battle to let the warrior throw javelins. When she slipped, his hand grasped her belt, drawing her back from falling between horses' hooves and chariot wheels. While he drove, he moved, leaning to one side or the other, leaving space for her to go around him. After a while, he pulled the horses up.

'It *is* like a dance,' she enthused.

'But for two,' he said, 'like fucking.' He took the tie off his hair, shook it out, something else for her to grab hold of. 'Now we go faster.'

Faster they went. Skaaha yanked a practice spear from the holder, used it to propel her from platform to pole and back, or to balance, not sure enough yet to attempt a throw. As the afternoon wore on, she stopped noticing the rough ground charging away beneath them, stopped looking down for footholds and began to trust the knowledge of her feet. Now the charioteer tested her, veering the chariot unexpectedly in different directions. It became a game, if she could stay on. Every time she missed her footing, he caught and pulled her back.

'I keep you on,' he said, as the wind whistled between their faces. 'You kill the enemy before they kill me.'

'Ho, Skaaha!' It was Terra, at the edge of the field, with a bow and quiver of headless arrows. 'Stop this.' The arrow zinged past, glancing off the charioteer's shoulder. Giggling, Terra drew the bow again. Skaaha had no shield. Her charioteer swung the rig around, heading at speed towards the stable.

'Go for her,' Skaaha yelled, spear poised.

'And die?' he shouted back, grabbing her wrist. 'Get the shield.' The one he'd removed from the chariot was propped against the stable wall.

Trusting him to hold her, Skahaa swung out, horizontal, and snatched it up. Now she kept her eye on the flight of Terra's missiles, batting them away while the charioteer put distance between them. 'I want her,' she shrieked.

'Can't charge archers,' he muttered. 'They go for the horses. Then we stop.' Terra chased after them, taking position in the middle of the field, firing at will.

Grabbing the spear again, Skaaha leapt forwards, running along the pole to the yoke between the ponies' withers. Settling herself crouched, back foot further down the pole, face between the animals' heads, spear gripped at her side, she poised the shield to protect the ponies. 'Lie down, and go straight for her,' she yelled. 'Fast!'

The chariot turned, horses urged to the gallop. They charged, the smallest target, heading towards Terra. Skaaha stopped the next arrow with her shield. Terra ran to a better position. The chariot turned towards her again, close and closing. Skaaha's shield shifted to meet the next arrow, then she raised her shoulders, aimed and threw the blunt spear. It smacked into Terra's back as she ran.

'Ach,' the young woman complained, raising her hands

as they circled round her to a halt. 'I should've dodged or cartwheeled.'

Skaaha leapt down, grinning, to throw her arms round the other girl. As they kissed and hugged, the charioteer walked his exhausted horses back to the stables.

'You like Hiko?' Terra grinned, nodding at the departing man.

'Och, you' – Skaaha dunted her friend – 'can you think of nothing else?' Certainly, she was aroused and excited by the session. Much of that was due to her developing mastery, the exhilaration of conquering speed and danger. Part of it, too, was from working in harmony, her safety secured by the considerable skills of another. But, yes, there was lust, the response to flesh, muscle and skin in close contact, the pleasure of touch. 'He really can drive that chariot,' she said.

'Uh-huh,' Terra agreed, 'among other things.' Chuckling, they headed for the river. 'And we share the charioteers, without jealousy.'

Skaaha watched Hiko stripping the horses of their harness. He worked with authority. Though the distance was too great to hear his voice, she knew he spoke to the animals as he worked. His hands stroked them automatically, also speaking through touch. Men were beautiful to look at. She wondered if they knew it.

While Skaaha ducked herself in the swollen river before dressing, Terra sat on the bank, swinging her legs, chattering. An Icenian from flat southern fens, she'd leave the school when summer came to join a warrior chapter near her home. The mystery of land without rocks and mountains impressed Skaaha; she was full of questions for the strangeness of it and how anyone could find their way in it without landmarks.

Eventually, arms linked, they sauntered back to the broch.

'What's new with you?' Terra asked. 'Just work?'

'Just work.' Skaaha shrugged, ignoring the cold fist that squeezed her gut.

'Except tonight,' Terra confided. 'Wild party before Donal gets back tomorrow.' She chuckled. 'We've got two new students to induct.'

'I see blood. I see blood on the beach,' Jiya muttered. She sat cross-legged by the campfire, rocking. 'I see the blood of men, black rock stained red. I see –'

'Can you not shut your eyes then?' Fion complained, turning over in the heather and drawing his bearskin tighter round his ears to keep out the cold and the noise. 'How is a man to sleep when blood is shed on his dreams?'

'I see blood.' Jiya continued her chant as if he hadn't spoken. 'I see the blood of Fion –'

'Blessed Bride!' Fion swore, sitting upright. It was a dark night, the quarter-moon hidden behind heavy cloud. 'A wonder you can see anything at all in this!' They were camped on the point of Camas Malag, where the shore of Loch Slapin approached Torrin. 'I could be in the bed of a woman, with soft hair in my face instead of heather, and sweet words in my ears instead of –' It was his turn to be interrupted as Thum came out of the darkness to shake the sleeping body of Vass.

'They're showing light at Doon Grugaig,' he said.

Vass was instantly awake. 'What do you hear?'

'Nothing. Even the seals sleep.'

Fion was already on his feet, urinating on the fire to douse it, before Vass and the others joined him. Now it was pitch dark, only the grey sheen of water to see by. On the shore, by their boat, Vass held them back from boarding.

'Be still,' he said, listening. Brochs were impenetrable once the great doors closed. If Doon Grugaig had time to get their farm folk inside, there was no rush. They'd sound the war-horn if marauders approached. The lamplight from inside the broch flickered as its thatch skylights intermittently closed and opened, a distant star on the tip of the peninsula down the opposite coast. No sound came across the water, just the gentle wash of waves.

'Look.' Thum nudged him. Nearer to them, another light sparked up from Doon Liath, further into the estuary. Warned by Grugaig's, their people would be in, the doors barred. But they wouldn't show their own light unless . . .

'There is a boat coming up the loch,' Vass said. 'That's what they see.' Torrin was the most likely destination. He glanced behind him, towards the faint flickering from the ever-burning flame of Bride. It guided pilgrims. It was also a beacon for enemies. 'We wait,' he said.

'I will win.' The new girl shook the dice in her cupped hands.

'Not with that,' Misha grinned as the dice clattered into the tray. The party was in full swing. Eefay and several other girls danced a reel. In the absence of druids, not due back from their own sabbaticals till morning, the charioteers provided music. Skaaha had joined them on the hand drum, inexpert with the spoon-shaped bone but growing in confidence with every mouthful from the drinking horn beside her. Food still piled on the low table. Ale and mead flowed freely.

Terra had taken charge of the gambling, determining forfeits. Whooping, she scooped up the dice. 'If you can't beat three,' she said, handing them to Misha, 'we'll hang you by your heels over the hearth.'

No one was ever sure if Terra was joking or not, until the forfeit was called. Misha held her cupped hands at her ear, muttering as she shook. The dice rattled on to wood.

'Seven,' she yelled, clenching her fists in the air.

'She put a spell on them,' the new girl accused.

'I'll put a spell on you,' Misha retorted, 'if you don't take that back.'

Skaaha put the drum down and squatted beside the furious warrior. 'She only meant your luck is magical,' she said soothingly, putting an arm round Misha's shoulders. 'Isn't that right?' she said, offering the new girl an out.

'I meant she cheated,' the newcomer said.

With a roar, Misha launched herself across the board, only

to rise, floating, above her antagonist's head. Eefay, detached from the dancers, had grabbed her wrists. Skaaha, standing now, had a grip of her ankles. 'Caledonians do not cheat!' Misha shrieked as the two seniors walked her, suspended between them, away from the beginner. The dance music ceased. Everyone watched.

'Nor do we kill new students,' Eefay warned the dangling girl.

'You owe a debt, warrior of the Brigantes,' Terra told the newcomer.

'Brigantians pay no forfeits,' she retorted. 'I am Cartimandua, heir and daughter of a queen.'

Howls of mockery rang round the room. Terra smiled, waiting for it to stop. 'As are we all,' she said mildly. 'But to claim Misha cheats makes your life forfeit.' The Brigantian objected. Misha roared to be let loose. Terra held up her hand for silence. 'However,' she continued, 'her honour will be satisfied with a duel.'

'Duel! Duel! Duel!' the students chanted as they crowded round, eyes gleaming in the hearth light.

Skaaha glanced at Eefay, who seemed unperturbed, and set Misha's feet on the floor. Blood wasn't shed among the students, except by accident. Wars had been started for less. Terra had surely gone too far. To refuse a duel meant a humiliating loss of face. But the newcomer knew nothing of how skilled Misha was, or with what weapons, and the speed of the second-sun warrior must have been alarming.

Cartimandua's arrogance wavered. 'You try to fool me,' she said, 'but I will fight' – her haughtiness became smug – 'when my superior commands it.'

Disappointment cooled the excitement of the watchers. Donal was absent. There were no druids. Even as keeper of the school, Eefay, as second daughter of a warrior queen, could not claim superiority. Terra considered the arrogant girl. Misha's honour required recompense, or blood would spill.

'The Brigantes' allegiance is to Brigit, for whom they're

named,' Terra said, 'Brigit, whose name in these parts is Bride and whose islands lie offshore.'

'That's why I'm here,' Cartimandua agreed.

'Then you'll accept the command of the goddess?'

A howl of delight rose from the students. Cartimandua was caught. Eefay whispered in Skaaha's ear. Relieved, Skaaha stepped forward, pushed the dark hair back off her neck to reveal the triquetra.

'That would be me,' she said.

Cartimandua's mouth gaped like that of a dead fish. Her face paled.

'You will duel,' Skaaha commanded, 'with mead.' Laughter exploded round the room.

'Mead?' Misha and Cartimandua repeated, almost in unison. Eefay and Terra had already filled the drinking horns.

'Drunk horn for horn,' Skaaha confirmed, as Cartimandua was helped to her feet. Horns were placed in both girls' hands. 'Last one standing wins.'

The Ardvasar warriors did not wait long. Soon, a third light glimmered on the opposite shore, closer than the last – the skylights of Doon Ringell. Something came up the loch, an unknown vessel, its progress recorded by watchers on the brochs. Under silent orders, the warriors left their boat to move on foot through grass and heather to the next bay, directly in front of Torrin. Six of them, and Jiya, deployed themselves behind rocks on the shore. The other seven took up fire stations on the perimeter, where dry broom and gorse would easily catch flame. No one relished fighting in the dark.

This time, the wait unnerved. Whatever travelled up the water towards them alarmed the watch-keepers. Preparing himself to fight, Fion, already on edge from Jiya's prophecies, began to entertain notions of monsters from the deep, legend becoming life. Perhaps they faced a ship of death rowed soundlessly by restless ghosts and the impossibility of killing what could not die. A faint creak made hairs rise on his neck.

Then a soft plash broke the rhythm of waves, the rhythmic dip of oars. What came towards them from the grey, dark sea was human after all. His grip tightened on the thrusting spear. They would fight shadows till the fires bloomed behind them. It was a situation none would choose. The danger from their own outweighed that of any close-knit group coming up the beach.

Wood scraped on rock. Feet splashed through shallow surf, the sound mingling with murmured voices in a foreign tongue. Fion breathed deep and steady, counting, certain the shallow-bottomed vessel had at least ten pairs of oars, twenty rowers. Nine . . . ten . . . Vass wouldn't let them all disembark before attacking.

'Hyaaa-aaaaa!' The war cry screamed from his commander.

'Hyaaa-aaaaa!' Every one of them took it up. Behind them, flints sparked.

Feet clattering down the stony beach, Fion bellowed again with his fellows. 'Hyaaa-aaaaa!' Alarmed shouts came from the shadowy figures, splashing back in terror to free their boat from the shallows. Fion drove his spear into the gut of the nearest enemy, yanking it out as the body crumpled. Some brave soul rushed him, the glitter of steel raised. Fion thrust again. The enemy boat was off the rocks. Oars splashed, finding water. Behind them fires flared as the dry shrubs caught light. Way to their right, the war-horn of Doon Beag, guardian of Torrin, blared into the night.

'Hyaaa-aaaaa!' Feet rattled over stones as the second wave of Ardvasar warriors pelted down the shore. There was nothing for them to do. The intruders' boat was out in the water. Those left behind were dead or dying on the shore. Jiya dragged one body to the nearest rock, drew her sword to take the head off it.

'Wait.' Fion stayed her hand. The man was still alive. A heavy torc glittered round his throat, his bloodied clothes richly dressed. 'He might be of some use . . .' A sharp pain thumped into his shoulder.

'Shields,' Vass roared, as a flight of javelins from the fleeing boat whistled down about their ears. Fion crumpled into Jiya's arms.

32

'Aye-yie-yaa!' The students of Glenelg cheered. Cartimandua staggered, steadied, staggered again then collapsed against a chamber screen, sliding down it to the floor. Misha stared bleary-eyed at nothing, swaying. Skaaha took the horn of mead from the girl's hands.

'You won, Misha,' she said. 'Time to sleep.'

Eefay called for broch workers to take the drunken girls and younger students back to Doon Trodden. The seniors settled to some serious play. Hiko, the charioteer, reclined beside Skaaha to watch her compete with Terra for the next forfeit. Another peat was added to the hearth. The pot-boy filled ale into horns. Roast pig and lamb were chewed over with each move. Dice rattled across the board. Boasts and witticisms, groans of despair and shrieks of delight filled the great room to the thatch. As the game neared its close, silence descended. The two competitors were neck and neck. One throw could decide the outcome. Terra passed the dice to Skaaha.

'Can you conjure up nines?' she taunted.

'My magic number.' Skaaha grinned, shaking the cubes and well-wishing four and five to appear. The dice bounced across the wood. Four and one turned over. A wish granted. *Be careful what you conjure, it may come to you.* Lethra's warning illustrated. The groan rose to the roof.

'Five!' Terra pounced. It was the number for humankind. 'Someone's ill-wishing you,' she rejoiced, taking her throw. 'Maybe it's me.' Neatly, as if conspired, the three and six faces turned obligingly up. 'Aye-yie-yaa!' she cheered.

'Forfeit! Forfeit!' The chant rose. Fists thundered on the tabletop.

Skaaha braced herself. To solve the problem of Carti-mandua, she'd claimed the role of goddess. Now Bride demanded her dues. Pain, humiliation, whatever endurance was asked, she would comply with good grace. Terra planked her elbow on the table. Chewing her bottom lip, she rested her chin on her palm to consider Skaaha. Lamplight glinted in her eyes.

'You owe a debt, warrior of Danu,' the Icenian said.

'Name it,' Skaaha retorted, copying Terra's pose so they were face to face. 'I will pay.' Terra gave forfeits in traditional triad form – a debt of three parts. She would not get off lightly.

'You will pay the debt to Hiko.'

So that was it. That explained the twinkle in Terra's eyes. Reclining beside Skaaha, the charioteer sat upright at the mention of his name.

'I will pay the debt to Hiko,' Skaaha responded, 'if he will accept it.'

Terra ignored the qualification. 'You will pay the second honour to manhood.' Her voice was cool and steady, face perfectly impassive.

Skaaha's heart fluttered like a heavy bird trapped in her chest. Her gut clenched. But she kept her breathing steady, let no emotion colour face or voice. A warrior feared nothing, not death, and not life. 'I will pay the second honour to manhood.'

A howl of disbelief came from one of the young women. 'How can pleasure be a forfeit?' Eefay elbowed the speaker. They had all witnessed the justice Skaaha meted out to Cut-eye. Graphically, it demonstrated how he'd dishonoured masculinity. Terra intended Skaaha to overcome that by paying service to the dignity of maleness. That service, easy for others, would be difficult for her. If she failed, she would be shamed.

The charioteers shifted uneasily. Despite their value, and the high regard warriors had for them, their right to comment, interrupt or advise was limited to work. Like most men, their opinions were seldom sought at other times. But Hiko could not stay quiet.

'I will accept the honour,' he protested, 'only if Skaaha wishes to give it.'

Skaaha held up a hand to silence him. Her eyes had not left Terra's. This had nothing to do with what she wished. It was a test of power, a battle of will. Loving Ruan, she had paid the first honour easily, her hands arousing him. Equally easily, she paid the third honour, drawing him deep into her womanhood. But, since Beltane, she had avoided this. Her friend had guessed, or knew. Truly, she was a witch.

The forfeit was not complete. Everyone except Terra held their breath, waiting for the third and final part. Skaaha, mesmerized by the Icenian's eyes, read the thought before Terra spoke the words.

'You will pay the debt,' she said, 'where we can witness it.'

Skaaha swallowed anger and panic. Already, her stomach heaved, remembering Cut-eye. But she wouldn't lose face. 'I will pay the debt,' she repeated grimly. 'Move the table.' Rapidly, the low table was whisked away. Skaaha stood, held out a hand to draw Hiko into the centre of the room. Cheering, the others quickly disrobed them and settled down, complete with ale or mead, and titbits, to watch. Out on the field, Hiko had been confident, certain of his role. Now he seemed discomfited. To put him at ease, Skaaha moved in close, putting her arms round his neck, glad of the familiarity of skin from that afternoon, smelling the faint tang of horse.

'You don't have to do this,' he whispered in her ear. 'I can refuse.' That was true. It would save face, but her humiliation would be great. He would be mocked, and Terra would just replace him with one of the others. There was only one way to proceed, begin as if the truth of intimacy was untainted and hope it became so.

'I want to honour you,' she murmured, letting her mouth brush his throat. 'And I have ghosts' – her lips touched his – 'which you can help me lay.' His mouth tasted of honeyed mead. Kissing soon sparked desire in them both. Urged on by raucous catcalls, Skaaha let her fingers track the bone of his shoulderblades and spine, the firm flesh of his buttocks. She allowed his hands, firm and warm on her skin, to explore at will, finding her responses, rousing his own.

Again they were on the track, wheels spinning, hooves thundering in their ears, gripping on to each other. Passion flared. At the point where it must grow into coupling or fade, she put her palm flat against his chest, over his heartbeat. 'Let me serve you now,' she breathed, fingers tracing the groove between his pectoral muscles, mouth kissing nipple then abdomen as she dropped slowly on to one knee.

Inside her, the voice of offence shrieked its rejection. Warring with it was the wish not to offend this beautiful man. Beautiful, he was, penis firmly erect, standing out from his pubis, vulnerable, strong and fine, very fine. A knot of revulsion grew in her gut, not at him, but from the memory of a slack jaw, sour flesh cramming her mouth. Fighting to stay in the present, with Hiko, she cupped both hands under his genitals, explored weight and shape with her palms and thumbs. His thighs trembled. Above her, he groaned. His fingers caressed the back of her head, played in her hair.

Failing to blot out the remembered stench of Cut-eye, the choking fleshiness, she couldn't put mouth or lips or tongue against the charioteer's cock. She tried to force the images away by borrowing past joy, the delight of Ruan in the ring of fire. And still she couldn't, could not ... A bowl slid across the floor, bumped against her knee.

'Butter him up a bit first,' Terra encouraged. Laughter erupted.

'Or let Terra do it for you,' Eefay shouted. More ribald hoots and giggles.

'Honey-buttered man,' another girl chuckled. 'We'd all eat that.'

'I'm ready to roll in a beehive,' one of the watching charioteers offered, 'any time you're hungry.'

Skaaha giggled. They were all crazy. Her tension eased. Scooping up the smooth, sticky butter, she rubbed it into

Hiko's scrotum, smeared his erection. Cheered on by crude and silly commentary, she began to lick it off, trying hard not to laugh. Absurdity made a game of the honour. Relaxed, she began to have fun, buttered fingers grasping his thighs and buttocks, nibbling his testicles, taking the sweetened shaft into her mouth, playing it with teeth and tongue. Tremors ran through the charioteer, his fingers clenched in her hair. Skaaha felt a rising sense of her own power. Mouth firm around his manhood, she rocked rhythmically, slipping it in and out. Delight howled from the warriors. With their hands, they drummed a matching beat on the floor. Eefay leaned over to place a horn of mead within reach.

'To wash him down,' she shouted above the din.

'Aye-yie-yaa!' The others shrieked with laughter, drumming a roll before resuming the rhythm.

Drawing back, Skaaha kept the stroke of the beat with her hand, lifted the horn from its stand with her other hand and swallowed a mouthful of liquid. Then she filled her mouth with it, and then with man. Lips sealed around the hard flesh, she sloshed the drink back and forth around it. Drops of mead dribbled down her chin. Hiko groaned, moaned. Part-swallowing the mead in her mouth so she wouldn't choke or splutter, she gripped his backside with one hand, caressed his scrotum with the other, and resumed the rhythm, eager, now, for his release.

He cried out, moaning her name. A shudder ran through him. Exulting in the pleasure she gave, Skaaha swallowed the last drops of liquid with his seed as it spurted out in absolute surrender to the honouring.

'Aye-yie-yaa!' the students bellowed, battering the floor. 'Aye-yie-yaa!' Eefay, and several others, rolled, hysterical with laughter. In the shadows beyond the firelight, two of them mounted charioteers.

Gently, her jaw aching, Skaaha released the man's spent organ and rose from her knees to hug him, her face and hands sticky with honey-butter, mead and man. Laughter and joy trembled through her as she kissed his throat and face.

'Blessings on you, Hiko,' she said. 'You're a beautiful man. The honour was mine.' She couldn't believe, and had to believe, for she had done it. The curse of fear was lifted. She had recovered the right of woman to fully cherish man. Someone began to sing. Drums picked up the beat. A pipe played. The girls danced. Terra pulled Skaaha into her arms.

'You did well, Danu warrior,' she crowed, hugging her.

'I did,' Skaaha agreed, amazed. 'I did, and you're a wicked woman.'

'Worldly wise, fearful of nothing.' Terra laughed, tossing back her long red hair. 'Some day I'll pay for it.' She pointed to the cauldron on the hearth. 'And you better wash before you sticky up everyone else you touch.'

Ladling water into a bowl, Skaaha rubbed her face and hands clean with a rag. The day had been long but rewarding. Her limbs ached as if she'd fought a dozen ghouls. Faintly, from above, she heard the watch-keeper on the walkway call out. Someone approached, and must have answered since no alarm followed. If it was Donal, she would learn tonight if her safety was assured or her peril increased. Hauling on her dress, she crossed the great room to the door. A robed figure climbed the stairs, carrying a druid staff. It was Ruan, the night chill still hanging round him.

'Late, but early,' she said. 'We expected you tomorrow.' He stepped into the lamplight. Before he spoke, his face told her all was not well.

'I must speak with Eefay,' he said. 'There has been a death.'

'And I want this man why?' Mara asked Vass, as she stalked around the wounded captive. No hospitality had been offered, the broch frowzy.

'He was their leader,' Vass explained, 'and might have information.'

'If I can make him talk' – she punched the man's wounded side, watched him fall, squealing, to his knees – 'or understand him when he does?'

'The druids will interpret,' Vass reminded her. 'They understood him well enough at Torrin. Nechta took a ransom message out to their boat under the white flag of Bride.' The priests at Torrin had also dressed the man's wound, and cremated his headless colleagues. 'He claims to be the son of their queen.'

'Then the ransom demand was suitably high?'

'It was. He's held against their good behaviour for six moons when they can present terms to you.'

'You did well.' It was rare praise. 'Take him down,' Mara ordered Corchen and Gila. 'Incarcerate him in the stockroom, where I don't have to see him.'

When the raider was removed from the great room, Vass took his leave. He was a man short and had no wish to dally at Doon Beck. Mara knew Skaaha trained at Glenelg. Donal was dead for disobedience that Vass did not believe. His queen's unpredictability made a liar of him, by omission. He told her only what he must, sharing nothing that could be withheld. It was a poor way to secure the island.

'Is Jiya still with you?' Mara asked.

The moon-crazed warrior was exempt from command, a free spirit. Why would Mara care? 'Yes,' he answered. 'She waits with the others at Torrin.' He had brought only a small escort with the prisoner. They hadn't come, exultant, to celebrate. That ought to concern her more than Jiya's whereabouts, that, and the poverty of household support from the clan. The tribe passed judgement on her worth. He was halfway down the stone steps to rejoin his men when she remembered.

'We're sorry about Fion,' she called down.

Vass kept walking, desperate to be out in good, fresh air.

Kya . . . Kya . . . Kya . . . a golden eagle shrieked and swooped overhead. Skaaha, searching the hill for Ruan, craned to watch it soar again. The moment stilled into eagle, she soaring with it, the weight of living and the forces of earth transcended. Seven days had passed since the chilling news of Donal's death, difficult, frustrating days. Ruan said little. The other druids returned to a wake, bringing word of the raid on Torrin, of Fion struck down. Mara crushed Glenelg but failed to protect the islands, harried by enemies. Out of respect for her father, Eefay refused to discuss the future till the wake ended and the school closed.

High above, the bird glided effortlessly through the air, its great wings spread against a cold, sharp sky. It was circling. Skaaha scanned the rocky hillside, looking for its prey. Ruan stood, planted on a rocky rise, arm outstretched. A leather gauntlet covered his forearm to the elbow. In his gloved fingers, he held a piece of meat. Stunned, Skaaha glanced upwards, saw the eagle fold its wings, roll over, and swoop.

Ruan held steady as the great bird dropped towards him. The risk was great. Eagles could kill a deer with one blow. As it approached and spread those great wings, the span as long as Ruan was tall, it seemed the bird might beat him to the ground. Instead, fluttering, it settled on his forearm, swaying to find balance, and began to tear at the meat. Immobilized with awe, Skaaha was certain Ruan spoke to the creature as it fed. When the food was done, the bird preened then spread its wings and rose, rapidly, into the autumn sky.

'How did you do that?' Skaaha ran to Ruan, calling as she went. 'Can I try?'

He removed the gauntlet. 'She's an old friend,' he said, 'visiting from Kylerhea, and the food is gone. You should have come earlier.'

'I would if I'd known.' Perhaps this explained his solitary evening sessions on the beach back home. She felt peeved he would keep such a secret. 'Wish I had.'

'I doubt she'd come down for anyone else,' he added. 'They have strong loyalties.' Together, they watched the soaring eagle vanish to a pinhead on the clouds. When it was gone, he pushed the gauntlet into his pouch. 'They even mate for life.'

'Do they? How strange.' The image of light and air still filled her head, the power of those wings. 'Why would they do that?'

Ruan shrugged. 'It must suit them.' They began to walk back across the hill. 'How well does Hiko suit you?'

Skaaha stopped walking. Since the party, she'd taken Hiko to her bed twice. But the wake was over. Mara sent no tutor to replace Donal. The students prepared to leave. She had just kissed Terra and Misha goodbye, taken leave of the others. There were more pressing things to discuss than who occupied her bed. 'Are you asking if I mean to marry him?'

'I ask what I intend,' Ruan said, turning to face her. 'He's a charioteer.'

'He's enjoyable, a fine man.' It was her turn to shrug. 'Fucking means we work the chariot better.'

'You, and all the other seniors,' he snorted. 'Where's your pride?'

'Set aside, as it should be.' She frowned. 'He's not mine.' Something was amiss. All warriors, male or female, fucked with their charioteers. It helped them move well together, but didn't bind them. 'A man can't be jealous,' she said.

'Can't he?' the druid snapped. 'Maybe we just control ourselves better than women.' He stalked off towards the trees. Skaaha ran after him, grabbed his arm and spun him round.

'This is foolish,' she said. 'Woman's capacity for pleasure is greater, that's all. Men are bound to one lover because they can't satisfy more. It's the way things are.' As a druid, Ruan couldn't bind to anyone, or marry, though he might copulate from duty or for pleasure. Maybe that explained why he thought like a woman on this. 'You didn't mind about Terra.'

'I did.'

'But you told me to take other lovers.'

'It's what I have to say.'

Skaaha was bewildered. 'Women are not eagles,' she said, 'except in spirit.' She wrapped her arms round him, feeling resistance. 'I love you with all my being,' she said. 'This you know. Here' – she placed his hand over her heart, spread his fingers – 'you live in here, with all those I love.' He began to soften. She nuzzled into his neck. 'You also live here' – she pressed her abdomen against him. His arms tightened round her. His cheek rubbed the top of her head. 'I'm the woman you taught me to be,' she murmured. 'I work, eat, play and fuck with others, as you do. It takes nothing away from us.'

'I know,' he groaned. 'Dear, sweet, blessed Bride, I know.'

33

They made love in the long grass as the day moved on and the creatures of the hill went about their business of hunting, feeding, drying or storing for the coming long nights. When the chill fingers of evening began to creep through their clothes, they rose, brushing off grass, and began to walk down the hill, hand in hand, through trees burnished with autumnal fire. Fallen leaves crunched underfoot. The twin delights of eagle and love-making slipped into memory.

'I came to ask what I should do,' she told him. 'I need to train, and I need opponents. Eefay and I already outguess each other. Misha offered to return with a warrior from the Caledones. But Eefay refused.'

'Rightly,' Ruan confirmed. 'The allegiance of Glenelg must be sworn to the Island of Wings. Unless Mara approves the tutor, the school can't operate.'

Skaaha snorted. If Mara sent anyone, it would be an assassin. 'Will Vass teach me, if I go to Ardvasar?'

'You can't go there!' The words exploded out of him, as if in anger.

'What is this thing with you?' She jerked her hand out of his. 'If I want to fuck with warriors, I will. You're my priest, not my wife!'

'It's not about that.' He caught her arm. 'You can't cross the water.'

'How do you know?'

'What?'

'The danger.' Her fury, already sparked, burst into flame. 'Did Eefay tell you? You won't interfere in this, Ruan. I'll deal with Mara when the time comes, after I deal with my loose-tongued sister!' She tried to tug her arm free, to charge down the slope through the trees and confront Eefay, but Ruan held her.

'She told me nothing,' he said. 'Be still.' They were close to the druid lodges. 'Go in.' He ushered her towards his. 'We need to talk.' He went to ask one of the other priests to fetch Eefay then returned to join her. 'Sit,' he insisted. 'I have something to tell you, and it seems you have something to tell me.'

Skaaha sat. His lodge smelled of herbs and perfumed oil, the same smell he had. Last time, it had stunk of vomit, hers, and then blood, as she writhed with pain. He'd held her, rubbed her belly and back with oils, apologizing over and over for the strong dose of abortifacient needed at that stage. When the agony eased, he washed her clean, burned the messed blanket. Then he taught her how to mix the weaker herbal brew that would prevent further pregnancies without causing pain or sickness. She was to take it over the fertile days if she wanted to mate then. If she forgot, it must be taken from copulation till bleeding. She'd been careful not to need it yet, till today.

'While we wait for Eefay,' he said, handing her a steaming cup, 'tell me the secret you've been keeping. I'll tell mine when she arrives.'

So she told him about Mara's visit to the cavern of Bride, that Bartok and his men came to Kylerhea intending to take her head, and Ard's revelation that Mara knew them. 'Now she's killed Donal,' she concluded, 'for disobedience, you said. I'd gamble my life it was because he told her I was here.'

A frown had creased Ruan's face as she spoke. Now it deepened. 'Why didn't you tell me this?'

'I didn't know who sent them' – she hesitated – 'or who to trust. Once I knew it was Mara' – she bit her lip – 'I couldn't tell you. The law won't help.'

He was silent for a few moments. 'The pieces fit together,' he said finally, 'but they're not evidence.'

'Exactly,' she agreed, 'and why would she want me dead?

I was a blacksmith, an asset to the warrior queen, and no threat.'

'Nor was my father,' Eefay said, coming through the door. 'The wake is over, Ruan. My school is closed.' She settled herself beside Skaaha. 'Now tell me why Donal died.'

'Skaaha is right,' the druid began. 'The fault is her presence here.' He didn't get much further. The telling of Mara's first claim prompted an outburst.

'She lies,' Eefay objected. 'The first Donal knew was when Skaaha arrived here, with you, long after Beltane.'

'I had no reason to train before,' Skaaha protested. 'Not till I was attacked, after you took me to Tokavaig, when Bride didn't let me die.'

'Your word isn't enough,' Ruan pointed out. 'It balances Mara's, so neither will count. But you do train here, together, as she said, without her knowledge.'

'Because of her!' Eefay exclaimed.

'That can't be proved either,' he said. 'But let me finish. Mara claims you conspire to overthrow her. She asks the druid elders for approval to enter Alba and bring you both to justice.'

The two sisters exchanged a look. 'Both of us,' Eefay said.

'Will they give it?' Skaaha asked.

'They might,' Ruan said. 'It will be a druid court, not warrior justice. They would expect to discover truth. The innocent have nothing to fear.'

'Except Mara,' Eefay corrected.

'The only fact is that Skaaha's here, training, as Mara claims,' Ruan repeated. 'She can't prove why. Nor can you. Donal's dead. Jiya and Ard are hardly witnesses, and they're kin. Mara's version of why she visited Bride's cavern and what she meant by *half those men* will be different from yours.'

'But she'll be believed.' Skaaha despaired. The queen's word carried weight. Mara out-thought her at every turn.

'Secrets do more harm than good,' Ruan chided. 'Keeping yours has strengthened her hand. She can claim you invent now. If you'd told me at the time –'

'She doesn't know I didn't,' Skaaha interrupted. 'She can't know if or who I told, or when.' Understanding followed in a flood of revelation. 'The court is a ruse. She'll never let us reach it.'

'Don't you trust me to protect you?' Ruan asked. Annoyance coloured his voice. 'It wouldn't have come to this if you'd confided in me.'

'I protected you,' Skaaha snapped. 'A dead druid makes no better witness than a dead warrior!'

'And will make a better one,' Eefay said, 'with the bog waiting, if she blamed the death on us. Look how she blames my father for his.'

Skaaha stood. 'If you want to protect me,' she told Ruan, 'train me to fight. Train both of us.'

Shocked, he also rose. 'You know I can't do that.'

Skaaha smiled. It was a warning sign. 'Not even for your beloved Danu?'

'That's unfair.'

'No, what's unfair is that you called her name in the ring of fire, even while my body received you, even when you professed to honour me. What's unfair is Mara might want my death because of the legend you played out then, that I am Danu.' Her words became a torrent, rage feeding rage. 'And what's truly unfair is that I go where you lead me, and when I challenge her, will become Danu just as you priests conjured me to be, fighting a threat to our people but wholly ill equipped to do so because you invoke the warrior goddess then play at peace!'

She stormed out of the lodge, banging the door behind her. Pots rattled on the shelves, the fire flared in the sudden draught, dust descended from the thatch. The door, unlatched, creaked open again.

'Good thing she's not upset,' Eefay said, getting to her feet to leave.

Ruan turned to stare at her as if he'd forgotten she was there. 'She means to challenge Mara?' he asked.

'That's the plan. Not the best, but all we've got, and it's lawful.' She gazed up at him, contemptuously. 'Warrior justice,' she said. 'Mara sent the outsiders for her head. Revenge is Skaaha's right. It's mine now too. My father's blood demands it. Tell that to your druid council.'

Fion was carried by chariot from the boat to Tokavaig sanctuary. His wound had been dressed by the druids at Torrin. Now, a fever gripped him. Although he had been brought for healing, his chance of survival looked slender. Weak from blood loss, his skin had the grey pallor of the dead. Delivered into the careful hands of priests, his strong body, strangely shrunken, trembled. The druids shooed the warriors away.

'I will stay,' Jiya announced, 'and make penance for him.' She squatted, cross-legged, outside the lodge they put him in and began to chant the song of healing.

Vass went to find Suli. The high priest was seated in the grove among naked, lichen-whitened branches. Mara's druid, Kirt, sat near by. Suli's head rose as if she listened. Before Vass reached her, or spoke, she answered him.

'Fion will not return to your chapter,' she said. 'Take your warriors home. This is no place for men of war.'

'And Jiya?'

'She will be robed while she's here. The guilt is not hers, though she feels it.'

Suli, in her own way, was as difficult to talk with as Mara. Vass fretted. Fion was close as a brother, yet Suli brushed his life off like chaff. 'Can we talk alone?'

'We are alone. Kirt is druid. I am he, he is me. Say what you must.'

'What of Donal, and Kerrigen's daughters?'

She seemed surprised, and stood, turning her milky eyes towards him. 'They are not your concern. We will address Mara's petition at Low Sun.' She raised her staff. 'If I strike you with this, Vass, you would see as I do. But that is not for you.'

'I would see stars,' he joked.

'Then maybe you do see, the shadow of change, at least. Go home. Do your work with the same good heart as always.'

It was a heavy heart, but she would share no more with him. All he could do was trust. The old woman chuckled.

'You arrive at a good place, my son,' she said. It was the only indication she gave of being his birth mother, the distance between them always great. 'I see a future for Fion,' she added, more gently, 'in this world. Now will you go?'

He bent down, kissed her soft, wrinkled cheek. She was so fragile, so frail, yet the toughest warrior he knew. 'Blessings on you, Mother,' he said, before walking away. When his footsteps faded beyond earshot, Suli seated herself again.

'There are changes coming, Kirt,' she said. 'And I'm blessed with little sight to see them all. But I see the way forward for you. Go you to Alba, to Ynys Mon. Tell Tosk what happens here.'

'And he will see further?' Mara's druid asked.

The old woman chuckled again. 'He will appreciate your news, more than Mara might if you returned to her.'

Breakfast, by flickering lamplight in Doon Telve, was sombre. That morning's routine, conducted clothed now the cold began to bite, took place on an empty field. The sisters ate in a broch unbearably quiet after the joy of returning students and their sad but equally raucous leave-taking following the noisy, bois-terous wake. Skaaha had never liked Donal. Now she felt guilty. Eefay sat opposite, head bowed, picking at her food.

'I've ruined your school and endangered your life,' Skaaha said.

'This is true.' Eefay barely looked up. She couldn't teach women, and Mara would ensure she didn't tutor men. 'You never were a liar, except about the Shee.'

'They might come for you yet.'

'Good. I'll take them on for training. Without students, food will stop arriving and the workers will disappear.'

'Don't.' Silence lengthened between them. ''Terra said we could go south, join the Iceni and train there for a time.'

Now Eefay did look up. 'Do you know why she came here? Same reason they all came. No warriors fight as well as those from the Islands of Bride.'

Skaaha hunkered up from reclining to a squat. 'So we're beaten!' She banged her fist on the table. 'Is that what you say – the daughters of Kerrigen, beaten by a jealous, spiteful bitch whose only talent is for telling lies?'

'She has a talent for murder.'

Skaaha threw herself backwards on to the goatskins and lay staring up at the gloomy, cavernous thatch, its skylights shut against the cold. 'Och, Eefay, we have nowhere to go from here.' She wondered what the friendless did – found a place away from folk; fished, farmed or hunted? It would be hard, having to do everything from making tools to cutting peat, but it was possible. Staying at Glenelg was not, not after Low Sun, not if Mara won her order from the druids. But if she did, they couldn't stay anywhere. It wasn't possible to run from druid justice. There were priests everywhere. Within a fortnight, every cell in Alba would be watching for them. They'd be brought home in chains, all the guiltier for having run away.

'I'm not guilty,' she told the roof. It didn't care. It was a roof. 'Not guilty,' she yelled. The thatch remained unperturbed. 'Fire!' There was no response, not even to the one thing that could cause its destruction.

The pot-boy scurried in. 'Where?' he asked. 'Where's the fire?'

'In the hearth,' Eefay said. She had finished eating, and was braiding her hair.

Skaaha jumped up and hugged the boy. 'You came running,' she crowed, 'because you are a person and know what to fear.' He began to back away. 'But the roof ' – she pointed – 'did nothing. Do you know why?'

The boy's mouth gaped like a gutted fish. He shook his head.

'Because it can't feel fear!' Skaaha announced triumphantly.

Eefay clapped her hands, slowly. The boy ran for the door.
'I know what it is,' Skaaha said, excited.

'A roof?' Eefay resumed braiding.

'I'm the roof.' She paced back and forth. 'At least, I'm not afraid of death. Not since Beltane. Life holds more fear.' Dropping to her knees beside the table, she leant forward on her elbows. 'Something changed, Eefay, and I know what.'

'So do I,' her sister commented dryly. 'You were a woman before breakfast. Now you're thatch.' She tossed back her braids. 'Good plan. No one can touch you if you're crazed.'

Skaaha snorted with laughter. 'It's not me.' She chuckled. 'It's Mara.'

Eefay's face crinkled. 'She's thatch?' She hooted, yelping.

'No.' Skaaha clutched her sides, giggling. 'That's the point.' Laughter choked her. 'Mara changed. *She's* afraid.' She banged the table, gulping air. 'That's why she wants us dead.' Tears trickled down her cheeks. 'All we need to know is why she changed.'

Eefay was helpless, howling. 'Could be,' she gasped, wiping her eyes with a sheepskin rug, 'you turning into a roof that scares her.'

It had been a long time since they giggled hysterically like children, and it was some time before it faded. Still in danger of further eruption, they walked down the stone steps to start the training session.

'You're not guilty,' Eefay said. 'Mara is, and she'll know it, whatever she tells anyone else.'

Skaaha halted. They were at the foot of the steps, just about to cross the stockroom, where the dung from the beasts was being cleared to the midden-heap outside. The sour-sweet stench hung warm in the cloying air.

'That's it!' she exclaimed.

'Don't start again,' Eefay begged. 'I'm still sore.'

'No, she *is* guilty,' Skaaha said, the thought rising with perfect clarity. 'That's why she's afraid. She's done something she thinks we know, or will guess.'

'She ordered your head.'

'Before that, before she came to the cavern. Jiya said that was jealousy, but I wasn't a rival, even as Danu. She came out of fear, to warn me off.'

'And you don't know why?'

'No.' They walked on, skirting shadowy piles of muck. 'If we could remember when she changed.'

'All I remember from Doon Beck is being scared of her.'

'Me too,' Skaaha agreed. 'But she changed, Eefay.' Something teased her memory, lurking in the shadows.

'Don't think about it,' Eefay said as they collected practice swords from the door-keeper. 'If we've asked the right question, the answer will come.'

Outside, Ruan sat on a rock, meditating among wind-tumbled fallen leaves. He stood when they came through the doorway.

'This isn't a time to let your standards slip,' he remonstrated. At his feet lay three oak staves.

Skaaha stared in disbelief. 'You're going to teach us?'

'I can't train you to fight,' he reiterated. 'That's forbidden.' He smiled as if he split a hair. 'But I can teach you how to defend yourselves.'

'With sticks?' Eefay queried in disbelief.

'It's better than nothing,' Skaaha said, taking one up.

The grip, in thirds, was similar to that of a thrusting spear, with hands opposing. Ruan was thorough in his teaching, making them stand still for the whole session, copying hand and arm movements until the staves felt like extensions of their limbs. They learned fast, experience already telling. Control, even of such a basic weapon, was pleasurable. Both were eager to continue after the mid-day meal, but he refused.

'Blistered hands won't help,' he said. 'Discipline will, and you have other lessons.' Skaaha's afternoon was spent with the oldest druid, continuing to learn the thirteen books of poetry. Eefay, who knew them all, worked with her chariot. The evening meal brought everyone together in Doon Telve: the two sisters, three druids and four charioteers.

'Nine,' Lana, the priest, counted when they sat down. 'There is no greater number.' She told a story of the sacred trinity, which had three parts and taught three truths. Skaaha tried to show no interest, but it was a fine story well told, and she applauded with the others the wit and wisdom of it. One of the charioteers took over, telling of a race with nine horses. The meal was less boisterous without students. Talk shifted from the learned to the practical. But it raised Skaaha's spirits. Life could continue at Glenelg, at least for the next two moons.

34

Next morning, staves in hand, Ruan walked them through the warrior steps. The familiar arm and hand movements became a system of thrusts, blocks, sweeps and strikes with the weapon.

'I never realized,' Skaaha yelled with delight, feeling confident and competent already with the new skill. A spear used in similar fashion would kill with ease.

'And now we do it this way,' Ruan said, turning them to face each other. Instantly, the sisters were rehearsing a battle where every strike stopped short of contact.

'It's magic,' Eefay crowed. 'How did we not know?' They had both performed the warrior steps, weaponless, since childhood. All warriors did.

Ruan had brought a hand drum, slung behind him. Now he pulled it round, took the beater from his pouch and began to drum. 'To the beat,' he said, marking time. When mealtime came, they were up to double time and not missing a stroke. By the end of the third morning, they moved so fast he gave up drumming. 'Tomorrow,' he said, 'do the steps three times in your routine, first as normal, second with staves at double time, third opposing each other at this speed. The session after breakfast will be free-style.' He walked away across the field, heading for his lodge.

'Does he ever say well done?' Eefay asked, chest heaving from exertion.

'Yes,' Skaaha said, drawing deep for breath. 'I guess we haven't yet.'

For greater space, the free-style session took place on the chariot-training field behind the broch. It brought another revelation. First, Ruan taught them to keep striking short so that training injuries would be avoided. Then he set them against each other, calling out instructions and advice. With their handling skills equalized by the new weapon, Skaaha's greater strength and speed meant she made two strikes to every one of Eefay's. For the first time, she was in advance of her sister.

The final third of the session was a demonstration.

'Attack me,' Ruan said, 'both of you, as you please.'

'Have you been cuffed by a bear?' Eefay asked. 'You'll get hurt.'

'Let's hope so,' Ruan smiled. 'We'll stop when either of you makes a hit.'

They began tentatively, but the druid blocked everything they tried. Before long, they ceased to care that he might be struck and threw every move they knew at him. None connected. Ruan moved like lightning, anticipating, blocking and returning every strike. They, on the other hand, often felt the light prod or thump of his staff, and would have been black and blue with broken bones if he'd intended injury.

'Did you know he could fight like this?' Eefay grunted as yet another strike was parried.

'He told me druids don't.' Skaaha ducked and swung.

'There's a lesson there,' Eefay hissed through gritted teeth. 'Don't doesn't mean can't.' Eventually, she threw her stave down in disgust. 'You couldn't do that if I had a sword,' she snapped, frustrated. 'I'd cut your staff to pieces!'

'Fetch one,' Ruan offered.

Skaaha wouldn't have bet either way, and watched intently. The priest simply avoided contact between his stave and the cutting edge of the sword, batting it away on the flat then tumbling or spinning out of reach to strike from a greater distance. Her sister was rapidly proved wrong. Fortunately, Eefay bore no grudges over battle skills. The bout ended with her in awe, determined to learn till she could equal the priest.

'What about you?' Ruan offered Skaaha the chance to try the sword against him. She declined. But, that evening, as the others told stories after eating, she returned to the field to practise with her staff in the dark. Two days later, when Ruan called them to attack, she was ready. Choosing her moment with care, while he was retreating to avoid a strike and Eefay moved in, she ran up behind him, vaulting on the stave. Turning in the air above Ruan's head, she swung the weapon round and down, hard. Briefly preoccupied with Eefay, the druid realized what was happening a moment too late. As he leapt aside, the blow caught his shoulder.

'Well done,' he groaned, wincing, as she landed. 'You put it all together.'

'Aye-yie-yaa.' Eefay danced, cock-a-hoop. 'We won, we won, we won!'

'I'm sorry,' Skaaha said, massaging the druid's injury. 'I realized the aerials you taught me were the same discipline, but I couldn't manage no contact as well.'

Tluck-tluck-tluck-tluck. Tapping sounded behind them from the stable.

'Don't apologize,' Ruan said. 'You did it here' – he touched the centre of his forehead – 'as you should, and took me by surprise. Don't expect to do it twice.'

'Twice,' Skaaha remembered. 'The outsiders came to Kylerhea twice.'

'So Mara sent them before?' Eefay asked.

'Unlikely,' Ruan said. 'They came to steal, took things from every house, and my lodge.' He frowned, remembering. 'Not clothes or food though.' Outsiders usually raided larders or stock, and stole clothing, especially as winter approached.

'If it was just theft,' Skaaha said, 'they'd have gone to the forge.' Kylerhea's wealth was stored there: tools, weapons and jewellery. Homes held only normal household goods. Druids had nothing of value, except knowledge.

Ruan agreed. 'Erith, or Kenna, thought they were searching for something else.'

'Or maybe they found it.' Eefay suggested. 'What was in your lodge?'

'Kerrigen's honours,' Skaaha answered. 'I sacrificed them the day after.'

'And they'd be no use to Mara,' Ruan pointed out.

'Yes, they would,' Eefay corrected, 'if she meant to stop our mother's spirit waking in the afterlife, or watching over us.'

'If she believed that,' Ruan said, 'then she feared the dead queen. Why?'

'I don't know,' Eefay snapped, 'except everything comes back to Kerrigen!'

Tluck – tluck – tluck – tluck – tluck. The sound, slowing now, continued.

'What is that noise?' Skaaha said, turning. It was familiar, like an old song. Outside the stable, Hiko had a chariot turned upside down, and was working on a wheel. She ran to him. 'Do that again,' she said.

'What, this?' He spun the wheel. *Tluck-tluck-tluck-tluck*. 'Broken spoke,' he explained. Dangling, it hit the axle with every turn. *Tluck – tluck – tluck – tluck*. 'Soon have it fixed,' he grinned, stopping the wheel to prise out the linchpin.

'Leave it for now,' she said, and called the others over. 'That's the noise Jiya made. You heard it,' she told Ruan.

'Yes.' He clucked his tongue. 'Tluck – tluck – tluck. It's similar.'

'Then I know what else the outsiders were looking for,' Skaaha said. 'Only it wasn't there. Not then.'

'Is this some other secret?' Ruan asked.

'You brought it to me.' She ran to the broch, leaving them to hurry behind. In her chamber, she hauled the broken spear from below her bed. 'It's Mara's,' she told Ruan. 'Donal said, and this' – she gripped the tattered blue cloth – 'is what's left of Kerrigen's sash cloak. The marks on it' – she swallowed hard – 'will be her blood.'

'You said it was an accident!' Eefay howled.

'It was,' Ruan answered, though he gazed at Skaaha, 'but you think . . .'

'I think Mara caused it,' Skaaha finished for him, 'with this spear. I think Jiya saw it happen, but she was crazed and can't remember. Kerrigen knew that ground as well as she knew her footing in the chariot. She wouldn't make a mistake.' *Skaa-haa* – Kerrigen reached out, not for help, but to tell her daughter what had happened.

Now it was Ruan who reached out, put his hand over hers and squeezed. Tears welled in her eyes. 'Mara did that, when she brought me home to the wake. That's when she changed. She hated us, yet she took my hand and squeezed it as if she cared, as if she were a friend.' A sob shook her body. 'But she'd taken our mother's life away, just to win a race.' Ruan gathered her into his arms, holding her as she wept.

'I'm going outside,' Eefay snorted, swishing the curtain, 'to hit something.'

Skaaha buried her face in Ruan's shoulder, weeping for the futility of her mother's death, a brave, beautiful warrior killed by envy; for the loss of self-belief, robbed from her ruined body in Kylerhea; and for her life, twice destroyed, her spirit broken on the wheel. While she cried, the priest held her close, rocking her as if she were that child she could never be again.

When the tears ran dry, the fullness of sorrow was gone. Loneliness filled the space, a wind howling in empty heavens. It was her familiar, a companion gifted by the goddess on a rock above the sea when Bride refused to let her die. It was also her strength, to care nothing for herself, trust nothing but the cold comfort of revenge. She lived only to take off Mara's bloodied head, to shake it in her hands.

'Skaaha –' Ruan began.

'Don't say it.' She put her fingers to his mouth. 'You want proof. I know it' – she pushed her fist into her solar plexus – 'here. Mara fears discovery. She would lose everything she gained. So she attacks me. Eefay would be next.'

'She was to be next. At least,' Ruan corrected himself, 'Mara invited her to Bracadale, just before she killed Donal.'

'She's clever,' Skaaha conceded, 'and her accusation means we're doubted. No one will believe the truth about her now, not from us, or Ard, or Jiya.'

'Devious,' Ruan responded. He stood. 'The guilty give

themselves away,' he said, 'by accusing others of what they do themselves. Come' – he offered his hand – 'let's find out if a spear can stop a chariot.'

Outside, Eefay had followed the same thought. Her chariot, inherited from Kerrigen, was hitched up. Beside it, four charioteers argued possibilities.

'The spear had to be thrown,' Eefay told Ruan and Skaaha, 'from alongside, or nearly that, to get between the spokes of the wheel and not bounce off.' She showed how the spoke would carry the spear with the turning wheel till it snagged below the frame. 'The wheel would stop. That would snap the spear, and the spoke.'

'And this had two new spokes when it came here,' her charioteer added.

'If you meant to slow it down,' Hiko said, 'that would do it.'

'But would it throw the driver out?' Ruan asked.

'The jolt would,' Eefay's charioteer answered, 'especially running fast and light with just one on board. You'd get lift on the other wheel then some bounce back. It would topple.' None of them was willing to risk injury, or the horses, with a demonstration.

'It could come down on either side,' Hiko explained, 'or flip right over.'

'If we couldn't jump clear,' the third man added, 'we'd get dragged with it.'

'And our heads kicked in by the horses,' the last one said.

'That's what happened,' Skaaha said, remembering her mother's injuries. 'Both.'

'Would hitting a rock do the same?' Ruan asked.

An explosion of derision from the charioteers told the answer.

'Chariots are built to go fast over rough ground,' Hiko said, 'balanced for it. No.' He shook his head. 'Other things could stop a wheel – a crash, a deep trench hole, broken axle or sheared linchpin, but not a rock of a size you wouldn't see and avoid.'

Skaaha's fists clenched, nails biting into her palms. She turned on Ruan. 'Did none of you ask these questions at the time?'

'We saw what we looked for,' he said. 'There were no witnesses.'

'There was one.' She spun the broken wheel on the upturned chariot. *Tluck-tluck-tluck-tluck.*

'It'd spin a while,' Eefay's charioteer offered, 'going over at speed.'

'That answer Jiya said you had' – Skaaha gazed at Eefay – 'to the spear? It wasn't a riddle. She meant the chariot.'

'Do nothing rash,' Ruan warned, 'or your own anger will defeat you.'

'There will be nothing rash,' Skaaha vowed, 'unless Mara can dance druids to her tune.' The accusation struck home. The council at Low Sun presented the greatest danger of being flushed out too soon.

Tluck – tluck — tluck —— tluck. The slowing sound picked up an echo from the glen, the softer clop of arriving horses.

'Ho,' shouted the taller of the two riders as they came into view. 'We leave for a few days and you break up a chariot?' It was Terra, with Misha alongside.

Shrieking with all the delight of excited children, Skaaha and Eefay rushed to greet the returning warriors.

'We got as far as Loch Laggan, where we should part,' Terra explained as she dismounted. 'For several days, we argued.'

'But couldn't go,' Misha chimed in, launching herself into Skaaha's arms. 'It didn't feel right, leaving you to face this alone.'

'So here we are,' Terra grinned. 'Company, witnesses or co-conspirators, we expect our reward in the next life.'

As they were bundled upstairs for food and ale, the gloomy tower of Doon Telve rang again with laughter, garbled questions and noisy replies.

'And Ruan is training us,' Eefay told them. 'Imagine!'

'He can't tutor.' Shock fixed on Terra's face.

'But he can,' Skaaha grinned. 'He was raised by warriors, so he knows . . .'

'He knows all right,' Terra agreed, 'but you shouldn't. Don't you know who he is?' Although the four of them were alone in the great room, huddled round the hearth for heat, she lowered her voice. 'He's a warrior priest,' she hissed.

Misha's chin dropped.

'Stories for children,' Eefay scoffed.

'No,' Terra said, glancing guiltily towards the empty doorway. 'Don't speak of it, but we have one with the Iceni, a woman, and I saw Ruan on the hill one night, practising.' She gazed at Skaaha. 'How do you not know? The staff gives him away.'

The question rapped on Skaaha's skull. Familiarity had blinded her. *You can't learn what he knows*, Jiya had told her, terrified. Warrior priests were legendary. It was said, in all of Alba, there were just thirteen of them, their purpose to preserve the faith even if the entire druid fellowship was wiped out, their duty to survive. Between them, they contained all druid knowledge. Their martial skills were ancient, drawn from the four corners of the earth, and in a lifetime were passed only to one other, their inheritor. Skaaha covered her gaping mouth with her hands. Legend also said Danu's lover was a warrior priest.

'There will be an old one somewhere,' Terra whispered, 'teaching him.'

Suli.

Skaaha might have called Ruan on it, as proof she was a pawn in a priest's game. But the game was hers now too, and since she hoped to win, he was her best ally. He didn't offer Terra or Misha training, and they, fearing bad magic, didn't seek it. A new pattern developed, packing the short days. Dips in the river after morning routines were brief. While Skaaha and Eefay worked with Ruan, Terra and Misha honed chariot skills. The rest period after dinner was turned over to learning the disciplines. Traditional battle skills filled the afternoons, the four girls pitting themselves against each other. The charioteers made willing commentators or, when the lack of a weapons tutor told, the students took turns to watch and correct each other, sharpening vital critical ability as they did.

Led by druids and charioteers, evening stories taught morals, heroism, faith and tactics. From board games with practised opponents they learned to think as fast as they moved, to plan ahead, to outwit, to win and to lose. Skaaha seldom slept alone, sharing the friendship of her thighs with those she favoured, or simply for companionship. Skills developed there too, from navigating desires and responses of others, or the tricky diplomacy of emotions, to the simple act of turning in bed in tune with another sleeping body.

By the time the first frost whitened the naked branches of the trees, Skaaha had transferred the tactics of the stave to a spear. Leaps, rolls and aerial twists were utilized to improve her combat skills with shield and sword. She could move like the shadow of her attacker to defend herself, or shift in opposition to attack with the speed of the wildest wind. There was only one opponent at Glenelg she could not defeat – Ruan, and he was leaving.

Outside the great door of Doon Telve, she clung to him, feeling the lithe strength of his warm body inside the thick winter cloak, face pressed against the side of his neck, breathing in the scent of herbs and perfumed oils.

'I need you,' she groaned. The school was illusion, novice fighting novice. 'I'm not ready for the battlefield, not yet.'

'If I don't go,' his voice thick with emotion, 'I can't speak for you.'

'Then go,' she said, stepping back abruptly to let him mount.

He caught her again, dropped a light kiss on her mouth then leapt into the saddle. 'If I'm not back when the snow comes,' he urged, 'go south with Terra as soon as it thaws. Don't wait for me.'

The instruction froze her. 'You'll be back.'

'I'll be with you,' he said, and kicked the horse away.

She ran to the end of the path, watching till he vanished round the foot of the hill. 'Live the day well, Ruan,' she whispered. Closing her eyes, she listened while the echo of hooves faded from the glen and her ears filled with the background roar of river water. She missed the sea, the open space of it, the bright, wide sky above.

'Are you crying?' Terra came down the path towards her.

'No, thinking of home.' She nodded towards the slopes. 'These hills are too close. I feel safer when I can see what's coming.'

'You'll know soon enough.' Terra linked her arm in Skaaha's and they walked back to the broch. 'Don't you trust him?'

'My life is in his hands. Do I have a choice?'

'You chose not to answer the question.' Terra grinned.

Skaaha laughed. 'Now you sound like him.' The voice of another red-haired friend spoke in her head. *Believe what you like. It won't change anything.* They were Freya's words, from another life. 'He's druid,' she said. 'If the elders order it, he'll take me to them in chains.'

35

'You teach what is forbidden?' Suli asked. They walked in the grove, wrapped up against the cold. The sky was iron-grey.

'Forbidden for most,' Ruan corrected.

'With few exceptions,' she amended. 'Tell me your reasons.'

'She asked,' he said, 'thinking my childhood and practice equipped me.'

'This is good.' The high priest glanced up at him. 'What else?'

He shrugged. 'It's from Danu we know these things. I return what we owe.' His task was to prepare her. 'If the islands are not secure, the faith is in danger.'

'Excuses.' Suli's eyes were opaque. 'Mara is the reason.'

Abashed, he nodded. 'Skaaha means to challenge her. She needs time, several suns of training, maturity. If these charges force her hand, she'll die.'

'You can't prevent that. Discipline is exercised, not gifted.' She moved on. 'The elders will rule on Mara's accusations. Skaaha is your concern. Teach her as you will, but she must not be led.' Her staff tapped the way ahead. 'Guided, but not led.'

'I made a mistake,' he confessed.

'You disappoint me. Just the one?' She chuckled. 'I expected several by this time.' The staff slipped, her footing missed. As she stumbled, Ruan caught her. Inside the thick robes, she was frail as a bird. 'Your faith failed,' she guessed.

'My courage.' He believed Mara would act whatever the ruling. 'I told her to go south, if the thaw came before I returned.'

The old woman sighed. 'Now you must stay with us till it does.'

'That's hardly fair,' he protested.

Her staff cracked off his shin. She had lost none of her speed. 'You talk like a child,' she snapped. 'That's what comes of living with them.' Anger made her walk faster. 'Don't confuse legend with life, or what's in your heart with law.'

He, too, was angry with his carelessness. Like knowledge, what was spoken could not be taken back. 'I came to address the council,' he said. The next words, hard to speak, would be harder to carry out. 'But I'll stay till the thaw.'

She slowed her pace. 'See it as a test, for both of you,' she advised. 'It's not you she must believe in, it's herself.'

Screaming – screams and smoke, the flash of blades, burning thatch, and blood – blood that bloomed on opening wounds, the sharp thrust of a spear. Skaaha gasped upright, hands clutching her gut, expecting to see blood ooze through her fingers. There was no blood, the only fire the flicker of night-lamps, the sounds of sleep. Stumbling to Eefay's chamber, she shook her sister awake.

'We must move to Doon Trodden,' she urged. 'Mara will attack whatever the druids decide.'

They moved come morning. Door- and watch-keepers were left at Doon Telve to raise the alarm if strangers approached from the coast. Sitting on a mound above the valley floor, tucked against the hillside, the second broch was easier to defend. A few strides from the door, a mountain stream supplied fresh water. Food, drink and fuel were rapidly re-stocked, a beacon fire built on the hilltop.

Along the valley, the higher farm broch was also alerted and prepared. There was always the chance of being caught outdoors, or the less likely possibility of falling back. The beacon there would carry a distress message to the warriors and tribes of Alba. At Doon Trodden, on the wall top walkway, defences were improved: quivers of javelin mounted; supplies of stones stacked in three weights – dropping, throwing and sling.

'You think of everything,' Eefay said, when she caught Skaaha discussing with the charioteers how they might push off the roof in the event of fire arrows.

'Not everything,' Skaaha said, taking her sister aside. 'Our friends will quickly become the enemy if the druids want us brought to court.'

'And we'll be locked in with them.'

'Not for long. They'll open the door. We can't ask or expect them to go against the law.'

'Then we'll surrender,' Eefay said. 'Two of us could hold the broch, but I won't fight my own people.'

Skaaha agreed. 'And as we surrender, we kill Mara.'

'How?'

'That's the "not everything" I haven't thought of yet,' Skaaha confessed.

The question preoccupied her as the longest night arrived, and kept her half awake throughout it. The men had vanished to their bonfire on the hill. It would be a good night to attack, when solstice fires rendered beacons useless. But none came. When the door opened at dawn to welcome the reborn sun, it opened on an altered landscape. Heavy snow fell in the glen, quickly masking everything in white. It arrived too soon for Ruan to have returned.

'Let it be a sign from Bride,' Skaaha muttered, as they ploughed down to the practice field. There was a stinging thud against her ear, a snowball thrown by a giggling Misha. The morning routine was forgotten as a fast and furious snow battle ensued. Sodden, chuckling and shivering with cold, they ran in to breakfast, returning in dry clothes to build an array of snowy enemies to attack during the training session. It was a fine day, happy and carefree, but it solved no problems. When night came, Skaaha slept alone and fitfully, waking before first light. Today, today surely, Ruan would be back with word.

Creeping downstairs, she armed herself with dagger and spear before going out. A wilderness of white waited, the river a black scar winding through it. Ankle-deep in snow, Skaaha crunched downhill and across the field. There was a spot midway between the brochs where deer came down to drink in the early morning. Keeping downwind, she crouched among scrub, spear resting shoulder-ready. A stone among stones, she waited, watching her cold breath smoke the air. Every sound was magnified, the creak and drip, the squeak and scurry, snuffling horses, and the soft steps of approaching roe, three of them, coming to the watering hole in the grey pre-dawn light.

However fast she was, they would be faster, leaping away as the spear left her hand. Does, in kid till Beltane, were not hunted, but these were bucks, breathing steamily in the chill, their darkened coats winter-grey. Lips parted to breathe silent, she let them test, settle, two heads dip. They wheeled back as she threw. The spear sang ahead of them into space where no deer was to find one filling it, thumping down, thrashing to rise. But she was on it, weight on the shaft, twisting in as blood came, through the scream, the thud of flailing limbs. Dropping down on to warm body, she slit its throat, watched dark eyes shine, shine and die into silence.

It was a silence that raised hackles on her neck. She was not alone in the field. Turning, she saw a bear, reared up in the far corner, a ripple of fur, and her too distant from either broch. The pointlessness of running or tree-climbing sucked out her breath. Then she saw that it was no bear but a warrior in his winter garb, stalking her. Rapidly, she slid the dagger into its sheath, twisted her spear free, still crouched, watching the man approach. Even through snow, that was a stride she knew.

'Fion,' she breathed, and stood. 'Fion!' she yelled, and ran.

'Ho, the hunter!' he hollered back, red moustache puffing outwards.

Half-way to him, she stopped abruptly. 'Throw your axe, Fion,' she shouted.

'It would kill you!' he protested.

'Throw it true,' she called, 'and I'll fuck with you.'

Fion threw the axe. Whup-whup-whup it flew. He grimaced, eyes shut, looked again. There was empty space where she had been.

She brushed against his back, slid the axe she'd caught into its holster, flung her arms round him from behind.

'Skaaha.' He let his held breath out, moved to clasp his hands over hers.

'Do not,' she warned, face between his shoulderblades, cheek against bearskin. Her hands clasped the dagger, point pressed into his centre below his ribs.

'You make a new way to fuck.' There was laughter in his voice.

'Tell me why you came.' If he moved, a slight tightening of her grip, it was to the grave. 'Speak.'

'Suli sent me,' he said, tense now. 'To recuperate, which I'd fine like to do.' He breathed too deep, wincing as the blade pricked his skin. 'Jiya's at the broch. I saw deer run and doubled back. Is this reason to attack me?'

'You threw the axe.'

'You told me to!' A pause. 'Persuasively.' Another pause. 'We brought the council of elders' judgement.' There was sorrow in his voice. 'You're banished.'

'Banished?' Skaaha dropped her hands, stepped round in front of him.

'You and Eefay, exiled from the island,' he said. 'Ach, Jiya promised she would tell you. That's why she went on.'

Ruan had failed her. He should have come to say so, not hid behind others. 'Can I never go home?'

'Not for two suns, then they'll consider it again.'

'Two suns?' Relief coursed through her body. She had been gifted time.

Fion put his hands on her shoulders. 'When I go back, we'll argue for sooner. This place is making you strange.'

'Not strange.' She grinned. 'Happy.' She threw her arms out. 'Blessed Bride, I love you,' she shouted to the skies. 'Oh, how I love you!'

'So now we fuck?' Fion asked, lifting her off her feet in a joyful bear-hug.

No flicker of feeling crossed Mara's face. She gazed steadily across the low table at the old druid's pale eyes. 'Banished,' she repeated.

'A severe punishment,' Suli said. 'But our security must not be threatened.'

'No,' Mara agreed. Her claim had succeeded but was a pyrrhic victory. Kerrigen's daughters still lived and, in accusing them, she'd shown her hand. She waved the new pot-boy, the third in as many moons, to pour mead into both their horns, waiting till he did, until she could be casual. 'What defence was offered?'

'None that affected our judgement,' the old woman said smoothly.

Nothing was tighter than a priest determined not to talk. Suli's placid face conveyed no emotion. The gaze of her blind eyes was disconcerting, as if she saw the thought behind what was spoken. Mara suspected a game was being played, the main player sitting opposite, blandly sipping the sweet drink.

'Kirt has not returned to us,' she said. Her druid had been replaced, a common occurrence, but one that might be intended to keep her in the dark.

'I sent him to Ynys Mon,' Suli explained. 'Tosk might shed some light on our concerns over Kerrigen's daughters.'

Panic fluttered in Mara's chest, quickly stilled. Tosk knew nothing, or he'd have spoken at the time. If Suli fished, it was in the dark. She changed tack. 'And if they return to the island, the punishment will be death?'

'Undoubtedly,' Suli agreed, 'unless there is reason for appeal. Time solves many things.'

Mara nodded. 'It does indeed,' she agreed. 'The wisdom of the goddess is great.' The meeting was over. She thanked the high priest for the honour of a personal visit, tried to look crestfallen when her offer of continued hospitality was declined, and saw the old woman safely out of Doon Beck.

'That's good news, isn't it?' Corchen asked tentatively as they watched the druid tap her way across the gentle slope, heading south to the black mountains.

'More than they imagine,' Mara said. There were many ways to flush a rat. 'But, enough of this. Take a message to Vass,' she instructed. 'His chapter is to attend here after Imbolc. They grow lazy. Training together every quarter will solve that, and our loss of Donal.'

'A fine solution,' Corchen enthused. 'The tribe will like it, and the warriors will enjoy the time together.'

Mara snorted, a short bark of derision. 'I don't intend to rouse lust,' she snapped, 'but to defeat our enemies.' Turning to head indoors, she halted, as if the thought occurred that moment. 'Before you go' – she pointed across the stockroom to the cell opposite – 'have our captive bathed, dressed and brought to me upstairs. When the ransom ship returns, diplomacy is better served if he survives.'

Admiration lit Corchen's face. Mara climbed the steps, grimly pleased with herself. Graciousness sat well on a warrior queen. The respect of others would increase. If Suli had different intentions, the wily druid underestimated her. The game grew longer, but not so long as the old priest might suppose.

Skaaha and Fion trudged to Doon Trodden, the kill slung between them on her spear. Sex in the snow had not materialized, so Fion muttered all the way about the rent in his tunic from Skaaha's blade. Men worked hard to win attention from women. Warriors had the advantage of glamour but were handicapped by impermanence and unsuitability as husbands. Marriage was rare, except with women warriors, and seldom outlasted parturition, which was the reason for it. The friendship of women's thighs was an infrequent joy, shared only at festivals or on tours of duty. Competition from the rest of his chapter meant Fion fussed mightily over his appearance.

'Right through my shirt too,' he complained, poking his finger into the cut.

'I'll have it mended,' Skaaha snapped as they approached the broch. 'We'll make you new clothes. Blessed Bride, I've said I'm sorry. Will you stop?'

The others met them at the door, cloaks drawn over their night clothes, coming to find her.

'Good hunting.' Terra grinned, flicking her shift up to welcome the warrior with her friend. 'A deer and a man.'

'Only half a man,' Skaaha muttered, as the deer was carried away for butchering, 'since he has a hole in his shirt.'

Jiya shrieked towards her. 'Exiled!' she cried, throwing her arms round her niece. 'How can they do this to you? Mara – Mara . . .' Her head shook.

'It's all right,' Skaaha soothed her. The warrior queen couldn't bring a force across the water now, not to attack them. 'This is good, not bad.'

'Is it?' Eefay sounded petulant. 'I was to come of age at Beltane.' A snort made her round on Misha and Terra, both of whom smothered smiles.

'You don't want a man,' Misha stammered, mystified.

'But it's my turn,' Eefay wailed. 'In two suns, I'll be too old for Torrin!'

Skaaha sighed. Yesterday, they didn't have two precious days. Now, time was a burden. 'No, you won't,' she assured her sister. 'You'll be just one sun older than I was, and even more beautiful because of it.'

The others assured Eefay this would be the case, the extra maturity adding to her stature. Mollified, she recovered dignity, and sense. She turned to Fion, raising the shift to her navel to assert her authority as she welcomed him.

'Bride is good to bring you to us, Fion,' she said. 'Glenelg needs a tutor.'

Eefay moved them back to Doon Telve. Despite her nightmares, Skaaha didn't argue. Ruan had abandoned her. The open valley was as close to home as she might come for some time. From the top of the broch, she could see the slight shimmer of sea far down the valley. Beyond it, the familiar mound of Ben Aslak sheltered the westward side of Kylerhea. The warriors settled into schooling the novices. Daily, the frozen glen rang with the clash of steel and Fion's good-natured shouts. Skaaha threw herself into training. Let Ruan hide, believing her a lost cause, she would not be beaten. Pitching herself against her exuberant, moon-crazed aunt, she discovered her own weaknesses, Jiya's experience telling even against unfamiliar aerial attacks.

'Good move,' Jiya yelled, as she brought her niece down yet again.

'Good and dead,' Skaaha groaned, face down in snow, severely winded and with Jiya's blind training spear prodding her back.

'You try too hard,' Fion called, coming over. 'How did you kill the deer?'

'I threw where I knew it would go,' Skaaha said, rising to dust off snow.

'Same here,' Fion said. 'Jiya sees what you will do. She fights that. Trust yourself,' he added. 'Know where she'll go and be there first. Make her follow you.'

'You make me.' Jiya grinned at the red-haired warrior.

'With these toys?' He laughed, slapping the blunt sword in his scabbard and waving the other three students over to watch while he tried to do just that. They were well matched, Jiya's speed equalizing Fion's strength. Often it was difficult to tell, in the swift flash of steel or clash of shields, who led or who followed. But if shouts and taunts were anything to go by, they were enjoying themselves.

'Gods,' Eefay muttered, attention rapt on the rapid action. 'They're gods.'

'We're so lucky,' Misha breathed, 'to have come back.'

Skaaha watched in despair. Mara could defeat both these warriors. If she was to stand any chance, so must she. But if she didn't try, and hard, how else could she achieve? *Like a leaf in the wind*, Ruan's voice answered from the past. It made no sense now, when death could drag her from the sky.

'He's right, you know,' Terra was saying. 'You don't trust yourself.'

'There is no reason why I should.' The truth spoke itself before she'd realized it. 'I failed to protect myself.'

'But you lived.' The Icenian swept her long red braids back off her face to glance at Skaaha. 'My foster-mother said everyone is trustworthy, if trusted with the right thing. She had a rhyme – trust a liar to lie to you, trust a thief to steal . . .'

'First blood!' Jiya yelled. 'Yield!'

There was no blood, the weapons blind, but Fion accepted the strike as defeat. First blood settled every dispute, even a challenge between champions.

'Aye-yie-yaa!' Eefay and Misha cheered.

As Terra raised her fist to compete next, Skaaha tugged her arm.

'There was no choice but to live,' she said. 'Here, or in the otherworld.'

Terra's hand touched the side of Skaaha's neck, fingers pressing warm against the tattoo of the goddess. 'Then trust Bride.' She grinned, and ran on to the field.

Skaaha watched her aunt and friend engage, the action fast and dangerous. Neither was tense, despite the demand on muscles, as if they danced – the same confidence she'd learned on the chariot. That was also how Ruan fought, without any discernible thought for himself, as if he could not be harmed. Death was the same as life to warriors of Bride, fearless in faith, the otherworld the same as this. She didn't trust herself because she was afraid, not of dying, but of failing again.

36

'Why did Jiya defeat you?' she asked when Fion came to stand with her.

'She fights to fight,' he said, 'not to win.'

'And you want to?'

'In battle, I fear nothing.' He shrugged. 'But in training?' He grinned. 'My shirt didn't want another hole in it.'

'Then maybe I try too hard.' Skaaha frowned. 'For much the same reason.'

Fion gazed at her, suddenly serious, considering this. He, too, had witnessed her broken body, the justice she had delivered at Kylerhea. His silence lengthened against the ringing of steel on steel from the field. Skaaha saw herself reflected in the mirror of his eyes, a shadow against the white snowline behind.

'Stop thinking, Fion,' she said. 'You're scaring me.'

'I am thinking,' he said slowly, 'there is only one thing you do wrong.'

'And that is?'

'You don't fuck with me yet.'

'Blessed Bride,' she swore. 'Is that all it takes?' Her voice rose in anger. 'And I suppose yours has the magic power of a druid's rod, so all I have to do is couple with it to become the greatest warrior on earth!'

The contest on the field faltered. Four heads turned their way.

Bemused, Fion tugged his long moustache. 'Maybe,' he finally got out, unwilling to deny a compliment to his prowess. 'But I was only thinking how fine it would be if you kept your word.'

Skaaha's outraged expression lifted into a wide grin. Her

shoulders crumpled. Shrieks of laughter shook her. Her arms hugged her belly as she howled, staggering in the snow, gulping in great yelps of breath. Chuckles infected the group, fighting forgotten. Even Fion laughed, a rumbling, hearty roar.

'Oh, dear,' Skaaha gasped, fighting for control and breath. 'Oh, dear.' And then she was away again, this time slapping Fion's chest as she tried to speak but was unable to, tears streaming down her cheeks, warm against cold. 'Oh, dear.' She put her hand into the warrior's great fist. 'Come on, Fion,' she gulped, and led him away towards the broch, still chuckling.

There was nothing she could teach him about the act of love. The musky odour of his skin raised forgotten memories from the rocks of Kylerhea, the roar of spume, a first kiss that flowered now into fullness. He was a great joy, tender and passionate, joking over awkward bits then seriously intense where it mattered. It was a loving savoured like a great feast, until she thought she might die of pleasure, several times, but didn't, and grew eager to know his, to draw him in, dissolving into orgasmic purity inside her.

'There's no rush,' he murmured, still holding back, stroking her skin. 'I can be your man a long time.'

'Rush?' The mid-day meal had come and gone. Lamps hissed, spitting softly in the silence, casting shadows on stone. Her fingertips traced the small indented hollow in his back, below his shoulder, where the javelin had pierced deep enough to threaten his precious life. 'Aren't you hungry?'

He offered to fetch food if she was, but his mouth and hands on her flesh put all thought of other nourishment to flight. The haste that haunted her, so out of place in this copulation, finally fled. There was nothing to win, to fight for or against. She clung to him in ecstasy, face buried in the well of his throat, or lay exhausted when he was spent, until her fire, or his, was roused again. Even in sleep, they wakened, limbs tangled, to lovemaking. For three days, they left the chamber only to ease other needs, stumbling back with warm water to bathe, snatch food or skins of ale.

It was Eefay who ended it, drawing back the curtain to announce there was a thaw, that Ruan had returned and she would like to continue tutored training, if they pleased. Dressing hurriedly, they stumbled downstairs, laughing as they tried to hold hands, one behind the other, fingers twined together. The dip in the river was brief, a cursory splash and scrub before they dressed rapidly again, now the cold nipped skin. Skaaha's face ached from the smile that kept forming on it.

'Warm up first,' Fion warned as they reached the field. They did the routine together, pacing themselves into it. Beneath the naked oaks, Ruan waited with Eefay.

'You took your time,' he said, when Skaaha reached them.

She wanted to be angry at his late return, to castigate him for the despair he left her with, but it was gone. Delight at his presence magnified her maddening joy. Her mouth curved insanely as she tried to speak. 'We would be half-way south,' she managed, 'if I did everything you said.'

He flushed. 'It's good you didn't go,' he conceded. 'Jiya's an excellent opponent and Fion has much to teach.'

She grinned like a fool and knew it. 'I wasn't going to run,' she said. 'Even before they came.' That pleased him. So did Eefay's decision to revert to traditional skills, where her strengths lay.

He suggested Skaaha resume their morning routines together. 'If you also join me in the evenings,' he added, 'then you miss no weapons training with the others.'

On the field, her companions already worked on unarmed combat under Fion's cheerful instruction. Time, he taught her to take it, the pleasure in the doing. Days, lengthening in the renewed sun, spread out before them. He was her man, she would tell him that, and if he lay with another woman now, she would kill both of them. The rap of Ruan's stave brought her back.

'Be in the moment,' he reminded. 'Is that not all there is?'

*

The vernal equinox arrived, a propitious balance. Far out in the bay of Bracadale a foreign ship struck its ochre sail and dropped anchor, waiting. It did not wait long. A coracle put out from the shore, bringing safe passage to Ullinish. A ransom was delivered to Doon Beck: gilded jars of coin, jewelled ornaments, fine wines and exotic foods. In the shy light of morning, Mara walked her captive down the beach. His language was not so difficult once she made the effort. He looked well fed now, dressed in fine robes made by her weavers, for a price. The deal struck for his release cheered her, the ransom more than adequate.

'You have the map?' she asked, as he stepped into the coracle that would row him to the waiting boat. But she knew he had, the instructions impressed on him over the last three moons. There was no need to trust him. His people had given much for his return and, for pride alone, he would act. All she need trust was human greed.

Above the tide-line, her warriors waited. It was the end of the first quarter. Before mid-day, the Ardvasar men would arrive for another week of training. Gila, the archer, stood with Corchen. In her hand she held a painted egg.

'This one's for you,' she told Mara. It promised new life. The eternal knot that covered the shell was drawn in red and gold, life through fire.

'A good omen,' Mara said, accepting the gift. Debts were paid on quarter days. She turned to watch the coracle bump against the side of the enemy ship, her captive climb aboard. Oars dipped, flashing, in the water. The ship moved slowly out to deeper water. The ochre sail rose, caught the breeze. Peace was all she wanted, peace from the vengeful haunting of Kerrigen through her dangerous daughters. By tomorrow morning, she would have it.

In Glenelg, the inhabitants raced hares or rolled their decorated eggs down the ancestral mounds. Bets were taken on both, all previous debts safely settled. Although their girls already bled, and they had no boys, a feast was still laid out in Doon Telve. A whole porker roasted on a spit. Falling between Imbolc and Beltane, this equinox was when first signs of adulthood were marked. It balanced day and night, another pinhead on which time stood, and changed.

At sunset, Skaaha and Ruan trained together on the hill. Around them, yellow gorse and broom blazed like fire. It was treasured time, silent apart from the thump and smack of staves, the air shifting as they leapt or spun. Birds, busy all day with breeding, settled to their evensong. The sky painted itself in red shades of sunset, clouds gilded with gold.

'You did well,' Ruan said when the session ended.

'Better,' she agreed. Always one step ahead, he advanced her ability without humiliation. Pleasure in her increasing skill replaced urgency. 'I drew first blood with Fion today.'

'And Jiya?'

'Not yet, she's faster in her madness, but soon.' She squinted at him against the last sunlight. 'So your days are numbered.'

He laughed. 'You boast like a warrior, at least,' he teased.

She blushed, smiling. 'We'll see.'

Screaming – screams and smoke, the flash of blades, burning thatch, the sharp thrust of a spear, and blood – blood that bloomed on opening wounds. Skaaha gasped upright, hands clutching her gut, expecting to see blood ooze through her fingers. There was no blood, the only fire the flicker of night-lamps, the sound of Fion's steady breathing beside her. Rising, she padded across the skins to the hearth, poured a horn of the druids' beech cordial left over from the feast, and climbed the stairs to the walkway to watch the stars.

The colour of the night sky promised dawn was not so far away. The watch-keeper cracked an eye at her and resumed dozing. An owl hooted among the trees. Overhead, Danu, the warrior, strode westward. Stars split the heavens, countless beyond imagination. A waning gibbous moon grinned in the east, lighting fields and forest. The sounds of night stirred, scatterings, shrieks, the soft whoop of owl wings, birds shifting in branches, a wolf howling far away, and the distant all-too-human cry of foxes that wasn't quite in the right place.

A shiver ran across her body as if the skin shrivelled on her bones. Dropping the drinking horn, she ran back round the walkway till she could see north. Fire glowed beyond the kyle. A pall of smoke drifted across Ben Aslack.

'Sound the alarm,' she yelled, shaking the slumbering watch-keeper. 'Kylerhea's burning!'

Before the war horn of Glenelg blared, she was downstairs, dressing rapidly. It was her lead the others followed, crashing down the stone steps to arm themselves while wakened workers saddled up their mounts. The druids came running to meet them outside the doors.

'They're under attack, Ruan,' Skaaha yelled, leaping on her horse.

'I hear it.' He caught hold of her bridle. 'Let the rest of us go. You and Eefay can't cross the water!'

'Come or stay,' she screamed back at him, drawing her sword to take his hand off if he didn't let go, 'but they won't die for want of me!'

For answer he leapt up behind her. 'Go!' He slapped the horse away.

Riding hard, rounding the hill, they confronted an orange glow. A dark pall of smoke stained the dawn. Across the sound, Kylerhea was in flames. Every roof blazed. The ride along the shore was longer than a lifetime. At the ferry, leaping from her horse and into a coracle, Skaaha pushed off with her spear as Ruan took up the paddle. Behind, a string of small craft followed. The current carried them rapidly over the water, into the crackle and roar of flame, to air thick with shrieks and moans, the din of terror-stricken beasts trapped in pens.

Pelting up the jetty, running low to avoid sparks and smoke, Skaaha stumbled to a stop. A body lay beside the path, forearm hacked open to the bone. Unfamiliar in death, neck bare of her strings of beads, Kenna lay like a broken thing, skirts ripped aside, a bloodied gash where her malformed male genitals had been. The noman's dead fingers still gripped an iron ladle like a club, the only weapon to hand in her home at night.

'Raiders,' Ruan muttered. 'They might still be here.'

Passing him her spear, Skaaha drew her sword and they ran on. Erith's roundhouse was in flames. Clumps of flaring thatch fell into it, setting beds and screens alight. Skaaha ran into choking, acrid smoke, eyes smarting.

'Cover your face,' Ruan yelled, tearing strips of cloth, soaking them quickly in the cold cauldron to wrap around his mouth and nose.

Erith lay on her back in the doorway of her chamber, dead eyes staring up at her burning roof, nightshift slashed across her swollen belly. The wound gaped, wet and bloody. Skaaha snatched up Freya's daughter from her cot, staggered outside, on to her knees, wheezing for breath, retching.

'Stay here' – Fion's voice in her ear – 'we'll get the rest out.'

Someone moaned, a body beside the path propped on a rock. 'Skaa-ha.'

She scrambled over, laid the gasping baby on the grass. It was Ard, face blackened, hair singed, one arm flung awkwardly behind. The other hand clutched his gut. He raised it towards her. Blood bloomed from the hole in him, where a spear had gone in. She pressed her own hands down. The warmth of his life oozed between her fingers. 'Ruan!' she screamed. 'Ruan!' Behind her, Lethra's blazing roof collapsed inwards.

They worked till daylight, dragging out the wounded, dead and dying. Gern was found unconscious near the forge. Lethra, pulled from her ruined house with just a knock on the head, cursed her survival. Yona, the druid, lived, but only just, her two fellows killed. Misha freed the animals from their pens, slaughtering those with injuries. Kenna's roof was the only one saved, a trick of nature helped by the sea-water Jiya and Terra carted up ladders to pour on to the smouldering thatch.

344

The growing light brought the small group of charcoal burners down from the forests. Wakened by the first screams, they'd lit the beacon on the hill then run away.

'There were too many,' Erith's youngest husband whispered, looking down at his wife's ruined body. 'They came in a great ship with yellow sails.'

When there was no one left to save, Skaaha ran back to be with Ard, bandaged now by the druids. She held his head in her lap, stroked his tormented, beloved face, and told him lies, all the lies that might make life beautiful again before he died.

'Erith?' he groaned, trying to rise.

'Is fine. Rest easy.'

'She had' – he shuddered – 'birth pains.'

'She's fine, and the baby. A boy it was . . . is. You have a fine son. She's on the green, with him, sleeping in a blanket. Hush now' – when he tried to turn to see. 'When you can be moved, we'll lay you with her. There are not so many hurt' – she kissed his forehead – 'it was the forge they came to raid.' That, at least, was true, the stores emptied. 'Things only, you'll make more, and more beautiful.'

'Go,' he gasped. 'Keep' – a great gulf between each breath – 'safe.'

'I will,' she promised more black lies, 'soon as you sleep.' His body relaxed in her arms. 'Soon as the tribes come to mend the roofs, soon as . . .' She was talking to herself. 'There now,' she said. 'Lie with Erith. I told you it would not be long.' Gently she laid his head on the ground, put a kiss on her fingers and pressed it to his mouth. Then she crawled away, hunched over the earth and beat her fists on the grass, thumping down over and over as if ferocity of feeling might kill the world.

'Skaaha.' Ruan's hand touched her shoulder.

'Do not give me pity,' she snarled up at him.

'I need your sword,' he said, his smoke-stained features bleak. 'There is a man and a child badly burned.'

She went with him. The adult writhed, unrecognizable,

naked skin blackened, cracked, his lips and eyelids gone, just a patch of pink flesh against his chest. The toddler, one pink arm against crusted burns, jerked. There was only one boy that age in the village, Kaitlyn's foster-son. His mother crouched near by, rocking, coughing, a tattered bandage on her arm.

'Hanick went to fetch him,' she sobbed. 'They didn't come out.'

'They won't live,' Ruan said, his voice hoarse, 'and their pain is great.' He held his hand out. 'Let me cut off their breath.'

'They're my people,' Skaaha said. 'I will do it.' She drew her sword.

When it was done, she walked away, sword glued in her hand, dragging through drifting ash beyond the ruined buildings to the foot of the hills. Weapons were made to defend their clans, not for this. Not for this. Her spirit could not hold what was happening here. Great circles of stone that had been homes smoked like hearths. Bodies lined the playing ground. The wounded huddled on the drying green. Among them, the druids worked, stitching, cauterizing, providing sips of brewed bark and herbs to dull the pain. Harsh coughs and howls of agony mingled with softer weeping. Nearby, a child whimpered.

She turned to look at the untouched hazel shelter of a latrine. Crossing to it, she pulled back the wicker screen. The boy inside drew in a sharp, frightened breath. His arms gripped his chest protectively. Tracks of tears ran down his face.

'Calum!'

'Don't cut me,' he squealed, covering his face.

'No.' Realizing she still held the sword, she sheathed it, dropped to her knees and held out her arms. 'You're safe now.'

'Bride,' he breathed, throwing himself at her. 'I knew you'd come.'

Thunder, there was thunder on the hill. Horses, so many horses, each with a warrior on its back, galloped down it. The boy in Skaaha's arms shook.

'It's all right,' she said, setting him down. 'Just stay behind me.'

The lead mount pulled up in front of her. Vass leapt down.

'What happened?' he demanded, gazing past her at the destruction.

She threw herself at him, beating on his chest. 'How did you let that ship pass?' she screamed. 'Look what they've done!'

'Raiders?' Vass gripped her arms. 'That makes no sense.' His warriors milled, dumbstruck. 'Mara returned their hostage only yesterday.'

'You didn't come,' she raged. 'They lit the beacon and you didn't come!'

'We rode from Bracadale' – he sounded bewildered – 'as soon as we saw smoke. Mara' – he waved a hand – 'called us up for training.' His voice changed. The grip on her arms tightened. 'You shouldn't be here,' he warned, pushing her away. 'Run.'

37

Skaaha stepped back. Women she knew rode among the men of Ardvasar. A horse edged through them. Skaaha's skin tightened till it might snap. Mara, haughty and arrogant, sat looking down at her. There was a strange light in her cold eyes.

'Well, well,' the warrior queen observed, 'our little renegade.' The edge of delight in her voice cut like a shard of glass. 'Take her!' she barked.

Skaaha drew her sword. The slash of steel echoed beside her, a second sword. It was Eefay's, her sister standing now at her side.

'Both of you?' Mara crowed. 'Better and better.'

Ruan leapt between them, arms raised to forbid attack. 'The ground of Kylerhea is sanctified for healing,' he shouted. 'You cannot pass.'

Mara's warriors hesitated. Jiya bounced up and down on Kenna's roof.

'You did this!' she howled. 'Slime-ridden bog bitch, I know you! I see you. Spawn of the swamp, I see what you do!'

'Shoot her down,' Mara ordered her archer.

'I can't.' Gila hesitated, unnerved. 'She's crazed.'

Still screeching obscenities, Jiya skittered down the roof, pelting over to join her nieces. The priests of Glenelg, stained with dirt and blood, hurried to stand shoulder to shoulder with Ruan. Misha and Terra, reeking of smoke, lined up with the two sisters, swords drawn. Fion stood alongside, axe in hand. In the morning light, skin blacked and eyes red-rimmed, they made a pitiful small band. The warrior queen leant forward over her horse's neck, glaring at Ruan.

'You can't save them with sanctuary, druid,' she said. 'By

the ruling of your own court, their lives were forfeit when their feet touched this island.'

Skaaha sheathed her sword. The time had come. Pushing past Ruan, she gazed up at Mara's hated face. 'You will have my life,' she said, strong and clear, 'if you can take it. I claim the right of combat.' A gasp of surprise or shock rippled through the mounted warriors. Beside her, Ruan tensed. Night and day, on the hill while they trained, they had planned for this. Now his hand touched hers, afraid it came too soon.

'Skaaha . . .'

'Is long dead,' she stopped him, still watching Mara. 'I am the instrument of vengeance' – her voice rose with her courage – 'Danu incarnate!'

Uncertainty flickered in Mara's eyes. 'You delude yourself,' she scoffed.

'That you fear me?'

'Ha!' the warrior screeched. 'Name the day.'

'The place of heroes,' Skaaha declared, 'after the wake for Kylerhea. If there is one shred of honour left on the Island of Wings, you'll meet me there.'

'Aye-yie-yaa!' the warriors shrieked. It was a powerful challenge.

'If my queen allows,' the archer, Gila, spoke, 'I will fight as her champion.'

'Then I stand as champion for Skaaha!' Jiya trumped her.

Mara waved her archer's offer away, gaze fixed on her challenger. 'The honour,' she spat the word, 'is mine.' A tight smile touched her mouth. 'You will need more than words, daughter of Kerrigen.' Her hands gripped her horse's reins. 'Bury your dead.' She pulled the animal round, kicked it away.

Several of the Bracadale chapter followed their queen. Others hesitated. Help was needed here.

'Go,' Vass said. 'This is our work.' His men dismounted.

'Thum!' Calum shrieked, darting out from behind the Glenelg line-up, running to embrace his brother.

Skaaha was surrounded. 'Stop,' she begged, refusing questions or concern. 'This is a wake.' The men of Ardvasar drifted away into the horror of Kylerhea, Thum to discover the loss of both his mothers, Vass of his brother. They would all of them find grief here, dead lovers, children, kinsfolk. Her life was the least concern. Mara expected her to be here, had delivered up her hostage to the raiders just the day before. The echoes with Beltane rang loud and clear. Mara's duplicity was without end. Sour smoke blew past Skaaha's face. The cold knot in her gut grew to encompass her heart, excising grief. Like Danu, the avenger, she was pitiless. Her challenge was not made too soon but far, far too late.

The ride north to the place of heroes took three days. They travelled at walking pace up the east coast of the island, overlooked by the hills of Alba across the water. Suli led the way, with priests from the cell of Bride, hand drums marking time. There was no joy in the procession to deliver up their young goddess. The Glenelg chariots, fetched over the kyle, carried Skaaha and her three companions. Standing upright, hair greased into coils, she was dressed for battle, torc round her throat, naked beneath her cloak and fully armed, the shield Ard had made shouldered on her back. Fion and Jiya, who rocked chanting in the saddle, rode with the Ardvasar men. Blaring war horns announced the challenge to the island people. Behind them, Lethra and Gern drove the fittest survivors from Kylerhea in a cart. Other clans followed on.

Ahead, the arena of champions lay hidden behind jagged walls of rock, a place of gloom and shadows where death was done. At the ridge of sentinels, the druids stopped. Skaaha glanced around at her companions in their chariots.

'Mind what I said.' She gripped her spear, leapt down. Ruan waited to speak with her. This was his land, the place of his birth and youth. He came on ahead, three days earlier, to prepare the ground. Before he left, she had him tattoo her left breast, erasing old scars.

Parting her cloak, he touched it now, checking, hand warm on her skin. 'You did well to bring her here,' he said. 'If truth can be won anywhere, it's in there.'

'I thought she'd refuse, or choose her champion.' As the drums of the assembled druids began to beat a war-dance, they walked on up the track together. Loose scree crunched underfoot.

'After that boast?' he said. 'You left her no choice.'

She smiled, without humour. 'Then I talk like a warrior, at least.'

He ignored the gibe. 'Fight like one too.' Blond hair flopped across his brow. 'Yield if she draws first blood. Suli will stop the contest.'

Fury punched through Skaaha's resolve. 'If Mara had mercy to give,' she snapped, 'Kylerhea would still stand!'

'Rage gives her the victory,' he warned. 'There's no dishonour in defeat, only in duplicity or cowardice.'

She calmed herself. 'Death is not defeat if Mara is exposed. The islands will be rid of this blight of jealousy, the people protected. Eefay will live. Our parents, and all those dead for Mara's failings, will be avenged.'

Ruan stopped walking. 'So you come to the land of heroes to sacrifice yourself?' They had reached the point of no return.

'I came to fight, with every weapon I have. Kerrigen was robbed of that.' They stood beside the pinnacle of rock that marked commitment, the last point before entering the arena where wisdom or fearfulness allowed a challenger to turn and flee.

'No change of heart then?' His words blew away in the wind.

She stretched her lips into a wide grin, and shrugged. 'Eefay wants to come of age at Beltane.' She couldn't touch him now, could not look back at her sister or her friends, at Fion or Jiya or Hiko, at any of the people who made life joyous.

'You go on alone,' he said. 'Suli will take the seat of justice when Mara comes.' His eyes were bluer than the early sky, and intense. 'Expect more trickery.'

'Blessings on you, Ruan,' she said.

He held her gaze. 'Live the day well.'

Before her towered a narrow gateway of rock through which only she and Mara, and the blind high priest, could pass. Two guards would be stationed to ensure no one entered or left until the contest was decided. Nobody outside could see or hear what happened within. It was why she'd chosen it. Skaaha squared her shoulders and, to the beat of druid drums, marched on through into the sacred ground.

Inside, a natural, circular plateau rose before her like a cauldron, flat-topped and brilliantly green, completely free of stones or scree that might trip or injure a fighter. Ruan had done his work. A wide grassy trough circled the raised ring of earth, into which the blood of heroes ran. High pillars of rock enclosed it, some pressing closer than others. There were no gaps where those outside might scramble to see in. Above the eastern ridge, the sky brightened with the light of the growing sun. It would be some time before it spilled over the edge.

Skaaha walked the rising path, paced out the arena, testing. Champions fought duels here, without onlookers to influence the outcome, so that true justice was done – the one judge, a blindfolded priest. Once engaged, no one could intrude; the contest ended by yielding at first blood, or death. She gambled her life that Mara, deluded by privacy and boasting to bait her, might reveal her crimes. Laying down her weapons, she cartwheeled round the plateau then tumbled back and forth, counting handsprings. Satisfied, she crossed to the far side, re-armed and sat, waiting while the drumbeats, fainter from beyond the looming cliffs, raised the lust for combat in her heart.

Outside, the horns of Bracadale announced the arrival of the warriors' queen. Flanked by Corchen and Gila, weapons shimmering, Mara rode in on her chariot at the head of her chapter, red cloak billowing, hair spiked white. A gold torc glowed round her throat. The tribe of Danu, trailed by others from the west, followed behind.

'When she goes in,' Misha whispered to Eefay, still standing erect in her chariot, watching the queen's approach, 'Skaaha said to get you to a safe place.'

'Did she?' Eefay made no move to go. 'I must've missed that, like I missed the bit where we decided it was the right time to roll the dice.'

Mounted alongside Fion, Jiya rocked in her saddle. 'I see blood,' she muttered, 'the blood of eagles falling from the sky. I see Skaaha fall –'

'Have a drink,' Fion cut in, thrusting a skin of ale into her hands.

As the horns fell silent, Vass dismounted, going to greet his one-time student. He was about to risk his own life, but something must be done. When Mara emerged victorious from this contest, war would engulf the islands. His men held her responsible for the loss of Kylerhea. Riven with grief for the deaths of Ard and Erith, he refused to inflame that belief, but he had seen the glint of victory in Mara's eyes when smoke was spotted in the south that day. Skaaha's claim to combat had pre-empted him, but if she failed, he would rescind his oath and take his men under Eefay's command. There was only one act of magnanimity that might preserve the peace.

'Rise above this,' he urged, walking with Mara to the gateway which he and Corchen would guard. Ahead, needing no blindfold, Suli waited. 'Draw first blood. Have your victory then send her back, as their blacksmith, to rebuild Kylerhea.'

'You ask for mercy?'

'For all of us. It will confound your enemies' – Bride would surely forgive his next words – 'and confirm your greatness. Let the past sleep.'

Mara paused at the pinnacle of no return. Her eyes were chips of ice. 'Concern yourself with the warrior in your ranks who dishonours his oath,' she said. 'I have my answer to Kerrigen's brat, and if you remember, she called me out.'

Forgetting himself, he caught her arm. 'Are you so lost, you no longer know the truth?' The point of a sword pressed in his back: Corchen's. He let go.

'When I see you again,' Mara said, 'I expect that hand to take off Fion's head.' She stalked on through the gateway, scattering scree behind her. The war horns of all the warrior chapters brayed again, fierce and deafening, announcing the duel between champions, of their queen and her challenger.

Inside the arena, the old priest tapped her way along a stony track that led to the ledge on which she'd sit. Mara strode up the grassy path on to the circle of green, cape flaring. Her opponent crouched, cloaked, on the far side of the ring. Either she communed with Bride, or regretted her mistake. Those who fought here were not forgotten, their stories told down the ages. Her own name would live on in triumph, Skaaha's in the ignominy of failure. Out of sight, beyond the perimeter, the drums and horns ceased, their echo clattering to silence round the cliffs. Suli stood on her ledge.

'In the place of heroes, we honour the rite of combat,' she intoned, 'the blessings of Bride afforded equally to all. May right prevail.' She sat.

Mara tossed aside her cloak. Still her opponent crouched. 'Do you mean to rise before I strike you down?' she taunted.

The girl shed her cloak and stood, shield on her arm. It was a fine piece, Ard's work, no doubt. Turning her spear upside down, Skaaha thrust it into the ground at her side. 'I have something of yours,' she said, lowering the shield. Her voice was steadier than it ought to be, her skin pale against the rock behind. A blue spiral tattooed around her left breast matched the pattern on Mara's cheek.

'My mark?' Mara scoffed, planting her own spear. 'You won't wear it long.'

'Long enough to remember you made me,' Skaaha said. 'But

I meant this.' She drew two rods from behind the shield, held them high. 'Your weapon,' she said, and tossed them into the centre of the circle. 'And this is mine.' She held up a tattered strip of blue cloth. They were not druid rods that landed on the grass, but the splintered remains of a broken spear. The cleaned head shone, the spiral running down the rib clearly visible.

It was a long time since Mara had seen that spear, since she had wrapped the parts hastily in Kerrigen's torn cloak to hide among the rocks before the others came. That same sense of dread rose now, of imminent discovery. She only meant to win the race, had sped back after crossing the finishing line, not to help the queen, but to help herself. That night, when she went to retrieve the pieces of shattered spear from their hiding place for burning, they were gone. So was Jiya, who'd been skulking in her madness.

'You murder for that,' the girl called. 'The druids said to return it.'

Mara glanced back towards the gateway. If they had the truth . . .

'There's no way out,' her opponent jeered. 'Only the bog waits now.'

It was lies. Mara reached for her sword. It must be lies. She'd be in chains, the contest stopped. They wouldn't sacrifice their goddess. Her blade swished from its scabbard. 'You talk riddles.'

'Jiya saw you,' Skaaha crowed. 'Kerrigen's blood is on this.' She waved the strip of cloth. 'Your broken spear wrapped in it. Her chariot gave up its secret.'

'Then you die first,' Mara snarled. Shield raised, she rushed forwards. Skaaha stuck the rag in her belt, yanked her sword free. Mara sliced. The girl's shield met it, clanging, slid the blade aside. Her eyes met Mara's, eyebrow raised, a brief, chilling smile. Mara froze as the girl spun away to the far side of the circle. She glanced towards the cliff face where the high priest sat, impassive, on the seat of justice, staff resting across her knees. The blind old woman's hearing was acute. Fear flooded the warrior queen like a chill in the blood. Had she damned herself by accepting guilt? Turning, she faced her tormentor.

Skaaha held the blue rag high. 'The victory is Kerrigen's,' she boasted.

'Not for long,' Mara corrected, ice-cool now, circling.

The rag was pushed back in Skaaha's belt. She advanced, swung her sword.

Mara fended. 'I smell fear,' she hissed, side-stepping to slash backhand.

The girl brought her shield down. 'The stink of your treachery,' she grunted.

Mara spun behind her. 'Or the stench of Bartok on you.' The girl turned fast. Their weapons sparked together. 'Was he any good?' She ducked as Skaaha's sword swept past her head, and thrust again. 'Or did you squeal' – again, the girl's shield was there – 'like your mother did?' She feigned a low slash then swept upwards. Skaaha somersaulted backwards. The ball of her foot, aimed to smack under Mara's jaw, missed. Satisfied, the queen watched her enraged opponent land. Now she knew her weakness. 'Nice move,' she said, voice devoid of feeling, 'for a novice.'

Skaaha raised her blade, touched it to her shoulder. Blood welled in the cut, depriving her opponent of first wounding. 'To the death.'

Mara leered. 'That, I promise you.' Changing tack, she moved fast. Her onslaught crashed repeatedly against the girl's shield while Skaaha's sword sparked uselessly on hers. Even in battle rage, Mara tested. The novice could defend but her attack was poorer. Each time she slashed the girl met it. Blow for blow, she was there, faster than Mara expected. 'Kerrigen died in error,' she breathed, 'fortuitously.' The stench of sweat rose between them. 'The rest was your fault.' She stepped back, breathing steadily. 'Now, I'll take your head myself.' Leaping forward, she chopped and chopped and chopped, forcing Skaaha to the edge of the arena. A tumble into the trough would finish it. Their shields clashed, swords locked, bodies close.

'The old one won't live to tell,' she spat in Skaaha's face. 'Another death on your conscience.' The girl wavered, muscles trembling with effort against the weight of the queen. She was strong, a strength that could outmatch Mara's, but her weakness was she cared. 'Ard must haunt you,' Mara taunted. 'Stuck like a pig while you hid.' She disengaged, stepped back, thrust at the girl's face.

Skaaha's shield came up. She sliced, furiously, for Mara's throat. Expecting it, the queen already swung to meet the mistimed blow, sword erect, grip firm. Steel rang. Skaaha's blade spun away into the dip, clattering on rock. Fluttering flapped above them. Their shields clashed. *Rau . . . rau . . .* Over the rims, their eyes met. The girl's blazed. Such desperation. Mara sneered. 'It's finished.'

38

'It's you who's haunted,' her opponent hissed. 'Kerrigen comes to feed on your bones.' Wings flapped. *Yip . . . yip . . . yipp.* Power surged through the girl. She pushed in, close. The bottom of Mara's shield yanked up. The top rattled under her chin, splitting skin, and the girl was gone, tumbling to the far side of the ring. Thrown back, staggering, Mara looked up. A sea eagle settled on the rocky rim. *Rau . . . rau . . . rau . . .* More of the birds soared overhead.

Mara's heart thundered. Trickery, it had to be more trickery. Blood trickled down her throat from the cut. First blood, drawn by a novice. Another eagle settled, flapping, strutting, and another. Shadows filled the sky. Shaken, she turned towards the girl, who abandoned her shield, propping it against the rising rock-face behind her, where the dip was narrow, and ran to yank her spear from the ground. Quartering smoothly, she faced the queen, weapon balanced in her hands.

Mara stepped sideways, positioning herself away from the trough. The novice made a second error by not rushing her. Breathing deep and steady, the warrior queen wiped the blood away with the back of her sword hand. Coolness returned. Omens could be read many ways. Kerrigen would watch her daughter die. The spear was a poor match for the sword of a master warrior, and she had a trick or two of her own to come.

Outside the shuttered rocks, the waiting crowd watched, awestruck, as eagles soared and circled. A dark cloud had descended on their lives when Kerrigen died. Now they had a sign, a powerful sign. Great magic was at work when the spirit of the dead came to witness for the living. It wasn't a corpse that brought the eagles, not yet. Although they could see nothing of the battle, they heard it rage, the clash and clatter of iron on steel. From her chariot, Eefay scanned the crowd, not the skies.

'Where's the archer?' she asked Terra. 'Mara's archer's gone.' Shouldering their own bows, they both leapt down, searching through the warriors. The woman they looked for wasn't there. With everyone's attention on the birds, they skirted the crowd, running in opposite directions round the foot of the rocky enclosure.

On the far side of the crags, an eagle flew too close. Gila ducked. Her foot slipped, sending scree spinning down. The birds made her nervous. They had arrived when she was half-way up the steep cliff. Now she neared the top. Her fingers searched the next handhold. On the ridge, a hooked beak turned, a bright eye blinked. The bird spread its wings, big as broch doors. *Rau . . . rau . . .* it barked. Then it lifted off, scattering stones down on to the archer's face. Gila pressed into the rock, held on.

Skaaha stood, feet spaced for strength, firmly planted on the ground. She wasn't alone, her mother here in spirit, seeking justice. Stillness swept through her, spear balanced between her hands. Mara was fast, but not as quick as Jiya in her madness. She was strong, but without the power of Fion. The high priest had sent good teachers. The queen's combat tactics were ingrained, swiftly instinctive, but no match for a warrior priest. Mara would not silence Suli, who could still best Ruan.

Everything in Skaaha's training distilled into this moment. There was nothing more to win. If the otherworld received her, she gained a new life. Mara's was over for eternity, her fate secured – execution by druids, the perpetual torment of the undead. *Deviousness will come*, Donal had said. She chose the place of heroes knowing Mara could not resist its pull. Justice was done. Kerrigen's legacy rested on Eefay's shoulders. The islands could find peace again. Fire surged in Skaaha's blood.

Her limbs felt loose, body confident of physical prowess. Now the battle began.

'Hyaaa-aaaaa!' she yelled, and ran at Mara, spear gripped firmly, aimed for the queen's centre. Mara's shield came round, braced to bat it away. Skaaha read her intentions – a sidestep to shatter the spear with her sword, meaning a second sword stroke to rake her opponent's unprotected flesh. On the last stride, she swung the spear into the two-handed grasp position across her body, parried Mara's sword, cracked her ear, thumped the queen's shins, spun behind and whacked the warrior's backside as she turned, too slow, to face her. Again, she smacked the flat of the sweeping sword, landed a crack on Mara's shoulder, and spun away.

High on the ridge, Gila peered over from behind a boulder. Far below, on a circle of green, Mara turned and turned, trying to fend off rapid smacks and thumps from a spear wielded like a stave in her challenger's hands. Frowning, the archer watched the dancing girl deliver humiliation to her queen. It was as if Mara fought a shadow, there then gone. Beyond them, on a ledge, the blind priest sat, a poor witness. Gila fitted an arrow to her bow and drew a line to her target, waiting for a moment of stillness. Beside her head, a stink drew her attention. On top of the boulder, the thigh bone of a calf mouldered, roped to the rock. *Yip – yip – yipp.* Wings flashed, a shadow dropped from above, hooked talons raked her head. Gila rolled over, fired the arrow. The sea eagle stuttered, fell and hit the slope, bouncing down.

Skirting the back of the formation, Terra turned towards the rattle of stone. One of the great birds tumbled down the incline. High above it, a figure moved.

'Bitch,' the Icenian muttered, searching for an accessible vantage point. When her eye found a flattened outcrop, she raced towards it, scrambling upwards in the uncertain hope of reaching it before Mara's archer could take her next shot. Up on the peak, the distant figure of Gila slotted another arrow to her bowstring.

Mara was tiring. This renewed girl had fiendish, unfamiliar skills. A flying roundhouse kick thumped her spine, the point of the spear stabbed behind her knee. She crumpled, shifting her shield as she fell to cover her exposed abdomen from the dancing Skaaha. The smell of earth filled her nostrils. Now she needed Gila, but no help came. Rolling, she swung her blade as her opponent leapt above. It barely nicked Skaaha's calf, but enough to cause a hesitation in the raining blows. Rapidly on her feet, Mara balanced low. Shield raised to block the spear from stabbing her face and shoulders, she spun sunwise fast, kicking out, and spun again, lashing up towards Skaaha's gut with her foot. The spear shaft cracked down on to her shin.

Braced on the rocky slope, Eefay squinted along her arrow, aiming carefully to target the assassin on the right above her. Mara's archer also took aim, over the ridge, down into the arena below. So her sister still lived, still fought. Even as pride flushed through her veins, Eefay hesitated. Skaaha's survival put a spoke in the wheel. Her older sister won every accolade. If she lived, Eefay would trail again in her wake.

Arriving on the flattened outcrop, Terra saw the enemy archer on the ridge draw back her bowstring, and cursed. Dragging her own bow round, her eye caught a second figure, below the archer, to the left. Relieved, she saw it was Eefay, arrow already aimed, bowstring taut, poised. 'Loose it,' Terra urged, soundless in case she alerted the target. What was Eefay waiting for? Her eye flicked back to Mara's accomplice on the crest. The bow snapped in her hands, the string loosed.

Skaaha somersaulted backwards beyond reach of the warrior queen. She was in control, not Mara, and delighting in her skills. Ard, somehow he surely knew. He, and Erith, and Kenna, and Hanick – their names were inscribed on her heart, every blow struck for one of the dead. In front of her, bleeding from numerous small cuts inflicted by Skaaha's spear, Mara gasped for breath, bruised and winded by the pace of attack. One mistake, and the warrior queen's guard was overcome. Time was on Skaaha's side. She intended to take it. Breathing deep, she balanced herself.

'Run out of threats?' she taunted.

On her ledge, Suli heard the hum of arrow slice through air. 'Skaaha!' she yelled.

Skaaha ducked sideways, too little, too late. Pain seared through her chest like fire, burning below her shoulder. She staggered back. Mara shrieked for joy, fingers tightening round the hilt of her sword.

On the scree slope, as Gila's bowstring snapped, Eefay loosed her arrow. Without pausing, she fitted a second flight to her bow. Below, on an outcrop, she saw Terra take aim, and fire.

Up on the ridge, reaching for the next arrow, Gila smiled, seeing the first strike home. A sharp stab burst through her neck, tore her windpipe. Choking as her chest burned, the archer fell back against the boulder, bow clattering from her clawing hands. A second shaft thumped into her chest, the iron head finding her heart.

'Hyaaa-aaaaa!' Mara screamed, leaping forward, sword poised. The mid-day sun spilled over the ridge, lighting the circle of green. Mara's blade shone as it crashed down on Skaaha's feebly presented spear. The shaft shattered in two, the pieces falling from her hands. Before they hit the ground, before Mara's swing completed and could turn on her, defenceless now, Skaaha dragged breath into her burning lungs and threw herself backwards into a handspring. Her fingers pressed the earth, felt wood, clutched. Blanking out pain, when her feet met grass again, she ran.

'Run,' Mara jeered, throwing her shield away to chase the wounded girl. 'There's no way out, remember?'

Skaaha was running, running not for the gateway but towards the cliff where her shield was propped, running into solid rock. The spar of wood grasped in her fingers was the broken head of Mara's old spear. She ran like time running out. Her feet lifted off from grass on to jagged stone. Momentum carried her up the sheer slope. Just before the force of the earth would drag her down, she bent her knees, pushed off and sprang backwards.

One day you'll leap and let fate choose your future. Jiya's voice from Doon Beck spoke in her head, from the day of her mother's death. She leapt, spinning, into brightness. Below, the warrior queen squinted up, the laugh dying in her mouth. A blaze of light blinded her – the sun reflected on the shield Ard had fashioned for his daughter. Her sword swung towards the shadow that soared above.

Skaaha turned in the air, kicked out. Her foot smacked the back of Mara's head, sending her reeling forward. As she dropped behind the queen, both hands grasped the broken spear shaft. With all her falling weight, she drove the point deep into Mara's back, between shoulderblade and spine, and held on. The ground hit with a smack. The queen thumped on top of her, dragged down, gasping, by the shaft of the spear still gripped in Skaaha's hands. Wincing from the tearing fire in her chest, Skaaha stretched out her foot, kicked away the fallen sword. The earth spun. Darkness rose. Blood from Mara's wound leaked over her.

Silence settled like a blanket on the waiting crowd. The grunts and shrieks of battle from behind the rock-face had ceased. Tension grew, taut as a harp string. They would only know who had won when the triumphant champion emerged through the guarded gateway. Sitting in the Kylerhean cart, Lethra clutched Gern's arm for support, the twin agonies of hope and fear written on their faces. Fronting the Ardvasar warriors, Fion's fingers touched his axe, freeing it in its holster. Beside him, Jiya sat rigid on her horse, finally still, finally wordless.

A slight breeze teased the red flags on Bracadale spears, the horsewomen as inscrutable as the other warriors around them. Guarding the gateway, Vass glanced at Corchen, standing by the other post. She, too, heard the crunch of stumbling feet approach from inside. A body loomed in the gap, hand clutching the rock. Filthy white, tangled spikes of hair clung to a bruised, bloodied face. It was Mara.

A few cheers stuttered among her warriors, mingling with stifled groans of dismay, rapidly strangled. The queen's scarred flesh bore no fatal wounds. Her breath shuddered. She jerked forward, pushed from behind.

'Don't think you escape,' Skaaha's voice snarled.

A gasp rose from the watchers. The shaft of an arrow jutted from the dishevelled challenger's shoulder, witness to perfidy. Buried in the stumbling queen's back, a shaft of broken spear bled profusely. Skaaha grabbed her opponent's hair, forcing the wounded woman to her knees.

'Mara sullied the place of heroes,' she called, voice rough, gasping, 'and made it a place of shame.' She paused, drew a groaning breath. 'Her death will not besmirch sacred ground.' Grunting as pain seared down across her chest from the arrow impaled between shoulder and throat, she dropped, slumping on to a boulder, still grasping the treacherous warrior's tangled hair.

Seeing their champion falter, fear rippled round the crowd. Hands clasped to mouths. Vass started towards Skaaha.

'Leave her be,' a voice warned. It was Suli, emerging from the gateway, staff tapping. 'Skaaha must finish this.' The end of her staff probed a loose rock. Bending, she lifted it, put it in the girl's limp hand.

Skaaha's fingers clenched around the stone. Adjusting her seat on the boulder, she bent forwards, yanked Mara's head up. Dazed, the queen struggled, unable to rise. Her eyes flickered, fearful. 'Know this,' Skaaha hissed in her ear, 'that you will die three times, and then for all eternity!' Driven only by the vengeance of justice now, she drew deep to still her pain, raised the rock to the extent of her arm, remembering another life beating iron in the forge. 'This death is for Kylerhea,' she roared, and brought the stone down with all the force in her to smash her enemy's skull.

'Aye-yie-yah!' the islanders howled. Tears ran down Lethra's haggard face.

Skaaha let the rock fall away, reached down to her belt, and drew out the blue strip of cloth from Kerrigen's cloak. Tugging Mara's lolling head back, she wound it around the stunned warrior's throat. 'This death,' she yelled, 'is for Kerrigen!' She jerked the cloth tight. Mara's body bucked against the sudden loss of breath. Skaaha twisted the rag tighter, holding with all her strength, breathing steadily, as the warrior queen thrashed. Her soul fought mightily to flee, feet scrabbling, scattering scree, hands clawing at the cloth, but there was no way out.

'Aye-ya! Aye-ya!' the warriors yelled. Jiya slid off her horse to dance.

Mara's limbs flopped, trembling. Before the gurgling ceased, Skaaha let go with one hand, gripping the garrotte tight with the other. Grunting with effort against the surge of pain in her wound, she reached forward over the twitching body to draw the dagger from its belt. 'And this,' she shrieked, 'is for Skaaha!' Yanking the limp head upright by the tightened noose, she dragged the short blade across a bulging vein in the queen's neck, slitting it in execution of the third ritual death. Blood squirted, pumping out the last dregs of Mara's life.

'Aye-yie-yah!' The roar from the crowd was deafening. The drums of Bride's druids began to beat in celebration. The war horns of the warriors blew.

Skaaha pushed the body away. It flopped forward, tipping over on the ground. 'There now,' she said, sucking air in, 'it's done,' and collapsed, letting the blessed darkness fill her head.

*

Weight pressed on her chest. She heard a snap, felt the thrust of agony fire through her shoulder. Robes brushed her cheek.

'Come now, child,' Suli said, tucking the broken, bloodied arrow shaft in her belt. 'You have felt worse pain. Sit up.' Hands helped her, Ruan's and Nechta's. Cool water washed her wounds, her bruised face and skin. Healing cream was applied.

'Ruan, did you see?' Skaaha grunted, still amazed. 'The eagles came.'

'Did you think they wouldn't' – his eyes glistened, unusually bright – 'for a goddess?' Her cloak was fastened round her shoulders, shield slung on her back.

'Ard protected me, as he hoped,' Skaaha muttered, gritting her teeth. 'The sun's light . . .'

'I think you had more help than you know,' Suli interrupted. Grasping Skaaha's elbow, she helped her rise. Despite frailty, her fingers gripped like iron.

'She meant to silence you,' Skaaha said.

'I was ready for her,' Suli said, unperturbed. Releasing her grasp, she freed the sling at her waist, swung it over her head. The stone shot thumped on rock above the gateway. A froth of feathers rose.

Skaaha gaped. 'You killed a sparrow.'

'Ach.' Suli tucked the sling away. 'Age dulls the ears. I heard mouse.'

Vass offered Skaaha her sword. 'The head is yours to take,' he said. Drums and horns ceased. Silence rippled like a tide through the onlookers.

Wincing, Skaaha grasped the hilt. Sun sparkled on the blade. Behind her, high above, white-tailed eagles soared, gathering to feed on a corpse sprawled on the ridge. She glanced down at the ruined body of her enemy. This was the moment she'd lived for, to raise that head in both her hands and shake it. Warrior foes were beheaded. Mara was unworthy of the accolade.

'I don't want it,' she said, then, raising her voice to shout, 'Let her go to the bog intact. Eternity should know her treachery.' Cheers bawled from the crowd, howling, becoming a great wall of sound.

'Skaaa-haaaa! Skaaa-haaaa! Skaaa-haaaa!'

Skaaha raised her sword in victory, and staggered. The chant faltered. Ruan ran to catch her. The wavering chant picked up again. Jiya danced, ululating. Thum stepped forward from the waiting warriors. Pride glowed on his youthful face. The beginnings of a moustache trapped sunlight on his upper lip. The chant frittered away, dropping to a murmur as he clenched his fist against his heart.

'I pledge allegiance to Skaaha!' he cried.

'No,' she protested, gripping Ruan's arm. 'Not me.'

Fion joined the young man, with a smile broad enough to split the stones. 'I pledge my allegiance to Skaaha!' he roared.

Vass stepped up beside his men, fist clenched to his chest, bellowing the oath. Corchen strode over to stand with them. Jiya beat her to it. One by one, warriors from the north, south, east and west chapters lined up to dedicate heart, sword and honour to their new queen. The watching tribes howled their approval.

'Skaaha, Skaaha, Skaaha!' they chanted as Thum and Fion carried her, shoulder high, to her chariot.

Ruan fell into step with Suli, to lead them back to Doon Beck.

'My task is over,' he said, 'my work done.'

'Huh,' Suli snorted. 'She has still to prove herself. The foreigners know the islands are weak.' Then she relented. 'Things are as they would have been. Bride is satisfied.' Her pale eyes turned to him, head cocked. 'Eagles?' she asked.

Ruan flushed. For the three days of his watch on the place of heroes, he had fixed chunks of carcases brought from Kylerhea up on the ridge so the eagles would come today at the same time to feed. 'It was too soon,' he excused himself.

'I thought death would come easier if she knew her mother's spirit watched over her.'

'You had no hope?'

'None.'

'Then where' – Suli's staff cracked across his ankle – 'was your faith?'

39

Boom-boom. Mara's body sank into the bog on the boundary of Bracadale. The great drum beat out in celebration. *Boom.* A feast waited at Doon Beck, meagre in expectation of her victory. *Boom-boom.* The people of Danu ran to fetch more food. Above Doon Mor, a bonfire of Mara's belongings burned. *Boom.* Answering fires flared across the island as Kerrigen's daughter was welcomed home. Standing with Skaaha on top of the broch, watching the moonlit festivities, Eefay was less pleased.

'I should be queen,' she objected. 'You didn't choose to be a warrior.'

Boom-boom. On the hill, people danced like fire shadows around the flames, ululating like Ban Shee.

'Time can't turn backwards,' Skaaha said. 'I am who I've become, as you are.' She slipped an arm round her sister's shoulders. 'Come of age at Beltane, and be queen of Glenelg. You're needed there. Where else will we train our warriors?'

Boom-boom. The smell of roast mutton drifted on the night air.

'Men, you want me to train the men?' Eefay's voice rose.

'I can't think of anyone better suited,' Skaaha grinned. 'Take Corchen. She's too slow to be of use to me but would make a fine tutor. Your school will be famous throughout Alba.'

Boom-boom. Barrels of beer were broken open. Voices called.

Eefay's face glowed. 'If I tell Nechta right now,' she said, 'they'll choose me to become Danu, won't they?' Without waiting for an answer, she ran down the stone steps to find the druid.

'A fine lesson in diplomacy,' Ruan said, coming over. He came to fetch her.

'My sister is a good teacher,' she said. So was Mara. Doon Beck smelt of neglect, the people's contempt.

Boom-boom. Ullinish spread out below, ghostly in the moonlight. The curve of the bay swept round from the flat-topped mountains beyond Idrigill Point to the towering black jagged peaks that sheltered Torrin. Whatever else changed, land, sea and mountains remained. The islanded loch of Bracadale was the harbour of her childhood, constant, reassuring in its disinterest. Her heart hurt with love of it. She had not expected to be here, had never expected to come home, or to stand on top of this broch knowing it was time, once again, for change. *Boom-boom.*

In the great room, lit by a low fire and guttering lamps, the dim space filled with chatter. Eager for counsel, the headwomen of the tribe ringed the table when Skaaha appeared. She flicked up her skirts in greeting as they did, and sat. Eefay bumped down on her left side, Ruan on her right. The Bracadale warriors filled the next few spaces. Opposite her, in the middle of the tribeswomen, Suli sat with Jiya. Vass and Fion, there by invitation of the new queen, reclined alongside.

Skaaha raised the ceremonial horn from its stand in front of her. It was not as heavy as she remembered, but to spill it would still be bad luck. The mead was as warm and thick as the silence that had settled. Skaaha drank and passed the cup to her sister. As it continued round the table, she steadied herself for the test to come. It came quickly, as soon as she replaced the horn.

'We won't feed warriors who don't protect us,' a farmkeeper warned.

'Not any more.' The boat-keeper backed her up. Mutterings of agreement issued from the other providers. The raid on Kylerhea was the last straw. They had lost kin, their source of tools gone. The islands lived in fear.

'I will deal with the raiders.' Skaaha silenced them. 'On my life,' she vowed. She began with the forge. It would be rebuilt inland, safely distant from the perils of the coast. With her experience, Kaitlyn could head it. She farmed ground near good water, bog and forest. Her new baby daughter ensured succession, and she had fostered Freya's rescued child. Gern, Calum and the other survivors would go there. The one house that remained on the kyle passed to Lethra, the crone, as a ferry post and small farm to succour travellers.

Heads nodded round the circle. There was wisdom in all of this. The change at Glenelg met the same response. A school there provided warriors at no cost to the island. Few boys had trained at Doon Beck of late.

'We must also secure Alba's future queens,' Skaaha said. 'If the people of Danu support it, women will train here as warriors.' She raised a hand to still the storm of questions. 'Doon Mor can house students. Doon Beck was Jiya's home. It will be hers again, as keeper of the new school.'

'Aye-yie-yaa!' Jiya hooted. 'I love it! We should have beer.'

The headwomen muttered approval. A school brought payment from the tribes of Alba whose daughters would also train there. With warrior tutors and students whose numbers compensated for novice skills, it provided protection and deterrent. Beer was liberally served.

Ruan put his head close to Skaaha's. 'Vass,' he whispered. Her uncle had lowered his gaze, covering his response by wiping froth from his long moustache. He would miss Jiya.

'I think so too,' she agreed. There was a tie between the old warrior and her moon-crazed aunt. His respect, and warmth, calmed her. 'Vass' – her uncle's head came up – 'the new school needs a tutor. I can think of no one better.'

'Aye-yie-yaa!' Jiya hooted again, thumping the table with her fist.

Pleasure lit up the chapter leader's face. 'You honour me,' he said.

'Then it's settled,' Skaaha said. 'Fion will lead the Ardvasar men and' – the corners of her mouth quirked – 'if he does it well enough, when I am ready for a child, I will marry him.'

Howls loud enough to raise the roof ascended to the thatch.

Fion beamed wider than the bay. As Vass slapped his shoulder in congratulation, the axe-man tossed the plait of red hair back from his face.

'I will lead like a hero,' he announced, 'then I will father one!'

'Marriage wasn't necessary,' Ruan murmured at Skaaha's side.

'He risked his life for me so the reward is high.' She leaned against him. 'But if any husband of mine is ever jealous,' she said softly, 'I will divorce him.'

'Where will we go?' a voice asked. It was one of the Bracadale warriors, the same question on all their faces. 'We're the queen's chapter. Where do you go?'

It was Suli's opaque eyes Skaaha met across the table. The old priest had not spoken. Yet she waited for this answer. Skaaha took time with it. If she stayed here, she'd walk in her mother's shadow, always Kerrigen's daughter, never herself. Three times Mara had taken her life away – from Bracadale, from Kylerhea, and from Glenelg. It was time to make life her own. The islands were the centre of the world, guarding the heart of the earth. Bride had surely saved her for this.

'We go to protect the faith,' she said. 'I will make my home at Tokavaig, on a landing gifted by the goddess.'

From all the islands, and from the north of Alba, the stone builders came. From every island house, able-bodied workers went to help raise up the fort of Skaaha on that vast stack of rock above the sea. While they worked, the druids chanted blessings, drumming the rhythmic beat of time. Children fell asleep, ears filled by stories of a winged warrior goddess who leapt out to sea and was saved by Bride to become the champion who would save them all. In fields, on boats, in homes, people told how they knew, when she emerged at Beltane, the spirit of Danu returned to watch over them. It was said the high priest sang Skaaha's castle into being. For three whole nights, the old woman sang unceasing through dark and through light as the stones grew. On the third dawn Doon Skaa towered over the waves.

At midsummer, when young men danced up the sun, the last stone was laid. Dramatic on its rock, the great fort could be reached only by Ruan's snake bridge, carved and strung to his instruction. Strong but delicate in appearance, the reed rope carried oak slats that shifted underfoot. Below, spume boiled over rocks. Opposite, on the clifftop, a guardhouse protected access. Daily, fine furniture and furnishings arrived as gifts. On the promontory, the settlement progressed.

Skaaha poached Hiko from Glenelg to run her stable, and auditioned women warriors from Alba who flocked to fill the empty spaces in her guard. Misha moved to train at Jiya's school. Instead of going home, Terra stayed to boost Skaaha's warriors, waiting for the raiders to return. They would be back, Skaaha was certain, before Sowen or come spring. While Doon Skaa grew, she prepared, travelling the islands, setting watches. Her chapter learned new tactics. The islands waited for sight of sails. It came with spring, at Imbolc, the festival of Bride. The ship sailed right to the rock.

'Ho, the castle!' a voice hailed them. 'A hag at Kylerhea stoned my boat. Said I was so behind times, she'd knock us forward to next moon if we set foot ashore!' The speaker, a small, round man, wore a long, brightly patterned coat and waved a cane. It was Beric, the tin trader, fallen foul of Lethra.

Skaaha directed him to harbour, sent Hiko to collect him in her chariot, and dispatched a rider to bring Kaitlyn to trade. It was a joy to see the colourful little man again, though his cheerful halloo soon changed. Seated round the hearth in the castle hall, generously fed and watered, he was deeply distressed by the loss of old friends.

'Erith and Kenna both? In my whole run, they were my favourite hagglers. Skinned my profit to the bone, but so sweetly I loved them for it. And Ard, was ever a smith so talented? As far as Egypt, you don't find jewellery like his.'

'Of course you never told them that.' Skaaha topped up his drink.

'Well, no, a man's got to eat.' He swallowed hard. 'But treasure lost, real treasure, and I'm right sorry to hear of it.'

The watch called out from above. Skaaha stood. 'That will be Kaitlyn.' She went to meet her friend at the bridge. Too much stirred: Ard beside her on Beric's boat, assessing Roman swords; her, not yet of age, anticipating Beltane; Erith with finely wrought jewelled bronze brought to Bride's cavern. A well of sorrow rose inside her for what was lost. So long as she lived it would not run dry.

But this was dangerous. *Be in the moment.* Beric gossiped wherever he went. Before he left, a different story must fill his head, of a fierce, stalwart people. He could see the fort, hear of the schools. Her friend would help. They would talk of trade, progress at the new forge, the virtue and training of their warriors.

The rider arriving at the guardhouse wasn't Kaitlyn. He leapt from a horse that had been ridden hard, ran across the bridge. It was a relay rider, bringing news.

'The raiders are back,' he said. 'Their sail was seen in the north yesterday.'

Running up the steps to the castle walkway, Skaaha scoured the western isles. There were no bale fires last night, no smoke now. The ship must have turned south, down the coast of the Island of Wings. Her heart hardened. That new story had begun. She knew exactly where the enemy was headed. Two riders later, it was confirmed.

As soon as the full moon rose, the boat slipped round the peninsula into Loch Slapin. The men of Harak had sailed this route before, into a trap that cost them dear. It was well-defended, evidence of protected treasure, wealth enough to repeat a risk. This time, they came prepared, and well-informed. The bright night that would reveal them to defenders also illuminated the foreign ground.

'You were right, Orek,' the captain murmured to the man at his side. 'They sleep.' On shore, the brochs showed no lights.

The king's son nodded grimly. He'd learned much during his captivity. The queen of this land was weak, blinded by jealous rage. She had him slaughter her own people, burn and pillage their forge. The wealth of that plunder had brought them back. If so rich a store could be sacrificed, this guarded shrine must hold much more.

Careless of creaking oars, they rowed in fast, past the beach where they'd been ambushed, to a cove just beyond that enticing flickering flame. The craft scraped on to pebbles. The men of Harak leapt, fully armed, shields raised, out of the boat, running up the slope towards the thatched roofs of homes ahead. There was no sound in the silence but their own feet. There was no sign of anyone awake, or of the warriors who met them the previous time. They would be in their cups, celebrating their festival.

A woman rose from the scrub, outdoors to relieve her bladder. She stood, naked in the moonlight, a dark spiral tattooed on her bluish breast. In her hand she held a short length of cord. Her mouth curved in a wide smile, though her eyes were cold. When she did not run, their feet slowed, hesitant that she showed no fear. From the shore behind, they heard the scrape of wood.

Several ghostly women with white flaming hair, shoulders to the prow of their boat, pushed it off into the water. Before they could move to save it, a screech erupted from the solitary banshee at their backs.

'Hyaaa-aaaaa!'

Shapes rose around them, more ghostly naked spectres whose empty hands flung forward. Thumps, cracks and clatters came like monstrous hail. Men fell, bleeding from broken heads. Those who didn't go down cowered below raised shields. A storm of stones rained from all around.

*

Skaaha walked to the hut in bright spring sunshine. She wore a fine white woollen dress, glittering silver earrings and a blue cloak pinned with a brooch that shone like the moon. Beric's presence had proved fortuitous after all. The trader would carry her message to the land of the raiders, and to every other land he visited. Greeting Terra, who guarded the hut, she put her hand on the catch and opened it.

The man inside gripped his hands together to stop them shaking. Twenty of them had left Harak on this raid. Half had died on that beach. His only company in the hut were their heads, hanged from the roof to dry. The young queen who entered was finely dressed and beautiful. Glossy black hair, braided round her head, tumbled in coils down her back. But she was the same woman as that naked she-witch who'd smiled so coldly in the half-light of that brutal night. His chains shook. Ten of them had lived, prodded here by swords and spears pulled from the ground. Turn by turn, she'd come for each one. Orek, the king's son, was taken out first, then the captain. Each time, those left behind heard screams, the terrified, tormented shrieks of men. Now, there was only him.

'You're well, I hope,' she asked, as his shackles were released. When he didn't answer, she smiled. 'You can speak,' she asserted. 'The reason you live is because you know my tongue.'

'I'm not badly hurt,' he muttered. His left eye was half closed, his lip split, body bruised. The red-haired woman warrior who came in with her yanked him to his feet. Stumbling, he was propelled out of the hut into daylight. The queen strolled alongside. A priest fell in behind. His presence brought no comfort. They headed towards the sea, skirting a high outcrop of rock. He could hear the wind howl high in the sky though the air was still, without a breeze.

'We have a custom in our country,' the queen said. 'Every spring, we dip rags in water and tie them, as our wishes, to a tree.' She paused. 'Do you do this?'

'No.' He shook his head, hands still trembling. They passed

the rock, the ground opening out to the sea. Ahead, a trader's boat waited beside a jetty. The trader, in a long, patterned coat, stood in the prow. Pale-faced, he stared towards them.

'You might like to tell your country of this custom,' she suggested, nodding for him to look back. The wind moaned louder here, almost human.

He turned. Behind the rocks they had passed was a wide grassy circle. In its centre, a massive oak tree spread leafless branches. High among those branches hung the naked bodies of men, hung by their hair. His nine companions swayed, hands tied behind them. Nooses lay slack around their necks, roped to branches to take the weight if the scalp tore from their heads. Every man, bruised and battered from that monstrous rain, bled from a wound where his manhood had been. Blood dripped to the gory ground below. Every one of them was still alive.

'Wishes work best,' the queen was saying, 'while they dry.'

Stumbling and retching, with that inhuman sobbing in his ears, he was hauled down to the waiting boat. On the jetty, the flame-haired warrior gripped his arms, as if to push him off on to the deck.

'Your boat was sacrificed in the sea,' the queen said. 'Beric will take you home.' Her hand grasped his hair, forcing him to look at her. 'You came to war against the Island of Wings. I let you live so your tongue will speak what it has seen.' Her eyes were dark as night. 'Tell your people the Land of Bride has a new warrior queen. Tell them she is the shadow of death. Tell them' – her voice rang hard as iron – 'I am Skaaha!'

Author's Note

'True knowledge exists in knowing that you know nothing.'

Socrates *c.* 470–399BC

Some names are spelt phonetically in Warrior Daughter. *The usual spellings are given below.*

Skaaha (Sgathach, Scathach) lived in the Iron Age on what became the Isle of Skye, just off the west coast of what is now Scotland. Island and country are both said to be named after her. There are no written records from her culture. She and her sister, Eefay (Aoife), are prehistory, their story preserved in oral myths and poetry until Christian monks wrote down the *Ulster Cycle* sagas between the eleventh and fifteenth centuries. Skaaha emerged for the first time in text, a vibrant, awesome leader, still respected a thousand years after she lived.

The *Cycle* tells of a fierce warrior, unbeatable by anyone in single combat, who taught the martial arts, and the art of love, to young men who proved themselves worthy. Her fort, Doonskaa (Dunscaith), later adapted as a castle, still stands, a ruin on its rock near Tokavaig. Skaaha lived between 200BC–AD200, so I chose spring of AD1 as her birth-date. *Warrior Daughter* tells her story, from the age of eleven until eighteen, and how she became that queen.

To write it realistically meant avoiding post-Roman and Christian influence, additions or opinions, though I often used what came next to deduce what went before. Archaeology and classical histories provided evidence and information. Anthropology filled the gaps. Britain was tribal, its land called Alba

(Scotland) or Albion (England). Since Skaaha lived on the margin between native Picts and Irish Gaels, I gave her lineage from both. Myths and archaeology indicate a settled society of artisans, food producers, warriors and priests, trading with Europe and beyond. Skaaha's culture is often described as Celtic, its people known for beauty, strength and ferocity. She was a warrior queen who preceded Cartimandua, queen of the Brigantes, and the Icenian, Boudicca.

Records of her warrior lifestyle come from Greek and Roman historians, enemy cultures. Of early Celts, Plutarch says, 'the fight had been no less fierce with the women than with the men themselves,' and 'the women charged with swords and axes and fell upon their opponents uttering a hideous outcry'. About two centuries later, Roman general Paullinus noted more women than men in Boudicca's army and, of the force defending Ynys Mon (Anglesey), Tacitus says Roman legions 'felt the disgrace of yielding to a troop of women'.

Archaeology confirms this. In 2001, burial mounds on the Russia–Kazakhstan border revealed remains of women horse-riders buried with weapons and warrior amulets. Dating from 600–200BC, other female graves were those of priests and warrior priests. A third type was of wealthy, powerful or highly regarded women. Among the remains of men, several had children buried beside them, though no woman had. Older by over a thousand years, the richest urns from Britain's Stanton Moor are women's, the only urns with weapons. From Scythians to Saxons, women warrior graves are found.

Tacitus wrote that Celts made no distinction between male and female leaders. Chieftain words are often genderless, often misinterpreted as male. Viking King Thorbergr was female. Before Skaaha, and among broch dwellers, there is no indication of hierarchy or central authority but of loose, independent communities who gather for celebration – signs of matriarchy. Eight hundred years after Skaaha, Celtic law was written down. The earlier status of women is clear. Violence against them was forbidden. They owned homes and property, and divorced husbands for snoring, drunkenness, obesity or impotence.

Women in Skaaha's culture were in charge. Those rights support matriarchies where only women inherit. Jeannine Davis-Kimball believes the Russian-border graves reveal women who protected property, managed spiritual welfare and led the tribe: 'They held strong positions in society. They controlled wealth, going back a long time. We're talking 2,500 years ago.' This wasn't rare. John Esten Cooke records the Iroquois as content to be ruled by women, their lives valued at twice that of men. Minoans had only female deities and priests. In *The Awakening of America*, V. F. Calverton notes that clan mothers were senior chiefs who selected, and de-selected, the lesser male chiefs.

Society arises from cooperation. To understand Skaaha's, I looked at modern women-led tribes. Peruvian Machiguenga men are docile. If aggressive or violent, they'd be avoided, driven away or killed. India's Khasi and Garo pass property and tribal office from mother to youngest daughter. Girls take the sexual initiative, boys are demure. In the Nagovisi matriclans of South Bougainville men share decisions but not wealth. There is no group authority or chiefs. In Taiwan, commune heads of the Amei are elected from elderly women. China's matriarchal Mosuo women, whose men also can't own property, practise 'walking marriage' and can choose multiple partners. They have no words for 'father' or 'husband', but also none for 'rape', 'murder' or 'war'.

In Skaaha's tribal Scotland, leadership passed through Pictish women until AD1230, when Alexander II, bent on ruling all Scots, ordered the murder of the baby girl who was heir to Alba's ancient female bloodline. It was the Romans who brought patriarchy to Britain. From AD43, they occupied England for 400 years. Two walls kept Scottish tribes at bay, ensuring little cross-culture interaction. As late as the fifteenth century, visitors such as Aeneas Sylvius and Don Pedro de Ayala decried Scotswomen's sexual boldness but describe them as absolute mistresses of their homes and husbands.

Skaaha's uninhibited sexuality is also documented. Druids share the same spiritual-erotic Indo-European roots as the ceremonial Vama Marga of early Hindu Tantra, and the pleasure principles of Sanskrit Kama. When the submissive Roman empress, Julia Augusta, commented on the free intercourse of women with men in Britain, the Pictish wife of Argentocoxus retorted that they fulfilled the demands of nature better, adding, 'We consort openly with the best men, whereas you let yourself be debauched in secret by the vilest.' Homosexuality was also common. In the first century BC, Siculus wrote that Celtic men openly enjoyed sex with each other, and were offended if refused.

Queen Medb, Skaaha's Irish contemporary, married many times but met her match just once, in Fergus mac Róich, the only lover able to replace her daily quota of thirty men. Mythic exaggeration maybe, but when choosing a husband, Medb said he must be as brave in battle as she was, generous like her, and not jealous, because she never denied herself any man she wanted and never would, married or not. In Skaaha's time, marriage wasn't lasting or limited. Brehon law lists at least ten forms: short, longer and multiple.

Julius Caesar, in *The Gallic Wars*, writes that British women often had ten or twelve husbands. Polyandry occurs, or has, in the Arctic, Africa, America, Bhutan, Canaries, China, India, Mongolia, Nepal, Sri Lanka, Sumeria, Tibet and the Polynesian islands. Although under pressure now from surrounding monogamist cultures, it limits offspring, increases family wealth and secures land ownership. Anthropologist Stephen Beckerman notes at least twenty current tribal societies who believe a child could, and should, have more than one father. Celts fostered their children to kin, a habit that continued in Highland clans into the eighteenth century. I made Skaaha an exception to throw up some reasons why they did.

Skaaha's nudity is indicative of normal practice. Despite fine clothes, jewellery, armour, shields and elaborate helmets, models show warriors naked apart from weapons. Classical writers record that they often fought wearing only gold torcs and armlets. Roman legions faced naked, blue 'painted' warriors in Scotland, nudity continued by later Highlanders. Privacy was unknown. Houses had no internal walls. Women wore nothing under those skirts raised in that universal gesture of dominance or contempt. Later stone Sheela-na-gigs expose vulvas with similar attitude.

Spiritual beliefs shape societies, but druids left no records, deliberately. *Warrior Daughter* incorporates all that's known about them. They cherished certain groves, springs, caves and streams, and celebrated the natural world. Votive deposits found in waterways suggest ancestor memorial, grief, mourning, hope or aspiration. Burial was rare. Goods from the few period graves relate to the deceased, just as they do today. Caesar said druids taught reincarnation, and enforced the law by excluding wrongdoers from festivals and society – the basis for those outsiders who attack Skaaha.

Caesar also wrote that druids received oral tuition for twenty years: 'They hold various lectures and discussions on astronomy, on the extent and geographical distribution of the globe, on the different branches of natural philosophy, and on many problems connected with religion.' While Romans distinguish druid, male, from priestess, women druids raise Ireland's Finn and advise Queen Medb. Strabo describes 'priestesses who were seers ... grey-haired, clad in white, with flaxen cloaks fastened on with clasps' killing prisoners. Tacitus writes of 'black-robed women with dishevelled hair like Furies, brandishing torches' and 'druids lifting their hands to heaven' who decry the Romans at Ynys Mon. Siculus wrote that druids threw themselves between two armies to bring peace.

The Hebridean islands, where Skaaha lived, may be the centre of druidism, claimed by classical writers to be in Britain. Iona is one of those islands. The heart of Christianity in

Scotland, its ancient Gaelic name is Island of Druids. There is a pantheon of Celtic gods who appear to derive from admired people who are mythologized after death, like saints, with supernatural powers. But there is no evidence of worship, no temples, no great idols, despite superb craftsmanship and buildings. Instead, druids held four major fire festivals which mark the agricultural year and celebrate the great triple goddess.

Bride, Danu and Carlin, or Brigid, Anu and Cailleach, embody primeval ideas, representing creation, war or life-struggle, and death. Bride, which means High One, was creator and source of knowledge. The Hebrides are named as hers. There are several Kilbrides, Bride Stones and wells. Widely known in Europe, a fine first-century AD bronze statue of her was found at Dinéault in France. As a competing creator trinity, what she represented was rapidly neutered by adoption into later Christian belief as St Brigid or St Bride.

The fourth festival, Lunasa (Lughnasadh), celebrates Telsha (Tailtui), the foster-mother. Legend says her foster-son, Lugh, set up her celebration and, with dubious logic, he later becomes one of many sun gods, in August when it's failing. In life, Lugh was a heroic warrior, probably attached to the existing first harvest festival with its child-fostering link to the autumn moon 'fostering' sunlight. Writing *Warrior Daughter*, it seemed obvious that Telsha was a second aspect of the central warrior-mother in Bride's three stages of life.

Just as solar feasts became Easter and Christmas, the festivals of Beltane, Lunasa, Sowen (Samhain) and Imbolc also linger. At miners' Gala days, a young May Queen fronts the proceedings, complete with consort. In August, Highland games proliferate. At Hallowe'en, people still dress in disguise to entertain as 'guisers'. Images of death abound. The crone rules, complete with broomstick, black garb and coned hat. The fire, a few days later, still burns an effigy. In spring, on her traditional 2 February date, Bride's eternal flame has become Candlemas.

Druids dealt with time. Equinoxes and solstices aren't easy

to discern. The expertise to date them, and predict eclipses, existed long before the Iron Age, charted in four Bronze Age gold 'hats' or cones. Calendar time, kept by the moon, needed corrective help, as its cycle averages 29.5 days. To prevent seasons creeping round, every third year lasted thirteen moons, the Ghost Moon of Skaaha's birth. In the Coligny calendar, the extra moon is counted twice every five years, eleven times in thirty, in autumn then in spring.

The authenticity of Skaaha's world is supported by archaeology: from the Wetwang female chariot burial to excavated mounds, roundhouses, caves and those specifically Scottish brochs, from skulls trepanned for unknown reasons whose owners lived on afterwards, to bog bodies quite clearly killed for some extreme crime. Although well populated, the only discovered grave on Skye from the period is a young woman's at High Pasture Cave near Kilbride, where Beltane is set. Cremation and excarnation, as practised in similarly rocky Tibet, seem the most likely forms of disposal.

I'm immensely grateful to those who so carefully dig up the past, to anthropologists such as Peggy Reeves Sanday and Jill Nash, the staff of Skye's museum and tourist offices, bird experts on Mull, and to Ian Armit, whose book, *The Archaeology of Skye and the Western Isles*, has been invaluable. Again, I'm in debt to Rennie McOwan for instantly supplying his article, 'Skye's Warrior Queen'. Thanks are due to my two sisters and eldest son, for their assistance as researchers during our time on the island, and to my good friend and fellow poet, Aonghas Macneacail, for first telling me of Skaaha and Eefay, about whom he has written a radio monologue and opera libretto.

I drew Skaaha's life from legend by exchanging mythical elements for likely facts, and have shown, through the oral tradition of storytelling in the novel, how that process originally did the opposite. But it's the island which inspires, with its long history part revealed and much obscured, a place where the mist of time is as real as that fog rolling down over the Cuillins. Doon Beck (Dun Beag) and other brochs can still be visited, now remnants of their former glory, their builders, purpose and how life was lived inside their dark walls to be guessed at and not known, like Skaaha herself. *Warrior Daughter* is my version of her early life, a story drawn from historical legend to bring from the shadows a woman, amazing and mysterious as the culture and land she inhabited.

Reference for Locality

The Archaeology of Skye and the Western Isles, Ian Armit: Edinburgh University Press 1996

Scotland – Archaeology and Early History, Graham and Anna Ritchie: EU Press 1991

Skye – The Island and its Legends, Otta Swire: Birlinn 2006

Isle of Skye – Rambler's Guide, Chris Townsend: Collins 2001

The Mediaeval Castles of Skye and Lochalsh, Roger Miket and David L. Roberts: Birlinn 2007

Ordinance Survey and *Nicolson's* maps of Skye

Additional Reading

The Ancient Celts, Barry Cunliffe: Oxford University Press 1997

A Brief History of the Druids, Peter Berresford Ellis: Robinson Publishing 2002

Britain BC: Life in Britain and Ireland before the Romans, Francis Pryor: Harper Perennial 2004

The Druids: Celtic Priests of Nature, Jean Markale: Inner Traditions 1999

The Histories, Cornelius Tacitus: Penguin, Classics edition 2005

Larousse Encyclopaedia of Mythology

Maiden Warriors & Other Sons, Carol J. Clover: *Journal of English and Germanic Philology*, 85, 1986

'Mythologie de la Brigitte', J. Christmann: *Bulletin de la Société de Mythologie Française*, No. 157, 6. Feb 2007, *Actes du Congrès de Château-Chinon*

Women in Roman Britain, Lindsay Allason-Jones: Council for British Archaeology 2006

A Group of Scottish Women, Harry Graham: Duffield & Company 1908

'The Development of Christian Society in Early England', Tim Bond: *Britannia Internet Magazine* 1996

Warrior Women: An Archaeologist's Search for History's Hidden Heroines, Jeannine Davis-Kimball: Little, Brown and Company 2004

Women Warriors: A History, David E. Jones: Potomac Books Inc. 2005

Battle Cries and Lullabies: Women in War from Prehistory to the Present, Linda Grant De Pauw: University of Oklahoma Press 2000

Chieftain or Warrior Priestess?, Jeannine Davis-Kimball: *Archaeology*, Sept./Oct. 1997

Women at the Center: Life in a Modern Matriarchy, Peggy Reeves Sanday: Cornell University Press 2002

Matriliny and Modernisation: The Nagovisi of South Bougainville, Jill Nash: New Guinea Research Unit 1974

'What Do Men Want?', Syed Zubair Ahmed: *New York Times* 1994

Sex in History, Gordon Rattray Taylor: 1954 (Book 1/2: *Mediaeval Sexual Behaviour*)

On-line Texts

Ulster Cycle – comment and translations: http://en.wikipedia.org/wiki/Ulster_Cycle

Celts – history and extensive links: http://en.wikipedia.org/wiki/Celt

The Gallic Wars, Julius Caesar – translation: http://classics.mit.edu/Caesar/gallic.html

The Pan-Celtic Goddess, Brigantia (Most High): http://www.celt
   net.org.uk/gods_b/brigantia.html

Ancient Nomads, Female Warriors and Priestesses, Jeannine Davis-
   Kimball: Centre for the Study of Eurasian Nomads, 1998:
   http://popgen.well.ox.ac.uk/eurasia/htdocs/davis.html

JANET PAISLEY

WHITE ROSE REBEL

Anne Farquharson is a Highland girl – tempestuous, bold, determined to be her own woman. Yet the clan Farquharson is threatened. The Highlands suffer at the domineering hand of English King George, while there are rumours that Bonnie Prince Charlie, exiled to France, is raising an army in a bid for the throne.

When Anne marries a clan chief and creates a shaky alliance, she is doing more than taking his bed. Soon she is drawn into the heart of a brutal and bloody conflict, and as the Jacobite rebellion escalates, she and her husband find themselves on opposite sides of the battlefield.

White Rose Rebel is inspired by the true story of a Highland heroine who risked everything for her country and its rightful king.

'A claymore-swinging, heather-igniting historical adventure' *Sunday Times*

'A powerful historical page-turner with a beautiful, feisty heroine' *Scotsman*

'An excellent fictional account... Paisley's creation of Anne Farquharson is a triumph' *Scottish Review of Books*

'A feisty heroine, romantic dash, and battle scenes of eye-watering gore' *FT*

'A hot-blooded riposte to the Highland machismo of clan history' *Sunday Herald*

ROSEMARY GORING

SCOTLAND: AN AUTOBIOGRAPHY

Scotland: The Autobiography is an account of the country's history told first-hand by those who witnessed it. Spanning 2,000-odd years of pivotal events, it is a compilation of vivid personal experiences from crofters and criminals, nuns and soldiers, scientists and artists, footballers and children. There are moving memories of battles such as Culloden and atrocities like the witch trials and clearances; there are great discoveries and inventions, like chloroform and the telephone, recorded by the men now famous for their breakthroughs; so too the moment when Robert Louis Stevenson knew he had a hit on his hands with *Treasure Island*, and Irvine Welsh gave his first interview for *Trainspotting*.

From the most prestigious men and women of their day to those at the bottom of the social ladder, *Scotland: The Autobiography* gathers voices from the distant past to modern times and allows them to be heard again. The result is a fascinating and uniquely lively retelling of Scotland's dramatic story.

'An unqualified triumph, superb, a real page-turner... What a stirring, dramatic, poignant story it has been' Alexander McCall Smith, *Spectator*

'History caught on the hoof and the wing by those who were actually there – a brilliant selection' Andrew Marr

'A triumph... will reward any amount of flipping and dipping. Rigorous and engaging in its sweep, Goring's meticulously edited anthology is full of moving, amusing and revealing detail. What an exemplary reclaiming of Scotland's past' *Scotland on Sunday*

'Goring has an ear for a riveting yarn, the emotion of human experience and the power of the voice to present history at its most striking' *Sunday Times*

'Fascinating and very valuable... should find a place in every Scottish home' Alan Massie, *Scotsman*

He just wanted a decent book to read ...

Not too much to ask, is it? It was in 1935 when Allen Lane, Managing Director of Bodley Head Publishers, stood on a platform at Exeter railway station looking for something good to read on his journey back to London. His choice was limited to popular magazines and poor-quality paperbacks – the same choice faced every day by the vast majority of readers, few of whom could afford hardbacks. Lane's disappointment and subsequent anger at the range of books generally available led him to found a company – and change the world.

'We believed in the existence in this country of a vast reading public for intelligent books at a low price, and staked everything on it'
Sir Allen Lane, 1902–1970, founder of Penguin Books

The quality paperback had arrived – and not just in bookshops. Lane was adamant that his Penguins should appear in chain stores and tobacconists, and should cost no more than a packet of cigarettes.

Reading habits (and cigarette prices) have changed since 1935, but Penguin still believes in publishing the best books for everybody to enjoy. We still believe that good design costs no more than bad design, and we still believe that quality books published passionately and responsibly make the world a better place.

So wherever you see the little bird – whether it's on a piece of prize-winning literary fiction or a celebrity autobiography, political tour de force or historical masterpiece, a serial-killer thriller, reference book, world classic or a piece of pure escapism – you can bet that it represents the very best that the genre has to offer.

Whatever you like to read – trust Penguin.